BLOODCRAFT

THE CRUENTUS CURSE SERIES, BOOK 2

AMALIE HOWARD

For the truest fans

"Monsters are real. They live inside us, and sometimes, they win."
~Stephen King

PREFACE

The Reii will rise when the world is at its close.
Vampyre Covenant XXV, The Book of Reii

PRISON OF LIGHTS

The magic rose to her command, her blood racing like wildfire in her veins as the creeping shadow unfurled in the corner, its eyes gleaming and vicious. Victoria suppressed a shiver as she stood against the side of the far wall, her body rigid. She swallowed hard, adrenaline making her ears throb. "You never should have ventured from whatever hole you call a home."

She'd marched into that dark corner of the room of her own free will, and now there was no doubt in her mind that it was now or never. She had no choice but to stand her ground. Fight or flee, as it were. She took a deep breath, pulling the magic that she would need to the fore as she faced her enemy square in the face.

"Die," she said, her heart in her throat. "You're going to die." The creature stared back at her, uncowed by her threats as it shuffled closer. "Don't say I didn't warn you. IGNIS CREMO," she yelled, leaping onto the bed and brandishing her arms wildly.

Her would-be attacker exploded as the fire spell ignited and charred its target until nothing remained but a blackened hole in the carpet. Victoria sighed with relief as she sank back against the pillows.

Stupid spiders.

The sprawling old Parisian château had its charm, but it also had its not-so-charming variety of sinister visitors, including this particular beast. Christian's home was impeccably decorated and furnished, but given its age, circa early seventeenth century, it was natural to expect some uninvited guests here and there, hiding in the most unexpected places. This one—the size of her fist—had practically hunted her down from the bathroom.

Well, at least it was gone. A hissing noise drew her attention and Victoria's eyes snapped open, her cheeks reddening as she noticed Leto's mirthful expression. Propping herself up onto her elbows, she glared at the cat that had been at her side since birth and scowled. He continued to make that silly hissing noise that sounded like laughter, and she flushed with embarrassment —he must have seen her showdown with the spider.

"What?" she muttered defensively. "It was the size of a house."

At least this one died a quick death, he replied, his mental voice sounding strangled.

"Shut up, Leto," Victoria said. "Before I banish you back to Maine."

She stuck her tongue out at him and flung herself onto the bed. Leto was an old and arrogant silver-furred feline, and, as she'd discovered last year, certainly far more than a mere cat. He was her familiar—her spirit link to a world full of witchcraft and magic.

Magic—as in real live witches and warlocks, spells and curses. No flying brooms though, which was a pity. She'd read *Harry Potter* along with everyone else in the world, and racing a broom around a Quidditch pitch sounded pretty fantastic. Then again, it wasn't like Victoria had much to complain about—she could teleport in the blink of an eye, heal any wound, cast a number of spells, and had a talking cat for a guide.

She'd inherited Leto from her grandmother's friend, Holly Milton. Despite his annoying tendency to disapprove of everything she did, he had been instrumental in most of her education in the ways of witches over the past year. Victoria sighed. Most days, she vacillated between being a source of disappointment or one of entertainment for him.

Today, it was obviously the latter. Victoria could see his body still shaking with silent laughter at her expense, and she bit her lip to keep from doing something rash, like tossing him out the window and testing the theory of whether cats did indeed have nine lives. She settled for some bland conversation instead.

"I really need to call Holly and let her know that we are okay," she said.

I am sure Holly is fine. You spoke to her last week.

"I know, but we've been here over a month now and I've only called her twice," she said. "I feel guilty."

Truth was, she missed Holly. She'd been a rock over the few months when things had gotten more than a little rough during Victoria's last year of high school in Maine. One of her best friends—who turned out to be an evil power hungry warlock—had tried to kill her. And that was *after* he kidnapped her and tortured her friends. It'd been a fight to the death, which thankfully had not been hers, or any of her loved ones, for that matter. All because of one teeny tiny curse.

A summer ago, it started with a random blood disease that had attacked her nervous system. The disease was parasitic—infecting her very cells and leaving the doctors baffled, even more so when she recovered in perfect health. In the space of the few weeks following, however, her entire world was flipped upside down. The mysterious blood disease wasn't a sickness at all. Instead, it was the precursor to the centuries old curse that had ushered in her magical powers … powers that everyone else in the world seemed to covet. Running for her life, the only person she could trust turned out to be a vampire.

A *vampire* … as in a blood-sucking creature of the night that preyed on people and stole the life from their veins, one with fangs and claws that never aged and feared the sunlight. Victoria smiled to herself. Christian wasn't all bad. Okay, well, he *did* drink human blood, but he wasn't a killer. And he wasn't just any vampire—he was a vampire royal who had risked his immortal life for her.

The thought of him made her blood tingle beneath her skin as it always did. The intimate nature of their relationship had drawn the censure of the Witch Clans and the Vampire Council, the governing factions of both species. She glanced at Leto. He'd been fiercely against them, too, and had only recently come to a reluctant acceptance of the fact that Christian wasn't going anywhere.

As if that wasn't enough to fuel the fire, Christian had a sadistic twin brother who wanted nothing but both their deaths and was still conspiring to usurp Christian's position as head of the House of Devereux. Lucian had been coveting Victoria's magic from the beginning, which led to why they were here, at Christian's family estate, just an hour south of Paris. Face the enemy directly and all that. Not that Victoria wanted to be anywhere near Lucian, but she could do a lot worse than spending the summer in the most romantic city in the world.

Not that she'd seen any of it either.

Victoria sighed and stared upward, her eyes tracing the intricate gold swirls of the crown molding on the ceiling. Upon his return to Paris, Christian had resumed his duties, mostly to keep an eye on his marauding brother and his vampire consort, Lena, who was now a member of the powerful Vampire Council. Victoria had accompanied him to Paris to learn about the Witch Clans, but she knew that Christian was obsessed with her safety. Thus far, she had yet to leave this drafty old castle or meet any of her own kind.

As a result, she was going stir crazy and killing insects for sport, while Christian insisted that it was not as safe as he would like. The night before, they'd had a huge fight about it. She had argued that she could more than take care of herself, but he hadn't budged an inch, and in the end, given that this was his territory, she had given in—if ungracefully—to his demands.

"I need to get out of here," she muttered, more to herself than to Leto.

You could always teleport to Holly's or Angie's, Leto suggested helpfully.

Victoria smiled as she thought how great it would be to see her friend Angie, who had started out as an enemy and had ended up becoming her closest friend. Or not, as she immediately imagined what Christian's reaction would be if she disappeared without telling him. She sighed. She had to get him to be reasonable or she'd just go back to Canville. Anything was a better alternative than being a prisoner in someone else's home in someone else's country, fighting abnormally large spiders all day long.

"Any more news on what the other familiars are saying?" she asked Leto, trying to change the subject to something that would distract the slow, angry simmer of her emotions.

Since their arrival in France, Leto had been communicating with other familiars that lived in the Paris covens. It irked her that *he* had been able to go out, but she was desperate for any information she could get, especially when Christian was being so overprotective and secretive. Victoria hadn't asked how Leto had known the other familiars—it was one of those things that went along with his endless knowledge of witchcraft. One of these days, she *would* get him to tell her his life story. Her attention snapped to him at his next words.

They are mobilizing, he was saying. *They sense that the Cruentus Curse is near.*

Victoria's body tensed at the mere mention of the blood curse that had haunted her for the past year, and Leto's mental voice shifted into a deep purr, dissipating the tension with some of his own special magic. She felt the rigidity seep from her shoulders.

They are looking for you to lead them, he added.

"Lead them against what?" she asked, frowning.

It is your birthright, Victoria. You are a witch queen. You must take your place among the Witch Clans.

She shook her head. "We've been through this before, Leto. I can't lead them. I can't even deal with my own life. And think about it. They'd never accept me given where I live or who I'm with, now would they?" Victoria's pointed reference to the fact that she was practically shacking up with a vampire—which was not condoned by either of their worlds—made Leto dip his head in silent acknowledgment.

Even so, you are the witch from the prophecy, the descendant of a legend. Who is to say you cannot make your own rules? You could make them agree, you know. He said the last part so quickly that she almost didn't hear him. But she did, and her eyes widened.

"I couldn't. Could I?"

Yes.

Victoria frowned in disbelief. "Forcing others to bend to my will?"

What's wrong with changing an antiquated belief so that you can live in your world on your own terms?

"But I *am* living on my own terms with Christian," she said, working through Leto's muddled logic. Sometimes she didn't know if he wanted her to heed his advice or whether he was playing devil's advocate and expected her to argue. What he was suggesting was barbaric. Tyrannical. She shook her head. "I don't think it's that easy. We're talking about millennia of mistrust between two feuding species. Witches and vampires are like oil and water—they don't mix."

Except for her and Christian. They were the anomalies ... the exception to the rule. They shouldn't be together. But somehow when they were, nothing else seemed to matter. From the very first moment she had met him, she had known that he was hers. Just as she had been his. Their road hadn't been an easy one. Love didn't always conquer everything—especially not other people and what they believed.

Victoria had once called their love "impossible" and that wasn't far from the truth. But despite the odds, they made it work because the alternative of life without each other was not an option either of them were willing to accept. She stared out the window, her heart aching. She could never leave him, no matter how lonely she got.

On cue, she felt the soft mental brush on her senses as Christian's car pulled up the long driveway leading into the estate. Victoria raced down the curving staircase to the foyer and flung herself into his arms as he was walking through the doorway. His blond hair was unkempt as if he'd scrubbed his hand through it a thousand times—as he was wont to do anytime he met with the Vampire Council—but his tired gray eyes sparked at the sight of her.

"I've missed you, chérie," he murmured, his lips soft against her temple.

Despite her pleasure at seeing him, Victoria couldn't help herself, the snappy comment slipping out before she could curb her tongue. "Well, you wouldn't as much if you took me with you."

Christian kissed the top of her head with a deep sigh, and she instantly regretted her outburst. It was no secret that the last few weeks had been hard for both of them. "I didn't mean to upset you," she said. "It's just ... hard. And lonely."

"I'm sorry, love," he said, tipping her face up to his. "But it's too dangerous. Lucian hasn't recovered from your blood attacking him or forgotten what happened in New York. He's unforgiving at the best of times. I can't take the chance that he won't retaliate in some way. At least here, there are safeguards in place for your protection." Something dark flickered in Christian's eyes at the memory and Victoria cringed. Her witch blood had tried to murder Lucian through possession of Christian, and despite his casual manner, she knew that he had yet to recover. She bit her lip as he continued. "But I do have some good news. I invited Aliya to have dinner with us tomorrow night."

Victoria brightened. Aliya was a high priestess of a witch coven in Paris, whom Victoria had briefly met during her last visit to Paris, and was someone that she had been looking forward to seeing during this trip to France.

"How did you get her to come?" she asked.

Christian smiled. "Simple. I told her you were here with me. She has been looking forward to spending more time with you since La Défense. And I know you have questions for her, too."

"I didn't think she would want to see me after the last time. I was pretty rude." She glanced up at Christian, a twinge of embarrassment winding through her. Aliya had had the unfortunate timing to be there when Victoria found out about Lena—Christian's vampire progeny—and Victoria hadn't left the best impression. She shrugged off the sour recollection. "I'm surprised she agreed, but glad. She's the only witch I've met, and I want to ask her so many things about magic and energy, and who I am, and ... you know ... all of it."

"I agree, it will be good for you," Christian said, shedding his jacket in the foyer and walking toward the back of the house. She followed. He sat on one of the chairs in the bright kitchen that looked out onto the rambling, expertly manicured gardens. Removing his cufflinks and rolling the cuffs on his shirt, he watched her with a smile on his face as she chewed the ends of her nails. "You have nothing to be nervous about, Tori," he said as if he could sense the anxiety spearing through her. "Stop driving yourself mad."

"But she knows about us. I sensed it that last time. Won't she be against it? Against us?" Victoria asked.

"Chérie, she accepted my invitation—our invitation—in full possession of all her faculties. If she does know, then perhaps she is withholding any judgment until she can make up her mind for herself. Now come here," he said in a deliberate voice that made butterflies erupt in her belly.

She complied, sitting in his lap at the table and winding her fingers through the soft strands of hair at his temple. "Yes, Your Grace?" she said demurely.

"I've been thinking about you all day, especially when I was stuck in that boardroom with a handful of very serious and grouchy Elders. All I could think about was this." His fingers grazed up her bare arm, making her pulse leap and the blood rush to the surface of her skin, every cell responding to his touch. "And this." They lingered at her throat for the briefest of moments before stroking across her jaw and mouth. Her lips parted against them, her tongue darting out to moisten his fingertip, and his silver eyes flared. Christian bent his head and she closed her eyes. "And especially *this*."

The minute he kissed her, she forgot everything. All she could do was melt into him, her lips parting beneath the pressure of his. Her body felt like it was separating into a thousand pieces as his mouth claimed hers, gently at first and then less so as desire took over. He nibbled her lips, drawing them between his, and then kissed her deeply. She arched against him. Christian's fingers dug into her arms, drawing her to him as the tip of his tongue traced a hot path down her jawline, and then lower still. Her heart caught and slowed, his hot breath fanning against the hollow of her throat. Her pulse there leapt toward his lips.

Stop now.

She didn't know whether the ragged thought was hers or his, only that it was a warning, a desperate one. Breathless, Victoria pulled away from his grasp, her fiery blood racing like a wanton river, and struggled to control its wild surges. She knew it was daring him to take it. That was what her blood did—it taunted and tortured. Inhaling deeply, she licked her tingling lips and stared at him, her chest heaving. Christian's eyes were stormy silver, latent hunger darkening their edges as his bloodlust rose in response to the dark call of blood. *Her* blood.

With a frustrated growl, he gently but firmly separated their bodies, composing himself with a harsh breath. Victoria sighed and leaned back against the table, watching a muscle work in his jaw. It should be getting easier, but it only seemed to be getting harder—*and riskier*—for them to be together. Every touch, every look, every *kiss* drew them closer to the edge of the abyss from which there would be no return—one mistake and one of them would die. Victoria took his cool hands in hers.

"I love you," she said as his hands trembled in hers. Touching his cheek, she climbed off his lap, putting some space between them. Despite the distance, she could feel her blood churning wildly, tempting him, inciting him to take it, and she shivered at the volatility of it. Her blood's siren call was near impossible to resist, and she knew how hard it was for him. He'd once told her that he'd risk the consequences of her blood's appeal because he couldn't deprive himself of never being able to touch her.

Seeing the savage transformation in his face and the tips of teeth pressing into his lower lip, she wondered whether he still thought the same. Christian stood and kissed her fingers, and with the ever-present apology in his eyes, excused himself from the room. Victoria watched him leave, his long, lithe body loping with an easy grace across the back gardens into the forest beyond.

The château sat at the edge of the Fontainebleau forest,

which, as in the days of old, continued to fulfill its function as a royal hunting park, for Christian's purposes anyway. She pressed a finger to her lips, the impression of his lingering on them. Sometimes she felt like the vampire, as if she were the one who couldn't get enough of *him*. And most times, she didn't know if those feelings were hers or those of her blood. Given the chance, her blood would devour Christian's very essence until there was nothing left.

It thrummed in her veins as if sensing her ominous thoughts, its hunger unabated and ever-present. It, too, was voracious and would consume anything to sate its dark thirst—even the one she loved. Victoria shivered, wrapping her arms about herself and staring toward the forest lost in thought. She wasn't afraid of Christian or the fact that he was a vampire. After all, she was more of a monster than he could ever be.

DESPERATE MEASURES

An hour away from Fontainebleau, Lucian stalked into the study of his palatial Paris apartment, seething with frustration. He poured himself two fingers of brandy and swallowed the amber liquid in one sip. Things were not going according to plan. Despite Lena's new position on the Vampire Council secured by the House of Devereux, it seemed once again, that he had underestimated the Council's suspicion of his motives. Lena had just imparted the news that the Council had been reorganized and enlarged.

With the death of Enhard, a respected Elder, the Council had been split into two groups, with the seven remaining Elders forming an additional line above the members of the general council. Together with the three vampires of royal blood, they were to be called the High Council. While the general council was expected to handle most of the standard affairs, the purpose of the High Council was to act as a final arbiter. In addition, the general council had also been expanded to twenty-five members. Previously a combined total of just twenty members, with the new changes, the governing body for the vampires was now a multi-layered organization of thirty-five.

The intent was not lost on Lucian. He knew that the reorganization was a calculated, strategic move by the Council to attempt to diffuse the power of the House of Devereux. His nomination of Lena had only forced their hand. They couldn't remove her seat, so they had gone the only route available to them—creating the High Council to discuss information that Lena and, by default, he, Lucian, would not be privy to.

To make matters worse, his brother's recent return to Paris meant that as a vampire royal, Christian would claim a seat on the High Council. Even though they both descended from royal blood, Christian was first-born and held the title of the Duke of Avigny. It infuriated Lucian that he wasn't the one to hold the station when Christian had never wanted it in the first place and had renounced their ways, to the point of disappearing in some desolate town in North America. And yet, they all revered him.

Lucian scraped his hands through his cropped golden hair, his mouth pulled into a sneer. And now, his prodigal brother had returned, and with a witch as his consort, no less. Although Lucian's own credibility with the Council was at an all-time low, given that they had unanimously voted for his execution just a few months before, he vowed that he'd find a way to rip Christian from his venerated pedestal. That witch would be the key.

Striding to the window to peruse the sea of bodies on the street below, a familiar ache started to burn in his chest. His jaw tightened. Perhaps a meal would calm his rotten temper. He'd just made up his mind to go for a stroll when the door opened and Lena walked in. Her pale skin held a becoming flush as she glowed with stolen radiance.

"Did you just feed?" he asked sourly.

Lena's mouth thinned at his tone, but she headed over to where he was standing. "Yes. Care for some?"

She embraced him, her blue eyes flashing at the sharp feral

hunger in his. Lena knew he liked it this way—it gave him a thrill to take something that she had just taken into herself moments before. Without a word, she tilted the long column of her neck backward in silent invitation. Her fingers bit into his shoulders when he sank his teeth into the side of her throat, feeling the still-warm life course into him as he crushed her unbreakable body to his.

It felt like hours before he emerged from the desperate feeding haze that enveloped him, but Lucian knew that it had only been moments. He felt better. Clearer. *Calmer.* As much as he liked taking blood directly from the humans, he enjoyed it this way, too. Something about the combination—desire and bloodlust—was an electrifying mix. He licked her neck, sweeping away the last weeping droplets from her translucent skin.

"Better?" she asked, fixing her hair and watching him, her expression unreadable.

"Yes, thank you."

Lena straightened and walked towards the fireplace where she sat down and studied him. The wound on her neck healed in seconds and the flush that had tinted her skin earlier disappeared, leaving her perfect face like pristine alabaster. Her long pale blond hair fell in a silky curtain over her shoulders. She waited for him to speak.

"What of the Council? Have they discussed Le Sang Noir?" he asked, taking the seat across from her.

"Yes and no," she said, her husky voice low. Lucian raised his eyebrows at her answer. Le Sang Noir was what the Witch Clans called the Cruentus Curse—the terrible blood curse that had been his obsession for decades. Only when he'd finally found it, his *brother* had been the one to take its power. And even though its terrifying magic had almost destroyed them both, Lucian could never forgive Christian for claiming what was meant to be his ... for always taking what was his.

His fists clenched as Lena continued. "The Council is close, based on what the Watchers are saying, but the Witch Clans have not been able to identify the witch from the prophecy. They are still looking," she added. "Even though she's right under their noses."

Lucian's brow furrowed. "I wonder why Christian hasn't told them who she is. He must know that it would bring him even more adoration that he already enjoys," he said. "Unless of course, he has some other purpose. I presume it must be something to do with protecting *her*."

Lena's eyes dimmed at the mention of Christian, but she shook her head in a careless shrug. "Either way, the Council has more pressing matters on its plate."

"What could possibly be more important than the blood curse that could hold dominion over the supernatural world?" he said. Lena inclined her head, studying her nails as if considering her words with care. Lucian frowned as her eyes met his. "Spit it out."

"The Council is considering your appeal, but they are also considering retaliation."

"Retaliation against what?"

"You." Lena's voice was so quiet, it was almost a whisper. "Even if they vote against execution, you will have to be punished for your part in the death of Enhard."

"I had nothing to do with his death."

Well, except for showing up at the crucial moment that had allowed a warlock to effectively dispatch the old vampire. It had been providential. He could have helped, he supposed, but Enhard had been a thorn in Lucian's side ever since he could remember. The fact that he'd been Christian's maker had only made his death sweeter. Hurting Christian gave Lucian a pleasure like no other. Even now, he savored the memory of the look on his brother's face the moment Enhard had met his end.

"Not directly anyway, and that old fool deserved it," he added.

"Lucian, the Elders' memories are connected. Enhard's last vision before he died was of your face. In their minds, you have already been tried and convicted. They knew how much you hated him …" She trailed off.

"Did they now?"

Lucian knew she had argued on his behalf that an obscure memory did not make Lucian Enhard's murderer, but most of the older members of the Council had clung to the idea so desperately that it'd been an uphill battle. Now they despised him, and Lena remained his only advocate. Lucian eyed the beautiful, composed vampire sitting across from him. He had never questioned her loyalty.

After Christian had left the House of Devereux, she'd had no one, and he had been the only one there for her. He'd taken her in at first as a means to punish his brother, but over the years, Lena had become his most dependable confidante. With benefits. Despite the fact that she'd forever be linked to Christian because he was her maker, Lucian had grown to trust her. Her lust for power and ambition rivaled his. And he knew that she loathed Christian with a deep-rooted, immeasurable hatred, which meant that she would never betray Lucian.

"When's the final vote?" he asked.

"In a few weeks," she said. "It has to be unanimous, so we do have a little more time."

"Time for what?" Lucian could see that Lena was getting at something, and the careful blank look on her face made him edgy. "Don't be shy, go on."

"To get on your brother's good side," she said. His face pulled into a scowl, and she placed her hands up in a placating gesture. "Hear me out. He's the only one the Council will listen to and he was there in that underground chamber. He knows that you did not kill Enhard. He is the only one who can vouch for you."

"No," Lucian snarled, standing so quickly that the chair beneath him slammed into the nearby wall. He stalked to the bar and poured himself another drink. "I would prefer execution than beg for his help."

"Lucian, please be reasonable. The Council will not delay a decision based on my vote alone. I will be overruled." Lena's voice was carefully modulated. She knew that if she pushed him too far, he would refuse just on principle. And of course he would. The thought of begging his brother to help him was ludicrous. Lena stood and walked toward him, resting her palm on his shoulder. "I don't want to lose you, Lucian. Just promise me that you'll at least consider it."

"There's nothing that would ever make me do that," he said, flinging her arm off with a violent shrug. "I would rather be burned in the fires of hell than beg my esteemed *brother* for anything. And you would do well to never mention it again."

Despite his ferocious threat, Lena stared at him and tried again. "Look," she began, "your brother's position as a royal vampire overlord on the High Council will afford him the authority to veto any decision of the Council. Even if he has to recuse himself from the vote given your relationship, he could prove without a doubt that Enhard had not died by your hand, and then you have a chance. Surely that's worth something." She took a deep breath. "Surely that's worth your life."

"I do not need him," he gritted through clenched teeth.

"You do, but your goddamned pride won't let you see beyond that."

"We are all damned, aren't we, my love?"

Her mouth tightened at his flippancy. "I'll call him. You won't have to do a thing."

Lucian watched in annoyance as she picked up the handset and dialed a number. She placed the call on speakerphone as Victoria's lilting female voice answered. Lucian ignored the twinge in his stomach at the sound of it.

17

"Hello?"

"Hello, may I speak to Christian … er … His Grace?" Lena asked, forgetting to use Christian's formal address. Lucian's mouth flattened.

"He's out. May I say who's calling, please?"

"It's Lena. I'll try his cellphone. Thank you," she said quickly and disconnected. She dialed another number. Lucian frowned, realizing that she had both numbers committed to memory, even after all these years. Despite himself, an unfamiliar bitter feeling coiled in his stomach, one he'd long forgotten.

It clicked on, the voice imperious. "Yes?"

"Christian, it's Lena," she said, her tone cautious. "I know I'm the last person you expected to hear from, but I need to see you regarding something important. It's about Lucian. I … we … need your help. Can you stop by?"

Lucian heard the dead silence on the other end of the phone line and knew that Lena had blindsided Christian with her blunt request. The silence deepened and he exhaled in an irritated rush. His brother would never agree to help him. His brows drew together and he was about to tell Lena to hang up when Christian spoke. "Where?"

"My place. You remember?"

"Yes. Thirty minutes." The phone clicked off.

Lena stared at Lucian, her look of triumph fading from her face at the glare on his. "My place made the most sense," she explained. "There are too many people watching your every step here."

At her reasoning, he fought to bring his roiling jealousy under control. Lena's apartment did make the most sense—they wouldn't be overheard, and she had guards of her own. He poured himself a liberal helping of brandy and drained his glass in a single gulp. It wouldn't matter if he drank the entire contents of the decanter, but the fire burning a path to his stomach kept his raging emotions at bay. "You're wrong about him. He won't help."

"He will."

"You better be right," he said and stalked out of the room. The door crashed into its frame behind him.

†††

CHRISTIAN STARED at the silver phone in his hand and wondered what Lena's game was. He pocketed the device, releasing his mental hold on the animal he'd fed from earlier. The deer bounded off on shaky legs into the woods. He debated what Lena really wanted. There was a chance that she wasn't playing one of her usual games and his brother really did need his help, but with either of them, he could never be sure. The last time he'd seen Lena, she'd been clear that her ... affections for him hadn't changed. But Christian wasn't interested in Lena. Not anymore. Not when he had Victoria.

As he ran back toward his house, he felt the soft brush of Victoria's voice in his mind. *Lena called.* Christian understood her hesitancy.

Yes, I just talked to her, something to do with Lucian. I'll be back soon.

You're going to see her?

I have to. I love you.

Okay, she said after a long pause. *I love you, too.*

Christian felt her withdraw, sensing the coolness at the end of their mental conversation. He sighed. Victoria had nothing to worry about. His courtship with Lena ended a long time ago, but he knew that Victoria agonized over the fact that he had made Lena into a vampire. It was something she could never expect to become. But what Victoria didn't seem to get was that Lena represented everything he hated about himself—her fierce love for killing went against everything that he believed. Lena belonged with someone like Lucian.

Christian didn't bother to head back into the house, instead sliding into the sleek car parked out front. He made the drive to Lena's apartment in Puteaux, a western suburb of Paris, in exactly half an hour. La Défense touched on the northern part of Puteaux, which made it a convenient location for Lena as most of the Council meetings took place at their headquarters in the Tour Areva in La Défense. Christian also owned a home in the nearby suburb of Le Vésinet, but he rarely used that residence, instead preferring the château in Fontainebleau where he and Victoria were temporarily ensconced. Lena's apartment was in a modern development overlooking the Seine River, and she was waiting for him out front as he parked.

"Lena," he said as he stepped out of the car. As always, she was impeccably dressed in a chic black suit. Her face was guarded as she leaned forward and kissed him in the French custom on both cheeks.

"Thank you for coming, Christian," she said. Lena's voice was melodic and contrasted sharply with the ruthlessness she was known for. Although she certainly appeared it, she was the furthest thing from delicate. Like the perfect predator, her beauty and her voice were the things that drew people to her. But for Christian, the soft tones of her voice only served to put him on edge. "There's a café around the corner. I was thinking we could go there. Unless you want to come up."

"The café is fine."

They walked in silence to the café and sat down at an outdoor table. The bruised twilight sky was clear and the streets buzzed with activity as the local Parisians enjoyed the balmy summer evening. Christian ordered a café au lait and sat back, his bearing impassive, giving no quarter to Lena. Whatever she wanted, she would have to come right out and ask for it.

"You look well," she said after ordering a black coffee. He inclined his head, but did not return the compliment, and waited for her to continue. Lena took a deep breath as she stared at him, her fingers drumming on the table's edge. "You weren't at the last few Council meetings," she began. "I am sure you are aware that the Council is close to convicting Lucian on murder charges for Enhard's death." She glanced at him, but he kept his face blank, and she rushed to continue. "I wouldn't contact you if I didn't think that this was impossible. You are the only one who can help him."

"What would you have me do?" Christian asked. He knew exactly what was happening with the Council and their decision to victimize his brother, and while there was no way he would let that happen, he wanted to see where Lena was coming from.

"You were there. He didn't kill Enhard."

"Yes, but he didn't save him either, which the Council would argue is the same thing. He could have easily, you know," Christian said. "Saved Enhard. But he chose not to, an act that led to Enhard's death. Does that not make him responsible in some way?" His voice remained flat, although it had caught slightly when he'd said Enhard's name. The pain of his death hadn't quite lost its sting.

"Yes, perhaps, but it doesn't warrant his execution," Lena replied in a heated voice. Watching the emotions play across her face, Christian was shocked at her vehemence. He hadn't realized that Lena cared so much for Lucian's welfare. They were the perfect pair, with the same values and the same ambitions, but he never understood outside of that connection what had held them together. Maybe, somewhere deep inside, she did care for his brother.

"Why are you doing this?" he asked. "Because we both know you're not here with Lucian's good wishes. So why do you care?" He was unprepared for the tormented expression that flashed across her face before she tried to conceal it.

"Because I do," she said, a defiant edge in her tone.

"I didn't think you cared *that* much," he said. "If you need my help, you need to be honest with me for once. Why do you care, Lena?"

She bit her lip and turned away. Christian sipped his coffee and narrowed his eyes at the crowd slowing to gape. He was used to attention, but this felt different. *Everyone* was looking at them. His eyes slid to his companion and he understood why. Of course people would stare—both blond and tall, the two of them made a striking couple with their flawless, predacious beauty. Like unsuspecting prey, people were drawn to them, oblivious to the danger they posed.

Lena glanced at him, and he shifted his stare toward her. He arched an eyebrow and repeated his last question. "Why?"

"Because …" Her voice faltered, her ice-blue eyes glittering with something akin to misery. "If I lose him too, then I have nothing." She pushed a wry smile to her lips. "You left me with nothing, but at least Lucian was there to pick up the pieces. Over the years, Lucian and I, well, it was more than I could hope for," she said. "And now, I won't give up on him. He didn't give up on me when …" She trailed off, but Christian knew what she meant. She meant when he did.

"Does Lucian know?" he asked.

She shrugged. "Perhaps."

"And does he feel the same?"

"In his own way, he does," she said. "You know your brother."

Christian leaned forward in his seat. Strangely, her honesty moved him. The vulnerability was so unlike her that it made him pause for a second. "I never gave up on you, Lena, you must know that," he admitted after a while. "You and I were cut from different cloths. You couldn't understand me then, and even now, I see that you still struggle to. I would have made you hate what you are, just as I do."

"But you made me into this," she said, her brows pulling together into a slight frown. "How could I not love it? Or you. Surely, *you* must know that."

"It was a mistake, for both of us." His voice was flat.

Lena's head drooped, and when he saw her shoulders shaking, for a moment he thought she was in tears. And then a chilling sound split the silence between them and he realized that she was laughing. The sound was brittle and empty. She raised glacial blue eyes to his and glared at him with veiled contempt.

"A little too late for a mistake, isn't it," she said. "For either of us."

"I guess I deserve that," he said. "But I can't change the past."

"No, Christian, you can't."

The moment between them passed as if it had never happened, and the vulnerability he'd seen faded, her features hardening into their usual icy and indifferent mask. Christian leaned back his seat and mimicked her blank expression. He had nothing to apologize for—Lena reveled in what she was. She'd wanted to become a vampire the minute she'd laid eyes on him and Lucian.

Lena's voice cut through the silence between them. "Don't get me wrong. You shouldn't be sorry. I love what I am." She waved a careless hand. "You're right, I can't understand how you don't love what we are. Immortal, unassailable, powerful, deadly." She grinned, her teeth white and perfect. The smile did not reach her eyes. "Help Lucian, Christian," she said forcefully, leaning forward and invoking the full force of her vampire compulsion.

In spite of himself, Christian felt its unmistakable magnetism. Damn, but she had become powerful. He raised an eyebrow at her boldness in trying to influence him and received one in return.

"Help him," she repeated, still persuasive, urgent. There was no request in her voice.

"You cannot compel me," he said. "If Lucian needs my help, he can ask for it and it will be given."

"You know he won't," she said, falling back into her seat.

"Then it looks like we are done here. The last I heard, my brother said that my biggest problem is saving people who don't need saving. I won't make that mistake with him again. He knows where to find me."

He stood, signaling the waiter for the check, which he paid, and walked away. Christian didn't look back even though he could feel the full weight of Lena's stare boring into his back.

DANGEROUS LIAISONS

D inner thus far had been a success. The staff had just removed the last of the dessert dishes, and Victoria and Aliya were retiring to the sitting room for coffee. Christian had thoughtfully decided to excuse himself, leaving the two of them alone. Victoria smiled at him as he pressed a kiss on her head, feeling the brush of Aliya's stare from across the room where she was admiring a Poussin landscape painting.

Their conversation over dinner had been light, more or less in the vein of what their summer plans were while in Paris, and although Aliya had been more than polite, Victoria could sense that she had many other questions, ones that remained unanswered from their last meeting. She and Christian had discussed whether she should share her secret with Aliya, and Christian had said that it was up to her. Victoria opted to wait and decide, depending on how things were going.

"These paintings are beautiful," Aliya said as she sat down in the armchair opposite Victoria.

"Christian's family owns many rare pieces," Victoria replied. "He's had a long time to collect them, I guess." She made a wry expression, and Aliya laughed. Her face seemed so ageless that it was difficult to tell how old she was, but Victoria knew that the high priestess had to be at least in her forties.

Aliya studied her, stirring her coffee. "Thank you again for the invitation to dinner. I was surprised to hear you were in Paris and delighted to accept."

"You're welcome. It was long overdue." Victoria took a deep breath, knowing that she would have to be the one to lead the direction of the conversation because of the way she had left it the last time. "I want to apologize for when we last met. I was upset at another situation."

"No need, my dear."

"I feel I must—my behavior was inexcusable, and for that, I'm sorry."

Aliya nodded her head with a gracious smile. "It is forgotten."

"Thank you," Victoria said, swallowing hard. She took a deep breath and made her decision. "Last time you asked me what my family name was," she said slowly. Aliya leaned forward in her seat, her eyes sparking with interest. "Well, it's Warrick."

Victoria didn't know what she was expecting, but it certainly wasn't the blank look that flitted across Aliya's face. If anything, Aliya looked confused. "I'm sorry. I don't recognize the name."

Victoria tried another approach. "How about the Duchess of Lancaster?" she asked softly, and was rewarded as Aliya's eyes popped and she flew out of her seat, hands clasped to her mouth. The Duchess of Lancaster was Victoria's ancestor and the legend of the Cruentus Curse was based on her, the last living record of the blood curse. "She was a Warrick, too," Victoria said.

Aliya sat back down in a daze, shaking her head. "It's impossible."

Her voice was raspy with shock, but as the minutes passed, Victoria could see the understanding dawning in her eyes as Aliya considered what had happened in La Défense. Victoria had blocked a Seer from seeing her unconscious mind and magically coerced a warded room full of vampires with her words alone.

"Is it true what you are saying?" Aliya asked when she finally found her voice. "Were you blood relatives?"

Her emphasis on *blood* was not lost on Victoria. "The Duchess was my great, great, great, great grandmother."

"And the curse?"

"Still alive and kicking, unfortunately," Victoria said with a dry look. "I'm sorry I couldn't tell you before. I didn't know who to trust and, well, there were a lot of things going on then that made it difficult for me to talk to anyone."

"Do you have any idea what this means, Tori?" Aliya said. "It's what everyone has been waiting for."

"Believe me, I know," she said.

"What do you mean?"

As Victoria launched the story of what had happened over the last few months with Gabriel and Lucian both trying to take control of her power, Aliya's mouth dropped open in disbelief. The mere mention of Lucian had hardened her expression. She obviously didn't trust him either. Victoria talked for almost an hour, and Aliya listened in amazed silence as the story of Brigid's amulet and the journal unfolded, and how Victoria had had to fight to gain control of the blood magic at the cost of her life as well as Christian's.

After she finished, Aliya stared at her in stupefied silence and cleared her throat. "You have no idea of the magnitude of what you are in the supernatural world. *Everyone* has been looking for you."

"I know," Victoria said quietly.

"And His Grace? What is your relationship with him?"

Victoria knew that Aliya was only trying to make the connections in her head—including the fact that she was here *living* with Christian. Clearly, she'd just announced that she was the wielder of the fabled and feared Cruentus Curse, and here she was, sitting in a vampire's home, of all places. She shrugged and exhaled. She didn't want to lie. "He's a friend."

Aliya's response was soft. "He is more than that, isn't he?"

As much as relations between their worlds were forbidden, this was her life and she loved Christian. She would never apologize for that, not even to secure the approval of a high priestess. She met Aliya's stare head on. "Yes."

Aliya exhaled slowly, nodding. "From what I know of His Grace, he does not appear to be like the rest of his kind. He has always treated the Witch Clans with respect and courtesy. Perhaps this will help to bring our people together."

Or tear it apart, a ghostly voice intoned, just as Victoria sensed the arrival of a new non-human presence. Another familiar. Victoria's eyes snapped to the large black spider dropping down from a silver strand of webbing to land on Aliya's shoulder. Of course it *had* to be a spider. She suppressed the sudden inclination to search for a very large boot.

"Tear what apart?" she asked, Aliya's familiar now staring at her with its eight gleaming eyes.

"You can hear him?" Aliya asked in surprise.

Victoria had forgotten that most familiars were only audible to their masters. "Yes."

She is powerful, the familiar commented.

Quiet, Dante, Aliya said. The spider bristled but remained silent, his eyes bright and intent. Aliya turned back to Victoria. "This is Dante. He is old and tends to speak his mind."

Victoria frowned, staring at the spider. She, too, was as surprised as Aliya that she could hear the thoughts of the familiar, but she was learning more and more how much her power surpassed those of ordinary witches. "Nice to meet you, Dante."

And you. With that, he disappeared into the curtain of Aliya's hair, but Victoria could still sense his presence. She wondered if Leto could, too, wherever he was.

"So please continue with your story," Aliya said, leaning forward. "Did the blood's magic tell you how to perform the offensive spells when you were under attack?"

"Yes and no. I don't need spells to perform magic, although the knowledge of the words made everything so much more powerful. Leto, my familiar, explained it to me. There's so much I don't understand about magic. I learned the hard way about energy and how it comes from life around us when the exiled witch on the mountain tried to capture me. Christian said you knew who she was?"

Aliya nodded. "Yes, she came from a very talented family, but when the mental illness manifested, she refused to have her magic removed and killed two high priestesses in the process. Mental weakness makes witches too unstable. Her magic was taken by force and she was exiled for her crimes. But from your story, it appears that she managed to keep some of it with her." Aliya's lips twisted in a wry smile. "I can't imagine how you were able to fight and survive. She was a powerful witch. But then, I guess so are you."

Victoria lowered her eyes, staring at the floor. She didn't want Aliya to see what was hidden there. The truth was, when she'd absorbed that witch's magic, it'd been revolting but thrilling. The blood had trilled in delight as the witch's life drained from her body, and she had *reveled* in it.

"Aliya," she asked, hesitant. "What happens with magic … say if someone takes it forcibly from you?"

"Like another witch, you mean?" Aliya said, and Victoria nodded. "One, it's almost impossible to do. But even if it were not, it is forbidden according to our laws. Magic is a part of us, and stealing it from another witch would be like taking a life."

"You take it away from insane people, right?"

"Yes, but not into ourselves. The magic is dissipated into the universe, the earth, and the air around us." Aliya smiled thinly.

"Not to make a comparison but it would be like a vampire pilfering life from others."

Victoria bit her lip, knowing she was pushing the limits. Aliya was far too clever to not get suspicious about the pointed nature of her questions, but she had to know. "I get that. But theoretically speaking, what would happen if someone were to do it?" Aliya's eyes snapped to hers, and she felt her cheeks getting hot and stomach souring—she'd gone too far.

The priestess leaned forward, a frown marring her face. "Is that what the witch tried to do to you up on that mountain?" she asked. Victoria swallowed her relief and nodded once, sickened by the lie. Aliya's sympathetic glance was almost her undoing. "The short answer is that they would die. We simply couldn't absorb someone else's magic. Magic is a complex structure, like our human DNA, and unique to each witch. There are no known records of anyone taking in another's magic for any extended period. How did it feel? Perhaps you mistook it for another spell?"

Victoria pursed her lips, trying to calm her racing heart. *She* hadn't died—she had taken the magic and wielded it against its master. "Maybe. But the only thing I can compare it to is power being drained from one source to another," she said, then sighed. She didn't even want to think about what she had been able to do with the witch's magic—it'd been an intrusion of the worst kind. She pushed it out of her head and forced a smile to her face. "I guess I have a lot to learn, don't I?"

"Would you like to learn more?"

Her spirits brightened. "Where?"

"We have a school here in Paris."

"A school for witchcraft?" Victoria said and then grinned. "Like a Hogwarts or something?"

A smile. "Not exactly, but similar."

Victoria ignored the slight skip of her heart. Learning more about her magic was an exciting thought—she'd meet other witches. She'd finally have a place to belong, somewhere to fit in. She didn't know how Christian would react to the news, considering how protective he was of her, but it was her life, after all. She took a breath and nodded to Aliya. "I would."

"Excellent. You should come tomorrow to my house. I'll arrange a meeting with some of the teachers and we will discuss who can start your formal education at the school. Perhaps something accelerated," Aliya said, as if recalling everything Victoria had told her.

A soft twitter inside her sleeve distracted them both as Dante crawled into sight. *Perhaps Pan? He is a new mentor, but has not been assigned.*

"Yes, I was thinking the same. Good suggestion."

Victoria cleared her throat, a wave of dread overcoming her. "Aliya, I don't want anyone to know … about me …" She trailed off in uncomfortable silence.

Aliya smiled kindly, though something like unease shifted in her eyes. "It will be your secret to tell."

Just then Leto sauntered into the room and jumped up onto Victoria's lap. She stroked him beneath his jaw and down his silver-furred back. "This is Leto. My familiar," she explained. "He's the one who got me through most of the earlier stuff, so I owe a lot to him."

The black spider peeked out from the folds of Aliya's shirt collar and met Leto's unwavering stare. Victoria almost grinned at the sight of the two familiars sizing each other up. Leto's head inclined in gracious deference and the spider acknowledged his greeting. From what Leto had told her, Victoria knew that the familiar of a high priestess often carried the same rank as she did, and etiquette followed the same lines among the familiars. Dante would certainly outrank Leto, at least within the Paris coven.

Suddenly, Dante went rigid as if something had taken control of his entire body. He slipped from Aliya's shoulder and fell in slow motion to the floor, reviving at the last minute to save himself with a swiftly released web.

"Dante," Aliya gasped, palming the spider. "What is it?"

The familiar ... it's very old. Dante hesitated as he crawled into Aliya's sleeve. *As in an Ancient.*

Victoria's curious gaze jerked to the spider. "What's an Ancient?"

Drawing a slow breath, the high priestess responded to her question with a stuttered one of her own. "May I ask about your familiar? How old is he?"

Victoria frowned, wondering why Leto wasn't being more forthcoming with their guests. Then she realized that Aliya wouldn't be able to hear him, as she'd been able to hear Dante. "Leto was my grandmother's. He does seem to have had a long life, doesn't he?" Victoria said as she stroked Leto's soft fur. He purred, but continued to stare at the high priestess and her familiar, his green eyes unswerving. "I wouldn't have made it far without him. Why do you ask? And you never answered my question. What's an Ancient?"

"Ancients are few and far between in our world," she began. "An Ancient means that a familiar can live far beyond their normal years. Age can always be extended by magic, but it isn't infinite, and only very few live beyond the lifetimes of their companion witches. Those who do are believed to have special gifts, carrying the spirits of ancient witch kings and queens."

Victoria snorted as Leto stiffened beneath her fingers. "And Leto? You think he's one of them?"

"Perhaps."

She snorted again, earning a soft hiss from the feline crouched on her lap. "He belonged to my grandmother, but I'm pretty sure she got him when she was a girl, so I know he's old, but he's not *ancient*."

"If you say so," Aliya said, but seemed unconvinced.

In a smooth motion, Leto stretched and jumped to the floor,

his gaze intense, with a long meaningful look directed at Aliya and her familiar. He sauntered away as if he didn't have a care in the world, leaving Victoria to offer excuses for his rudeness.

"I'm so sorry, not sure what's gotten into him lately." Victoria shook her head and shrugged. "He doesn't like strangers, especially since we've been here in Paris. Maybe you're right about him. He is kind of a grumpy old curmudgeon."

"No apology needed," Aliya said, rising. "It's late anyway, and we should get going. Please call in tomorrow and we will see how we can expedite your training. It's imperative that we start at once, given … what you are."

Victoria tensed at the wording, but she knew it wasn't malicious. "Thank you, Aliya. Thanks for listening, and well, for everything."

"It's my honor," she said.

As her guests took their leave, Victoria eyed the black limousine pulling away and noted that, like the vampires, the witches also liked to travel in style and comfort. She grinned. Well, at least she didn't jump on a broom and fly off … although Leto had told her that witches couldn't fly. Go figure, but one day, she intended to put that theory to the test. It was all physics and probability, really. That, and a really great spell.

Sensing the soft whisper of movement behind her, Victoria leaned back just as Christian's arms curved around her shoulders, drawing her to him.

"How did it go?" he murmured.

"Good, I think. I have a meeting with them tomorrow to talk about my magical education." She laughed, already breathless at the feel of his lean body braced against hers. "I'm quite excited," she told him. "I'm going to meet more people like me and learn about who I am." She paused, her humor fading slightly. "And maybe figure out a way to work this thing out between us."

"It's good to see you happy," he said, kissing the top of her head. "I know it's been difficult the last few weeks."

"Just a little," she said under her breath, earning her a playful swat on the arm as he turned her to face him. His slate colored eyes bore into hers. She almost shivered from the intensity of that look, her knees turning to putty as warmth suffused her entire body. The attraction between them hadn't waned a bit. If anything, it'd grown stronger, more combustible, and infinitely more treacherous. She licked dry lips and swallowed, watching an answering flare burst in his eyes.

"Stop staring at me and kiss me already," she said, her voice hoarse. Christian obliged, bending his head and brushing his warm lips across hers, but she pulled away until only their fingertips were touching.

"Not that way, the *other* way," she said breathless. *This way.*

Her mental voice was a gentle coaxing caress. Christian's eyes burned silver as she slipped past the doors of his mind, her essence twirling around his consciousness, so seductive, it overtook them both in seconds. Desire was like liquid heat, touching everywhere inside of them all at once. Christian gave as good as he got, returning her phantom caresses until she slid her hand up his arm and he broke away, the physical friction of her fingers ratcheting the tension to excruciating heights.

What's wrong? Victoria asked.

Christian didn't answer, his free hand moving to cradle her jaw, his thumb brushing across her lips. She could see the simmering want in his eyes, feeling it in the pulse of his fingers on her face. She knew that all he wanted to do was to pull her into his arms and kiss her for real—kiss her until neither of them could speak. But it was far too risky. As torturous as the mental kissing was, it was the safest thing for them.

The reality was neither of them could be trusted when things got heated—her perfidious *blood* couldn't be trusted—so they'd had to settle for something more controlled, less threatening. But as intense as the mental thing was, nothing could surpass the feel of physical contact, the feel of skin on skin, or the taste of his lips. She exhaled sharply, tearing her gaze from his, but Christian wouldn't let her go. Instead, he drew her closer, his hand splaying against her back, his natural vampire magnetism compelling despite himself.

"Christian—"

I want ... His gaze dropped to her lips recklessly. *More.*

Victoria blinked, responsive, her mind going blank for a dizzying second as an overwhelming surge took over her entire body, making her center hot and her knees weak. Her blood pushed hungrily beneath her skin, its desire almost as strong as hers. She wanted to say no, but everything inside of her screamed yes. It'd only be for a second. They were both in control.

Yes, she thought, sliding her palms up his chest.

Desire and hunger spun into the perfect storm as Victoria wrapped her fingers around his nape and held his head captive to hers. Christian's lips and mouth recreated every scorching step of their earlier mental exchange. His kisses grazed her cheek, nipped at her jaw, her ear, inhaling her scent and descending lower, pressing into the taut column of her neck as she arched toward him, lost in the near-forgotten feel of him. His tongue drew a hot path from her collarbone to the tops of her breasts and back up again, leaving a scorching trail wherever it touched.

Her blood was singing, the heat spiraling under her skin as Christian pressed forward, his teeth grazing her flushed skin. Despite herself and the vague warning at the back of her head, she arched backward, feeling her pulse humming beneath his lips, louder and louder as if inviting him in—daring him to do what he was made to do—consume her blood.

All her desires coalesced into a single, insistent command.

Take it.

The only thing that drew them out of their manic, seductive haze was Leto's crazed hissing and the vicious swipe of his paw against Christian's leg. Christian jerked out of her embrace with a harsh curse, and Victoria blinked with wide, dazed eyes, confused by his sudden withdrawal, her gaze sliding to Leto, who stood by, fury vibrating in waves off of him.

That was too close. His mental voice was a shriek. *What were you thinking?*

Staring at them both, Christian stumbled backward, his lips stained crimson, to collapse on the foyer staircase. Victoria's heart stopped.

"Oh my god, is that—" she whispered, terrified. "My blood?"

"No, it's mine," he said shakily, tasting the blood on his lips. "I think."

"What happened?" she said, her fingers fluttering to her neck to feel for broken skin.

They hadn't ever lost this much control, not to the point that Christian would willingly put either of them at risk. They both knew what her blood had done in New York when it had possessed him. But they had always been able to stop before. She shivered and met Christian's eyes.

"Don't you realize how close … I … you …" he whispered brokenly, unable to finish his sentence. "If it weren't for Leto, I don't know what would have happened. We were both in so deep. I wanted you so much that I barely even knew what I was doing. I think I was compelling you. You felt … malleable."

Victoria blinked. "But your vampire compulsion doesn't work against me. We tried it, remember?" she said, walking toward him and sitting down on the step at his side. She studied his face, noticing that he was keeping his mouth tightly closed. His body flinched at her nearness, as if he was struggling to hold on to his control. She slid to the far end of the step, putting some distance between them. "Right?"

"Yes, but this was different. This time you wanted it as much as I did. For the compulsion to work, you have to take it in. You have to *want* it to work. And you did. Your mind is too strong for it to work on its own. I compelled you, Tori. There's no other explanation for what just happened."

Her heart plummeted as cold realization set in. "My blood." She sighed. "It must have been my blood. I mean I could feel it flexing inside of me, but after a while everything just felt hot, and well, that's what happens when you touch me, so I didn't really think anything of it."

"Didn't you feel my mouth on your neck? My teeth?"

She flushed. "Yes, but you always do that, and you don't *do* anything."

"Tori, I was seconds away from ripping into you. If Leto hadn't warned us, I don't know what I would have done. Who knows what your blood would have done?" He broke off and Victoria knew he was thinking about the last time he'd drunk her rogue blood. Now, it'd be a coin toss as to whether the blood would have killed him, had he taken it, or let him live like the last time.

She swallowed and wrapped her arms around her middle. "Why would it let you compel me?"

"It wanted me to take it," he said. "I saw it flash in your eyes in the seconds after I kissed you. There's no other way you would have given in to the compulsion. Your magic would have warned you that a vampire was trying to compel you, and there's a reason it didn't."

Christian grimaced as a spasm rocked his shoulders. He raised stormy eyes to hers and she could see that they were turning feral, his hunger eating away at him until it would be the only thing he could feel, the only thing he could see. His face sharpened, the sculpted, angular planes almost razor-like, and his features took on a predatory quality. Heat bloomed in the pit of her stomach. God help her—he almost bit her, and still, she wanted him. He made her forget how to breathe, *especially* when he was hungry. She sighed and mentally caressed his cheek. He flinched away from her fragmented touch.

"Go," she whispered. "I'll be here." Christian disappeared within seconds with an apologetic twist of his mouth.

Leto walked over, rubbing against her legs. Victoria hadn't noticed his constant purring since she and Christian had pulled apart, but it helped to diffuse the rattled emotions swirling within her. She stroked his fur and felt herself calm even further. She stared into the green eyes that mirrored hers.

He's right, you know, Leto said, somber. *About the blood.*

But why would my blood want me to succumb to his vampire power?

It's a powerful curse you bear ... all it wants is its own freedom, and it nearly had that within its grasp, Leto said. *Distracting you both was clever. You need to be careful, Victoria.*

She narrowed her eyes at her familiar. *What do you mean it wants its own freedom?*

Darkness always seeks escape from its chains. The Cruentus Curse will do anything it can to twist you ... to make you its instrument instead of its master.

Couldn't I have been born a normal witch? She sighed. *You know, without all of this crazy, surreal existential blood curse crap?*

Leto stared at her. *You cannot run from who you are.*

I know, she said with an eye roll. *I wish I could find a way to stop torturing Christian like this.*

It's his nature, Victoria. He is a vampire and you are a witch. You knew that this was never going to be easy. I warned you, but you chose not to listen.

Victoria bristled at the blunt reprimand. *He loves me, Leto. And I love him. I am going to find a way to make this work, with or without you.*

They stared at each other in silent standoff. She knew he didn't approve of her relationship with Christian, even if he'd reluctantly come to accept it, but he was out of line. It was *her* life, regardless of her stupid bloodlines or his unsolicited opinions on the matter.

Leto's moods had become unpredictable since they'd arrived in Paris. One minute, he was the normal snide cat she knew, and the next, he was a stranger condemning her with blazing, unfamiliar eyes. She figured that it had to do with Gabriel's torture and its effect on him, but the erratic behavior unnerved her, which was one of the reasons why she hadn't pushed him earlier with Aliya and Dante.

Someday you will learn that there are greater things than this childish infatuation, Leto said and stalked off. She stared after him in disbelief even after he had rounded the corner to the living room.

"Childish infatuation?" she repeated in an aggravated mutter. "What does that even mean? Why doesn't the talking animal make sense?"

The talking animal can still hear you.

Then do me a favor and talk to your familiar friends so we can figure out how to stop my rogue blood from trying to get my boyfriend to kill me.

THE ART OF WAR

Lucian crashed his fist into the glass countertop in a rage, watching the glistening cracks shatter outward in a concentric shape. He wanted to smash the whole thing to pieces. The Council was treading way beyond its authority, and if they thought that antagonizing him or the House of Devereux was the best course of action, then so be it. In hindsight, he probably shouldn't have let Enhard die—arguably, he'd been one of the few more rational influences over the Council, and many of his colleagues had followed his lead in his respect toward the House of Devereux.

His House was powerful in its own right, but noble blood remained noble in the vampire realm, and Lucian took full advantage of it, just as he had in his human one. Still, he wasn't naïve. He knew that despite his aristocratic lineage, squaring off against any Elder would be suicide. For such mature vampires, their age gave them considerable advantages, like strength and speed, infinite regenerative powers, and invulnerability to most forms of damage. Another Elder could kill an Elder, but that was unlikely. The only vampire immortal stronger than an

Elder would be the Reii, the original vampires. But it wasn't like Lucian knew any of them.

Like most modern vampires, he was skeptical about their existence. The Reii were more myth than reality. Choosing to slumber the centuries, it was said that they remained in seclusion because the weight of immortality had become too much to bear. Lucian snorted. He would never tire of power and immortality. If he were Reii, *everyone* would know of his presence. He thirsted for power so much that it consumed him.

A knock at the door interrupted his thoughts.

"Yes?" he said, pouring himself a brandy. A tall, thin vampire walked in, Kristos, one of Lucian's most trusted advisors. He looked at him expectantly. "What is it?"

"My lord," Kristos said, bowing. "We have found the girl you've been looking for."

"What girl?"

"Le Sang Noir, my lord." Lucian's eyes jumped to Kristos's face, a muscle beginning to twitch in his jaw. He was sick of their incompetence. He'd already found the witch from the prophecy—Christian had taken Victoria from right beneath his nose and she remained under his protection. It was over. He gritted his teeth, suppressing his desire to heave Kristos across the room.

"Le Sang Noir is finished," he gritted through clenched teeth. "It doesn't exist. It's a myth, a fable, a *lie*." Spit flew from his mouth as his fury echoed in the room. He would rather them believe it was an urban legend than discover that his brother, Christian, had been the one to find and wield the power from the prophecy. Kristos shrank back from Lucian's anger, but stood his ground.

"I insist, my lord, you need to see this witch," he said even as Lucian glared daggers at him. His black eyes glittered in response and Lucian paused. The urge to inflict damage hadn't gone away, but killing Kristos wouldn't solve anything and would leave him without allies. He massaged his brow and studied the contents of his glass.

"Kristos," he explained. "Le Sang Noir has already been found. The power is useless. No one can harness it. It's too late. The witch you found is not the one from the prophecy. This, I know. I have seen it with my own eyes."

Kristos remained wary, as if he didn't want to antagonize Lucian. "Perhaps not, but I have not seen this level of power in a long time. Her magic could be useful if she is rogue. No coven, no family." He pressed on. "She kills without words. I saw her slay a handful of dark creatures with a single look. Her face was so pale and her blood as black as her eyes."

"What did you say?" Lucian said, spinning in a reaction so quick that he had Kristos' neck in his hand against the wall in a heartbeat. His snarling face was inches from his. "What did you say?" His voice was deadly soft.

"I saw her slay—"

"No," Lucian interrupted him. "About her blood?"

"She had a wound," Kristos choked, barely able to speak from Lucian's death grip. "Her arm was dripping blood. It was black."

"Could it have been a trick of the light?" Lucian said, loosening his hold on the vampire.

Kristos rubbed his bruised neck with one hand. "Maybe. The hour was late."

"It had to have been a trick," Lucian muttered. Victoria was the witch from the prophecy. He had seen Le Sang Noir in action, seen it take control of his brother. Kristos was wrong, he had to be. But ... what if he wasn't?

The niggling thought wriggled its way into the folds of his mind. Could Le Sang Noir appear simultaneously? Could this witch be part of the same family? He shook his head. No, the prophecy had never spoken of another, and after all his years of research, he would have known if there was a chance there could be more than one manifestation of it. It was too sporadic, too rare.

But even if it weren't possible, Lucian didn't want to take any chances. He needed to amass an army. And Kristos was right. A powerful witch as an ally could be just what he needed. A forgotten whiff of Victoria's seductive blood assailed his memory and he stifled it with brutal force. He needed to put Le Sang Noir out of his head once and for all—that part of his scheme was over. Victoria would never leave Christian's side, nor would she put her lot in with Lucian. Resentment simmered in his bones, and that was the only basis for his decision.

"Where is this witch?"

"Montmartre."

Lucian stared at Kristos. "No coven, you said?"

"We've been tracking her for six weeks, my lord. She's alone."

"You're positive." It was not a question and Kristos nodded, his black eyes unfaltering. Lucian walked over to the window. He could smell the earthy summer scents of the wind and the colorful wafts of people floating within it. He felt the hunger stir in his throat at the sight. His desires—power, blood, immortality—overwhelmed him, merging into one single writhing mass. He blinked, silencing the clamor in his belly, and turned to Kristos.

"We can't take her by force if she is as strong as you say," Lucian mused. "We need another strategy. Does she have any friends?"

"No. She lives alone. I must warn you, my lord, that she seems quite demented, talks to herself."

"An exile?"

"It's possible. We've seen her kill others of her own kind, completely without conscience or motive." Kristos paused, looking puzzled for a second. "Her magic is strange, not like we've ever seen, which is why I think you should see her for yourself. She's powerful, but raw. Perhaps she can replace the one who died."

Lucian glared at him. Victoria had dispatched her easily. Too easily. A surge of anger ripped through him at the thought of all that power at his undeserving brother's fingertips. His fingers curled at his sides. He hated to be reminded of Victoria's power, and the fact that she had so effortlessly killed a witch loyal to him made his blood boil. He was just about to tear into Kristos as the door opened, distracting him.

"Get out," he said instead.

Lena entered, the scowl on her face deepening as it centered on Kristos. She glared at him with a dispassionate look as he walked past her. Lena didn't care much for him, Lucian knew. She thought him slippery and shifty. She bared her teeth at him, hissing under her breath as he raked her body insolently from head to toe.

Her eyes narrowed. "One of these days, you'll be out of Lucian's favor and you'll see just what happens to anyone who stares at me that way."

"I look forward to it," Kristos taunted and walked away.

Lucian grinned, forgetting his anger. Lena would make quick work of Kristos, but for now, he needed him. He would enjoy watching her rip the vampire to pieces once he'd served his purpose.

"News?" he asked Lena.

"Nothing new from the Council," she said, draping her lithe form on the arm of a black chair. Her lips were blood red and her color was high. Lucian's scowl returned. "What's the matter? What did Kristos have to say?" she asked him.

"He claims to have found an exiled witch," he said. "He insists that this one is alone and powerful." He shrugged. "I suppose it bears looking into." Lucian sat on the sofa across from Lena, tapping his hands in agitation against his leg. "With the Council making these changes and trying to entrap me at

every turn, things are going to be more difficult than we anticipated. They are cutting us off at the legs, leaving us weak and
useless."

Lena remained silent, watching him. He knew that with all
the unwanted attention from the Council, things had indeed
become more precarious for her in the last few weeks. They
were keen on his execution, and Lena remained one of three
vampires in opposition. By law, execution required a unanimous vote, and the first time the Council had brought it to the
table, there'd been at least ten against the execution. Now, there
were three. It wouldn't be long before she was the only one
standing in the way. The Council could move for a vote of no
confidence given her loyalty to the House of Devereux and that
would be the end.

"Lucian," Lena said, interrupting his thoughts. "I met with
Christian."

"And?" His voice was ominous, despite his shaking fingers.
"Did he agree?"

"No," she said. "Not directly. He wants you to ask him."

"Of course he does," he seethed, the corded muscles in his
neck bulging from irritation at the foolish burst of hope he'd
felt. He wanted nothing from his brother. "I don't need his help.
I would rather face execution than beg for anything from him.
Is that what you told him? That I would plead for his
assistance?"

Lena recoiled from his fury, but held his gaze. "No, I did not.
And I know you would rather die than ask for his help. But I
would rather you didn't," she said, pulling herself to her feet and
walking towards him. She took his hands in her own. "You're all
I have. If we have to beg Christian's power to save you, then we
should do so without a second thought. The Council is too
close. I fear the next vote will be the deciding factor. We need
him. *You* need him. You need to forget your pride, Lucian.
Please."

Lucian looked at her earnest elegant face and stroked her cheek. His hand drifted to her neck and he caressed it lightly before grasping it between his fingers, throttling her sudden gasp. Her eyes widened at the rage barreling through him. His mouth pulled tight as he leaned forward. "Don't you ever presume to represent me in such a manner. Do you understand?" he whispered, his face scant inches from hers.

Lena didn't flinch. Instead, she ignored the grip of his ruthless fingers and tipped her chin in defiance. "I'll do what I have to, to save you from yourself. Even die at your hands."

She never cowed before him, but in this moment, Lucian wanted to snap her pretty little neck. His voice was silky. "That can be arranged. I told you before, Lena. I don't need saving, by you or anyone else." His other hand brushed the fullness of her lower lip. "You really should not have gone to Christian," he said, moments before his lips descended, capturing hers in a brutal kiss. He wrenched her neck to the side and sank his fangs into her skin, feeling himself calm as her cool blood flowed over his tongue and into the back of his throat. She didn't struggle and after several minutes he pulled away, his lips rimmed in red.

He lifted a careless eyebrow, releasing her. "Was it as good for you as it was for me?" Lena's eyes flashed venomous fire as her palm cracked across his face, snapping his head back. He eyed her, but made no move to strike back. "I suppose I deserved that," he said mildly.

"If you ever touch me like that again, I promise it will be the last time you *ever* touch me," she erupted, her voice shaking with vitriolic rage.

Lucian stared at her and inclined his head in the mockery of a bow. Strangely, he was as disgusted as she was. He was furious over her suggestion that he grovel before Christian, but he knew why she felt it was necessary. Soliciting his brother's help was the last thing he wanted, especially after their previous encounter, and *especially* after his bold last words that one of them would die at their next meeting. The plain truth was that if the Council did agree on his death, Christian would be the only one who could veto it.

His only other alternatives would be to run away or fight. Running away wasn't an option—he'd rather die than become hunted by his own kind. Fighting was possible, but only if he had the time to amass an army to face the retaliation of the Council. But time was a luxury he did not have and Lucian knew it. He glanced at Lena's blank face and felt a momentary twinge of remorse for his behavior.

"I'm sorry." His apology was terse, and despite her surprise, Lena accepted it with a gracious—albeit wary—nod. "I'm on edge lately," he explained curtly, "and I didn't feed today. It's been days, but I shouldn't have done that."

"Fine. Just don't do it again." She turned towards him and flashed a short smile. "In fact, if you hadn't been so premature and so angry all the time, you would have received your gift, and things would have turned out so much better."

"My gift?" Lucian asked, confused. Lena's brow furrowed for a minute as she issued a mental command. The door opened and an olive-skinned, buxom young woman walked in. She was dressed in a mini skirt and a skimpy top. Her face was lined, belying her youthful, lush body, and her eyes were glazed, helpless against Lena's vampire compulsion.

"Compliments of Place Pigalle," Lena said with a smile, indicating the area of Paris that was famously known in its day as the Red Light District, whose side streets still teemed with occasional prostitutes. Lucian smirked.

"Slumming, Lena?" he said, quirking an eyebrow.

"Well, if you don't want her—"

"I didn't say that," he interjected.

The hunger rippled through him so quickly that his face transformed in seconds and he walked to the woman's side. Lucian could smell the salt of her skin, hear the thick mesmerizing thump of her pulse. She smiled beatifically at him as he led her to the sofa. It took only moments before he sat back looking refreshed and revitalized. The woman slumped at his side, unconscious, as he wiped the remnants of her blood from his lips.

"Feeling better?" Lena asked.

"You know me too well."

She took a breath, not moving from her position across the room, as if she were considering her words. Absently, she rubbed her hands across her throat where he'd bitten, and Lucian recoiled. The skin there was unmarred and had already healed, but he regretted his brutal reaction. He owed it to her to hear what she had to say and so he waited.

"I know you hate Christian," she began. "After all, we have a long history together. You, me, him, and I know you dislike the fact that he made me."

Lucian flinched, wondering why she was bringing up painful, ancient memories. She *had* chosen Christian over him, even before he had made her a vampire. Lucian often wondered if he had been the one to petition the Council to make her a vampire instead of Christian, whether she'd have accepted him as readily as she had Christian. He forced his jealousy back— she, like everyone else, had fallen for his brother first.

"You chose him," he said flatly.

Lena sighed. "Yes. I chose him then, but I'm with you now. Regardless, I want you to know if I have to make the same choice between both of you now, I would choose you, Lucian. I stay here with you because I *want* to be with you. For no other reason. Do you understand that?" Lucian nodded, shaken by the feeling in her voice. He knew that she put up with his violent mood swings and his cruelty—because she *did* care for him in some way. Lena continued. "I meant what I said earlier. I'll do whatever it takes to ensure that the Council doesn't execute a death order on your head. If I have to beg for Christian's help, I will. If I have to crawl, I will, no holds barred. And I don't give a damn what you do to me because of your stupid pride, do you hear me?"

He crossed the room then and kissed Lena's neck in exactly the same spot he'd mauled so savagely before. "I'm sorry," he said. "And I understand. Forgive me?"

She nodded, standing in his embrace for a few minutes before pulling away. "We need to talk."

"I thought we just did," he said, walking over to pour himself some cognac. "Drink?"

She ignored the invitation. "That was personal. This is different. Lucian, the next Council meeting is in a few weeks. You need to speak with Christian before then. He won't listen unless you do it."

"He wants me to beg." It was not a question. Lucian's voice was tight.

"No, he knows how you feel about saving people who don't need saving, remember?" She softened her next words, as if noticing the sudden shift in his mood. "He needs you to ask him, Lucian. That's all. No more, no less. Don't make it more than it is."

Lucian jerked a hand through his cropped blond hair. She stared at him and he sighed. "Fine," he said, pinching the bridge of his nose with his thumb and forefinger. "I'll talk to him."

As he said the words, he saw the relief cross her face, and for the first time, felt a root of worry take hold. It took a lot to make Lena anxious. If the Council moved faster than either of them anticipated, his house of cards would be quick to come tumbling down. He'd speak to Christian and put the rest of his plan into place.

So far, if he was successful in instigating a coup against the leadership of the Council, he'd have the allegiance of three of the seven vampire Houses. He could call in blood favors with one more, which left only two to deal with, House Arcan and

House Vesily, both of which were formidable opponents. To go up against them would be difficult, but not impossible. If he secured Kristos's witch, that would bring an added advantage and the benefit of surprise. He'd have to move quickly, and if anything, Lena's sense of urgency demanded it. Lucian smiled grimly. He had a lot to do in not a whole lot of time, but at least he planned to go down swinging.

He'd give them the showdown of their lives.

SCHOOL OF WITCHCRAFT

Victoria was openly admiring as she took in Aliya's modern and architecturally stunning home. After living in Christian's beautiful but old château, Aliya's house in Saint Cloud, a western suburb of Paris on the left bank of the Seine River, was a breath of fresh air. The loft-like open space and brightly colored accent furniture were pleasing to the eye. Red throw rugs dotted the hardwood floors and entire walls were cased in windows trimmed with stained glass, looking out onto small but colorful gardens. The space was bright and inviting. And it suited Aliya perfectly.

"Do you live here alone?" Victoria asked. The house seemed quite large for one person.

"For the most part, although my partner does visit from time to time," she said with a grin that made her look very young for a second.

Victoria blinked at the sudden transformation of her face. "I have to ask, if you don't mind. How old are you?"

"I am sixty-two," she said. Victoria smothered her gasp. She'd have guessed her to be in her early twenties. Aliya smiled, inclining her head and preempting Victoria's next question. "It's part of the high priestess induction rites. We don't age like other people. It's for the good of the coven really, not a lot of turnover in leadership."

"How long do you live for?" Victoria asked, curious.

"Two centuries on average, give or take a few years," Aliya said as they walked outside to the waiting car.

"Wow," Victoria said and then lapsed into silence as the driver pulled off smoothly. Now that they were on their way, her nerves were starting to get the better of her. "So where are we going? Is it close?"

"The school is located in Neuilly-Sur-Seine, not far from here. It'll take about thirty minutes. Do you have anything you'd like to know before we arrive?"

"What's it like? The school, I mean," Victoria asked, grateful for the chance to get some answers. "Is it only for people like us?"

"It's like any other learning facility, I suppose, only with a different curriculum. Most of our students attend regular school and come here for supplemental classes when they are of age." Noticing Victoria's look, she continued. "Most witches come of age when they are thirteen, some later, when formal training in magic begins before they join their respective covens."

"Are there many of you? Covens, I mean."

"Yes, although they're not as segregated as they used to be. We have intermingling from covens all over the world. People come and go as they please. Communal living, you could say. We share the same rules and principles, and for the most part, our ways and laws are the same across the globe. The chosen high priestess of each coven meets monthly in a secret location. They are the ones who unite the covens everywhere and uphold the true circle of leadership. They're called moon priestesses."

"Are you a moon priestess?"

"Yes."

"Why are there no high priests?" Victoria asked after she'd digested the surprising information on the coven hierarchy as well as the fact that Aliya was one of the coven's most powerful leaders.

"Because our society is matriarchal beneath the guidance of the Goddess Mother."

Victoria nodded slowly, her mind racing. "Right, that would explain how my grandmother's name was passed down to me. What about warlocks? How do they fit in?"

"Warlocks are … another type of group. They serve dark magic, and although they respect our laws, they are not bound to them. Some we call friends, others, well, that's another matter entirely."

Victoria couldn't help thinking of Gabriel. He was a rogue warlock who'd been consumed with securing the Cruentus Curse for himself. She'd bet anything that he wouldn't have been a friend to the witches or held himself accountable to any of their laws. Gabriel had only been out for Gabriel.

"Who is the Goddess Mother?" she asked after a beat.

"She is the source and end of all human life," Aliya said simply. "The epicenter of who we are begins and ends with her."

"Oh." Frowning, Victoria wondered whether Aliya's Goddess Mother had anything to do with her family and the curse. She hesitated and then asked the question that had been on the edge of her tongue since she'd arrived in France. "Aliya, what do you know of the history of the Cruentus Curse?" Aliya smiled as if she'd been expecting the question. She made sure that the partition behind the driver was closed before answering.

"It's an old story," Aliya began, "which means we don't know how factual it is. Much of it has become legend rather than truth."

Victoria nodded, leaning forward in her seat. She'd heard bits and pieces from Leto, but it'd always felt disjointed to her. "Please, I'd like to hear it from you."

Aliya shot her a searching look before diving into the tale. "Thousands of years ago, a daughter was born to Circe, one of the Goddess Mother's favorite moon priestesses. Her name was Thaia and she was destined to be a moon priestess. Thaia was beautiful and pure of heart. Many sought her hand because of her beauty, goodness, and charm, but Thaia did not choose any of them. Instead, her right to a consort was stolen from her by a demon, one that spirited her away to his dimension."

"A demon?" Victoria gasped.

"Yes. This demon was a powerful spirit demon that captured Thaia against her will. After almost a year of fruitless searching, Circe and the Goddess Mother were finally able to track the beast to his dimension. But they were too late. The demon had forced Thaia to become his consort and she'd died in childbirth, bearing a daughter who was forever cursed with the demon blood of her father. Circe and the Goddess Mother took the child and punished the demon for all eternity for his crime."

"What did they do?" Victoria said, lost in Aliya's story.

"No one really knows. He was banished from his dimension and this one, never to be heard from again."

"And the baby?"

"The baby grew to be a powerful witch when she came of age at sixteen." Aliya paused and looked Victoria full in the face. "The witch born of Thaia and the demon was the first Cruentus Curse witch."

Victoria huffed, her hands fluttering to her throat. "So you're saying that my b … blood is from a *demon?*"

"That is the legend. It is also said that the Goddess Mother saw the child as an abomination. Her impure demon blood and her untapped volatile power could not be controlled, so she tried to kill the girl soon after her magical awakening. But Circe, despite being bound to her oath as a moon priestess, helped her granddaughter escape. To protect her, Circe attempted to banish the girl's demon gifts with a spell. It worked ... partially." Aliya's eyes were sympathetic as she paused. "The transfer of the blood curse became sporadic, every few hundred years, as you know."

"I see." Victoria sighed, sinking back into the leather seat in a daze. The story made uncanny sense. And the more she thought about it, the more plausible it became—with its blackly red color, insane power, and terrifying ability to think for itself, blood like hers *had* to be demon blood. Which meant that she, too, was part demon. Her blood trilled softly and she shivered. Witches and vampires, she could handle, but *demons?* They were worse than monsters. And she was one of them.

Victoria swallowed past the surge of bile in her throat. "So you're saying that demons exist?"

"Yes."

"In this realm?"

"Not often. They rarely stray from their own dimension, but warlocks and dark witches summon them as part of black magic rites—in which you have to give up a part of your soul for the summoning." Aliya's face was tight as if caught in some awful memory, but as quickly as it'd come, her expression morphed into a bright smile when the car slowed. "Ah, we're here."

The limousine rolled to a stop in front of a gated estate. The golden sign on top of the entrance read *Belles Fontaines*. Victoria frowned, noticing that the forbidding perimeter fence on either side of the gates was mounted with high-tech surveillance equipment. It looked like a prison more than a school. From what Leto had told her, modern covens were esoteric and communal in nature, shrouded in secrecy like a specialized kind of cult. A small voice in her head reminded her that nothing good ever came out of secret organizations, but she shoved the warning away. The gates were designed to keep people out, that was all.

The car glided past the gates and meandered along a tree-lined street. She turned to stare at the black steel bars of the gate closing behind her, and a sour feeling invaded her stomach. She flushed at Aliya's questioning look and directed her gaze to the surrounding landscape. She could be in a different place. It was strange that this hundred-acre wooded estate existed so close to the center of Paris, yet seemed to be worlds apart. The car swung left down a side street and pulled to a stop in front of a stately gray mansion.

"Here we are," Aliya said, exiting the vehicle. "This is the main house."

"This is the school?" Victoria asked as they walked into the building.

"Yes, Belles Fontaines." She smiled at Victoria's look of surprise. "It's imposing at first, but we value our privacy for what we do here. The awakening of a witch's power is no small matter, and the students need a lot of room for practice. Much of the training takes place outside."

Victoria frowned. "But if you value secrecy, won't regular people be able to see what's going on?"

"There's an illusion charm around the perimeter," Aliya said, gesturing with her hands. "All anyone would see are tree tops and your standard estate property." She smiled. "As you will no doubt discover, magic has its uses and benefits."

Aliya walked down the entrance foyer to a room marked REGISTRATION, which was bustling with activity. Although there weren't many students here yet, as this was their summer period, Aliya explained that preparations for the forthcoming fall year began early. After a few greetings, she led Victoria into another room off to the side with a door marked HEAD-MISTRESS and ushered Victoria in to meet Madame Starke, a diminutive woman with a mop of black curls and penetrating green eyes. She looked like a forest imp, more girl than head-mistress, until she spoke. Her voice was low and resonant and demanded attention. Victoria could feel the power emanating just from the tenor of it—leaving no doubt in her mind that she was a force to be reckoned with.

She introduced herself. "I'm Victoria Warrick. My friends call me Tori."

Aliya had warned earlier that she'd had to confide Victoria's true identity to Madame Starke, so Victoria was not surprised to see her person subjected to a thorough and piercing assessment. The woman's stare stripped away her defenses like they were nothing, and Victoria's paper-thin confidence dissolved in seconds. This woman had the power to decide her future and whether she would be accepted as part of the school. Fighting the urge to flee, Victoria regarded her in tense silence until the headmistress finished the lengthy perusal.

"It is an honor to have you here, Mademoiselle Warrick," she said finally. "As you must expect, the nature of your"—she paused, searching for the right word—"ancestry is interesting, to say the least."

Victoria swallowed hard—*interesting* hardly covered it. And the less people knew about her ancestry, the better. "Thank you, Madame Starke," she said in a wary voice. "If you don't mind, I would rather not have my identity be common knowledge."

"*Bien sûr.* Of course." Madame Starke nodded. "Only senior staff will know about your background for their own protection, and yours, should anything untoward happen." Her manner turned brisk, authoritative, as she opened a folder on her desk. "Now, Aliya suggests that you would benefit from some of our accelerated courses. She has also said that you've gained some rudimentary knowledge from your familiar. Is that correct?"

"Yes, I'm familiar with the basics, but I'd also like to understand more about magic and its use. I am not accustomed to your laws and rules, and I'd like to know them." Victoria hesitated. "I know I'm not a part of your coven, but it's important for me to appreciate how it operates."

Madame Starke was nodding as Victoria spoke, a hint of a frown drawing her brows together. "Excellent. We have already assigned you a mentor. Here's your course schedule for the next few months. You'll start immediately."

"My mentor?"

"A senior graduate who has to complete a year of apprenticeship, which includes mentoring younger students," she said. "I'll introduce you to him in a moment. And as discussed, it's your choice to take anyone into your confidence regarding the Cruentus Curse." Victoria flinched inwardly at the mention of it, but displayed no outward reaction. "You'll also need to do a standard assessment examination, which is required for any new matriculating students."

"Assessment?"

"Yes, we need to gauge your abilities."

Victoria bit her lip, fear making her stomach dip at the thought of showing what she was capable of. She didn't want to hurt anyone, or worse, be ruled a danger to people at the school.

"*All* my abilities?" she asked. Madame Starke's answering nod was firm, but Victoria thought she saw something wary flash in their depths for the barest moment. Anxiety or maybe concern, but she couldn't be sure. Just as she was about to object, a knock on the door interrupted them, and a tall young man walked in.

"Ah, Panthèse. Perfect. This is Victoria Warrick, the new student we discussed. I trust you will take her under your wing."

"Of course. Call me Pan," the boy said in a jaunty voice, clasping Victoria's hands in his. Something warm and familiar leapt between them, putting her instantly at ease. She stared at him with a shy smile. Pan was the most beautiful boy she'd ever seen. Spiky white blond hair framed his heart-shaped face, making him look almost elfin. His eyes were as blue as pansies, and his ears—oh my god—her eyes snapped to his. Pan winked and grinned at her slack-jawed expression.

"Ah, I see you've noticed my Achilles heel, my fatal flaw," he said with dramatic flair. "That's what happens when there's elf blood in the family. It shows up in the most unexpected places." He waggled his pointed ears and Victoria giggled in spite of herself. She liked his unaffected warmth already.

Madame Starke cleared her throat. "Pan, her assessment is this afternoon, so if you could escort her through the basics of the school program until then, that would be most appreciated."

Victoria's eyes widened at the timing. She'd expected some time to prepare, talk to Leto, and figure out how she could perform magic without going blood crazy. "Wait, what? This afternoon?"

"The sooner, the better," Madame Starke said. She straightened, her manner becoming dismissive. "It was a pleasure, Victoria. Please do let me know if you have any questions about our school. Pan will take it from here."

"Thank you."

In a daze, Victoria followed Pan outside, saying goodbye to Aliya, who had some business to attend to. Pan chatted nonstop during the brief tour of the academic program and the premises, and she struggled to take it all in. After the tour, she decided to explore at her own pace since Pan needed to check in with his advisor.

"Don't worry, I'll find you."

"How?"

"You'll see." He smiled and winked.

Victoria shook her head, grinning at his confidence. Part of her blood's magic included a special cloaking ability, but she was interested to see how he would fare.

The compound was picturesque, its perfectly groomed grounds stretching for miles with flowering trees and shrubs dotting the landscape. Victoria looked up at the overcast sky and wondered about the magical ceiling. She mentally projected herself upward until she could sense the pliable barrier, shimmering all around her like silvery blue dust. It was complex magic.

Awed by the sheer intricacy of it, not to mention the power behind it, she floated back to herself and continued her walk, studying the map in her hand. The buildings were arranged in a star shape with the main house at its top-most point. They were all connected by walkways leading to a central circular building. As she walked toward it, other tree-shrouded groves caught her attention, and she realized that they were outdoor classrooms. The thought of participating in an open-air class with other Belles Fontaines students made her smile.

Aliya had explained that most students matriculated when they came of magical age, usually between thirteen and sixteen, and that magical training had to be concurrent with regular academics. Since she'd already graduated, she would only focus on the magical piece. Victoria looked at the small handbook she'd received. There were five years in total, not including the apprenticeship year, and were split from rank one through rank five She would not participate in any of those, as her handbook was clearly marked Advanced Program, which meant that she'd be studying with other specializing students. Unless, of course, she failed her assessment.

Great. Not that she wasn't putting enough pressure on herself already.

She leafed through the book. The Advanced Program was a fast-track placement that occurred after rank five Not everyone made it into the AP classes, and some chose to not to specialize, but for the most part, witches entering the program had to specify their area of study in addition to taking General Magic Theory. From what she could see, the specializations ranged from Elemental Magic to Healing Charms to Quantum Spatial Magic to Crystal Enhancement. Luckily, she would have a few weeks of accelerated immersion before most of the other students came back in September, and maybe she'd be lucky enough to figure out a specialization before that.

If she got that far.

Victoria pushed open the door to the massive central building surrounded by tall gray columns. She exhaled when her eyes adjusted to the dark as the huge arena came into view. Stadium seating surrounded an indented gym-like center as big as a soccer field, scattered with all kinds of apparatuses, pads, and weapons.

"Illustro," she said, and all the lights in the darkened hall came on. It looked exactly like a medieval dueling ring, except without sand and blood. Climbing down the steps to the railing around the enclosure, she stared in fascination.

"Whoa," she whispered.

A voice behind her made her jump nearly out of her skin. "It's impressive, isn't it?"

Victoria whirled around so quickly that she almost tumbled over the side, but relaxed when she saw that it was Pan. "What is this place?" she asked.

"It's an exhibition ring. Each week during the term, we have all kinds of competitions. Students can earn extra credit in various classes—telekinesis, shape shifting, you name it. We also have duels, where any student can challenge another student, within the same rank, of course. It's all supervised so no one gets too badly hurt." He grinned noticing her shocked expression. "It's a healthy way to settle disagreements."

Victoria stared at him, belatedly realizing that he'd found her just as he said he would. She frowned. "How did you find me?"

Pan smiled wider. "Ah, that's my specialty," he said in a sham mysterious voice. "Guess."

"I don't know—smell?" she guessed. He shot her a patronizing look at her response and Victoria flushed, but then she remembered the witch who had found her on the mountain because of her heat signature. "Heat radiation?" she asked and he shook his head. "Fine, how did you do it?"

"You're no fun. Come on, be inventive!"

"Projection?"

"Now we're getting somewhere, but no."

"I give up."

Pan flung his arms wide. "The trees."

"The trees?" she repeated.

"Yes, I can talk to them and they talk to me."

Victoria stifled the giggle that rose in her throat, her face twisting into a sarcastic expression. "Yeah, right. You saw me come in here, didn't you?"

"I'm serious, Victoria. I talk to trees, plants, bushes, and flowers." He paused. "Why so surprised? They're living things, too, and can communicate just as well as anyone. It's why I was placed in the Advanced Program. I study Dendrology. It's a rare gift."

She stared at him. "I'm sorry, I didn't realize that was even possible," she apologized, despite feeling like he was playing her. "And my name's Tori."

"Here, I can see that you don't believe me. I'll show you." Pan gabbed her arm and pulled her out of the building. He waved his hand above his head, and sure enough, the branches swayed, rustling in the wind as if in response to Pan's special brand of magic.

Victoria glanced up into the boughs of the trees stretching above them and shook her head in wonder. "Now that I think about it, it makes sense. Out of every living thing in the world, why would they be any different?" She smiled. "So what are they saying now? I can hear their leaves rustling, but that's about it."

"They're saying, 'Pan, your friend is greener than we are. But she's oh, so pretty,'" he said with a mischievous grin.

"No, they're not." She laughed, drawn in by his playful teasing. Feeling determined to hear them on her own, she focused and summoned the blood magic to her center, but all she could discern was a muted whispering and a few indecipherable words. Still, her eyes widened in surprise—they *were* talking, although it seemed to be in a language she didn't understand. "What are they really saying?" she said. "I don't understand their language."

Pan shot her an incredulous look. "You can hear them?" She nodded, and this time, it was Pan's turn to look surprised. "You truly are gifted."

"Where are you taking me, anyway?" she asked, blushing at his comment and noticing that they were headed back to the main manor house.

"I was sent to fetch you for your assessment," he said in a fake ominous tone. Despite his jovial eye roll, Victoria felt a nervous weight settle in her stomach as they walked toward one of the other points of the building. Her blood swirled restlessly, as if it, too, knew that something was in the wind. She quieted it with an unspoken command. There would be no display of rogue blood magic today, not if she could help it.

"Here we are," Pan said, depositing her at a door with some steps leading down into what looked to be some kind of basement area. There was a sign on the door that read ASSESS-MENT IN PROGRESS. Victoria's stomach soured even more at the thought of what lay beyond the entrance.

"Good luck, Tori," Pan said, opening the door and ushering her inside. He shot her a wicked grin. "Try not to die."

On that parting note, Victoria made her way down the stairs, her heart pounding so wildly she was afraid it'd leap out of her chest. She entered a large room, where Madame Starke and four other people were waiting.

"Ah, Mademoiselle Warrick, you are right on time." Madame Starke introduced her to the other four people, all of whom were various teachers and department heads—Mademoiselle Claret, head of Offensive Magic; Madame Didier, teacher of

Curative Magic; Monsieur George, teacher of Defensive Magic; and, finally, Monsieur Thornton, head of Spatial Manipulation. Victoria committed the names and faces to memory and hauled a deep breath into her lungs to calm her rattled nerves. This was it.

Madame Starke smiled encouragingly. "Don't be nervous. The Assessment includes a run-through of the basic spells, including teleportation, shielding, attacking, and defense, as well as elemental magic using earth, air, fire, and water. We will understand if there is something you haven't learned yet, given your lack of formal training. Just take it slow and easy."

Victoria took another deep breath and the examination began. The basic spells were simple enough, and she sailed through that part of the evaluation. Transformation and tele-portation were also easy, and she showed off a bit, the magic flowing like breath within her. Her control of elemental magic was adept, and only now did she understand the true strength behind her power—it was elemental *demon* magic. Distracted at the turn of her thoughts, she didn't realize that Madame Starke had asked her a question.

"Sorry?" she said.

"Would you like to take a break?" Madame Starke repeated.

"No, thanks. I don't need one. Let's continue. I'm not tired."

In the defensive magic part of the review, Victoria impressed her evaluators by producing a solid protection charm with her lightning quick shield magic. Her curative powers in the midst of an attack impressed both Monsieur George and Madame Didier, and her ability to simultaneously cure while blocking offensive poison spells, sleep spells, confusion spells, and petri-faction spells, was outstanding. Although Victoria wasn't familiar with the formal spells themselves, she was able to perform the magic by envisioning what she wanted to do, as she'd done in the past. And that was without engaging the blood magic. She knew that with the blood magic, her spells were a thousand times more effective.

As the evaluation wore on, Victoria felt the fatigue start to set in, but she wasn't inclined to stop. She wanted to push through it. The final part of the review was the offensive magic portion. A shiver passed over her skin. In defense, she'd only had to shield or deflect. This was different. She needed to assault *them*. Victoria was surprised to see both Madame Claret and Madame Starke get into attack positions and she took a deep steadying breath. She touched the amulet resting at her throat as she relaxed her center. It'd be the one thing that would protect them if things went south.

Both women shouted "PROTECTUM!" at the same moment as Victoria released simultaneous stunning spells in their direction. The protection charm would defend against spells like poison, but not against physical attack spells. However, they both deflected the stunning attack easily and circled her.

"IGNIS CREMO," Victoria shouted as two mini-tornados of fire encircled the two teachers. Their defensive spells were quick, but not fast enough. Victoria cringed as Madame Claret gingerly rubbed and healed her scalded arm.

Knowing she was being evaluated, Victoria went through the gambit of elemental attack spells—earth, wind, fire, and water—and each successive time, her attacks got stronger and stronger even as she felt herself growing weaker. But she refused to delve into the backup power of the amulet. Technically, it'd be cheating because its magical energy didn't belong to her. A gift from her ancestor Brigid, Victoria had only summoned its full power when she'd had to subdue the blood magic.

Preoccupied, she barely noticed the two teachers make eye contact and switch formation. Suddenly Madame Claret grabbed her by the arms as Madame Starke shouted a corporal binding spell, which held her arms frozen against her body. "EVINCIO!"

Victoria's nails dug futilely into her palms as she struggled against the invisible magical bonds. Her blood swirled and she stifled the immediate desire to invoke it. A burning pain scorched her body as one of the witches threw a poison spell toward her. In agony, she bit her lip and tasted blood. Liquid adrenaline flooded her brain as the blood magic suffused her entire body. Victoria didn't hear the sounds of Madame Claret's screaming as she stumbled back, clutching her horribly blistered body from the magnified and rebounded poison spell, courtesy of her blood.

The other teachers regrouped into a protective circle as Victoria fought for control. When threatened, the blood magic's instinct was self-preservation at any cost, and it would even operate independently of her, if necessary, to achieve that goal. As if understanding Victoria's struggle, Madame Starke moved, casting a shield spell around the teachers. It wouldn't help them, Victoria knew. Sure enough, the blood magic surged, and the shield burned red before disappearing.

"You can't run and you can't hide from it," she said. "Why did you incite it?" she said, clutching her middle with both arms.

"What do you mean?" Madame Starke said, eyes narrowed. "Incite what?"

"It will stop at nothing to protect me," Victoria said, even as she felt the magic coalesce within her. "It's my fault. I was tired and careless, and it took over. I should have stopped when I was able."

"Mademoiselle Warrick, are you all right?"

"You need to leave," she begged, gasping and sinking to her knees. "Please, for your own safety."

The teachers exchanged a worried look, but Madame Starke stood her ground, her lips in a thin white line. "We can defend ourselves."

"You cannot."

"Mademoiselle Warrick—"

"Haustum anima," her lips murmured, and before she could stop herself or move, every single one of the teachers fell to their knees beside her, struggling for breath. The spell was an unfamiliar one, but from what she could tell, the blood magic was draining the very essence from their bodies. She could see it in their sunken eyes and abnormally taut skin. They had minutes left, if that. In horror, Victoria dove into the reserves of the amulet and absorbed its power.

"Desino!" Victoria commanded as Brigid's magic restored her fading energy, forcing the blood magic to release its demonic hold. "It's okay. I've got it under control now. I'm sorry." Her teachers stared at her with varying degrees of shock and fear. Victoria clenched her fingers, unsure of what to say or do next, but then stood weakly, holding her palms outward in a non-threatening gesture. "I was overtired and thought I could push through. I should have remembered that the curse gets its own ideas when I'm worn down."

"It does that?" whispered Monsieur George in disbelief as he, too, rose.

Victoria nodded. "That and more." She looked around at their dazed expressions. "That was a sliver of what it's capable of. I've seen it possess a non-magical person and perform spells via its host's body and mind." She registered the expressions of stunned horror and shrugged. "Then again, my blood has also healed me when I was unconscious and about to die at a crazed vampire's hands."

She paused, noting the looks on their faces as if they were only now coming to terms with what they'd invited into their midst—the Cruentus Curse—an unpredictable raw magic that no one, not even them, could defend against. Victoria glanced over at Madame Claret, who was still covered in hot oozing blisters. She swallowed hard. Both she and Madame Didier had tried to cure it, but it was blood magic, and the demon curse would be extremely hard to heal. It would take weeks, if not more, she knew. Madame Claret recoiled as she approached.

"May I?" she asked, cringing at the teacher's panicked expression. "I only want to help." After a beat, Madame Claret nodded. Victoria touched the woman's clammy skin and murmured, "Curo," her forehead wrinkling from the effort of the spell. Almost instantly, Madame Claret's skin cleared and the feverish redness disappeared.

Both women stared at her with incredulous expressions as Madame Claret studied the now healed and unblemished skin of her forearm. "Unbelievable. This was the same curse I sent your way, yes?"

Victoria nodded, her mouth twisting in silent apology. "My blood has a habit of redirecting poison spells and making them less defensible by ordinary magic. I'm so sorry."

She could feel their stares of the two witches boring into her back as she crossed the room to where Madame Starke was waiting. Victoria's heart sank. She knew exactly what the headmistress was thinking. She didn't need to read her mind to discern it—she was a danger to all of them and to anyone else around her. They were going to kick her out. She could feel it. They were too afraid and her blood's magic was too unpredictable. She was nothing more than a liability.

"I know what you're going to say, but please give me a chance. You can see that I can control it." Despite the stony look on the headmistress's face, Victoria made one last ditch effort. "Madame Starke, I need to be here. I need to learn who I am … it's the only way for me to not just control the Cruentus Curse, but for me to understand it. Please … I'm begging you."

Clearly unmoved by her pleas, Madame Starke eyed her. "We'll need to convene an assembly, Mademoiselle Warrick. It will have to be a staff decision. Yes, you have shown that you can control it, but it was not without incident," she said with a pointed look in Madame Claret's direction. "Furthermore, it appeared beyond your command of it and that is concerning."

"I understand," Victoria said in a soft voice. "Thank you, and I'm sorry, again."

Monsieur Thornton escorted her to the front of the building, where the limousine was waiting. She shook his proffered hand and apologized yet again. To her surprise, he grinned at her. He was a short, bald man with a bushy beard and equally bushy eyebrows, but he had an unaffected smile and twinkling brown eyes.

"You've got my vote, Mademoiselle Warrick. I would like to learn more about how you don't suffer the after effects of teleportation. And this magic you control—it's magnificent! It would be a travesty to not explore your talents further." He winked. "I will do everything in my power to make sure we see you tomorrow."

"Thank you," she said.

Inside the car, Victoria fell back against the seat, exhausted, and wondered whether she had blown it or if she would indeed get a second chance as Monsieur Thornton had implied. She twirled the amulet between her fingers, feeling its warmth seep into her skin. Without it, she knew beyond the shadow of a doubt that the blood magic would have killed everyone in that room.

Victoria recalled the new life-draining spell that it'd cast earlier and shivered. It was getting stronger. If she didn't learn how to control it, and soon, who knew what it would be capable of?

NECESSARY CHOICES

"Have you seen Leto?" Victoria asked the housekeeper for the third time and received the same negative response.

Normally Leto didn't disappear for days at a time, even while renewing old acquaintances of his, but this time he'd been gone for at least three days. And while Victoria wasn't too worried for his wellbeing, she hadn't been able to communicate mentally with him, and that made her nervous. The last time she'd been blocked from mental communication, Lucian's witch had tried to kill her. This time was different. It felt like Leto was consciously blocking *her*, even though she knew that was impossible. A familiar could not block its master. She shook her head. She was imagining things. He could be anywhere, perhaps in an area that had a spell on it to prevent mental communication.

Christian looked up from the paper he'd been reading at the breakfast table and studied her as she paced back and forth, chewing on her lip. "Tori, I'm sure Leto is fine. He's a magical creature, one who can look after himself if he has to. You are going to wear a hole in the carpet with all your pacing." She shot him a dark look and plopped into the chair opposite his, grabbing her untouched cup of coffee. He eyed her. "Why are you so fidgety anyway? Haven't they called yet?"

"No, and I've left Aliya three messages like a super-stalker over the past week," she said. "All joking aside, I think I scared them. They were afraid. I could sense it. I wouldn't be surprised if they said no."

"They're going to call. Now come over here and I'll make you feel better," he said, placing his newspaper on the side table as if deciding that she needed some cheering up. He lounged back in his chair, uncrossing his legs and watching her with heavy-lidded eyes. He waited and then repeated himself. "Victoria, I said come here."

"I'm not in the mood, Christian," she replied, distracted by the mouthful of cold coffee she'd just sipped. In the next instant, the breath flew out of her as she felt her body lifted in strong arms and moving with inhuman speed toward the living room. Sighing at his high-handedness, she looped her arms around his shoulders as he sat down in a comfortable armchair. It had taken all of half a second to move across the entire house. She could teleport with magic, but his vampire speed was still impressive.

"Now, isn't that better?" he said. "I'd like to whisk you far away from here, but you'd probably flay me alive if I took you away from the phone."

"I'm sorry," she said. "You know this means a lot to me."

"I do, but have patience. There's no way they will say no. The power you wield is far too enticing to weigh against any risk, you'll see. Their intentions may be well meant, but people still covet what they don't have or don't understand. Your magic is something that they can't afford *not* to take in."

"Keep your friends close and your enemies closer?"

"That's not what I meant. It's in their best interest to keep you close as their ally. In case you haven't noticed, the relations between our worlds are, at best, tenuous."

"Are they? I hadn't noticed," Victoria said, a delicious shiver running through her at the feel of his hands kneading the length of her spine. She lowered her mouth to the hollow at his collarbone and inhaled his spicy cologne. "But you may be right. I think we may need some vampire-witch bonding, you know, to foster proper liaisons."

"Is that so?"

Christian's pulse leapt beneath her lips as his entire body went perfectly still. She smiled. "Yes. Are you going to do something about it? Or are you just going to sit there and try not to breathe for the rest of the morning?"

Christian let out the breath he'd been holding and chuckled, bending his head to her cheek. He grazed the skin there and moved to nibble gently on her earlobe. Victoria's body jumped in silent, reflexive response as all *her* breath left her body in a soft burst.

"Now who's not breathing?" he whispered back.

"Maybe we can both forget about breathing for a while," she said as his lips covered her own. At first, the kiss was gentle. But as she twisted her body on top of his, arching towards him, it became more insistent, more demanding. He drew her lower lip into his mouth, and Victoria sighed against him, dissolving into his embrace. Desire detonated between them like an atomic explosion. They were both flirting with disaster. But Victoria couldn't stop him, not when she wanted it as badly as he did. Sleeping in separate rooms was torture enough.

"I cannot get enough of you," he whispered, his voice husky. Drawing away from her mouth, Christian trailed kisses down her jaw, across the delicate bones of her neck, above the deep V of her camisole. Her breath hitched as his lips traced the edges of the lace. Every part of her thrummed with sensation. Christian's free hand slid up her rib cage as he nudged the silk material aside. Victoria's neck arched backward, her body held in place only by the brace of his palm at her back. His fingers turned icy against her skin and Christian froze, a muscle pulsing wildly in his clenched jaw at the bared expanse of her throat.

The silver in his eyes shifted into something feral and she moved backward, acutely aware of the rigidity of his body as she did so. His nostrils flared responsively, animalistic and primal. She could see the tips of his incisors pressing beyond their edges. It wouldn't take much to push him over the edge. Deep down, a part of her wanted to. It wanted to take the risk—to give in to the pulsing demands of her all too human body. But of course, that would be stupid.

"I wish we were normal," she whispered.

Christian made a noise caught between a laugh and a growl and nipped at her earlobe. "At times like this, being supernatural is supremely overrated." He stood, taking her with him, his lips grazing her cheek. "I'll be in the forest."

She sighed. "I'll be in the shower."

A very, *very* cold shower, she amended, admiring the violently bunched muscles beneath his shirt as he moved away. He was all lean leashed strength. She had no idea how sexual hunger translated into blood hunger, but somehow it did. The two seemed to be inextricably linked. Every time they made out, he invariably started to change when things got too hot and heavy, which seemed to be happening more often than not. She'd had more cold showers than she could count in the last month.

By the time Christian returned, the afternoon sun was already descending into the skyline, dropping long fragmented shadows into the gardens. He'd been gone a long time, but had checked in to let Victoria know that he had been over to the Council headquarters to meet with David, one of the Elders. Apparently Enhard had named Christian as his sole heir and there were some papers that he needed to sign because of it. His face was tight as he walked into the lounge room.

"Are you okay?" Victoria asked, looking up from where she was reading with Leto curled on her lap.

"I see you found him," he noted with a glance toward the sleeping feline.

Victoria nodded, her gaze sliding back to Christian. His face looked strained and worried. "What's the matter?"

He raked a tired hand through his hair, tension emanating from every part of him. His eyes met hers. "Four vampires have been murdered."

"Murdered?" Every cell in her body froze.

Christian nodded, his lips thinning. "They're convening the Council first thing tomorrow morning, an emergency meeting. One of the vampires killed was an overlord, the head of a House. Two others were old and powerful, and the last was a female."

Victoria was horrified. "I don't understand. How? Why?"

"I don't know, but what makes it strange is that they were all killed at exactly the same time."

"What does that mean?"

"It means that it was an attack. A carefully planned and well-orchestrated attack," he replied. "There were no signs of a struggle, none at all. The strange thing is that there were servants in other parts of the house and none of them heard a sound. But the bodies were charred to blackened bones in the space of an hour."

"Do you think this has to do with what's happening between the vampires and the Witch Clans?" she asked. "Or is it because I'm here?"

Christian's rejoinder was tired as he absently rubbed the tense muscles in his neck. "I don't think so. It seems too abstract to be connected."

Something troubled Victoria. Something he'd said about the

bodies being charred and blackened. "Christian, when vampires die … don't you disappear? I mean, disintegrate to ashes?" she asked.

"Not always. The older we are, yes, certainly. But in this case, they were discovered in the same condition as if they'd been attacked by flash fire," he said, pausing, trying to find the right words to explain. "But it was so precise that there was no blood, no broken bones, nothing out of place, and no damage to the space around them. Their bodies were shriveled and bone-dry as if they had been demolished from inside." He glanced up as she gasped aloud. "I probably shouldn't be telling you this."

"If it turns out to be connected to me or the Witch Clans, then yes, you should," she reminded him. "So what are the Council members saying?"

Christian conceded her point with a grim nod and continued. "There are three theories at this point. One is an attack from another House, other vampires. But it's not likely. There'd be other marks. The second is an attack from the warlocks trying to assert their position." Christian kept his expression shuttered as if the last thing he had to say was by far the worst. He cleared his throat. "The third, which is looking to be more and more of a strong possibility, is that the clans have mobilized."

"What are you saying? That the *witches* murdered the vampires?" she asked, unable to keep the sarcasm from threading into her tone.

Christian shrugged, his face giving away nothing. "Why is that so hard to believe? We've committed untold wrongs against them. Take Lucian, for example, in his conquest of Le Sang Noir. He has stopped at nothing to get what he wants. They demanded his head for his crimes and we refused to give in. Or, worse, let's consider the fact that perhaps someone has found out about us—someone important who wants to make an example of us."

The blood drained from her body as she digested what he was saying. "But that's insane. Why would anyone murder random vampires because of you and me? We aren't hurting anyone, and hardly anybody knows that I'm here. It doesn't make sense."

"Because of *who* you are, Victoria," he said simply. "And because of who I am, too. We are visible now, and the truth is many people do know, witches and vampires alike—Aliya, the Belles Fontaines teachers, Lucian, Lena, the Council. What exists between us is not accepted, and there are many people who will take it to extremes to keep us apart." He stared at her, his eyes intense. "I don't have to remind you of what happened with Gabriel." Having made his point, Victoria nodded. She remembered Gabriel's response all too well. He'd been furious that she'd chosen to be with a vampire, saying that she had debased herself and disgraced her lineage. His rage had been obscene. She shivered at the memory.

Christian sighed as he correctly interpreted her expression. "People aren't as open as you'd expect in the supernatural world. Here, there are worse bigots than in the human world, and they are vicious and deadly." Christian walked forward and cradled her face in his hands. "This is fine for as long as we are here and protected within these walls, but what if I am away and you are alone?"

"I can take care of myself," she said. "They can't hurt me."

"Oh, chérie, but they can, through me." He held her shoulders, staring into her eyes. He lowered his voice to a near whisper. "Would you die for me?" Victoria's stomach sank as she realized where he was going. He brushed a thumb over her cheek. "You don't even have to answer that. I can see it, right here, written all over your face. The thing is what if someone— anyone—uses me to get to you? Can you be strong for who *you* are? And forget me—us—if you have to?"

"Why are you saying this?"

"Because it's the reality, Tori. War is brewing and there won't be anything we can do to stop it once it starts."

"War?" she said dully.

"A truce can only hold us in check for so long. Given any chance, either side will grasp the opportunity to dominate the other. These murders are the proof they need."

"Who? The Council?"

"Yes."

Victoria knew that getting upset wouldn't help the cause. Christian's worry could only mean one thing—the Council *already* believed that the Witch Clans were at fault and were considering retaliation. And given what Lena and Lucian already knew about her, the Council would use Christian without qualm to secure her loyalty and the power of Le Sang Noir. Or vice versa.

She understood his fear, but there'd be no question—she'd choose him in a heartbeat over all others, even her own kind. There was no way to explain the depth of what she felt for him, the connection between them. He'd stood by her when she'd been alone, stood *up* to her when no one else could. He had believed in her when she hadn't been able to believe in herself. No, Christian had nothing to worry about.

"Tell me what the Council said," she said as he poured a glass of cognac. His fingers clenched around the stem of the glass as he considered her request. He wanted to protect her, she knew. But hiding the truth from her was a worse alternative. "Please, Christian. I can handle it, I promise."

He scrubbed his free hand through his hair and drained the contents of his glass. "David believes it was an attack coordinated in secret by the Witch Clans. The evidence is too clear. There is no way another vampire could have killed four vampires without leaving some indication of a struggle." He paused, taking a deep breath. "Same for a human attack. There would be other identifying marks. That leaves only one viable alternative—a magical attack. Only a spell could have caused such a precise result."

"What about the warlocks?" Victoria asked, her throat dry. "You said that they've been lurking around. Could they have done it?"

Christian nodded. "I asked the same question. David agreed that it was a possibility, though a slim one. They simply wouldn't risk a war with the Witch Clans. Tori—" He paused, staring at her as if he had more to say.

"What is it?"

"I don't know how I feel about you spending so much time at the school when we don't know who's behind the attacks. I know you can protect yourself, but if anything happens while you're there, I won't be able to enter the campus without an escort. And if something were to happen, they'd view me as the enemy. *I* couldn't protect you."

Despite the panic slinking around in the pit of her stomach, Victoria took a deep, calming breath. His fear for her safety was evident and if things didn't get resolved, she knew it would only get worse. She thought through the facts he had presented. "You don't need to be worried about protecting me. You know more than anyone that I am more than capable of taking care of myself. But I'm certain there's a logical explanation, so let's not be rash or hasty to accuse the Witch Clans or to stop me from enrolling at Belles Fontaines." She was proud that her voice didn't waver once, but Christian didn't look convinced at her reasoning.

"At least here you are safe."

"Here I am trapped," she blurted out and then felt instant regret at the stricken look on his face. "I didn't mean it the way it came out. I need to learn about my abilities and I can only do that at their school."

"It's too dangerous," he said stubbornly.

Victoria rose and stood in front of him. She placed her

hands on his shoulders. "That's not your decision to make. I am not some lost little girl you have to protect. I came to Paris to be with you *and* to find people like me."

"There's no one like you," he said softly, his eyes storm-wrought silver. "And your life will be at risk."

"But it is *my* life. I won't stay cooped up in this place for fear of what could happen. Soporo," she added under her breath, but knew that the spell would probably not work—Christian, for some reason, was immune to any of her healing magic, much less a simple calming spell. But he seemed to relax after her words, more so from the ministrations of her fingers as she kneaded the tension from his neck and shoulders. Christian sighed, bringing his forehead down to rest lightly against hers as his hands dropped to encircle her waist. They stood there for an eternity in the silence before the ringing of the telephone jarred them apart.

He stirred, and Victoria tightened her arms about him. "No, don't get it," she said. "Just keep holding me and maybe everything ugly will disappear."

"It's Aliya," he said.

She frowned. "How do you know?"

"Caller ID."

She dropped her arms and raced toward the phone. She answered and listened intently. The strength drained from her limbs as she grasped the phone with bloodless fingers. Christian was at her side the moment she disconnected the call. She knew he would have overheard the conversation. "Did you hear?"

He nodded. "Some. I was trying not to, but she said something about an accident?"

"One of the high priestesses and her familiar have been attacked. The familiar is dead, but the witch is unconscious."

"Attacked by whom?" Christian asked.

"They don't know. She was insensible when they found her. Aliya said they're hoping they can find something that can help identify the attacker." Victoria stared at him, her eyes wide. He touched her wrist and she swallowed convulsively. "Christian, her body was drained of blood."

His features were inscrutable as he returned her stare. "Were there any marks?" he said after a few minutes.

"None, but you said that your saliva has healing properties," she replied without thinking. "Wait, I didn't mean—"

But Christian cut her off with a weary hand. "I see they've already jumped to the same conclusion as you have," he said in a flat tone.

"Isn't that the same as you did earlier?" she retorted, responding to the blame in his voice.

Christian's lips thinned into a flat line. "Victoria, they have no way of knowing that a vampire was responsible for anything, and unless their seers were indeed able to delve into the witch's unconscious mind, there is no conclusive evidence that a vampire was guilty of the crime."

His hand dropped away from her body and he turned to pick up the discarded glass of cognac he'd been drinking earlier. He refilled it and watched her over its rim, his irritation obvious. She didn't have to read his mind to know what he was thinking —that she was naïve for believing Aliya without proof.

"You blamed the witches earlier."

"Not exactly," he said. "You're twisting my words. We came to an *assumption* by a process of logical elimination."

"And so did they," she said, resenting the feeling of being backed into a corner by his attitude and his thunderous expression. "Her body was *drained* of blood. Doesn't that mean anything to you?"

"Not necessarily by a vampire. Could have been anything."

"Well, we'll soon find out, won't we?" she snapped through her teeth at the indifference in his tone.

They stood staring at each other in combustible silence, until Christian's mouth twitched and he burst into low laughter.

"Come on, you know you find this as ridiculous as I do," he said. "Here we are dividing the field of battle, sighting off against each other. Witch camp versus vampire camp."

"What, you find it amusing that someone was attacked?" she said. "Have you no respect?" Christian crossed the room in two long strides to stand directly in front of her. She held her ground, mutinous, and braced herself for a scathing response, but his voice was gentle.

"Tori, what's the real reason you're firing up at me? I know it's not because you think a high priestess was attacked by a vampire," Christian said. "Are you angry because I questioned Aliya's opinion? Making this some kind of us versus them situation? What's wrong? Tell me what happened." She clenched her jaw and studied the floor, fighting the tears already welling behind her eyes. He always could see right through her. "Tell me everything Aliya said," he repeated, forceful, tipping her chin up. "All of it this time."

She looked away, but answered in a monotone whisper. "Aliya said they haven't made a final decision about me based on the attack. They're convinced it was a vampire because of the way her body was empty of blood and life and"—she broke off, meeting his eyes—"and they think that because I live with you, a vampire, it will be a threat to their security." She glanced at his impassive face, trying to read anything from his blank expression. It was like staring at a brick wall. She licked dry lips and pushed ahead since there was more. "I can train with them if I agree to live with Aliya."

"And if you stay here with me?"

She swallowed hard. "Their answer is no."

"So it's worse than I suspected. It's already begun."

"Christian—"

"So what have you decided to do?" he asked, his voice devoid of inflection. Her heart crumbled at the defeated look in his eyes.

She cleared her throat, fighting the growing lump there. "I was thinking that the school is so close to Paris anyway, and because Fontainebleau is so far that it would make sense to move closer, at least for a few weeks until things calm down," she said miserably.

Victoria didn't want to hurt Christian, but this was what she had come to Paris for—to find out who she was and learn about others like herself. But his wounded expression made her want to throw herself into his arms and swear that she'd never leave, that that would never be a choice she would make. But she *couldn't*. She stepped towards him and touched the face that seemed to be chiseled in granite. His eyes betrayed nothing, but a muscle leapt in his jaw at her touch.

"They're not giving me a choice," she said.

"You always have a choice."

"Can't you see that I'm not leaving you—this is *not* an us and them thing. It's what makes the most sense for right now," she said, pressing a kiss to his lips. "You have to trust me."

"I understand," he said, but his words were empty, mechanical. Victoria kissed him harder, pressing herself against his uncompromising length and silently pleading with him to understand her reasoning.

"Kiss me back, Christian," she whispered against his mouth. He was fighting her, but she needed to show him that she wasn't leaving him for *them*. Stung by his passivity, Victoria tried to make him feel something, anything. She kissed him with all the passion she could muster, with a combination of inexperience and sensuality that normally made him crazy. This time, it didn't.

Please, Christian.

It was her achingly raw plea that fractured the barrier between them. His lips softened and he groaned against her mouth. Crushing her body to his, Christian seized her lips in a hard, possessive kiss that went on and on until she was clinging to him, breathless and shattered. How could she possibly be away from him for so long? They broke apart and she met his eyes. They searched deep, as if trying to see into the most secret parts of her. She flushed from the intensity of it.

"Do you need to go out?" she whispered, hesitant.

"No."

Surprised, she watched him. Normally after such a passionate exchange, he'd already be shifting, but strangely enough, apart from his rapid breathing, he seemed perfectly composed. It was strange.

"How come?" she said.

"I don't know," he said in an equally surprised voice. "I felt myself compartmentalizing what you said earlier about leaving, and when you kissed me, all I could think about was resisting you—something I've never done." His words held a note of bewilderment. "The hunger was there. I could feel it twisting in my gut, but somehow it stayed under control."

"What does that mean?" She frowned. "I thought you couldn't control the change?"

"I don't know," he repeated. "A vampire *can't* control the hunger once it takes over. It owns us until we satisfy it, and it's near impossible to suppress once we're past a certain point. This felt different, as if I wasn't even hungry in the first place."

"Well, I'm glad," she said softly. "I hate to see you in any kind of pain because of me. And I'm sorry about this, Christian. I really am. But you know how much this means to me, and the only way I can start training is if I live temporarily with Aliya."

Christian brushed a tendril of hair out of her face. "So I guess it'll be like when we were dating in Maine, sort of." His light tone took her by surprise, but she grasped at it like a lifeline.

"We'll see and talk to each other every day. This is what I came here for," she reiterated. For some reason, she needed him to agree, to support her decision, to let her know despite being apart, that they were going to be okay. She needed to hear it from him.

"I know," he said, kissing her forehead. "What am I going to do without you?"

"The same as I am—think about you every single minute we're apart." Christian smiled at her response and wound his arms about her.

"So when do you leave?"

"Tomorrow," she said, her heart sinking at the thought of being away from him so soon. As such, she was completely unprepared for Christian's wicked answering smile.

"Perfect. Let's go upstairs and see what else I can compartmentalize."

TRUTHS UNVEILED

Christian entered the boardroom on the top floor of the Tour Areva in La Défense, Vampire Council headquarters, and nodded to David, who was waiting with four other men, whom Christian recognized as the shell corporation's attorneys. Two of them were vampires, the other two human, although they could well be vampires for the ruthless way they operated. They greeted him and he sat down. As always whenever he met with Council members, Christian looked the part he was expected to play—that of vampire royalty. Dressed in an expensive, tailored navy suit, he wore no jewelry, save for a heavy onyx ring emblazoned with his ducal crest in gold, which he twisted on his finger as he waited for them to begin.

"Your Grace, as you are aware, Lord Enhard Markham has left his entire estate to you, which comprises a number of commercial and residential properties across the world, including several here in France. It also includes a substantial cash settlement. The value of the estate, including all assets, is approximately forty billion Euros." The attorney paused and Christian nodded for him to continue. "As is customary, the

Council will receive thirty percent of the liquid assets and thirty percent of the property, at your discretion. The total of the liquid assets due to you is ten billion Euros."

Christian didn't bat an eyelash at the staggering sum. One of Enhard's fondest passions had been playing the stock markets across the world, and the value of his portfolio and cash liquidity came as no shock to Christian. He was, however, completely stunned that Enhard had left his entire estate to him. As a Council Elder, Christian had assumed that Enhard would have bequeathed his entire estate to the Council itself. It wasn't as if Christian needed it. He had more money than he could ever want or need for several lifetimes over.

Still, Enhard's parental gesture left him in a state of curious emotion. The closest thing he'd had to a father, Enhard had taken him under his wing, teaching him most of what he knew, and had saved him from himself countless times. There'd been instances when Christian had the distinct impression that Enhard was hiding a secret, something related to *him*, but it was always fleeting and the moment had always passed before Christian could ask him about it.

The thought of never again seeing his face or talking to him when the need arose was a sobering one. Enhard had been one of the only Council members he could trust with his life. He clenched his fingers as a spasm of pain rolled across his insides, but kept his face composed—displaying any emotion in his position was tantamount to weakness. His thoughts were interrupted by the attorney's voice.

"Lord Markham left you a sealed envelope, to be opened upon his death," the man said, pushing a manila envelope across the table. Christian noticed that David was staring at him with a strange expression on his face, but it disappeared before he could process it. The rest of the meeting passed quickly as they finalized the rest of the estate transition. For the most part,

Christian's own asset management team would handle the bulk of the transfer into his portfolio.

As the attorneys filed out, Christian held the manila envelope between his fingers, lost in thought, not realizing that David hadn't left the room with the others until he sat heavily in the chair to his right. Christian regarded him in silence. Like most vampires, David was youthful, his boyish looks preserved for eternity, but his eyes were ancient. Those eyes had seen a lot. Christian waited for the old vampire to speak.

"Enhard's death was a great loss to us," David said after a beat. "I know you held him in high regard, and he felt the same about you." He hesitated, staring at the envelope that Christian held. "What you will find in that envelope will not be easy to understand. You'll have many questions." David placed a cool pale hand on Christian's sleeve. "I am at your service, Your Grace."

"Please call me Christian."

"Do you know how old I am, Christian?" David asked.

"Several millennia, I imagine."

"I have lived over two thousand years," he said with a sad smile. "I have seen so many beginnings and ends, ups and downs, and the rise and fall of many great things and many terrible things. And still, in our world, there are vampires that are so much older and far more powerful than I, ones who have become the fabric of legend."

"The Reii," Christian said, his voice soft. *Had Enhard been Reii?* he wondered briefly before dismissing the thought as improbable. Enhard would not have been killed so easily if he had indeed been Reii. No, such vampires did not exist.

"Yes, the Reii." David said. "The father of who we are." Christian remained silent, wondering what David was getting at. "How much do you know about them?" the old vampire asked. At Christian's raised eyebrow at the suitability of the time and place for a mythology lesson, David interjected, "Humor me, please."

Christian conceded after a glance to the timepiece on his wrist. "Not a lot other than the stories we all know. They are said to be powerful with dark magic abilities and live in seclusion for hundreds of years at a time. I fail to see the point of this," he added, an impatient note creeping into his voice. He had a lot to do and sitting in a darkened boardroom with David discussing what constituted vampire folklore was starting to grate on his nerves. A strange light settled into David's eyes and he leaned forward.

"How long since you last fed?"

"I don't know. The usual, a week or so," he responded in a bland tone, although he was taken aback by the abrupt and improper question. But even as he said the words, Christian realized that he was wrong. He hadn't fed in over three weeks because it had been three weeks since Victoria had left. He hadn't thought much about it. He'd been so busy with the daily Council meetings and working with the task group assigned to the vampire murders, that he'd barely noticed any signs of hunger. And yet, here he was, as strong as ever with no feeling of deprivation. Perhaps it was the stress of the murders combined with Victoria's absence, but it was baffling.

He frowned. "Perhaps longer," he admitted. Vampires were driven by their constant, consistent need for blood, especially ones as young as he. In his world, at barely two hundred years old, he was considered a fledgling, and blood would remain the center of his universe until his strength evolved with age. His frown deepened as his gaze snapped to David's. "Why do you ask?" he said, suddenly wary.

"It's already happening, isn't it?" David said, his eyes narrowing as he leaned forward to peer at Christian's eyes. "Did you always have those?"

"What are you talking about, David? You're speaking in

riddles," Christian said, forgetting decorum. He had no time for games, not even with an Elder.

"Your eyes. Those black rings," David said. Christian blinked, inhaling sharply as David bent closer, nodding to himself. "Curious. I distinctly remember your eyes being gray."

"Why does this even matter?" Christian evaded. "It's insignificant."

"Perhaps, perhaps not. When a vampire is transformed, our physical traits do not change. How did you come by them? Or, more importantly, when?"

Christian rubbed his brow with the heel of his hand. After Enhard's death, David had been the only one to know of Victoria's true identity, but he didn't know the exact circumstances of what had happened in that room in New York City or the fact Le Sang Noir had completely possessed Christian, a vampire, with no qualm or consequence.

He sighed. To refuse to explain would put him in the untenable position of lying to an Elder, one whom Christian trusted, but he had no idea what recriminations the truth would bring. In few words, he explained to David what had transpired in the tunnels in New York and watched as the aged vampire collapsed back into his seat.

After several minutes of tense, fraught silence, David spoke. "Well, that would certainly explain a lot of things," he said. He stared at Christian and shook his head. "You took Le Sang Noir. No wonder ... so accelerated, unprecedented ... given who you are." David could barely string the words together, rambling almost to himself. "Do you have any idea?" He broke off, shaking his head in disbelief again.

"It was nothing." Christian didn't blink an eye. He didn't know what David was getting at about "who he was." The fact that he was a royal had no impact on the effect of Le Sang Noir. As far as he was concerned, it was no longer inside of him and had left no permanent damage, thanks to Victoria.

"I fear, my boy, that it is a little more than just nothing. Open the envelope, and as soon as you've read its contents, we will talk then. There will be much to discuss, I expect," he said as he stood, effectively ending their unexpected tête-à-tête. Christian looked up at him in surprise. After David's cryptic response, he'd expected a lot more than "open the envelope and we'll talk later." But that was exactly what he got as the door swung closed behind the Elder.

Christian stared into space, recalling the odd conversation that had just taken place. Obviously the contents of the letter had to do with who Enhard was or some secret that he'd taken great pains to keep hidden, although not from the other Elders it seemed. At least not from David. He twisted the parchment in his hands.

The envelope was formally addressed to him: To His Grace, Christian Thierry François Devereux, Duc d'Avigny, from Lord Enhard Markham. He took a deep breath, wondering what in the world Enhard would have kept from him, and opened it in one swift movement. Naked pain slashed through him as he recognized Enhard's familiar script. It was precise and scholarly. The letter was dated the day before he died. Clenching his jaw, Christian began to read.

CHRISTIAN:

If you are reading this letter, then things have not turned out as carefully as I had planned. Obviously, I have not lived to be thousands of years old, nor am I living in carefree vampire retirement on an exotic island with a harem of beautiful people at my beck and call. Although, I am hopeful even in death, if I am lucky, that it will be more of the same – at least, that is my fervent hope. What else do we have to live for, as vampires, if not an afterlife of hedonistic pleasure?

. . .

CHRISTIAN BIT back a smile at Enhard's twisted sense of humor. He was as straitlaced as they came, but on the odd, infrequent occasion, especially when he was uncomfortable, he had a blasé way of phrasing things that would make Christian choke in mortified surprise. The ironic hilarity bubbling in his throat fizzled as he continued reading the letter.

THERE ARE SO many things left unsaid, important things that I meant to tell you, but missed our windows of opportunity. I convinced myself that you were still too young and that there would be time. But alas, time has come and gone. And here we find ourselves – you reading this hasty, poor excuse of a letter, and me, gone to some other place where I am unable to fulfill my duty as your guardian. But so be it. I can't change the past nor alter the future.

CHRISTIAN PAUSED, swallowing. His palms were clammy, his heart pounding. He couldn't imagine what Enhard's secret could be, but given the circumstances, he instinctively understood that it had to be something vital, something important. Breathing hard, he continued.

I AM WRITING this letter because I do not know what will happen in the next few days, but I will protect you with everything in me if need be. My life is yours. There are so many things I wish to say, but there are two above all that must take precedence here.

Firstly: Victoria. She came here tonight to save you and to solicit my help despite my earlier, less than acceptable, treatment of her. If I hadn't seen the depth of her love for you with my own mind, shared in that brief moment when she linked our thoughts, I never would have understood. It is astounding ... and humbling. She is strong, as is her love. Protect it, guard it, defend it. For most likely, you will be forced to in the coming days. You have my every blessing for your happiness together.

Secondly: Your legacy. You may not recall it, but when we found you near death and changed you nearly two hundred years ago, unlike your brother, you rejected the vampire blood from your maker. I've never told you this, but it was my blood that you rejected.

CHRISTIAN PAUSED, the letter almost dropping from his blood-less fingers. Enhard had changed him, or *not*, as he seemed to be implying. Christian forced himself to finish reading.

YOUR REFUSAL as a human to change was unprecedented amongst our kind and your spirit was indomitable, fighting my blood as if it were the devil itself. I had never seen its like. You fought for weeks, alive but not, somehow caught in a shadow world between life and death. Your condition was too unfamiliar, too unnatural, and many of the Council Elders were afraid of what you represented – a worse kind of fiend than we were. They wanted your execution. But someone did save you, Christian. Someone saved you, as I could not.

Your maker's name was Sezja.

AS THE NAME filtered its way into his chaotic thoughts, Christian felt an odd sense of knowing, of familiarity. *Sezja.* The name itself meant "protector," he knew. He closed his eyes, focusing on the name. Shadowy images flashed through his vision, as if summoned, and his body jerked with each vivid memory.

A striking olive-skinned face with dark, intense eyes, red lips, and long black hair resting like a silk curtain across his chest ... eyes so ancient, they tore through him ... the gentle murmur of her voice, musical, calming, mesmerizing ... a conscious choice made in seconds, soft acquiescence ... a sliver of pain at his neck ... pure consuming pleasure ... the feel of warm blood on his lips ... the dark earthy taste of it ... and then so much burning agony that his entire body twitched with phantom recollection.

Sezja.

His maker.

When Christian opened his eyes, his hands were gripping the sides of the chair so tightly that the steel beneath the leather had distorted like putty, the letter resting forgotten on the table. He held it with shaking hands.

SHE WAS the one who changed you, possibly the only one who could have reached you where you had gone. She gave you her gift. In case you have not already guessed, Sezja was Reii.

IN COMPLETE DISBELIEF, Christian had to reread the last sentence, and then reread it again. A Reii. How was that even possible? His maker was *Reii.* He didn't believe that they existed, but obviously he was being proved wrong. If he took Enhard's words for truth, then he was made by one of them. It was unfathomable. In a daze, he forced his attention back to the letter.

INASMUCH as you must be shocked, do not be. The Council summoned her at the time because no human soul had ever rejected the gift of immortality so fearlessly, so viciously. When she made her offer, you took it. If you hadn't, you would have died.

And so you became a child of the Reii, an immortal son of Sezja, born into the mantle of the most exalted, and the most revered, in our world. As far as memory serves me, you were the first vampire that she has sired in over five thousand years, and your rebirth was the first and last time I ever saw her.

So this, my son, makes you a child of the Reii.

From the little I do know, in the Reii world, it is said that you will inherit their memories and their strengths in some form or other after several hundred centuries, when your vampire body can withstand the transformation, when your mind is strong enough to control and command the dark magic that binds you to them. In your case, that will not be for a long time as you are relatively young, but you must still be prepared.

In my absence if it is so fated, David will help you understand what to expect. You may not know it, but he is only three generations removed from the Reii and has gone through a watery version of the change himself. Yours, I fear, will be much more powerful as a direct descendant, but still, he has promised to be there for you in my stead.

I know you must be confused. Please believe that I did not intentionally mean to conceal this from you. The time was never right, and now, if you are reading this letter, it is too late for both of us. For that, I apologize. I wish I could be there when the time comes, but I will be there in spirit. You are born to lead, Christian, born into a power that ordinary vampires can only dream of.

Despite not being your true maker, it is my hope that some small part of me still exists within you and was not lost. I am so honored and proud to have been your mentor and friend. I love you, my son.

Enhard

. . .

CHRISTIAN SLUMPED BACK into his seat, drained and utterly devastated. His throat was clogged with emotion at Enhard's last words. *My son.* He inhaled deeply and reread the letter, considering the facts before him. He was a Reii, or would be in a few hundred years. Unless...

Christian sprang to his feet, suddenly understanding David's earlier cryptic comments about when he'd last fed and that something was already happening.

Because something *was* happening!

But that was impossible. Enhard had written that nothing would happen for several hundred years, until his body was strong enough to withstand the transformation from vampire to Reii. He closed his eyes and her name brushed across his senses like silk... *Victoria.*

Christian's knees buckled and he sank into the chair. "Le Sang Noir," he whispered. It was the only explanation for his recent and accelerated changes. No ordinary two hundred-year-old vampire could survive without feeding for three weeks, and yet he had. And he'd been able to hold himself back far longer with Victoria the last time they'd been together.

Somehow, Le Sang Noir had awakened something within him, far earlier than Enhard had ever expected, and now, he was changing, altering, becoming. He recognized the unfamiliar feeling burgeoning in his stomach as mind-numbing, heart-stopping fear.

With a harsh inhale, Christian rose and folded the letter back into its envelope. He walked to the receptionist, who eyed him with barely veiled interest.

"Where is Lord Argyle's office?"

"I'm sorry, Your Grace. David has left for the day," she responded, blushing prettily. The invitation in her eyes was unmistakable. Christian ignored it.

"Where did he go?" His voice was stricter than he'd intended and her smile faltered.

"He didn't say, Your Grace."

A flurry of activity in the lobby near the elevators drew his attention. Several of the Council members had congregated there, and as he focused his attention in their direction, the words he overheard rooted him to the spot.

"... four more murders."

BENEATH THE SURFACE

"**F**ocus, Tori. You're not paying attention!" Pan admonished. "We've been working on this shield spell for hours."

"I'm sorry," Victoria said with a guilty flush. "It's just that I haven't spoken to Christian in days and I can't help feeling that something is wrong."

"Ah, yes, the boyfriend," Pan said in an overly dramatic tone. "And when am I going to meet this elusive creature who has captured my magnificent Tori's heart?" he said. "I'm starting to think he's your *imaginary* boyfriend."

"He may well be, for all I've heard from him lately," she muttered, wiping the sweat from her brow. At Pan's grin, she shook her head and sighed. "He travels for work and I rarely get to see him," she explained, fearing that Pan would see right through her lies. There was no way she could confide in him— or any student at Belles Fontaines—that Christian was a vampire. He wouldn't understand. No witch would.

She'd gotten around the security issue by moving in temporarily with Aliya in Saint Cloud, but being away from Christian was starting to affect her more than she cared to admit. It was making her edgy, and she couldn't focus when she was worried about the slew of murders, and whether he'd be targeted next. She couldn't prove who was attacking the vampires, but she guessed that the Council was growing more convinced that the Witch Clans were behind it.

What made it doubly worse was that the Clans were also being targeted. Three more witches had been found dead, their bodies drained in the same way as the others. That put the total death toll at twelve, eight vampires and four witches. Tensions were high and only getting higher as suspicions escalated to new heights. They were days away from declaring an all out war.

The first witch, who had been rendered unconscious, had died soon afterwards, and Aliya had been unable to get any information that could help identify the killer. What the seers had divined had been inconclusive—spotty images of a single assassin who moved incredibly fast and was very powerful. Naturally, the conclusions of the High Priestess Circle went in much the same direction as those of the Vampire Council. They suspected the vampires of masterminding the attacks.

In passing conversation, Aliya had mentioned to Victoria that they'd invited peace talks with Council representatives and were awaiting their response. Their intent was to prevent all out war, but things were slowly spiraling out of control as the body count rocketed. Everywhere Victoria went, people were discussing the murders and laying blame on each other's doorsteps. It was turning into a circus.

Already, the school had had to intervene when a teenage witch retaliated against a vampire in the seventeenth arrondissement. It had taken officials on both sides to stop the incident from garnering unwanted human media attention, but they'd been successful. Since then, unofficial vampire and witch patrols were put in place to prevent volatile situations from erupting, and a curfew had been ordered for any underage witch or vampire.

"Tori!" Pan chastised in exasperation. "Where are you? You're in the clouds."

"Sorry, I have a lot on my mind," she said, frowning. "Doesn't it worry you about these murders and the fact that we're about to jump into an all out war with the vampires?"

"I'm pretty sure there won't be a war without some pretty heavy negotiation up front. Plus, we don't even know if it's really the vampires murdering us. It could be anyone. Could be the warlocks. I have a distant cousin who is really, really evil. Like he tried seven times to murder me in my sleep evil."

"But the vampires also think we are killing them," Victoria said, and Pan's eyes narrowed in sudden awareness.

"Where did you hear that the vampires think that?" he shot back.

Victoria stifled a guilty flush. "It was something that Aliya said," she said.

Pan grabbed a hold of her shoulders, and she pulled away. "What are you hiding? I can see it all over your face."

"Look, can we drop it? Let's just work on the spell, okay?"

"We've tried the spell to death and you can't block me. I get through every single time. This is way more interesting, I think," he teased. Victoria wanted to smack the smirk off his face.

"More interesting," she said softly, warningly. But Pan didn't notice or he was too busy strategizing on how he could find out what she was hiding. She smiled. "Come and get it then."

His eyes widened and a grin split his face at her arrogantly issued challenge. "You do realize what you're asking, right?"

"Yes."

"To be clear, you want me to attack you."

"Just get on with it, hero," she said. Pan's blue eyes flashed in challenge. He threw an energy blast so fast that she barely had time to repel it.

"REDITIO!" she shouted, watching the ball of energy flip on itself and fly back towards Pan. He dodged it easily.

"Is that all you got, transfer?" he said as he teleported to stand directly behind her. Victoria felt the shift in the air and teleported herself just as a pillar of fire scorched the ground where she'd been standing.

"Try again! Why don't you bring it instead of talking such a big game?" she cried breathlessly.

Pan hissed, smirking at her challenge. Suddenly, he became invisible and struck out, landing her flat onto her back. The wind whooshed out of her. Victoria tried to get her bearings, righting herself, but all she could see was a blur as he spun around her in a blinding circle. His speed generated a cool wind that buffeted her on all sides. Victoria started to move and real-ized that Pan's spin was part of some clever holding spell. Her body felt sluggish as if she were suspended in invisible quicksand.

"What is this?" she asked. Even her voice sounded tedious and drawn out. The air felt thin, making her gasp for breath.

"An air retention spell. One of my own making. Like it?" He laughed aloud as she struggled against the powerful bonds. She couldn't deny that it was a daunting spell, trying everything in her power to escape it. He was inventive, she'd give him that.

"RESOLVO," she cried, trying to break up the root bindings of the spell. It didn't work.

Pan laughed, enjoying her predicament. His laughter was tinged with a madness that made a tendril of fear curl around her—he was enjoying this too much for her liking. "Now if I were truly an evil witch, you would be dead meat right about now," he crowed.

Victoria pushed against the magical restraints and her fingers barely moved. She could feel the blood rushing beneath her skin, begging to be set free. The blood magic would destroy the spell with no holds barred, but she'd promised Aliya that she wouldn't engage it. And true to her word, she hadn't.

But lately the problem had become separating the blood magic from her own magic—it felt more and more like they were becoming one and the same, and it terrified her. She intuitively understood that it was a natural progression. The more she used her magic, the more in tune she'd become with it—*all* parts of it. The blood was hers, after all, and eventually when she grew strong enough, its magic would become an innate part of her, too. But for now, it was too raw, too unpredictable ... too untrustworthy.

A jeering voice interrupted her thoughts. "Still think I'm talking too much?" Pan said, his tone growing deeper and rougher as if the lack of oxygen was making her dizzy. Even his features seemed to shift—his cheekbones elongating and his eyes bulging. She was going to pass out if she didn't do something. She blinked as Pan leered at her. "Try to block this! AMNIS CINCTUM!" he cried. A rushing wall of water rose out of nowhere like a spinning cyclone, drawing closer and closer toward her as if it were a noose. She struggled harder, willing her body to move.

"RESOLVO!" she shouted, more forcefully this time. The spell thinned, but not nearly enough to release her. Victoria felt the blood surge within her as the magical mountain of water cinched tighter. She could hear the rushing in her ears, and as she looked at Pan's unfamiliar expression, she felt the bloodlust fill her eyes.

"EXSCINDO," she shouted.

Like the pop of a light bulb, the wind around them winked out of existence as energy coalesced into her center. Victoria felt it building, and the second before she released it, she whispered "PROTECTUM" in Pan's direction. The silence was deafening in the seconds before the counter spell exploded outward, completely obliterating the two attack spells and taking Pan with it. His body rolled in midair and crashed into a nearby tree.

Released from her bonds, she raced breathless to Pan's side where he lay dazed but unhurt. The smell of sulfur hung thick in the air from the charged energy particles that had annihilated the wall of water.

"Are you okay?"

"What did you do?" he said, gasping, his face back to normal. "And why am I not completely pulverized? You should hear what the trees are saying now." Victoria glanced at the trees in the immediate vicinity and noticed that their leaves were browned and wilted. She winced.

"Curo salus," she said, waving her hand. *I'm sorry*, she added under her breath. Pan's eyes widened as he heard her voice the spell and listened to silent voices in his head. The leaves of the trees returned to their lustrous vibrant green as if they hadn't been scorched in the first place. Pan's eyes widened until they were huge blue orbs.

"Seriously, who *are* you?" he whispered. Victoria was saved from having to answer as Monsieur George, the Defensive Magic teacher, teleported into the glen.

"Everyone okay? We felt a very powerful shift in energy." He glanced at Victoria, and she flushed in delayed guilt. Pan's eyes narrowed as he noted the silent exchange and cleared his throat, rising on unsteady legs.

"Actually, Monsieur George, it was my fault. I attacked her with a tricky combination of spells and her shield charm caused them to rebound. No one was hurt." The teacher stared hard at Pan and then looked at Victoria, who returned his stare evenly.

"Fine," he said with one last searching look at Victoria and vanished as suddenly as he had arrived.

"Thanks, Pan," Victoria said.

An irrepressible smile lit up his face. "It's the least I could do for that protection charm you put on me at the last minute. That was quick thinking. The trees told me," he said.

"What else did they tell you?" she asked in a small voice.

"That you're one badass witch and I should rethink teasing you going forward."

Victoria bit her lip. She knew he was joking, but a small part of her had known exactly what her counter spell would have done to Pan and it'd been easy to protect him. Perhaps her magic was coming together, after all.

He walked beside her and poked at a speck above her lip. "You're bleeding," he noted. "Did you hit your nose or something?"

Victoria wiped the tiny smear away quickly. "Must have," she said.

"So, Super Witch, I think we should call it a day."

"Don't call me that," Victoria said with a frown. "I think that's a good idea. Any chance you can give me a ride to Aliya's? I think she already left."

Pan nodded, and as they walked towards the parking lot, Victoria could feel his preoccupied gaze on her. She knew he wouldn't just let it go, but she was hoping that he would. No such luck. The minute they got on the road away from the school and prying ears and eyes, his glances became more searching.

"So what really happened back there?" he asked eventually.

"What do you mean?"

"Come on, Tori, you know what I mean. We're not near the school so you can be honest with me. What was up with that bit of really advanced magic? You know, a spell that counter-attacks offensive spells and simultaneously destroys everything in its path? I've never seen—or felt—anything like it." Victoria was silent. Pan continued speaking, unable to stop himself. "On top of that, I felt the power surge right before you cast it and there's no way you should be standing after a spell that intense.

You should be unconscious. Not unless you were a high priestess ... by the Goddess, that's it, isn't it? You're some kind of high priestess prodigy!" He looked so pleased with his own conclusions that Victoria remained silent, grateful for the reprieve. Pan stared at her. "So are you?"

"Something like that," she evaded.

Satisfied with his own deductions, Pan didn't push the matter as they drove the rest of the way to Aliya's house, each preoccupied with their own thoughts. Slowing at the top of Aliya's driveway, Pan whistled, breaking the silence and looking in his rear view mirror.

"Whose car is *that?*" he said.

Victoria spun around and noticed the sleek, black Lamborghini that was pulling in behind them. On cue, she felt the familiar brush on her senses. It had been far too long. She melted into it.

I missed you. Her heart skipped a beat and she couldn't stop the warm blush that colored her cheeks. *I thought we could go to dinner. I already spoke with Aliya.*

"Now what's the matter with you?" Pan said as he parked in front of the garage. Trust Pan's attention to detail not to miss a thing. "You've gone all blotchy."

"Nothing," she said, smoothing her hair and trying to sneak a glance in the mirror before getting out.

Pan arched an eyebrow. "Why are you preening? Do you know whoever owns that sex machine?"

"Sex what?" Victoria sputtered, but Pan had already stepped out of the car. She opened her passenger door and got out.

"Oh. My. Goddess," Pan's stage whisper was loud in the silence. "Who is *that?*"

Victoria turned in slow motion and braced herself. She hadn't seen Christian in three weeks, even though they'd spoken often. With her daily training and his evening hours with the Council, it'd been impossible to get together. All the bones deserted her body in the second that their eyes connected, and her breath disappeared altogether as he pressed a soft kiss to her cheek. She grasped his arm for support, the touch of his body making her fingers tingle and burn.

Conscious of Pan, Victoria found her voice. "Pan, this is Christian, my ... ah ... boyfriend. Christian, this is Pan, my mentor at Belles Fontaines."

"Very nice to meet you." Christian's cultured baritone was warm and courteous. "Tori has told me a lot about you."

"And me, you ... um ... she's told me a lot about you, too." Pan's voice was breathy. Victoria had never seen him act so oddly, like a lovesick puppy, and suddenly she had a delayed epiphany—Pan liked boys, and, well, Christian was ... *Christian.* She glanced at Pan with a smirk. She wondered whether he'd guessed that Christian was a vampire and whether his opinion would change then.

"You can come inside if you're finished gawking, Pan," she said under her breath in his direction. He could only open and close his mouth and Victoria had to laugh. In Christian's presence, she felt exactly the same way.

Christian, for his part, didn't seem affected by Pan's look of adulation, and watched as they walked into the foyer. He did not follow them and waited outside. Victoria glanced at him inquiringly. His answering look was meaningful and she immediately understood.

I thought that was a myth. About being invited, I mean, she said mentally.

It is. This is just common courtesy.

She rolled her eyes and stuck out her tongue at him. *No need to be snarky about it. I'll get Aliya.*

Aliya came to the door, a curious smile on her face. "Your Grace, what an unexpected pleasure."

"May I come in?" he asked politely. She looked taken aback, but smiled at his consideration and nodded for him to do so.

Aliya would of course know that vampires didn't need permission to enter someone's home. Christian was being polite and making a point at the same time that he was aware they considered him an enemy.

"Can I get you some refreshment?" she asked. "Cognac, if I recall?"

Christian nodded his thanks. Victoria trailed behind them, heading to where Pan was waiting in the living room. He wore the same beatific expression on his face and she nearly laughed out loud.

Sorry about Pan, she said.

He is harmless.

"So ... cool car," Pan said, interrupting their silent conversation.

"Thank you," Christian said, taking a seat opposite them. "How is the training going?" Pan leapt at the chance to enter into conversation with him just so he could stare at Christian openly instead of hiding his furtive glances.

"Good, although Tori knocked me on my butt today with an amazing spell. I don't even know where she pulled it from, but it was fantastic. She protected me from it at the same time, which in itself, was also extremely advanced." His words came out in a wild, breathless rush. Christian raised an eyebrow, a polite smile curving his lips.

"Advanced, was it?" he said. Victoria could feel his glance settling upon her and, this time, her whole body tingled. She was sure that everyone would be able to see right through her. The thought of having dinner alone with Christian made her giddy. She hadn't realized how much she'd taken him and his company for granted, and she'd missed him dreadfully in the last few weeks.

She excused herself from the room to get changed, deciding on a simple black dress. She dressed quickly, conscious of Pan's escalating level of adoration. No doubt by the time she got back, he'd have evolved into a stage five clinger. Checking herself one last time in the mirror, she took a deep breath before finger combing her hair into a simple updo and returning to the living room. Pan was still babbling about her performance, the divine adoration on his face making her stifle a giggle.

"Tori clammed up like a vise after I asked her about it. My guess is that she's some sort of prodigy that they're grooming for some important role." Pan paused and shrugged. "I feel pretty honored they chose me, but I'm sure she could teach *me* a few things."

A clear voice interrupted them as Aliya returned with the drinks. "Who could teach you?" she said.

"Tori could." Pan's voice trailed off as he saw Victoria standing there. He gave her a sly wink and a furtive thumbs up.

Victoria's insides warmed at the frank appreciation in Christian's eyes. She sat beside him this time, conscious of the lean stretch of his thigh inches from hers. The fifteen minutes it took for him to finish his drink felt like hours. She let Pan prattle on and nodded her head at appropriate moments, but she was intensely focused on the man at her side. The slant of his fingers curving around his glass. His slow measured exhales. The way he, too, was intimately conscious of her.

"Ready?" he said as he drained the last sip, turning the full force of those silver eyes on her.

Her insides combusted. "Yes."

"Have a good time, Tori," Aliya said. A slight frown creased her forehead, but it smoothed out as a smile took its place. "Nice to see you again, Your Grace."

"Your *Grace?*" said Pan in a disbelieving whisper to Victoria. "That's too delicious for words. Looks *and* a title, in this day and age, too." She rolled her eyes at him. Playing into his overt teasing, she winked.

"I know. Every girl's dream, right?" she said.

"Every boy's dream, too."

"I'm right here, you two," Christian commented dryly. Pan and Victoria burst into laughter. "Time to go," he said, firmly taking her shoulders and twisting her toward the door. He extended his hand to Pan. At the first touch, Pan's eyes widened and he stepped back clutching his hand as if stung, looking from Christian's suddenly stoic features to Victoria. Recovering his composure almost immediately, he said bluntly, "You're a vampire."

Christian returned his stare levelly, the barest hint of a smile playing about his lips. His eyes were mocking. "Yes."

"That explains a lot ... for me, I mean," Pan said, blushing wildly. He looked from Christian to Victoria to Aliya and bit his lip. "Looks like I really put my foot in it, didn't I?"

Victoria took pity on him and smiled reassuringly as Christian went out to the car, hugging him. "You're fine, Pan. It's okay, really."

"I am going to wring your lovely little neck next week," he muttered.

"For what?"

"For *what*, she asks! For not telling me that you're dating a totally hot, totally steamy duke who happens to be a sexy as hell vampire, that's what!" Pan shrieked in her ear. Christian's lips twitched, even though he was on the other side of the driveway.

"It doesn't bother you?" Victoria asked, curious. It was not a response she was accustomed to when people found out about her and Christian. Pan shot her a disparaging look.

"Why on earth would it bother *me*?" he said. At her blank look, he sighed and waggled his ears. "I'm gay. I'm one-quarter elf with a smidge of human blood in there somewhere. I'm a witch. I don't judge."

"Oh."

"Now go. Prince Fang Charming is waiting." Pan winked and shoved her out the door. "Don't do anything I wouldn't," he called after her as she slid into the car's luxurious leather interior.

Christian drove slowly down the driveway and gave her a wicked smile that made her stomach do ridiculous somersaults. "So do *you* think I'm a 'sexy as hell vampire'?"

Her gaze flew to his. "You heard that?"

"Super vampire hearing, remember?" He grinned at her discomfort. "So?"

"So, what?"

He raised an eyebrow.

"Yes, you are sexy as hell. Happy now?"

"Very," he said. He glanced at her shaking shoulders as she struggled to keep a straight face and then burst into laughter. "What's so funny now?"

"Pan." She chuckled. "Could he have been any more into you?"

"He seems like a nice young man," Christian said.

"You're only saying that because he worships the ground you walk on." She poked him in his ribs. "You're his super hot, super steamy vampire duke, remember?"

"I can't help it if people fawn over me like besotted admirers, can I?" he said staring at her in a way that made it clear he was referring to her, not Pan.

"You wish," she said giggling, punching him in the arm and wincing as her fist connected with solid muscle. "Ouch." He grinned at her. Victoria rubbed her hand and twisted to face his chiseled profile, her expression suddenly turning serious. "This is wonderful. I haven't felt so free in days, and I really, really, *really* missed you."

Christian grasped the hand laying between them on the center console and kissed the backs of her fingers. "I know exactly what you mean," he said with a slow breaking smile that turned every cell in her body into fire. She stifled her worries and vowed to enjoy the time with him, regardless of what was brewing between the Witch Clans and the vampires. Tonight would be theirs and theirs alone.

"By the way, I told Aliya that I would be staying with you tonight," she said, her voice shaking slightly.

His hand tightened on hers. "Good, because there was no way I was going to let you go."

ALLEGIANCES

"**K**ristos, where is this witch?" Lucian asked imperiously as they walked the darkened streets of Châtelet-Les-Halles, a not very savory area of Paris at night. Not that Lucian was worried. He *was* one of the unsavory elements that wandered the streets after dark, but he was getting irritated that this witch hunt had been largely unsuccessful thus far. Their search had led them from Montmartre all the way to Les Halles with no sign of the witch.

"Just up here, my lord, not far."

Kristos disappeared around a shadowy corner and, suddenly, there was a guttural scream. Lucian dropped into a careful crouch and streaked across to a shadowed corner. His vampire senses on full alert, he peered around the corner of the building. Even with his vampire eyesight, it was strangely difficult to see in the gloom—something didn't feel right about the air. It shimmered like heat off a hot road, making everything blurry. The haze was magical, he was sure of it. Lucian blinked and forced his eyes to focus. He could only make out indistinct shapes, but the smell of blood and fear was thick in the air. Another guttural groan slivered through the space toward him. Lucian slipped closer, keeping his back to the edge of the building, his footfalls quiet in the dark alley. He inched around the side.

The alley was empty.

Except for what looked like Kristos hanging splayed in midair against a building at the far end. Lucian strained his senses forward but could discern no threat or movement, and he crept forward until he was a few feet away from the suspended body.

"Kristos? Are you all right?" Lucian's whisper was harsh in the deathly quiet. There was no answer. Kristos's face twisted, his mouth opening and closing with no sounds emerging. His eyes rolled back in his head and his body jerked spasmodically as if tied to an invisible string. The hair on the back of Lucian's neck prickled and he glanced around, keeping his body low. He snarled, sensing movement behind him, and spun with inhuman speed towards the threat.

It was a young waif of a girl. She was barefoot and her long dark hair was a snare of tangled curls. She looked to be twelve or thirteen. She tipped her head to one side like she was listening to some silent voice in her head and watched him curiously.

"Who are you?" Her voice was bell-like and it sounded far younger than she looked. Lucian straightened.

"Did you do this to him?" he said, not answering her question.

"He tried to kill my friend." A thin black snake curled between her fingers.

"Your friend is a snake?"

"My dearest friend." Confusion marred Lucian's features before comprehension dawned. The snake was a *familiar*. This girl must be the witch that Kristos had been talking about. Lucian relaxed his aggressive stance, although he remained wary. His objective was to approach the witch, not put her on the offensive. He spread his hands in a gesture of goodwill.

"My apologies for my companion. He was wrong to try to do what he did." The girl tipped her head again in a funny fashion, as if listening to her inside voice, and watched him with unblinking eyes as if waiting for him to continue. "My name is Lucian. I was looking for you, as a matter of fact."

"Why?"

"Because I think I can help you." The snake writhed protectively up her arm to twine about her neck. It hissed in his direction, a forked tongue flicking out as if tasting the air. He spread his hands in a placating gesture once more. "I know you don't have any reason to trust me, but I can help you understand the changes that are happening to you, young one."

Her eyes widened at his statement. Now Lucian understood what Kristos had tried to explain about the girl. She must be barely thirteen, which meant she'd only recently awakened. That would explain her lack of control over her abilities. Lucian blinked. She was strong. He could feel the raw magic surrounding her as if it were extensions of her body.

"What would you help me with?"

"With your awakening," he said.

Her small body shook with tremors. She seemed overcome with emotion. Lucian stepped closer and closer again. The girl was laughing. Her body heaved as her laugh turned manic, the hollow sound distorting in the alley. Kristos made choking noises behind him, but he could barely turn to look, his attention was caught by the slight figure in front of him. Something felt wrong—every cell within him warned against danger, but Lucian only arched an arrogant eyebrow. This was a child-witch. He would kill her without a thought if it came down to it.

"Exactly how old do you think I am?" she asked him, cocking her head to the side.

"Thirteen?" Her smile widened.

"What else do you see about me? How do I look to you?" Lucian frowned. Something about her voice was different. It sounded like she was swallowing gravel. The black snake had wound its way around her throat, its shiny scales shimmering between the curls of her hair. Its head rested on level with her left ear.

"How you look?" he asked. She nodded. "You look like a young girl with black ... hair and a black snake."

"And you look like a vampire." She bared her teeth in an ugly grin and suddenly Lucian felt something clammy take hold of his insides. He dove to the side just as the snake launched itself toward him, its fangs glinting and lethal. He rolled swiftly and eased into a crouch as the black cobra flared the wings on either side of its head and hissed.

"I am no threat to you," Lucian said. "We can help each other."

"I doubt that."

Before his very eyes, the small girl started shifting. The haziness surrounding her became indistinct and he squinted. She seemed to be growing, thickening. The air around her settled and in her place stood a burly looking man. A man! The snake had slithered back to its master's feet and slid up his leg. Even from a distance Lucian could see the telltale black mark that streaked from lower lip to chin. His eyes narrowed.

"Why the pretense, warlock?"

"Hunting." His voice was thin, gravelly. The warlock laughed. "Hunting for the thing that's been on a killing spree against my kind, and I find you and your friend soliciting a young, defenseless witch in a very seedy part of town. Interesting, no?"

"Your kind?" Lucian said coolly. "The warlocks hold no allegiance to the Witch Clans."

"We do when it suits our purposes, and right now, our

purpose is to ally against the vampires." He grinned again. "No more hunting little witches for you, my friend."

The warlock swung his arm in a wide arc and Lucian dodged the ball of yellow fire with inches to spare. He twirled and risked a glance at Kristos, who hung limply against the wall. His body was gray, as if he'd been leached of blood and turned to stone. If he weren't already dead, he would soon be. Lucian snarled. They'd been careless to fall into this trap, but it was too late for regrets now. He faced the warlock squarely, feeling the change take over. His jaw tightened, his teeth lengthening.

"You should know that I am also no fledgling vampire," Lucian said, straightening. He snarled, baring lethal fangs. "I am a vampire overlord. You risk war against us on a guess that I am the one who has killed witches? Your idiocy will not go unpunished."

"Then this should be fun. War between the clans and vampires is just one piece of the puzzle for us. The more of you and them dead, the better."

"The minute I die, everything about this unfortunate meeting will be transferred to the Vampire Council. Your words, your face, your intent, everything."

Then the warlock did something that Lucian did not expect. He laughed in his face. It was a sound of genuine mirth. Lucian stiffened.

"Then all they would see is a strong, powerful vampire overlord and a tiny just-awakened witch defending herself. You've already been known to attack defenseless witches, haven't you, Lord *Devereux?*" The warlock's smile was calculating, and Lucian faltered for a second. Understanding ballooned like a delayed explosion. The warlock had known all along who he was ... because he had *tracked* them from Lucian's house. This was all a set-up, a clever machinated trap—one designed to drive a wedge between the vampires and the Witch Clans. Even though Lucian was persona non grata with the Council, his death would be the proverbial nail in the coffin.

Lucian glanced to the right, calculating the odds of escape. Slim, but still a chance. He gathered his strength.

The warlock's grin widened.

Lucian feinted to the left and the warlock mimicked his movement. He spun to the right and almost collided with the warlock, who had teleported to block his escape via the right side of the narrow alley, forcing Lucian to somersault backward. Lucian dropped into a crouch. He would tear his way through the warlock if he had to.

"INCENDO MALEFICUS!" the warlock shouted. The black fire exploded into the wall behind Lucian as he leapt out of the way, only to consume Kristos's inert body. It crumbled to nothingness, leaving nothing but a blackened smear on the greasy red brick wall. Lucian growled. There was a way he could get the true images of this warlock to the Council, but it was one that he refused to consider even in the face of death. He would rather die than call his brother for help. He resorted to diplomatic entreaty instead.

"Why don't we talk about this? You are obviously very powerful, as am I, and we could be here all night." The warlock did not answer, but tipped his head to the side, in much the same way as the slight girl had done earlier. The action seemed incongruous with his burly appearance.

"We could, but I prefer to do this quickly."

"Wait."

"Goodbye, Lord Devereux. Your death will inspire a flurry of blood vengeance that we, the warlocks, will only welcome. The enemy of my enemy is my friend, and the outcome of war can only be in our favor. We welcome that, for the vampires have always been a silent enemy and the Witch Clans remain our greatest foe. We will watch you kill each other."

Lucian laughed and the sound was as mocking as the one

that had preceded it from the lips of the warlock. "You think my death will ignite war? Hardly."

"You are a vampire royal. We know exactly who you are."

"Then you have mistaken me for my brother. He is the royal, not I."

The warlock curled a lip. "You, your brother, it matters not. You are the overlord of House Devereux, one of the seven."

"Fallen, my friend. A fallen vampire whose death will do nothing for your cause. The clans will celebrate my death and the Vampire Council will concede for political reasons that my death was truly a sanctioned execution for my crimes against the Witch Clans," Lucian said. He laughed again. "You are only doing them a favor, one they will thank you—or the Witch Clans—for."

"I have my orders. You must die."

The warlock's hands spun in a circle above his head, and Lucian could feel the shift in the air as energy rushed toward the man's body. The snake was wrapped around his chest and torso. Two pairs of eyes burned holes in his direction.

"EVOCO ... INFENSUS ... SIMULACRUM ... DIABOLUS ..."

A spectral shape began to form in front of the warlock and, for the first time since he had encountered the witch/warlock, Lucian felt a tendril of fear curl up his spine. That chant meant that the warlock was summoning something. Lucian was well aware of his limits when it came to demons and his chances of escaping alive were slim to none, especially cornered as he was.

"Wait," Lucian said, but the warlock ignored him.

"EVOCO ... INFENSUS ... SIMULACRUM ... DIABOLUS ..."

The shape expanded and began to solidify. The smell of sulfur stung the air as the beast, ripped from the bowels of its dimension, answered its master's call. Lucian gritted his teeth, his lips curled back in panic.

"I said wait! The vampires have Le Sang Noir ... what your people call the Cruentus Curse." The warlock froze mid-incantation, the spectral demon shape remaining indistinct and cloudy. Its smell was still rank, but there was no further solidification. The warlock frowned as he tried to maintain the summoning while at the same time trying to focus on Lucian.

"What did you say?" he said in a hiss.

"You heard me, warlock."

The man's eyes narrowed, as if assessing his words for truth. "What of it?"

"They have it in their possession. Le Sang Noir ... the ultimate weapon against us all. You think a war between the vampires and the clans will help your position? Once they are done with the clans, they will do the same to everyone who stands in their path, including you. You have already lost!" Lucian's voice was a desperate growl.

"You talk of something you know nothing about, vampire."

"Don't I?" Lucian laughed in the warlock's face. "I've seen it with my own eyes. The witch's blood is black, it smells like your heart's deepest desires, and it is wielded by the descendant of the Duchess of Lancaster, who looks very much like her, I must say."

"You've seen it? You've seen her?" The warlock's sharp whisper was disbelieving. His eyes narrowed. "But yet you live to tell the tale?"

Lucian scowled. "She was too busy killing other *warlocks* to attack me, one by the name of Gabriel. If you kill me now, you will lose a potential ally in your cause." The warlock's face remained impassive as he considered Lucian's offer. The shape beside him writhed as if caught in between dimensions.

"*You* want to align with us? Why should I trust a word you say? You are a vampire and bound to your own kind."

"Not if my own kind has turned against me," Lucian said. "I want to be on the side that wins. If that means you, then yes, I will join you."

"And the Cruentus Curse?"

"I can point you in her direction. I know where she can be found."

"And you think that she will allow herself to be taken? If she is who you say she is, then she is more powerful than the clans and the warlocks combined."

Lucian smiled. "She is, you see, but I know her greatest weakness."

"Why should we trust you?" the warlock growled.

"Because you have nothing to lose. You are welcome to kill me later if what I say is not true. Take me to the one who leads you."

A keening sound pierced the air and Lucian realized that it was the half-summoned demon begging to be released, either back to its dimension or into the world it'd been called to. The warlock's attention sprang back to his task. The cloudy vapor swirled as he negated the final steps of the spell. The shape disappeared. Lucian exhaled slowly, relief flooding him. He kept the arrogant smirk on his face.

"Any tricks and you die," the warlock warned.

Lucian knew that he was playing a dangerous game, but he'd always had a special gift for understanding what drove people. The lust for power was the same, no matter the species, and it was the one commonality that bound them across worlds. The basis of a plan formed in his head. He'd help the warlocks in return for amnesty and would convince them of his loyalty. He would give dogs his allegiance if it furthered his own cause—he wanted to eliminate the Council and assume the mantle of their leader. Lucian was a brilliant strategist, more so when his life hung in the balance. He'd sought a witch to win over to his side and, instead, he'd found a coven of warlocks who were playing both sides for their own endgame. Their goals were the same.

Only the rules had changed.

And Lucian was, if anything, a master opportunist.

He approached the warlock, his head held high with no fear

in his expression or demeanor. The snake hissed at him, but Lucian ignored it. He raised an eyebrow.

"Are we going or not?" he said, his voice dripping with purposeful, barely veiled contempt. Arrogance would be the key to this performance. It implied strength and a disdain for death. Only the weak were afraid and displaying fear would be his downfall.

The warlock's eyes narrowed, but he grasped Lucian's shoulder. His smile was not encouraging. "TRANSEO."

At the last moment, Lucian felt something materialize at his back and turned instinctively toward the pull. All he saw were two glowing red eyes before he was drawn into the teleportation spell. The distant grumble of a predator deprived of its prey reverberated through the teleportation tunnel and Lucian shook his head. His fear was making him imagine things. The warlock had dismissed the demon he'd summoned.

Despite his bravado, Lucian *was* afraid—he knew that he was taking an enormous risk, but as far as he could ascertain, the outcome of meeting with the warlocks could only be to his benefit. He had something they desperately wanted and, in return, he would negotiate for immunity from any attack. It was better than anything he could have come up with on his own, short of convincing Victoria to help him, which he knew she'd never do. But she was weak where his brother was concerned … and no one knew that better than Lucian. She'd told him so herself.

Lucian smiled. His dear brother would be his collateral.

IN TIMES OF LOVE AND WAR

Christian stared at the young woman sitting across from him at the table. Victoria looked poised and beautiful as if she had come into herself these past few weeks. Her skin glowed with vitality, her eyes bright. Her newfound confidence made the blood in his veins surge in response. Seeing her alone had been long overdue. He missed not having her at the château, not feeling her curled up beside him on the sofa, not hearing her laugh in that dreary old house. It was empty without her.

He'd known that it would have come down to this—that the Witch Clans never would have agreed to teach her if she had remained with him. And so he'd agreed to let her go, but Christian had felt a warning deep in his bones from the start. They didn't want him in her life. He was a threat and his presence made her unpredictable. As a pair, *they* were even more unpredictable—a sentiment expressed by both sides.

"So," he said over the rim of his wineglass. "How is training?"

"Good," she said with a smile that lit up her whole face. "The school term starts in a few weeks and I'm rapidly catching up to where I need to be."

"That's good. Do you like Pan as a mentor?"

"He's great. Doesn't treat me as if I'm some kind of freak or second coming. I like him a lot, actually. We've been sparring quite a bit lately, and it feels like I'm starting to get a better hold on my magic." She paused, meeting his eyes. "The blood part, I mean."

"I'm glad," he said softly. "I've missed you, Tori."

She blushed, the heat suffusing her face. "I miss you, too."

"Do you?" The two words slipped out before he could help himself, and he regretted it the instant they did. He wished he'd just nodded instead and focused on the goddamned weather or some other mundane *safe* topic. But they'd been apart too long and the span of time had been ripe ground for insecurities to flourish on both sides. His, particularly.

Her eyes narrowed at him. "What do you mean? Of course I do. Do you think I like going home to Aliya's?"

"It occurred to me."

She stopped eating and stared at him, a host of emotions flying across her expressive face. "How can you think that? This is as hard for me as it is for you, can't you see? I want to call you every minute of the day, and when I can't reach you, it tortures me to think of where you are ... and who you're with."

Christian could see the vulnerability in her eyes. "I'm part of the Council, Tori, and most of my time lately has been spent there. You know that."

"But so is she." Christian didn't have to guess to know to whom she was referring. "Are you with her? With Lena?" Her voice choked on the last word as her eyes fell to her plate.

He frowned, genuinely surprised at the question. "Why would I be with her? She's with Lucian. Tori, you know that that is over. We've been through this."

"Sure, we have. You're only her maker—an age old connection that transcends all other bonds." She eyed him. "I've learned a little more about what that means."

"And what do you think that is?" he asked evenly.

"That you are forever linked."

"Which does not mean that I am *with* her. Lena has made her choice, and I have made mine. We are both at peace with what that is." Christian felt strange as the words left his mouth because he realized that they weren't true. At their last meeting, Lena had made it more than clear that she would always be open to a dalliance with him, but Christian was not interested, not even to take the edge off his loneliness.

Victoria was watching him closely and he kept his face expressionless. She resumed eating, her voice nonchalant. "You must take me for a fool, Christian. Call it whatever you will, woman's intuition, but that vampire is in love with you. Always has been and always will be. When she snaps her fingers, you go running."

"I do not return her feelings," he said. "And that's hardly fair."

"She called when I was still at the château, remember? She wanted to talk to you about something and you left so it had to have been important. When she needs you, you go."

"She wanted to talk about Lucian. The Council is bringing him up on charges and they asked for my help. That is all. Tori, what is this really about? You've been cagey all night and now you're picking for a fight. Why don't you tell me the truth and come out and say what's wrong?"

Victoria set down her fork and stared him right in the eye. "Maybe everyone is right about us. About us being from two different worlds and all. Maybe it will be better if we ... have some space."

Christian felt his whole world transform into one made of fragile glass. He hadn't expected this, not so soon. It'd barely been a few weeks and they'd already succeeded in driving a wedge between them. "Is that what you feel or what you're being told to feel?"

She swallowed, a rush of tears welling in her eyes. "No, of

course not. But it seems like you're keeping secrets from me and we swore never to do that. You always said that you would be honest with me, no matter how hard the truth was to hear."

"So did you. You accuse me of something and yet you do the same. We haven't spoken in days and you lay the blame at my doorstep. It goes both ways, my love."

She eyed him and swallowed hard, pain flashing through them for a moment before it was eclipsed by something else. He frowned as she wiped her mouth with her napkin and drained the contents of her glass. "I want to leave."

With a sinking feeling, Christian signaled to the waiter for the check. The owner of the restaurant brought over the bill personally, exchanging pleasantries while the hostess retrieved their coats. He escorted Victoria into the waiting car and slid into the driver's seat. The silence between them was charged.

"Do you wish to return to Aliya's?" he asked politely.

"Don't do that with me," she blurted out. "Take that bland aristocratic tone and pretend that I'm one of your servants from the nineteenth century. You are not a duke anymore, Christian, and this is the twenty-first century. Talk to me, please."

"You seem to have made up your mind. What else is there to say?" He shifted the car into gear and pulled out of the parking lot. "I shall deliver you back to your home."

"You are so stupid," she seethed. "My home is with you, not with Aliya. And you should know that and if you don't, I will have to remind you." She unbuckled her seatbelt as he took the turn to enter the Champs-Elysées.

"What are you doing?"

"Reminding you," she said as she climbed over the gear console and settled herself in his lap.

"Victoria," he said, struggling to concentrate as the backs of her thighs pressed into his, her knees straddling him.

"Drive," she said into his ear. "Take me *home*."

He held his breath as a sudden push of magic pressed the

accelerator into the ground and the car sped forward. "You're going to get us both killed," he said as she sucked on his earlobe. "Or arrested."

"You're immortal and I'm unkillable, so that's hardly a possibility. As far as being arrested, well, that would be a first." Her mouth trailed along his jaw and set itself to his, her tongue sweeping inside as if confident of its welcome there. Christian kissed her back, his body responding as only she could incite it to, and fought to focus on the road. But it was a losing battle— he was so starved for her that he could hardly concentrate. The car swerved out of control, veering across the divider into the opposite lane, straight into the path of an oncoming truck.

Christian swore under his breath as Victoria's mouth tore from his, and her eyes flashed black before the entire car fragmented into pieces. The Champs-Elysées and all its lights disappeared until they were in a vacuum of nothing, the world spinning around them as if they were the center of the universe. Victoria clung to him, her eyes wild with excitement, and glued her mouth to his. His hands left the steering wheel, curving around her hips and drew her closer. She was the one driving now. He closed his eyes and let go as everything winked into silence.

When he opened them, they were parked in front of the château. She still straddled his lap, her face flushed and her eyes diamond bright. "What did you do?" Christian asked.

"I didn't think you were driving fast enough, so I teleported us."

He stared at her in incredulous surprise. "You teleported an entire car?"

Victoria's smile was full of secrets. "I told you I was getting stronger." She reached over and unlocked the door, sliding over his legs to step out of the car. She hooked an arm over the door and leaned down. "Your turn."

He moved so quickly that her intake of breath was audible,

snatching her into his arms with inhuman speed until they were in the foyer. He couldn't move his hands fast enough, sliding over her rib cage and back, dragging her closer. Her mouth found his again and he was lost in the pure sensation of her.

"Wait," he said. "We need to talk."

"I don't want to talk," she insisted. "Everyone talks all the time. All I want to do is *feel* and remember for myself what it means to be here." Her hands roved over him, too, cupping his back and sliding provocatively down over his trousers. Christian's breath caught at the insistent pressure of her fingers. His body leapt to life and she pressed hers along every inch of him as if reveling in the power she had over him.

In the haze that surrounded them, Christian felt that something wasn't right. "No, Tori. Stop, this isn't you. This is your blood coercing you to get what it wants."

Her eyes went wide as she pressed an inch away. "You don't want me?"

"No, of course I do, but this is moving too fast. I can't think about controlling myself and we both know that I have to, for both our sakes."

"I can control it now," she said. "The blood."

His eyes narrowed, his hands sliding to hold her shoulders and keep her at arm's length. "What is it you think you want?"

"You."

Christian sighed, desire leaping like flame inside of him at the single word and the languid look in her eyes. "We both know that that can't happen, Tori. Your blood will kill me or possess me."

Her hand slid around to the front of his pants, her voice a seductive whisper. "Your body doesn't seem to share your concerns. Aren't I worth the risk?"

Christian groaned and pulled her to him. He could have sworn he saw something triumphant flash in her eyes, but he couldn't be sure. He set his lips to hers, his mouth slanting against hers, coaxing them open. She met him hungrily, arching up against him and clutching the lapels of his coat. His mouth slid to her throat, her pulse flicking beneath her skin like a beacon. He could feel his teeth lengthening and pressing through his upper jaw, and he paused, his hand splaying wide against her back as she arched backward.

In one smooth movement, Christian swept her up into his arms and vanished up the stairs. He sat her on the edge of the bed, watching with hooded eyes as she undid the fastenings on the black silk dress. He knew he was flirting with danger, but he was too far gone to care. She stood, the front of her dress gaping open and displaying tantalizing glimpses of bare flesh draped in black lace. Sliding off his jacket, her fingers made quick work of his buttons. And then his shirt was off, too, as her palms slid hotly against his skin, slipping lower along his ridged abdomen to the band of his pants.

"Tori," he whispered.

"Shhh," she told him, drawing him backward to the bed. "I know what I'm doing."

Her hands reached around behind her back to unclasp the black lace bra as she shrugged out of the dress to her waist. Christian's breath stalled in his throat at the perfection of her body laid bare before his eyes. Her hands tangled in his hair as she drew him down. His mouth closed over the peak of her breast, making her gasp and throw her head back. Christian's fingers skipped down her flat stomach, easing the rest of the dress down over her hips until she lay there in nothing but an indecent strip of black panties.

"You are so beautiful," he said. "Perfect."

A glimpse of the old Victoria emerged as she blushed furiously and pulled the satin sheet over her. "Are you okay?" she asked him, reaching up with her fingers to trace his lips and pressing them into the tips of his elongated teeth.

He drew back a hair's breadth, knowing that the slightest

pressure of their razor sharp points would draw blood, and nodded, surprised. Normally, by this time he would be rushing into the woods to relieve the hunger that would almost be tearing him apart. But now, all he felt was desire. He felt the hunger, too, but it wasn't oppressive. He sucked her forefinger into his mouth and watched her eyes flare in response. Her free hand slid to his belt buckle, working it loose as Christian stepped out of his pants and boxers and slid between the sheets.

She blinked at his nearness, that shyness appearing in her eyes for a scant second before it was eclipsed by something else, and she straddled him as she had in the car, only there was nothing between them. At some point, she had removed the last bit of her clothes and Christian's breath failed him at the intimate press of her skin upon him.

Her dark hair fell into her face and he brushed the lock away, staring up at her. "Are you sure?" She nodded, her lip caught between her teeth. "I don't want to hurt you," he said.

"You won't."

His hands slid on either side of her hips, adjusting himself beneath her. He paused, uncertainty warring within him. "Tori—"

She made the decision for him and slid her body atop his, her eyes going wide as he met her downward movement with an upward thrust. She froze, an agonized gasp escaping her lips, her fingers digging into his hands resting firmly at her sides. Christian held himself perfectly still, not moving an inch until she stirred and her eyes fluttered open. Pain shadowed their depths. He eased away gently, pushing them both onto their sides facing each other. Their bodies were intimately cradled together. "Do you want me to stop?"

"No, it's what I want," she said. "Please."

"Why?"

"Because I want to give myself to you while I'm still me."

Christian raised himself up on one elbow and stared at her. "What do you mean while you're still you?"

She traced a finger across his chest, making the muscle there leap reflexively at her light touch. "I wasn't honest before about the blood magic. I can control it more, but I feel it changing me, too. We are becoming one and I have no control over that." She paused, as if she had more to say, and Christian waited. "Aliya and the others say that you only want me because of Le Sang Noir."

"Do you believe that?"

Her voice broke, her eyes shifting away. "I guess I needed to know for sure if you wanted me for me."

"Victoria," Christian said gently, turning her chin so that she couldn't move her face away. "I *love* you. It's not just about wanting you. How could I not? You take my breath away. But I care about you, not just about a physical connection between us. Surely, you know that by now?"

She turned her face away. "I do, but when we are apart, it's hard to silence the voices … the ones that tell me you only want me for what I can do for you. I wanted to see if you would risk it all, even your death." He didn't respond and she continued. "You asked me once if I would die for you, and you're right, I would have."

"But now?"

"They need me, the Witch Clans. They need the Cruentus Curse. I can't abandon them. I can't abandon my people."

"I would never ask you to."

"I know you wouldn't, but you're a vampire royal, and you have your own people to consider. They would always come first, wouldn't they? Your loyalty should be to them."

"It's not a question of loyalty. I will do what is best for everyone, but your safety will always come first. You are the only thing that matters."

She flung herself back onto the pillows, a frustrated sigh

leaving her mouth. "But what if you can't, Christian? What if you can't please everyone? Our people are on the brink of war, and while they haven't asked me to declare or prove my allegiance, I suspect that it is coming."

"No one can force you to do anything you don't want to do," he said gently. "Or who you want to be with."

"I don't want to lose them," she said, her gaze fluttering to his. "And I don't want to lose you either. But deep down I know I can't have both. Love in times of war is like wearing your lover's heart on the outside of your body. Anyone can target it and strike you down. Our enemies won't stop at hurting you to get to me and hurting me to get to you."

"What are you saying?"

She bit her lip. "That this has to be goodbye."

Christian felt coldness take hold of his body as her words hammered into him like nails. "So this is why you wanted to …" He trailed off and pulled himself up to sit at the edge of the bed, rubbing a hand through his hair. He reached for his trousers. "I understand. This is the consolation prize. Thanks, but no thanks."

"Christian, please." She placed a hand on his arm, stalling him. "That's not it at all. I wanted you to know that you'll always have this part of me."

He turned to her, his voice inflectionless despite his slowly fragmenting heart. "When we make love, it won't be to say goodbye, Victoria. It's a pledge between two people who love each other, who can't bear to be apart on any level, emotional or physical. Giving my body to you is *my* pledge to you, and it's not something I take lightly." His voice shook with emotion as a savage anger tore through him at the realization that she had used him to assuage her own guilt. "You don't get to take my love for you and twist it as you see fit. You can believe all you want that your intentions were pure, but you know deep down why you're doing this. You know the truth.

You feel guilty because you didn't choose me. You didn't choose us."

Christian could see her flinching against the harsh bullets of his words, but he didn't care. He felt nothing. She'd already made the decision for both of them. He stood and tugged on his trousers, when a huge weight shoved into him from behind and a blow smashed his head sideways. Reacting out of pure instinct, he snarled and shifted into full vampire mode. Knowing it was her, he forced himself to temper the surge of fury pouring through him, but Victoria was having none of that. Her eyes flashed violent fire as she drew her discarded dress over her head. He could feel the oxygen being sucked out of the room, rushing toward her like flame and feeding into her spiraling rage. Tiny blue frissons of static electricity hovered over her body. Christian knew she would never hurt him, but a moment of real fear licked along his senses as he watched her struggle for control.

"Twist your love for me?" she seethed. "How is offering myself to you a fucking *consolation* prize?"

"Isn't it?" he countered coolly.

She flew at him, her magic lending her such brute strength that it took all of his considerable power to restrain her. "I will never forgive you for this," she hissed, trying to shrug off his hands at her shoulders.

"Forgive *me*?" He stared down at her furious face, the searing heat of her blood seeping out of her skin and scorching his fingers. "For what? For not letting you use me? Or for not making it easy for you to live with the choice you've made?"

The magic poured out of her in waves, making the flesh of his hands peel away. He kept them there, watching her all the while through the agony until bone became visible beneath the charred skin. Her eyes flicked to them and widened in horror. "Release me," she begged. "I don't want to hurt you."

"It's too late for that," he said in a dull voice, his arms falling to his sides. His burned injuries healed almost instantly. He didn't think twice about the unnatural speed of his recovery, but she did.

"Instant healing?" she blurted out, reaching for his hand. Her eyes shifted over him and she pushed out with her mental awareness. Christian felt the press of her power and, for the first time, consciously blocked her from him. A mask fell over her features, but he could see her surprise shimmering behind it.

"You're not the only one who is changing," he said, pulling his shirt over his shoulders. He swallowed, not meeting her eyes. "I'll take you home."

"No need," she said, hiking her chin. "Goodbye, Christian."

He stared at the space where she'd stood long after she teleported from the room, wondering if he should have done things differently. Perhaps he should have taken what little she'd offered and been content with that. He'd known that it would eventually come to a choice, but what he didn't know was that Victoria would have chosen them over him. Not without a fight, anyway. He felt hollow as if someone had scooped out his insides with a trowel, leaving only the shell of his body behind. Love didn't always conquer all—sometimes it fled in the face of fear. He didn't blame her. War was coming, after all.

"C'est fini," he murmured. "It is done."

HEARTBREAK WARFARE

Victoria teleported all the way to Maine, back to Holly's house, and huddled on her old bed. She didn't care that she hadn't returned to Aliya's or that someone would notice her absence. The Witch Clans kept track of everyone's whereabouts, including hers. What would they do? Send her to detention? Ban her from the coven? Truth was, she didn't give a rat's ass what any of them would think. She had already let them influence her far too much. She had let their doubts and suspicions in, let their mistrust of Christian color what she felt for him.

And because of them, she'd left him.

Victoria knew she had made a mess of things. Her deepening control over the blood magic had made her overconfident that they could finally be together, even if it were just for a short while. Christian was right. What she had offered had been a break-up consolation prize. She hadn't intended to go there and throw herself so shamelessly at him, but she couldn't bear to end it without letting him know how she felt underneath it all—that she was his, body and heart. Selfishly, she had always wanted him to be her first. He was meant to be her *only*.

She wrapped her arms around her knees, rocking back and forth. Her body was tender from the little they'd done. She had expected that it would hurt, but that brief physical pain had been well and truly eclipsed by the brutal coldness of Christian's response. His rejection had hurt more than anything she'd thought possible. It still did, even though everything he had said was true. She had used him to relieve her own guilt, to make herself feel better about breaking up with him. She wanted the solace and comfort that being with him would bring, not caring about what the aftermath would be like.

She almost smiled through her misery. He was so old-fashioned that he called it *making love*. A faint blush heated her cheeks as she remembered the surprising feel of him against her. It had been everything she had imagined and more. Victoria frowned as she thought of Christian's control. It'd been a two-way street. Though she had control over her blood, she did not have any control over his vampire impulses. He was the only one who could suppress that. And unlike all the other times when things had gotten hot and heavy between them, he had. Other than his teeth lengthening, he hadn't gone feral. He'd been calm and in control, able to resist his hunger.

Her frowned deepened as curiosity won out over misery for a brief moment. Christian had said that he was changing, too. She wondered what that meant. At the end, when she had reached out toward him, she had felt an ancient strength about him—layers and layers of inherited power—one that had not been there before. Her blood magic had burnt the skin off his forearms and hands, and he had healed in seconds. An injury like that would have taken days to heal for any ordinary vampire, which clearly he was not.

She wondered whether Christian's extraordinary newfound power had anything to do with Enhard's death. Not that he would ever confide in her again. Anything between them was now gone. God, the look on his face as she told him it had to be goodbye had almost brought her to her knees. He had looked broken and utterly devastated. Yet, deep down, a part of him had known that she would be the one to break it off, because in the end, he had let her go.

Victoria stared at the girlish decor and the pink bedspread of her old room. Helpless tears sprung to her eyes as she wrapped the blanket around her shoulders and wept as if her heart were breaking. Because it was. Perhaps she truly was weak. She lacked courage and conviction. She couldn't even stand by the one who loved her, who had stuck with her through everything. Instead, she had turned tail and ran because it'd been the easy thing to do—the *safest* thing to do.

"Tori? Is that you?" Aunt Holly's welcoming grin faded from her face as she took in the scene before her. "Oh, my darling, what is the matter?"

Victoria's tears turned into a full on deluge as she fell into Holly's arms, sobbing her heart out. "We broke up."

"Why? What happened? What did he do?"

"He didn't do anything. I broke up with him. It was getting to be too much—the school, the witches, the magic, all of it. Everyone is ready to kill everyone else. There are murders and each side is blaming the other. And I'm caught in the middle because you know ..." She sniffed. "Because of what I am."

Holly brushed a strand of hair out of her face. Her wrinkled face was compassionate. It was amazing that she hadn't gone crazy months before, after a demented warlock had kidnapped her, when Victoria and Christian had divulged that creatures like vampires and witches roamed the human world. She's taken it in stride. Of course, her best friend—Victoria's grandmother—had been a witch, too, so it wasn't all out of the blue. Victoria had wanted to wipe her memory of everything that had happened, but Holly wouldn't let her. She had argued that she had seen too much throughout her life to stick her head in the sand and pretend bad things didn't exist. And now, Victoria was deeply grateful that Holly was aware and could offer comfort.

"I thought you loved him? Christian?"

"I do, but it's complicated. He's part of the Council. His loyalty is to them, not to me."

"Child, I've seen the way that boy looks at you, and his loyalty is and will always be to you. He loves you. And you love him. You're letting people and politics come between the two of you—something you swore that you would never do."

"I know." Victoria sighed. "I didn't expect it to be so difficult. The Witch Clans don't trust the vampires, and they are afraid of me, too. I guess I was trying to prove that I am one of them and on their side. I wanted them to accept me. I was an outsider all my life and for once I feel like I belong somewhere ... that I have a place in the world."

"You've always had a place in the world," Holly said gently. "And you will always have a place here with me."

"I know, Aunt Holly."

"Have you eaten?" she asked, and Victoria nodded. "Let me fix you some tea. You wash up and come downstairs. Everything will get better, I promise."

Victoria nodded as Holly left the room. She stripped slowly and walked into the connecting bathroom, turning the shower to hot. She stared at herself in the mirror, remembering the start of her senior year so many months ago. She'd been just a girl then. Now she was so much more than that, more than she ever expected to become. Despite the changes, her reflection looked the same—dark wavy hair and pale brown skin—except for her eyes. The green seemed weighted down as if they had seen far too much in a short space of time. They looked too weary and too old for someone who had only just turned eighteen. She stepped into the shower and let the scalding hot water run down her body. She washed herself slowly from head to toe, letting her sadness and her memories rinse away with the sudsy water.

By the time she was finished, Victoria had a newfound sense of clarity. She had done what was best for both of them. Now they could be strong for the people who needed them. Grabbing a towel, she stared at the steam-clogged mirror, her eyes catching something forming in its depths. An indistinct shape loomed forward, two bright eyes shimmering for a scant second before the shape vanished. She blinked. There was nothing there but cloudy vapor.

Were you going to tell me that you'd left?

She nearly jumped out of her skin and whirled around, only to see Leto glaring at her from the doorway. Her fingers crackled with suppressed magic. "I could have killed you!" she yelled and glared back at the cat, her eyes narrowing. "How did you get here anyway? Did you come with Aliya? Did she send you?"

No one sent me. You summoned me.

Victoria frowned. "Summoned? How? I didn't think that was possible … to summon live creatures, I mean."

It is not, but as you can see, here I am, Leto said. *I shall add it to your increasing range of talents.*

"I didn't summon you, Leto."

A part of you did or I would not be here. What has happened?

"I broke up with Christian," she said tonelessly, sweeping a brush through her wet hair. "And I needed some space. This is the only place I don't feel hunted or stared at." She turned to eye the cat. "And where have you been? You've been gone for days and days."

I have business.

"What kind of business?" she snapped. "As my familiar, any business of yours should also be mine. I need to know where you are at all times, Leto." Something leapt to life in his eyes, a sharp green surge that made Victoria pause. It looked like anger, but then again, Leto had always been moody, even more so after what had happened with Gabriel. She softened her voice and reached for a fresh pair of jeans and a sweater. "Are you okay? You seem agitated."

I was summoned across the Atlantic on a whim. How do you think I am?

"Grouchy, apparently." She turned to stare at him, resenting his accusatory tone. "And as I've told you already, I didn't summon you. You're behaving as if I drew you away from something drastically important. What? Did I interrupt your fourth catnap for the day?"

He eyed her, his green eyes boring into hers in a fiery stand-off. She gritted her teeth and held her ground until he looked away. His head bowed slightly and she knew that it was his way of apologizing. *It is better this way*, he said.

"What is?"

That you have ended it with the vampire prince.

Her hands stalled over the button closure of her jeans. "Vampire *what?*"

Oh, I take it you haven't heard? Word via the secret grapevine is that your ex-boyfriend is the child of a Reii.

"A what?" Victoria was starting to feel like a broken record. A dumb one. She frowned and sat on the edge of the bed. "Explain."

A Reii. They are very ancient vampires—the most powerful of their kind. One of them was his maker.

She knew what the Reii were, but wasn't Enhard Christian's maker? She narrowed her eyes at the silver feline. "How do you know this?"

I have my sources.

Victoria thought back to the primeval sense of power she had felt earlier and Christian's newfound ability to control his hunger so easily with her. "I thought Enhard was his maker?"

So did he.

"I thought the Reii were extinct? No one has ever mentioned them before."

Leto moved his shoulders in a very human shrug. *They are— were—thought to be extinct. No one has heard of them in centuries. The one that made him was one of the few remaining. She hasn't been seen since she turned him. It is a mystery whether she is still even alive.*

"Why did you call him a prince?"

The strengths of the Reii are revered by the vampires. In the old days, they were rulers of their people—kings and queens of the blood. The new Vampire Council governed by the various vampire houses is an invention of modern times, meant to distribute their power equally. Vampire kings and queens were a thing of a past, until now.

"Have you told anyone of this?"

He stared at her knowingly. *Like the Witch Clans?*

"Yes."

No, but this will not remain hidden for long. Lord Devereux's power will become a new weapon for the vampires. And should war arise between the witches and the vampires, they will look to him for leadership. He eyed her. *Just as the Witch Clans will look to you.*

"I'm not going to fight Christian," she said. "That is absurd."

You won't have a choice. You have made your position clear, and you are as much a weapon for the Witch Clans as he is for them. If it comes down to it, Victoria, will you sacrifice your people to their enemies over whatever paltry feeling you may have held for one vampire?

Victoria felt the blood drain from her body at his words. Leto was right. She would have no choice but to fight. If the vampires attacked and Christian was on their side, she would have to defend her people. She couldn't let thousands of witches be slaughtered because … because she had loved the enemy. *Still* loved the enemy. Her breath caught as a fresh wave of agony overtook her. The loss was raw.

"Go," she growled to the cat, pushing her hand out toward

him, the magic rushing through her body like wind. "Go back to whatever you were doing."

Victoria, wait, Leto began.

But she couldn't look at him. He reminded her too much of what she had just done, and she needed to be alone with her grief. She had to put Christian where he belonged—in the past. She closed her eyes and willed him back to Paris. When she opened them, the familiar had disappeared.

She walked over to the white and pink antique dresser and picked up one of the framed photos that Holly had kept. It was one that someone had taken at the masquerade at the Rainbow Room in New York City—she, Angie, Charla, and Gabe. Christian hadn't gone. She traced the faces of the people in the picture. Strange to think that two of the smiling faces were dead —both casualties of the enmity between vampires and witches that raged on the sidelines of human existence. It seemed like a lifetime ago. And it seemed that history was about to repeat itself.

She picked up a photo set in a silver frame. It was one of her and Christian. Contrary to what most people believed, vampires could be photographed. Frozen in time they looked so happy, untouched by anything but what they felt for each other. She had been so naïve to think that their love could survive all the outside influences. Here in Maine, they had been sheltered from all the hate that divided their species. Their love had blossomed and grown, only to be ripped apart by those who didn't want to see them together.

And she had let them.

A tear dripped on the glass of the photo frame. Christian looked so unbearably handsome. Anyone with a heart could see the connection between the two of them—one that was evident even in this glossy photograph. She saw it in his hands, in his eyes, in the way his body braced protectively around hers. She placed the frame face down on the dresser and wiped the tears from her face before leaving the room. The sooner she put Christian out of her mind, the better.

On the way downstairs, she heard voices, one of which she recognized. Her heart soared with delight.

"Angie!" she said, rushing into the room and pulling her friend into a warm hug. "You're here? I thought you moved back to New York?"

"Grad school," Angie said, smiling back.

"You look great," Victoria said and she meant it. Angie's dark hair had been cut in a pixie style and her eyes glowed with happiness, a far cry from the sour and miserable girl she'd been when they'd first met. Notwithstanding that she no longer had the dark cloud of her evil warlock brother Gabriel hanging over her, Angie looked like she was enjoying life.

Her friend's eyes narrowed as she stared at her. "What's wrong?"

Victoria knew that Angie was using her special sight, the one that allowed her to see her aura. It was a gift that had been the bane of Angie's existence—permitting her to see the truth of what people were—vampires, witches, werewolves, or any manner of supernatural creature.

She swallowed. "I'm fine."

Angie exchanged a glance with Holly, who suddenly busied herself with an excuse about getting fresh herbs from the garden. "I can see that you're not fine. Your colors are mottled, so much unhappiness. What's going on? And be honest because I can tell when you're lying." Angie's face was fierce, despite the compassion layered in her eyes.

"I broke up with Christian," Victoria said, proud that her voice didn't waver. It seemed that the more she said it, they easier it became. She took a breath at the expression on Angie's face.

"Why? You two love each other."

"It's complicated."

Angie frowned at her. "I hate that word. It's a word that *complicates* everything it is used to describe. Last I knew, you and Christian were closer than ever. What happened?"

Victoria collapsed on the nearby window seat and stared out at Holly puttering at the far end of the garden as Angie took a seat opposite at the kitchen table. "Everything happened. School, the clans, the vampires. There's been a slew of murders. We're on the brink of war. Being with Christian seemed to be too much of a risk."

"For him or for you?"

Her gaze snapped to Angie's. "For *him*."

Angie drummed her fingers on the table. "Are you sure about that? Pushing people away is easy to do instead of standing and fighting for them."

Victoria swallowed and reddened. Angie always could cut right through the heart of the matter. "It's not like that. I—"

"Then what is it like?" she asked gently. "Talk to me, Tori."

Victoria closed her eyes. On the one hand she knew she could trust Angie. She trusted her with her life. But she didn't want to betray sacred covenants of the Witch Clans. She took a deep breath. Angie had sacrificed more than enough for her in the past, including being tortured by her own brother. She deserved the truth. "The witches don't think it's safe for me to be with him because of the Cruentus Curse. They're worried that if things do come to war … that … that …"

"You'll choose to be with him," Angie finished.

"They're afraid of me." A tear slipped down her cheek. "Who wouldn't be? I'm a monster who can kill with a thought."

Angie moved to sit beside her on the bench, taking hold of her hand. "You can also heal with a thought, Tori. And you're no monster. We've both seen more than our share of those." She paused, her eyes unfocusing slightly as she stared at Victoria. "Your power has grown a lot in the time we've been apart." Her voice softened. "I remember the first time I saw you and you were just coming to terms with your magic and what you were. It was so chaotic, like a shimmering rainbow of black and red."

"And now?" Victoria prompted.

"Now it's mature. The black is there but it's layered in so tightly with the rest that it's almost all one color." She blinked and her eyes settled on Victoria's face. "You're in control, Tori. And I know that's what you're really afraid of—that you'll lose control and put everyone you love at risk. But you won't."

"How do you know?"

"Because I know my friend. And I know that she'll put herself in harm's way before hurting anyone she loves."

Angie stroked her back as Victoria hugged her, the first tear joined by another and another until there was veritable deluge pouring down her face. "I slept with him," she whispered into Angie's shoulder.

"What? With Christian?" Angie nearly toppled off the window seat, her eyes going wide with alarm. "Like sleeping or the other thing?"

She nodded. "The other thing."

"But I thought you couldn't."

"Me, too," Victoria said, flushing to the roots of her hairline. "I initiated it and we did, but then we didn't really finish. It's hard to explain. But he didn't bite me and I didn't go blood crazy."

Angie's brows slammed together. "That's weird."

"Yeah." Victoria stared at Angie. "I know I'm stronger, but he said that he had changed, too. And I sensed it. That he was more powerful. He didn't have to run off to feed as he usually does when we make out."

"And then what happened?"

"And then I opened my big mouth and said I wanted to … you know … before we broke up. We fought. I used magic."

"Wow."

"Trust me, I know." Victoria swallowed again, her heart

swelling on a surge of regret in her chest. The look in his eyes had been excruciating to witness. It'd been damp with betrayal and sadness—emotions she had caused. She'd hurt him just enough so that he would let her go.

"Are you okay?"

"Physically, yes. Emotionally, I don't know. I feel shattered inside, like I'm coming apart into a million pieces and I can't stop it."

They stared at each other in silence until Angie cleared her throat. "I'm going with you. Back to Paris."

Victoria shook her head. "You can't. It's too dangerous. And what about school?"

"It's orientation next week," she said. "And plus, if there's some mega-supernatural war erupting in Europe, I'm pretty sure that school isn't going to matter once this shit hits the rest of the non-humans back the United States."

"Angie—" Victoria began.

"I'm doing it. You need me. You're emotionally vulnerable and I know you trust these witch leaders, but I don't. Everyone wants a piece of you because of what you can do, and I'm the only one who can protect you."

"How?"

Angie tapped the side of her head. "I can see what they are and what they want, remember? You don't know who to trust and I'm going to help you with that." She shook her head decisively. "Nope, it's settled. I'm going with you and there's nothing you can say about it. Trust me, the witches will be thrilled to have an Aurus in their midst, but I am there for you, no one else." She smiled. "And I've never been to Paris, so there's that."

Victoria threw her arms around her friend, the prospect of returning to Paris suddenly no longer so daunting. "Do you know how much I love you?"

"I do," Angie said. "But promise me one thing."

"Anything."

"You'll rethink this thing with Christian. You two belong together and you're far stronger together than you are apart. You always have been. And if you're right about a war coming, then you two will need each other more than ever."

"But the Witch Clans want me to lead them."

"Then lead them," Angie said with a grim smile. "But on your terms."

THE PRICE OF POWER

Within seconds, Lucian and the warlock teleported to another dark greasy alley that mirrored the one they had just vacated, and Lucian gasped as his body regulated to the transfer. The warlock started moving toward the west end of the alley and Lucian followed, straining his ears to see if he could determine where they were. A few sentences in French caught his attention. They were still in France, he guessed, Paris even. The smells were the same. He expanded his awareness. From what he could tell, they were on the northern edge of Paris, near Saint-Denis, one of the northern suburbs infamous for its crime rates.

Lucian suddenly wished he had fed before going on Kristos's fool errand. He also wished that he could communicate with Lena, but she was bound to Christian, not him. And since he was known for disappearing for hours on end, she wouldn't think twice about his absence. Lucian felt exposed, but he hadn't become as powerful as he had by being cautious or scared. He gritted his teeth—if he were going down, he'd take as many of the creatures with him as he could. He followed the warlock to a crumbling stone church covered in demonic looking gargoyles. He blinked and swore that one of them twisted its gruesome stone head to mark his approach.

"Wait here," the warlock said as the heavy studded doors opened to admit them.

Lucian nodded curtly, his face impassive as the doors shut behind him. The inside of the church had been gutted except for the stained glass windows, which cast colored puzzles along the dusty floor. It was quiet and empty, yet Lucian knew that it would not be. They were there in the silence, hiding in the darkness. His skin crawled as the sensation of danger intensified.

The warlock returned and crooked a finger for him to follow. Leaving the vaulted main room, they descended down a stone staircase. The air was not musty, which made Lucian think that this was a passage that was used often. Again, he felt that prickle of awareness along his senses as if hundreds of eyes were watching his progress. As yet another wooden door slammed shut behind him, Lucian was well and truly trapped inside the den of the enemy.

They arrived in a large underground chamber nearly double the size of the upstairs room. His eyes shifted across the space, noticing the long table standing at one end and what looked to be a blood-soaked marble altar on the right side. He couldn't help himself. Self-preservation rose within him. His fingers shifted into claws, his teeth elongating at the threat that pressed on all sides of his body. A feral change overcame his face as the beast inside surged forth. Dark magic shifted in the space and he readied himself.

"Calm yourself, vampire," a laughing voice said. A laughing *female* voice. "You will not be harmed."

"You're a woman," Lucian burst out as the owner of the voice came into view. She was stunningly beautiful and tall, almost as tall as he was. Her hair was the color of flame, her eyes like ice chips. Clad in a voluminous gown of pale silver, she exuded sexuality and confidence. Power, too. He could feel it emanating from her like a wave of heat. Lucian knew that she was old and she was strong. He was no stranger to magic and he could feel the very air pulsing in response to her presence. "I thought all warlocks were men."

"Most assume the same." She smiled, her teeth white and perfect. "We do not discriminate by gender. Warlock is simply a misunderstood term. I am Freyja."

Lucian's eyes narrowed. "Norse?"

"If you wish." She waved a hand, indicating the stone-faced warlock who had transported him at her side. "Roan says you have something you desire to share." They were the only three in the room, but Lucian was not foolish to believe that they were alone. He was already supposed to be dead and the only way out of this trap would be to use his tongue. Freyja indicated that he should sit as she strode to the end of the long table. "What is it?"

"Did you give the order to kill me?" Lucian asked instead, following her lead and sitting as if he didn't have a care in the world.

A smile shifted across her lips. "Yes."

"Why?"

"Because you are a chess piece, Lord Devereux. Although it appears that you have now advanced from pawn to knight and that intrigues me." She crossed long shapely legs, the soft material outlining the sleek silhouette of her thighs, and leaned back in her chair. Lucian felt something respond deep in his nether regions as the electricity crackled between them. In another world when she didn't want him dead or he didn't want to rip her head off, he could see them engaged in another kind of discussion—one that included this very same table along with considerably less clothing. He'd rarely had dalliances with other supernatural creatures, but for her he'd make an exception. Lucian shifted forward in his seat, letting his eyes flare, and was rewarded with a tiny quirk of her eyebrow as the chemistry between them climbed another notch.

"Your vampire compulsion does not work here," Roan snapped.

Freyja's eyes flashed. "Leave us."

Roan did as she asked, staring with malevolence at Lucian the entire way past. Lucian was not cowed by the warlock's antagonism. He let his smirk show, remaining idle in his chair.

"He does not like you," Freyja commented. "None of my people do. They know what you are capable of. There aren't very many people in Paris who haven't heard of the infamous leader of the House of Devereux. Your methods are … notorious."

"And you?" Lucian asked with a lazy smile. "What is your opinion?"

A vaulted eyebrow. "Of you?" Lucian nodded and Freyja stood, closing the gap between them. She slid a hip on the edge of the table inches from him and leaned down. The scent of her —warmth and spice—curled around him. Freyja's fingers trailed along the collar of his black coat. Her voice was husky. "I think, Lord Devereux, that you are hanging by a very thin thread. Either you are lying about the existence of Le Sang Noir and trying to avoid your very real execution, or you are telling the truth and want something in return." Her voice lowered, as did her fingers, trailing down button by torturous button. "So what is it that you want?"

Lucian's eyes did not leave hers, despite the sheer torment of her fingers. His entire body felt leashed, as if held on some invisible string connected to the lightness of her touch, seeping through layers of brushed wool and silk. "Amnesty."

Her hand settled into his lap and Lucian inhaled sharply. "Come now, Lord Devereux. Surely you do not expect me to believe that is all you want. I can smell it on you—your desires, your cravings, your need."

"Power," he bit out, the slight pressure driving him to distraction.

"At least you were honest this time." She eyed him, the grip of that diamond gaze almost as powerful as that of her hand. "What are your terms?"

Lucian stood swiftly, closing the gap between them. His hand curled around her hip as he attempted to turn the tables in whatever game she was playing, but before he could even draw a breath, a bolt of energy threw him on his back several feet away. She eased off the table, standing to face him. He crossed the room in the blink of an eye, but as he reached her, she teleported out of his grasp.

"Did you think it was going to be that easy?" Freyja laughed, her voice echoing in the cavernous room. "Trust me, Lord Devereux, I know everything there is to know about you, and while you are correct that a diversion between us would be … interesting, I assure you that I am not like your usual conquests."

Lucian fought a wave of humiliation, his desire turning to acid in his blood. Either he'd been incredibly transparent or she'd read his mind. She had played him like a fiddle—seducing him with her words and her eyes and her hands, and he'd been careless, caught up with lust like an errant schoolboy. He snarled and shifted toward her. Freyja wasn't slow in confronting him. He dodged a second bolt of energy with inhuman speed and spun to avoid another.

Rage and desire surged through him as the maddening scent of her filled his nostrils, mingling into an explosive cocktail that fired his blood. Games or not, he wanted her. He grinned and charged, keeping his gaze on hers. Magic users moved with their eyes, not with their bodies. He ducked beneath a fire spell, spinning like a cyclone toward his head, and rolled until he was only a few feet away. The air around her shimmered as she teleported once more, but Lucian closed his eyes, following the magic surge with his vampire senses and spun backward. When Freyja reappeared at the far end of the room, he was right there, his fingers closing about her slender—oh, so beautiful—throat.

"What are you going to do now?" he asked, pressing her into the heel of the altar at her back and taking pleasure in the scrape of her shoes on the floor. His eyes slid to the pulsing vein at her neck. Her blood would be rich, he knew, from the magic that flowed in her veins. He could smell it rising in tantalizing wafts with each stroke of her pulse. His teeth lengthened in automatic visceral response.

Freyja smiled at him, her mouth shaping an incantation that made a wild rush of vivid green fog surround them in a haze. The wisps of mist cut into his skin like touches of pure sunlight. Lucian didn't flinch, even though they burned his flesh raw. He was used to pain—it focused and motivated. He pressed closer until his mouth was inches from hers, so close that he could taste the warmth of her exhale. Her eyes widened even as he felt her pulse quicken beneath his fingertips … with excitement, not fear.

His thumb slid along the taut column of her neck and he licked his lips slowly and deliberately. "And I assure you that you know nothing about me."

Lucian stepped away, releasing her throat and watching the acid fog flicker and recede. He steeled himself and held his transformation at bay, his features returning to normal as his vampire strength healed the blisters on his body. "Now that we have that out of the way, shall we proceed to business?" A smile crooked her lips at his arrogance, but Lucian was done with the games. "I offer you information on Le Sang Noir in return for destroying the Vampire Council. You get what you want, and I get what I want."

"And what is it you think we want?" she asked, signaling to an invisible servant. Within seconds, another warlock appeared with two glasses—one filled with a clear liquid in a flute and the other golden colored in a whiskey glass. She took the first and the man approached him with the second. Lucian shook his head, refusing the drink. He wanted all his wits about him.

"War," he said as the servant melted from the room. "You want the witches and the vampires to destroy each other so you can be rid of your two greatest enemies."

She eyed him over the rim of her glass, her eyes shadowed. "If you are correct and that happens, there won't be much left for you to inherit."

"Whatever is left, I want it. Those are my terms."

Freyja nodded. "Tell me who she is."

"I want your bond."

"You have it." She strode forward and grasped his forearm. Lucian felt the surge of energy binding her word to their agreement and had to restrain his sense of triumph. His strategy worked. "Now divulge your information."

"Why do you want the witch from the prophecy so badly?" Lucian asked, his eyes narrowing. Something in the warlock's tone was anxious, fretful even. "For power? With her on your side, you can have absolute control."

"She is dangerous."

Lucian shrugged. "Tell me something I do not already know. I saw her blood possess another vampire to the point of making him do its magical bidding."

"You have seen the Cruentus Curse in action?"

"Yes."

Freyja frowned. "And yet you live to tell the tale."

Lucian smiled. "My brother saved me. He was the one it possessed, you see. She gave him her blood to save him and it did. Only it had other designs for him once he was under its spell. He almost killed everyone in that room with that blood magic, until she exorcized it." He could see the disbelief in Freyja's eyes. His tale sounded fanciful to his own ears, but it was the truth and he hadn't spoken of it to anyone, not since that fateful day in the underground room in New York. He shook his head. "Trust me, I know how it sounds, but it is true."

"And the witch?"

"She is more powerful than the Witch Clans and the warlocks combined. And her power was only fledgling when I saw her last."

"Is that why you were looking for her?" Freyja asked and smiled at the look on his face. "That was part of our plan. We heard you were looking for young witches. Roan's idea, actually, and it worked."

"I lost my last witch to her," Lucian snapped. "I needed a replacement. Magic has its uses, even to us vampires." He knew he had nothing to lose by confiding his plot to her. "I wanted to use the prophecy to retake control of the Vampire Council, but her loyalty was to my brother, not to me. He was the one to take the power of her blood into himself."

"Her loyalty?" Freyja asked with a frown. "You said that she offered it to him. Why would she do that? Knowing he was a vampire?"

Lucian smiled and played his hand. "Haven't you heard? She is my brother's consort."

"Consort?" Freyja repeated.

"Yes."

"A witch and a vampire," she breathed. "It is forbidden. The Clans would never allow it, nor would the Council."

Lucian winked with a lewd grin. "See? Not as farfetched as it seems. And forbidden or not, neither the Council nor the Clans can stop them. She compelled an entire room full of vampires at our headquarters with a single word in a room warded for magic."

"How do you know it's her?"

"I saw her blood with my own eyes," he said. "I smelled it, too, when she teleported from vampire headquarters a hair's breadth from my fingers. Black as midnight and as decadent as the blood of the Goddess herself."

Freyja's eyes widened. "Where is this witch now?"

"Alas, that is where I cannot help you. She is training with the Witch Clans. It took them longer than I expected to pull them apart, but they have succeeded. They refused to teach her about her magic unless she left my brother. And she did. And as far as I know, he wasn't very happy about it, but he agreed because it was what she wanted. They didn't want a vampire having undue influence on the wielder of the Cruentus Curse, you see."

"I fail to understand how that helps us, Lord Devereux, if what you say is true and that she is no longer with your brother."

Lucian walked to the table where the servant had left the glass of whiskey. He raised it in a toast and drained the contents. "We have both lived so long that we have become jaded, don't you see? It's true love, Freyja." Sarcasm dripped from his every syllable. "They *love* each other to the point of destruction. And this little witch will do anything for my brother and vice versa. Get my brother and you get her."

"You would sacrifice your brother?"

"I would sacrifice my firstborn son if I had to." He smiled. "Most of the rumors you have heard about me are true."

Freyja lifted an arm and, suddenly, a dozen warlocks pooled from the shadows, including the one who had brought Lucian here, Roan. "You have heard this vampire's testimony. He speaks the truth."

Lucian exhaled. Of course he had spoken the truth. Any witch or warlock worth his or her salt would know when someone was lying. And he wasn't about to risk his neck by telling falsehoods or exaggerating what he knew, not with the most powerful warlock he had ever met. He felt a twinge of guilt for what he had done, but he did not owe Christian anything. He was doing him a favor, after all. Christian had never wanted to become a vampire and now he would be free from his curse.

"What are you going to do to her?" he asked Freyja. "The witch."

"She is dangerous."

"You said that already," he said dryly, raising an eyebrow.

"Not that it matters to you, vampire, but her powers upset the balance of magic on this plane. She is—as the humans say—a ticking time bomb, one with the potential to kill every supernatural being in this realm."

"So you mean to kill her."

"Yes."

She eyed the warlocks in the room. "We have a new target. Lord Devereux's brother. His Grace, the Duke of D'Avigny."

Lucian felt his stomach clench at the sound of the title—yet one more thing Christian had stolen from him. Jealousy burned within him with the force of a thousand suns. Christian had always been the bane of his existence, and when he was gone, it would be the beginning of a new era … a new start without the shadow of his brother looming over him. He raised his chin and squashed the remnants of any guilt. Christian would get what he deserved.

"He is not to be harmed," she warned her followers. Her gaze fell on Lucian. "And Lord Devereux is now under my protection."

Roan's lips curled over his teeth and Lucian could see his fingers clenching into fists at his side. He was not pleased by Freyja's announcement, Lucian knew. They did not trust him and with good reason—he had killed thousands of them over the years. When this was all said and done, he would make sure that Roan was added to the list.

Freyja addressed him. "What is her name?"

"Whose name?" Lucian asked, distracted.

"The name of the witch."

He cleared his throat. "She is the descendant of the Duchess of Lancaster." The room went silent at his announcement. Every witch or warlock knew the stories of who she was—and the blood madness that had consumed her. If they doubted him before, they did not now. He could smell their collective fear. He kept his smile carefully contained, keeping his face expressionless. "Her name is Victoria Warrick."

THE IMMORTAL SON

C hristian felt the tug deep in the marrow of his bones. Lucian was in trouble. They had always been connected as twins, but the vampire connection between them was even more powerful. He fought the immediate urge to rush to his brother's defense. Lucian had made it clear that he didn't want his help. He was so stubborn that he'd rather face execution at the hands of the Council for his perceived crimes than ask for help. And now, even though every cell in his body warned that his brother was in jeopardy, Christian ignored the insistent pull of it.

Standing in the massive boardroom in the Tour Areva of the vampire headquarters, he surveyed the city of Paris, his eyes pausing on the elegant lit frame of the Eiffel Tower. It was one of his favorite monuments, along with the Notre Dame cathedral, also visible in the distance. He'd planned to take Victoria sightseeing to all of his favorite places, but they hadn't made the time. He swallowed hard, his fingers clenching at his sides. And now neither of them would have that chance. She was gone.

Composing himself, he focused on the matter at hand—Enhard's letter. He'd read it a hundred times, but hadn't found the answers he'd sought. He had asked his assistant to summon David. As if on cue, he felt the Elder's presence, swirling among all the other energies in the building. Christian frowned—being able to distinguish identities was yet another new development in his growing array of skills.

The power worried him. He knew nothing much about the Reii other than they were the founding fathers—the original vampires—of their race. They were powerful, their blood undiluted by time or generation. And it seemed that he had been graced with their strengths. He knew that it had to be because of Victoria's blood—it was the only thing that explained his accelerated changes.

Enhard had written that he would inherit his maker's memories and her strengths, but only when his body was able to control such tremendous and dark power after many, *many* years of life as an immortal. It seemed that Victoria's blood had expedited that, spreading within him and forcing him to evolve or die. And so, he had evolved ... enough to inherit a legacy he had no inkling of.

"Your Grace," David said as he entered the room. He bowed in deference, even though at the moment he was by far the stronger vampire of the two. "You wanted to see me?"

Christian glanced at the old vampire and nodded. Enhard had said that David was only three generations removed from the Reii. He held up the letter. "Please, have a seat. You know what Enhard wrote in here." He paused. "Of the truth of my maker."

"Yes."

"And you also know what I have told you about Le Sang Noir and what happened in New York. Do you believe that it caused me to evolve?"

"When you took Victoria's blood, did she remove it completely?"

"As far as I know," Christian replied. "Although it has left an indelible mark." He jabbed a finger toward his eyes. The black ring around the silver of his irises had not disappeared and was a daily reminder of how potent the blood's magic had been. He fought back a shiver at the visceral memory of it and turned his attention to the Elder. "Enhard wrote that you went through a version of the change?"

David nodded. "When I had lived seven centuries as a vampire and was old enough to withstand my inheritance, I did."

Christian withheld his gasp. He had barely claimed two centuries as a vampire and he was nowhere near that age … nowhere near ready. "What was it like?"

"Overwhelming," the vampire said with a rueful smile. "The memories were fragmented, agonizing to piece together at first, but it became easier. And the gifts, they came more gradually."

"What kind of gifts?"

"My sensory abilities sharpened a thousandfold. I developed psychic powers and was able to read people, see their truths and lies, understand their desires and their fears. My speed … well, let me show you." He smiled and blinked, but did not move.

Christian's eyes narrowed on him. "Are you going to demonstrate?"

"I already have," David said, opening his fist to display a strawberry. Christian turned around in disbelief, his gaze falling on the fruit platter sitting at the far end of the table on the other side of the room. He was a vampire with formidable vampire strengths of his own and he hadn't seen David move.

"Do it again," he commanded.

David nodded. This time, Christian felt the slight disturbance in the air, but he still did not see David leave his chair. The only indication that the vampire had moved was the glass of water now sitting at the edge of the table.

"Impossible," Christian murmured, even though he could see evidence of David's speed in the materialization of the glass.

"Enhanced speed, enhanced strength, enhanced everything," David said, taking a casual sip of the water. "Everything you were able to do before, you can do it better. Shifting into other forms will be like breathing. Advanced healing. Super strength. And as you have no doubt already discovered, you do not need to feed as often." The vampire eyed him. "But you will still need to feed, Christian. Blood, as always, remains our one sustenance. And the more you use your new powers, the more quickly your strength will drain."

Christian paced, his mind spinning with the new knowledge. "What of dark magic? Enhard's letter said that the Reii have control over it."

"I expect that the presence of such magic is what Le Sang Noir responded to in you. Your powers of compulsion will grow. Few will be able to resist your will, animal or human." David eyed him. "And you will be less susceptible to the magical powers of witches."

Christian froze, thinking back to Victoria's fire and frowned. Her hex had been powerful, but he had barely felt it. A lesser vampire would have been incinerated and turned to dust. But he had withstood the spell and healed.

"You will also have the power to call on other vampires and the ability to communicate with the dead."

"Call on them how?"

"You can take their strength, drain their power if you had to." David flexed his fingers. "If you needed my power, you could command it."

"But I am not your maker. How is that possible?"

"Because you are a Reii and that power transcends any other bond." David leaned forward in his chair, threading his fingers together on the table, his eyes thoughtful. "With the threat of war looming on the horizon, this could not have come at a better time. The witches have their weapon, and now we shall have ours."

"Their weapon?" Christian said carefully. "You mean Victoria."

"They won't hesitate to use her for their own ends, Christian. You have to see that. No matter what you feel for the girl, her loyalty will always lie with her own kind. Enhard told me of what lies between you and we shared the same concern. Relations between our species are forbidden for a reason. No good can come of it, no matter your feelings on the matter. Love in times of war is a liability."

"No need to worry. It is finished between us," Christian said in a dead voice. He cracked his knuckles in a nervous gesture, desperate for something to drink, anything to numb the rawness of the feelings surging through him. He stalked over to the wet bar at the end of the conference room and poured himself a liberal drink. He drained the glass and poured another.

"That is for the best."

Christian frowned and faced the Elder. "Regardless, I won't hurt her, if that is what you are suggesting. Even if we are on the brink of war, there is nothing that will induce me to harm her in any way."

"What if it is to defend your people? Her powers are legendary. If she loses control, it's not just the vampires who will be at risk of total destruction. Everyone else will be as well —the witches, humans, everyone. There will be nothing left."

"If the Reii were so strong, why didn't they stop the Duchess of Lancaster?" Christian asked.

"I do not know why the Reii chose to stand aside and watch their progeny get massacred, but that is what they did. From what I can gather in the memories that were passed on to me, they chose not to awaken and come to our defense."

"Why?"

"Because we had grown lazy, fat, and indolent. Our ranks needed to be culled. The last time any of us even *saw* a true Reii was when you were made." He shrugged. "We don't know why she appeared for you, of all people, but Enhard knew that it had to be kept a secret. The truth of your lineage would have put you in terrible danger from the other vampire houses. After you accepted the change, no one saw Sezja again. For all we know, she could be dead."

"She isn't." Christian's words were quick. He didn't know how he knew that fact, only that he did. Sezja—his maker—was alive somewhere. He also sensed that he could find her or summon her if he needed to. Such was the bond between a maker and his progeny. He wasn't sure he was ready to face her, though, not when the knowledge of his vampire birthright was so fresh.

"Christian, one more thing. At peak strength, you can walk in the daylight for prolonged periods." David smiled. "It is one of the better perks of our bloodline."

Christian stared at the expanse of the glittering city below as David's words sank in. He couldn't fathom walking in sunlight without pain. For an unguarded moment, he thought of Victoria and walking hand in hand with her through the Tuileries in daylight. He imagined the sun glistening on her hair and the warmth of it on her skin as they strolled through the gardens. The scenic vision metamorphosed into one of a war-torn Paris with Victoria standing on one end and he on the other, thousands of innocents caught in the cross fire. With a stifled sigh, he shoved the image away.

"What of my progeny?" he asked David, pinching the bridge of his nose. "Lena. Will she have accelerated powers?"

David nodded. "Yes. Less than yours, but hers won't manifest for centuries yet." He hesitated. "Once word gets out about your new strengths, it won't be long before she finds out. Others, too, will seek to control her, namely your brother."

At the mention of Lucian, Christian felt the same twinge in his blood—the one he'd felt earlier signaling that his brother was in danger. He was alive, but the threat was still present. It didn't make sense. What was he up to?

"Speaking of Lucian, have you heard from him?"

David shook his head. "No."

"When is the vote scheduled for the final appeal?"

"In three weeks."

Christian nodded, clasping his hands behind his back and striding toward the table. He knew that Lucian would not be executed, especially if he gave his testimony to the Council that Lucian hadn't directly killed Enhard, but the punishment would be severe. They had tolerated his machinations long enough, and too many vampires on the Council felt that Lucian needed to be put in his place. What had happened with Enhard had been the last straw. As much as Christian wanted to protect his brother, he knew that Lucian would have to pay some price for his actions.

Given his relationship with the accused, Christian had been recused from the vote, but at the very least, he suspected they would strip his brother of his leadership over the House of Devereux and of all his material assets. Exile was also an option. Other brutal punishments had spanned the gambit over the years—a thousand silvered lashes, trial by fire, teeth removal, which was by far the cruelest sentence short of death since vampire teeth did not regenerate.

Christian wondered whether his change in status would affect the outcome of the vote—it was no secret that he would defend his brother to his last breath, if it came to that. He also knew that that was the reason Lena had come to see him. She wanted him to convince the Council to spare Lucian. He had considered it, but he understood more that his brother needed to face the music or he would never stop. And truth be told, if Lucian wanted his help, he'd have to damn well ask for it.

He glanced at the clock on the wall. The High Council was due to meet in a quarter of an hour, a meeting that both he and

David were expected to attend. It was to discuss the recent slew of murders and whether they were going to declare a full out war against the Witch Clans. Tensions within the general council were already mounting, and the emergency meeting of the High Council had been called to determine the appropriate course of action.

"Thank you, David, for your counsel. I'll meet you shortly in the grand hall. I need to make a phone call. I trust I can count on your discretion."

"Of course." The Elder hesitated in the doorway. "Your Grace?"

"Yes?"

"For what it's worth, I did like Victoria," David said. "Very much. And I know how much you cared for her. Sometimes, these things are simply not meant to be, no matter how hard we wish for them." He stopped, as if considering his words. "If there was anyone who could have brought our people together, it would have been the two of you. I know that Enhard believed that with all his heart."

Christian couldn't hide the pain that slashed through him and he took a strangled breath to compose himself. He nodded mutely to David before the vampire took his leave and slumped into one of the chairs, staring into space. He wondered if Victoria would still hear his thoughts across the miles and he had to fight to keep the wall he'd erected in place. He wanted nothing more than to hold her, to bury his face into her sweet-smelling hair, and to forget about the outside world. His fingers clenched into fists as the need surged within him like a writhing beast. It was worse than the hunger. The walls of the conference room started closing in on him and Christian leapt to his feet. He didn't look up until he was in the heavily shaded outdoor courtyard on the roof.

Once outside, Christian felt better. He flicked out his cell phone and dialed his brother. It went straight to voicemail. He didn't bother to leave a message. He called Lena next, but she had no idea where he was either. There was another way for him to contact his brother, but Christian was loath to use it. The sense of danger was still there, though, lurking beneath the surface of his skin. He sighed and pushed his awareness outward.

Lucian.

He waited, knowing his brother could choose not to respond. It would be just like him to ignore the mental communication. To his surprise, an answer came back rapidly.

To what do I owe the honor, brother?

Christian bristled at the sarcasm, but kept his voice monotone. *I sensed you were in trouble.*

You sensed wrong, Lucian replied. *As you can tell, I am quite well.*

Where are you?

Paris.

Lucian was being deliberately vague and, for a moment, Christian wanted to know where he was. Lucian had many friends in dark places and Christian knew that he wouldn't accept the Council's decision without a fight. Lucian would go down kicking and screaming, taking as many as he could with him. Christian wouldn't put it past him to seek clemency from other species who hated the vampires.

Lucian—

What is it? Lucian drawled. *Worried for my wellbeing? It's a little too late for brotherly concerns, isn't it? Don't worry about poor little Lucian. Turns out he can look after himself after all.*

Now isn't the time for your riddles and your games, Lucian, Christian snapped. *We are on the brink of war with the witches.*

A laugh. *Oh, I know. I just hope for your sake when that happens that you are on the right side. Soon your luck will run out, and I will be there to pick up the pieces of what should rightfully be mine.*

Where are you? Christian asked.

Making new friends. Now bugger off, mon cher frère, before my friends get offended.

The link was abruptly severed and Christian frowned. The threatening feeling was there, roiling beneath the surface. He shrugged it off. If his brother didn't want his help, then there was nothing he could do. He only hoped that Lucian didn't do anything foolish, especially anything that would strain the already tenuous relations between the vampires and the witches. But Lucian could only be counted on for doing what was in his own best interests.

He thought back to his newfound gifts and how he had been able to sense David's arrival earlier. He took a deep breath. Time to put his new abilities to the test. Christian closed his eyes and focused on his brother's essence, tracing it backward through the hundreds of other energies pressing upon them. In his mind's eye, he came to a shadowy alley where he could see a half-consumed body hanging against a blood-spattered wall—Kristos, his brother's first in command. Dark shadows congregated around it as if consuming the vampire's remains. They froze, sensing his presence, and Christian recoiled. His brother had been here, but then he had simply vanished. There was no other trace, which could only mean one thing—he'd been teleported somewhere.

The question was by whom?

Christian snapped back into himself. Lucian had always had a fondness for witches and using their magic to further his own agenda. Had he found another? He focused on the alley again, pulling it clearly into his head. This time, he noticed all the details he had missed—like the scuffle marks on the wet ground and the faint smell of sulfur in the air.

Suddenly, the shadows converged upon Kristos's body scuttled out of the way and he turned to study them. Something had scared them. He peered closer. The wraiths were staring at *him*.

Because he was standing right there in that alley.

He could feel the cobbled stones pressing into his shoes, see the layers of grit on the surrounding brick walls, smell the rot coming off of Kristos's half-eaten body. He tapped the toe of his shoe against the ground, hearing the clipped sound echo off the stone, and watched as the wraiths retreated even further.

He'd been so sharply focused on the memory of the surroundings that he hadn't even realized he had moved. But he had—he had crossed whole districts in the blink of an eye. Christian shook his head, trying to orient himself. He was indeed standing in the very same alley he'd been so intent upon in his head as if he had willed himself there. What he had done was impossible—vampires couldn't teleport.

But they could fly.

And he was the direct descendant of a Reii.

Was it possible? Had he flown without realizing it? He shook his head. He'd worry about that later. Right now, he needed to figure out what had happened here with his brother and how he had disappeared. The odor of sulfur was faint, but he traced it back to a spot near the darkened end of the alleyway. Something—no, someone—had summoned a demon, or had been in the process of summoning a demon. He frowned at the marking on the cobblestones. The beast hadn't fully materialized. Still, the only creatures that summoned demons were warlocks.

What was Lucian doing in the company of *warlocks*?

A clicking noise behind him had him spinning to confront a threat, but there was nothing there. The clicking sound echoed again, and Christian squinted into the darkness, watching as something took shape. He readied himself, but recognition took the place of worry as a familiar feline shape sauntered into view.

"Leto, what are you doing here?" he said, although not expecting an answer. The familiar only communicated through his master, and she was not here. He would have sensed her in a heartbeat. The cat sat, staring at him with intense green eyes, as if it could see right through him. Christian shrugged. "I don't suppose you've seen Lucian?" He jerked a head at Kristos. "Or whatever killed him?"

The familiar eyed him, unblinking, for several long moments before sauntering off without a backward glance. Christian shook his head. There was never any love lost between them, but without Victoria there to translate the cat's thoughts, they could be strangers. It was odd, he thought, that the familiar had been so indifferent, almost as if he hadn't recognized him. Then again, Leto had changed since they had come to Paris, becoming more and more disconnected over the weeks, so much so that Victoria had thought to mention Leto's ambivalence to him.

He glanced at his watch, noticing that he was going to be late for the Council meeting. Time to see if he could get himself back to La Défense in one piece or come up with some fantastic excuse as to how he ended up on the other side of the city. He wasn't quite sure how he had done it the first time, but he guessed it had to do with visualizing a target destination.

Inhaling slowly, he drew the rooftop garden into sharp focus in his head and, after a few seconds, felt his body rise off the ground. And then he was moving so fast, it seemed as if the world was rushing past in an indistinct shimmery blur. The cool air pushed against his face and the city of Paris twinkled like a sea of lights below him. He barely had a chance to savor it when the obsidian shape of the Tour Areva loomed into view, and he was right back where he started. It had taken him all of three seconds to fly eight miles. Christian grinned.

Now *this*, he could appreciate.

A WEB OF BETRAYAL

Victoria paced the noisy halls of Belles Fontaines while she waited to see the headmistress. Madame Starke was not usually late, but today she was. Considering that it was the start of the fall term, Victoria wasn't surprised. She glanced around at the bustling hallway filled with fresh new faces. Their ages spanned the gambit—the wide eyed ones were the newest while older students moved with quiet, poised confidence.

The energy was palpable and there was a lot of it. Victoria could feel the power pulsing in every waking heartbeat. She closed her eyes and let her body feel the crush of all the diverse energies until her skin tingled with it and pings of electricity crackled across her own flesh. Knowledge surged inside of her —she could control them all if she had to. She blinked, shocked at the random thought, and then steeled herself. Her blood was no doubt responding to all the magic. She quelled its impulses with a silent command.

"Enter," Madame Starke called out.

"Bonjour, Madame," Victoria said politely. "You wanted to see me?"

"Ah, Victoria, yes, I did," she said. "Thank you for waiting. As you can see it's quite busy. Today is your first official day of classes and I wanted to check in that you were feeling comfortable."

Victoria's eyes narrowed at the strange choice of words. Feeling comfortable? She stared at the woman, seeing nothing but concern reflected back toward her. Perhaps it was a genuine question. Or perhaps not, as she studied the diminutive but powerful woman sitting behind the desk. Madame Starke was ruthless when it came to protecting the students of her school. No, she was asking whether her trust had been well placed in allowing Victoria to attend the school when her magic was by all standards uncontrollable.

Victoria nodded and swallowed through the sawdust taking residence in her throat. "I am."

"Good. If you feel out of sorts today, it is imperative that you see me or one of the other teachers at once."

"I'm not sure what you think is going to happen."

The headmistress eyed her, her eyes unreadable. "What I don't want to happen is a repeat of what occurred in the examination room."

"I won't hurt anyone, if that is what you are implying."

"I am not implying that you will," she said smoothly, not responding to the anger in Victoria's tone. "I'm asking that you try to stay calm and don't make me regret allowing you to attend Belles Fontaines."

Victoria drew her annoyance under control. She shouldn't be surprised that they were still afraid of her. She had, after all, neutralized a team of advanced teachers during her assessment. "Understood."

"Excellent. Panthèse will escort you to your classes for the rest of this week."

Madame Starke pointed to the door, which opened as if on command, allowing a waiting person to enter. Pan grinned at her, his blue eyes glowing in his face. Victoria smiled in response. At least she had one friend who wasn't terrified of her or what she could do.

"She hates me," she said to Pan as he accompanied her to the building at the third point on the star configuration of the school.

"She does not."

"You don't understand how she looked at me," Victoria said. "As if I was going to murder every last one of the students in the school in cold blood."

"Are you?" he deadpanned.

"No," she blurted out and then laughed at his droll expression. "Maybe just one."

"Bring it, Super Witch."

Victoria frowned, her eyes snapping to his. "I told you not to call me that."

"Why?" Pan grinned. "It's what they're calling you, don't you know."

"Who's calling me that?"

"The trees," he said in a quiet voice, all trace of humor disappearing from his laughing blue eyes. "They know all your secrets. They see what you can do, and they tell me that there hasn't been someone like you in centuries."

"Oh, have they?" she asked, not meeting his eyes. "What else do they tell you?"

A glowing orb racing toward them high in the sky interrupted Pan's answer. The odd-looking meteor collided with the magical barrier that surrounded the school in a bright shower of sparks. The shock of it threw Victoria and Pan to the ground, the earth trembling beneath them. The explosion was followed by another and then another. It couldn't be coincidence.

"What the hell is that?" Pan said, his neck arching upward and his palms resting in the dirt.

"Fire spells," Victoria said. "We're under attack."

"Attack?"

Victoria eyed him, panic registering in her center as she felt the concentration of magic outside the school walls. She pushed her consciousness forward, but slammed back into herself as another series of flares cracked into the school's protective sphere. "Warlocks. We have to warn Starke. Quick, Pan."

"Warlocks?" he gasped.

"They've surrounded the school."

"But how is that possible? We're warded for invisibility. No one knows that we are here unless you *go* here."

She glared at him. "Well, they know and they're here. We need to get these kids to safety. Now move."

The barrier chose that exact moment to disintegrate as huge firebombs pierced the interior. Flames and billowing smoke sprouted everywhere, consuming buildings and bodies in equal measure. Screams erupted, and Pan dove into motion, scooping up fallen bodies and running toward the main building. Victoria did the same as she approached a sobbing girl who couldn't have been more than twelve.

"Are you hurt?" she asked.

"My leg," the girl whimpered. Victoria stared past the smoke and retched in horror. The entire lower half of the girl's left leg was missing, severed by a metal piling from a nearby roof. Victoria bent and touched the bleeding stump. "CURO."

She couldn't bring back the leg, but she could stop the bleeding. She saw a young man running toward them and signaled to him. "She's lost her leg, but she's conscious. Help her to the main building." She didn't ask. She commanded. The boy nodded, grasping the girl in his arms and disappearing down the path.

Victoria flexed as four bodies appeared directly in front of her. They weren't students or teachers—that, she was sure of. They also weren't witches. They were warlocks. She could smell it on them.

"Mademoiselle Warrick, stand down."

The voice came from behind her and she turned to see Madame Starke, along with a line of determined staff flanking her, including Monsieur George and Madame Claret.

She met the headmistress's eyes. "But—"

"I said stand down," the woman hissed as she deflected a blow meant to maim. "Get behind us."

"I can help."

But her answer was drowned out in a rattling noise that made almost every witch drop to the ground clutching their heads in agony. All except her. She strode forward, her magic protecting her with every step and pushed a hand out. The blast of power seething from her fingers incinerated the bodies of the four warlocks. But before she could blink, four more materialized to take their place. And then a dozen more teleported into the courtyard and filtered into the shadows.

Her senses tingled as she recognized a familiar essence. *Vampire.* Victoria frowned, honing in on it. It was Lucian. She knew it as she knew her own body. What was he doing here in the presence of the warlocks? She shook her head—perhaps she was mistaken. She focused on the lone body standing at the periphery, hoping that he was in the wrong place at the wrong time. But she knew better. Lucian was always out for himself, no one else. He was the one who had led them here.

Fury surged along her veins, her hands spreading forward. "Ignis cremo." The fire spell surged forward in violent precision, contacting two of the warlocks opposing them as the other two spun out of the way. A poison spell speared toward her and she dove to avoid the blast, a protection shield spell darting from her fingers at the last moment. She crouched behind a large shrub beside Monsieur George, the defensive magic teacher. He was covered in soot and blood, a large gash on his cheek leaking crimson onto the white collar of his shirt.

"There are too many of them," he shouted.

"How did they get in?"

He shook his head. "I don't know. They attacked from the top, which is the least protected area of the dome. The barrier is meant to conceal, not to defend."

Victoria glanced over her shoulder, but couldn't see the group of teachers who had been there before with the head-mistress. "Where are the others?"

"I don't know. Our line of defense collapsed soon after we arrived, but I think they retreated to defend the main building. Madame Starke and the others are still out here."

"What do the warlocks want?"

He stared at her. "What they always want. Power."

The bush they were hiding behind went up in a spire of dust as it disappeared, leaving them both exposed. They took off in opposite directions, Victoria flying behind a small shed. She tossed a protection spell toward the professor, deflecting an attack from a nearby warlock as he, too, dove for cover. The professor sent a grateful look in her direction and proceeded to fight off a barrage of poisoned spikes.

Monsieur George nodded to her. "Go," he shouted. "Get yourself to safety. Find Madame Starke. I can hold them off."

Victoria stared around wildly, seeing the gray-clad bodies sliding in and out of the thick fog. "I can't leave you. You're outnumbered."

"Go. Don't stop and don't look back."

Despite her reticence to leave him, Victoria took a deep breath and raced back along one of the paths toward the main building and froze as it came into vision. Warlocks surrounded the entire building. She ducked behind a large sapling and pulled herself into the lower boughs where she was out of sight. She wished she had Pan's gift to speak with the tree. Instead she pressed her palm against its rough bark and begged for its assistance to camouflage her. To her surprise, the branches closed in, holding her in a makeshift cradle and blocking her from sight. Her fingers gripped the rough sides of the trunk, gratitude filling her. She had the perfect view of the entrance to the main building.

A statuesque woman in a flowing red dress approached through the clearing smog. She was a warlock, Victoria knew. A powerful one. She could sense the magic rippling in the air around her as she walked. To her surprise, Lucian followed in her wake, and Victoria's breath caught in her throat. She was right—he obviously was helping them. Her stomach dropped as she realized what that meant—he had told them about her ... about who she was. Which meant that they were here for her.

"You know why I am here. Surrender the Cruentus witch," the warlock in red said, her voice ringing through the courtyard like the sound of bells.

Madame Starke appeared, flanked by two of her senior teachers, Didier and Claret. Victoria wondered for a second whether Monsieur George had survived the assault. "We do not know what you are talking about, Freyja."

Freyja.

The sound of the name sent thrills through her body. She did not know the warlock, but something inside of her knew what that name meant.

The woman in red laughed. "But of course you do," she said. "You are harboring her here."

"The Cruentus Curse is a myth."

"Then why do I smell the fear in your blood?" Freyja waved a careless hand. "If it were a myth, do you think I would risk war against the Witch Clans? If so, you misunderstand me. Now, cease your games and give me what I want or I will raze your precious school to the ground and all of the innocent lives within." She smiled, those cold red lips stretching into a grimace across her face. "You know you cannot protect them. There are too many of us and too little of you. That blood will be on your hands."

Starke opted for a different tactic. "I do not know where she is."

"But you admit that she is here."

"I will tell you nothing," Starke snarled, her hands twitching at her sides.

Freyja looked unperturbed. She flicked an arm and one of the sheds near the end of the six-pointed star went up in flames. A bolt of energy flew from Madame Starke, but Freyja deflected it easily with a shield spell. Victoria felt her blood boil. She was about to swing herself down from the tree when someone appeared between the warlocks and the witches.

Her heart hitched with recognition as Christian's lithe form took shape. She almost lost her grip on the branch—her feelings were so raw and so sharp that the sight of him made her physically weak. Her eyes consumed his features—the slope of his brow, the rise of his cheekbones, the sleek curve of his lips. She remembered the touch of them on hers with visceral feeling. It made no sense that he was here right now, and yet, there he was. Standing there and looking so imposing and so strong that it was all she could do not to run to him and beg him to hold her.

Victoria blinked as reality set in. Had he teleported? As far as she knew, vampires weren't able to use magic. Apparently those in the courtyard felt the same and stared at him with varying measures of mistrust and surprise, emerging so coolly in their midst.

"Enough," he said.

"This does not concern you, vampire," Madame Starke snarled.

"It does if whatever this is draws more attention from the humans than it already has." He waved a hand. "Your cloaking glamour is gone. You risk discovery with every passing second."

"The vampire is right," Freyja drawled. "Give us the witch and we will be on our way with no more bloodshed."

Christian's eyes flicked to his brother, who stared back with supreme unconcern, a smirk playing about his lips. Understanding dawned as he realized the same thing that Victoria had —*Lucian* had led the warlocks here to her doorstep. Christian's brow furrowed for a brief moment before blinding rage eclipsed it. His fury was only evident in the white outline of his clenched fists, but Victoria felt the push of it even from where she was hiding.

Christian's voice was calm when he spoke. "What have you done, brother?"

"She does not belong to you," Lucian tossed back.

"Of course not. She belongs to no one."

"Then you should not care."

"I do not care," he said mildly. His cold response was a blow to Victoria's gut. "I am here for one purpose—to avoid a conflict with the humans. The odds are not in our favor. There are billions of them and tens of thousands of us. Everyone needs to calm down and take a step back. Think about what you are doing."

"You think you can take us all on, vampire?" The snarling comment was from a warlock standing to the right of Freyja. His eyes flared and a scream lodged in Victoria's throat, but the stunning spell bounced harmlessly off Christian. Her eyes widened as the warlock fell to his knees, his eyes bulging from the rebounded hex. Victoria's blood reared in her veins, responding to the pull of the dark magic … magic that was coming *from* Christian. Leto's words came back in a rush—he was a vampire prince now, a son of one of their original vampires.

Christian released his hold and the man rose, gasping for breath. "You do not want to test my will."

Freyja raised a hand, something flashing across her face. "Impressive," she said. Her glance flicked to Lucian, who was staring at Christian with a disbelieving, incredulous look. But instead of focusing on either of the brothers, she turned her attention to Madame Starke, who had been watching the entire exchange with silent, calculating eyes. "Give us the witch and we will go."

"No."

"I can feel her presence." She lowered her voice, but her words filtered back to Victoria, making her body go ice cold. "Odette, she is a threat to everyone."

"And what will she become in your hands?" Odette Starke shot back. "A weapon against the Clans? We know your endgame, Freyja. It has been the same since the dawn of time. Your hatred of the Witch Clans will outweigh any shred of decency you have. Le Sang Noir will rise to defend our blood-lines, and there is nothing you can do about it."

Victoria felt her blood surge as blue fire flicked between the line of witches that had now grown ten bodies deep. This was going to be a bloodbath, with Christian standing at its midpoint. She had to stop it. She took a deep breath and shim-mied down to a lower branch when a hand stopped her descent.

"You can't," Pan whispered as he climbed up the branches beside her. Her eyes widened at his bloodstained face and he shook his head. "It's not my blood, don't worry. I am fine."

"I have to help them."

"You can't. Super Witch or not, you'll get yourself killed."

Her eyes met his and she wrestled with telling him the truth. Pan wouldn't hurt her, she knew. He was too guileless, too transparent. And he was bonded to the trees. They already guessed who she was and it would only be a matter of time before Pan found out. She inhaled sharply and made her decision.

"You don't understand. They're here for me."

"What do you mean?"

"I'm the Cruentus witch, the one from the prophecy."

Pan stared at her, a shadow slinking through his clear blue eyes. His fingers fluttered against her arm and he pulled her in for a hug. His hands spread wide at the place between her shoulder blades and she was completely unprepared for the electrical shock that speared from his fingers, covering her body in a wide net. Her eyes popped as Pan leaned back, blowing something that looked like golden dust into her face.

"I know exactly who you are, little bird," he whispered. "Time to go home."

MASTER OF DECEPTION

Christian felt Victoria's departure the minute she teleported. All he sensed was a swift spike of fear the moment before she disappeared into thin air, but he expected that was because of what was happening. He'd been aware of her presence the whole time as if she were a tangible force anchoring him to her. He was glad that she'd stayed hidden because he hadn't known what he would have done if she'd gotten hurt. As much as he wanted to prevent war from erupting in the middle of Paris, he wanted to protect her, too.

He stood between the immovable bodies of the warlock and the headmistress of the school, knowing they, too, would have felt the shift in the magic. "Victoria is no longer here," he said.

"How do you—?" the one called Odette Starke snapped.

He let his eyes meet hers, not deigning to answer. She knew full well how he knew. She'd been the one to insist that Victoria and he separate so that she could attend the school. It hadn't been Aliya's idea—although she had been resistant to the two of them as a couple, she'd come to understand the bond that lay between them. No, it had been this woman. Christian wondered at her endgame. She'd manipulated Victoria like a pawn, making her want to belong so badly that she'd given up everything to do so. And now, when the warlocks had made their play, she pretended ignorance.

He turned to his brother. "Come with me."

"I'm not going anywhere."

Christian flexed his newfound influence and his brother's eyes widened at the compulsion. "You will accompany me, by force or by any other means necessary."

"Who do you think you are?" Lucian gritted as he fought Christian's unspoken command.

"Your brother and your liege."

"I owe you no allegiance."

Christian assessed him with cool composure. "Then why does your blood bend to mine? You are bound to me. Now move."

"Freyja," Lucian said, his eyes darting to her. "Are you going to let this happen?"

"You have fulfilled your purpose," she said.

"We had an agreement."

"Which shall be honored, but you mistake my intentions if you believe I will enter into a blood feud with the vampires, least of all your brother. You would do well to follow his wishes." With that, the warlocks vanished into thin air, leaving Lucian standing there alone. He turned to run, but Christian halted him in his tracks.

"How are you doing this?"

Christian didn't answer. He nodded coldly to Odette Starke and grasped Lucian's arm before taking to the skies.

They arrived at the rooftop of the Tour Areva in seconds and Lucian pushed away from him, his face purple. "Since when can you fly?"

"It's a recent development."

"It's because of her, isn't it?" Lucian snarled. "Le Sang Noir? The blood you took that you claimed was so self-serving?"

"No, and her blood is self-serving."

Lucian raked a hand through his cropped hair. "Lies. Your powers have accelerated. Powers of compulsion, flight. What else can you do, *brother*, because of that bitch's blood?"

Christian eyed Lucian, watching the unrestrained emotions play across the face that was a mirror image of his own—jealousy, rage, confusion, and frustration combining into an unrecognizable mess. There was nothing that he could say that would make his status palatable to Lucian, he knew. His jealousy would consume him as it always had.

He cleared his throat. "My maker was Reii."

"Reii?" Lucian exploded. "Since when? Enhard was your maker."

Christian shook his head. "No, Lucian. My maker was a woman called Sezja."

"Since when? He gave you his blood."

"She did, too. Her blood displaced his."

"That is impossible," Lucian said, stalking to the edge of the platform. "You seek to deceive as you have always done. Admit it. Your powers are because of Le Sang Noir. You tried to warn me against it because you wanted to keep it for yourself. You don't think I can see right through your lies? The Reii haven't existed for years, and now you claim to be descended from one of them? You are deluded."

"I don't care if you believe me or not," Christian said. "What were you doing with the warlocks? They cannot be trusted."

"Just as my own people cannot be trusted," he shot back. "Should I sit quietly in my rooms and await my execution? Is that what you want? I did not kill Enhard, but I am a target for the entire Council."

"You have brought this upon yourself with your constant scheming for power. You think whatever agreement you have made with the warlocks will be your answer?" Christian strode to Lucian's side, grabbing him by the lapels of his jacket and forcing his brother to look at him. "You must be accountable for your actions. The Council only seeks justice."

"Justice?" Lucian scoffed, shrugging off his hold. "Trust me, none of them know the meaning of that word."

"I do."

"And yet you seek to see me fall to the same fate."

"I am on your side. Can't you see that?" Christian hissed. "You are the one blinded by your lust for power, by everything you think you don't have. The warlocks cannot be trusted—they want one thing. War."

"Then let them have it," Lucian said, storming toward the elevator. "Mark my words, brother. You and your Council will rue the day that you crossed me. And as far as trust goes, you broke that the moment you chose a witch over your own flesh and blood."

"I didn't choose anyone over you, Lucian."

"Didn't you?"

Christian couldn't believe his brother's obtuseness. He softened his voice as the elevator doors slid open and Lucian entered. "We are brothers first, bound by something deeper than blood. Does that not mean anything to you?"

Glacial silver eyes reflected into his. "No."

The doors glided shut, obscuring Lucian from view. Christian sighed. His brother would be his own destruction. He couldn't see beyond his own agenda, and whatever plans he had with the warlocks would only put him—and the entire House of Devereux—in jeopardy.

He pinched the bridge of his nose with his thumb and forefinger. Victoria's identity was no longer a secret and he knew that things would only get worse. Everyone would make a play for her—the witches, the warlocks, even the vampires. Lucian hadn't given up on his claim either.

Striding to his office, he slammed the door and braced his forearms against his desk, recalling the sliver of fear he'd felt the moment she'd disappeared from the grove at Belles Fontaines. He couldn't help himself—he pushed out into the void, settling into the connection between them that had yet to fade.

Victoria? Are you there?

No answer. He tried again, but there was nothing but emptiness.

The door to his office crashed open and his assistant, along with three frazzled Council members, rushed in. His mental projection slammed back into his body as he eyed their rude entry with a raised eyebrow. "What is it?"

"Four vampires murdered in southern Paris," the closest one gasped.

"When?"

"An hour ago."

Christian frowned. The timing coincided with the attack on the school, but he couldn't prove that it'd been the warlocks. And if they were looking for Victoria, why would they attack the vampires? The correlation made no sense, which meant that it had to have been a random attack.

"Their bodies?"

"Calcified. They've been turned to stone."

Stone. That was new. The previous victims had been burned to ashes. Christian's frown deepened. "Find out if any witches have been killed."

He watched as his assistant pulled something up on the device in her hand and nodded a few minutes later. "Three killed in the same area two hours earlier."

It was too coincidental, as if someone wanted them to believe that each side was targeting the other. It had to be the warlocks, and if Lucian's involvement confirmed anything, it was that he'd never align himself with the losing side.

"Get me Aliya on the phone now," he snapped to his assistant before looking at the three council members. "And convene the full Council."

"But, Your Grace—"

Christian silenced the young council member who spoke with a frosty glance. "Do not question me. Now."

She and the two others bowed their way out of the room. "Yes, Your Grace."

"I have the high priestess on the line," his assistant said.

Christian nodded for her to leave the room, and only when the door was closed did he speak into the handset. "I trust you have heard the news."

Aliya's voice was even. "Yes."

"We are being pitted against one another," he said. "I give you my word that we are not attacking your people, and I can guess that you can do the same for yours. The warlocks are plotting against both of us."

"What about rogue vampires? Can you vouch for them?"

Of course she meant his brother. She would have heard about the attack at the school, the one with Lucian at its helm and flanked by a contingent of their common enemy—the warlocks.

He spoke urgently into the phone. "We have to stop this, Aliya. The Council is on the brink of voting for war. Think of the consequences, of the collateral damage. So many innocents will die. Is that what you want?"

"Of course I don't. No one wants war, but it is becoming inevitable. The Clans are mobilizing, too."

He cleared his throat. "And Victoria?"

There was dead silence on the other end. "She's not with you?"

"With *me*?" He fumbled for the words. "Aliya, Victoria ended things several days ago. I haven't seen her since. I sensed her at the school earlier this morning, but she disappeared. I assumed that she teleported to safety."

"She did not," Aliya replied, dread saturating her tone. "No one has seen her, so we assumed that she was with you. Your vampire wards make communication impossible."

Chills raced across his spine—had his brother succeeded in his plot? Christian pushed his senses out, trying to see if he could sense her presence anywhere, but it was as if she had vanished off the face of the earth. She simply did not exist. "I cannot sense her."

"We have to find her," Aliya said. "Whoever has her has to be someone she trusted. She would have put up a fierce fight otherwise."

"She must have been caught unawares," Christian agreed. "Aliya, say nothing of this to anyone. We don't know who to trust. I will check back in with you in one hour. Please contact me at once if you hear anything."

He placed the phone back into its cradle, resisting the urge to break it into tiny unrecognizable fragments. Victoria was in danger. Somehow, she'd been taken. His hands fisted at his sides. It didn't matter that they weren't together—Christian would move heaven and earth to find her. But first, he would start with his brother.

†††

At the House of Devereux, Lucian flung the human host away from him and wiped his red-rimmed lips with the back of his sleeve, his gaze falling to Lena lounging at the entrance to the foyer. The other vampires in the salon twittered, watching the interaction between them with unveiled interest. Lena's eyes slid to the prone body of the young boy slipping in slow motion from the lounge he'd just vacated. The boy moaned, barely conscious, and Lena's mouth tightened in obvious disapproval. Lucian shrugged. He was beyond reproach, hers even. The boy was lucky he'd let him live—he'd wanted to drain every last drop from his body.

"To what do I owe the honor of your visit?" Sarcasm dripped from his words, and the twittering increased. Lucian smirked—he enjoyed having an audience.

"They are convening the Council," she said, approaching him and ignoring his baiting. "To decide whether or not to go to war against the Witch Clans."

He poured himself a brandy and studied the amber colored liquid swirling in the glass. "So?"

"*So*, they will need you. They will need every able-bodied vampire to make a stand against the witches. This is your chance, Lucian, to redeem yourself in their eyes."

"If you believe that you are a more of a fool than I thought."

She eyed the other house vampires listening intently to their conversation. "Is it true that you were consorting with the warlocks?"

"Word travels fast," he said dryly. "I'm hedging my bets, sweet."

"With Freyja?"

"Jealous?" he taunted. "I assure you I only have the usual interests in Freyja and, while a dalliance would be interesting, I'm more concerned with my survival."

"She is not to be trusted."

"You sound like my brother," he flung back.

"More vampires have been killed and we are suffering losses on both sides, Lucian," Lena said fiercely. "Pretend to be oblivious if you must, but people are dying. If we go to war with the Clans, the cost will be too great to consider. No one wants that, not even me."

"Now you really sound like Christian." He waved a careless hand. "If the vampires go to war with the witches, it will only be to my benefit, and yours, if you so desire. That is the deal I have worked out with Freyja—my inheritance."

Lena froze, her mouth parted in surprise. "What did you offer in return?"

"The witch from the prophecy, of course."

"Lucian, are you mad?" she whispered. "She is a weapon that they won't hesitate to use against us!"

He smiled slowly. "I know."

"What about your brother? The rest of the vampire houses? Are you willing to let them all die?"

"Every single house celebrated the idea of my execution," he said. "And my brother? Why the sudden concern? Changing your mind again about which brother will bring better odds?" She flinched against his words, but he didn't stop, relishing the shocked look on that perfect alabaster face.

He crossed the distance between them until she was backed up against the far wall. She stood her ground as his body pressed mercilessly into hers. Her gaze flitted to the others in the room, but their eyes remained averted. Lucian's grin was lazy. They wouldn't help her if she screamed for mercy—they'd relish the show. "Is that it? You want to leave me, too?"

"No, I've made my choice."

"Have you?" he whispered, lowering his head to brush her long neck with his lips. The hot scent of her filled him and he opened his mouth upon her skin, dragging his tongue across the expanse of creamy flesh. His palm slid down past her waist to curve around her hip as he drew her against him. He nipped his way up her throat to her jaw and set his mouth to hers. He could feel her reticence and it made a swell of rage rise within him. He tore his mouth away and braced his hands on either side of her head, resting his forehead against hers. "If that is the case, why do you tremble so?"

"I am afraid for you."

"Afraid for *me*? Why, pray tell?"

Her hands slid up his shirtfront in a placating gesture. "Lucian, this is madness, what you are doing. Everyone will die if Le Sang Noir is unleashed. It will be a repeat of the bloodbath with the Duchess of Lancaster, and no one will be spared."

Fear glittered in those transparent eyes of hers. For as much as she was a brutal killer, Lucian had always been able to read her. She was lying now, and the way she was looking at him as if he was beyond reach was the final insult. If she didn't want to join him, she would die with the others. "I already told you—I have a plan."

"Freyja will betray you the first chance she gets. Why can't you see that?"

His voice turned honeyed. "And you think trusting my brother offers a better chance?"

"I do."

His fingers dropped viselike to her throat. "Then die with him."

Lena's eyes bulged, but she was no match for his superior strength. Her legs kicked out and Lucian pressed his body into hers, restricting the movement, while his fist tightened inexorably. Lucian imagined how he would end her life in exhilarating detail. He would crack each bone until he felt satiated, then he would drain her body of every last drop of life, and finally, he would cut off her deceitful, treacherous head. His eyes dilated with pleasure as her struggles intensified. Damn but she was strong.

Her knee rose to catch him in the groin, dislodging his tight hold for one moment. She fought him like a hound from hell, scratching, biting, kicking to get away from him. He threw himself on top of her and they went rolling across the floor, their captive audience darting out of their way. Lucian settled his weight on hers, still gripping her throat and watching the fight fade from her eyes.

His free hands slid down to the clasp of his trousers. "Once more for old times' sake?"

She spat at him and turned her face away. Lucian couldn't

help himself. Readjusting his grasp, he bent down and sank his fangs into the flesh at the base of her neck. Her blood flowed past his lips into his mouth as he pulled deeply, sapping her strength with each swallow. After several long moments, he pulled away.

"Such a pity," he told her. "A waste, really." He gripped her chin, his thumb sliding along the flawless skin there. "He said his maker was Reii. If that were true, you would be such an asset. I understand only too well the bond between a maker and his progeny. I see the answer in your eyes—you will always choose him over me."

"Your jealousy has made you blind," she whispered, a bubble of blood frothing at her mouth. "I gave everything to you."

"You *will* give everything to me, sweet."

He bent his head just as the door to the apartment crashed in on its hinges and a hammering force drove into him. Lena's body rolled to the floor as Christian's fists pounded into his sides, making him gasp.

"Get out," Christian snarled to the vampires in the room, and they scurried like rats toward the doors. "What are you doing, Lucian?"

"Tying up loose ends?"

"You have lost your mind," Christian said, slipping his arms beneath Lena's shoulders and knees and placing her on the bed. He bit his wrist and let his blood flow into her mouth, waiting as she pulled it to her lips and sucked on it. Color bloomed in her wan cheeks, and he gently drew his hand away, returning his focus to his brother.

"What were you thinking? Lena has been nothing but loyal to you, and you punish her to within an inch of her life?"

"Punish?" Lucian drawled, cracking his knuckles and hooking one leg over the other in the chair. "Dear brother, if you hadn't interrupted us, your precious progeny would be dead."

Anger sparked in Christian's eyes. "You dare too much."

"It is my right—she belongs to me. She swore fealty to me. If she breaks those oaths, her sacrifice is her death. Just like in the old days when loyalty meant more than life."

"I was always loyal to you, Lucian." The weak voice came from the bed as Lena drew herself into a sitting position. Lucian blinked at her swift recovery, his gaze sliding to his brother's. He had drained her nearly dry. His stare flicked down to his brother's wrist that was now healed but still stained with blood.

"I may have been too hasty in my reaction." Lucian stood with deliberate slowness and walked toward the mantel, where he poured himself a stiff drink. He lifted an inquiring eyebrow in Christian's direction, but didn't wait for an answer before filling a second glass. He offered it to him. Christian took the glass but did not drink. "You are right, dear brother, after all."

"About what?"

"About us being bound by more than blood. Truce?" He could see Christian wavering, considering his peace offering for truth. But his shoulders relaxed a smidge and Lucian knew that he had won. He placed his drink down and pulled his brother into an embrace, his eyes flicking to Lena. "I am sorry."

Lena moved fast, her hand outstretched as she emptied the syringe into Christian's neck. Christian stumbled backward, bucking against him, but Lucian held fast. A cold smile blossomed on his face as the liquid silver sank into his brother's bloodstream, incapacitating him like nothing else could. Christian's eyes rolled back in his head and he hung like a dead weight.

"Are you all right?" Lucian asked Lena, his fingers caressing her face. "I am sorry I was rough on you, but your performance was spectacular."

"Thank you." Her eyes were shadowed as she stared at the limp body of her maker. "What are the warlocks going to do to him?"

"Use him to get the witch."

"How do you know they won't kill him once they get what they want?"

Lucian eyed his longtime accomplice. "I don't. Do you care?"

Her eyes hardened. "No."

"That's what I thought," he said with a smile. "If what everyone says is true, soon my late brother's gifts will manifest, and you will be one of the most powerful vampires left. We will forge our own history together."

KEEP YOUR FRIENDS CLOSE

Victoria lay cocooned in a wide heavenly soft bed, silk
sheets pressing against her legs. She could see blue
skies and hear the sounds of the ocean, the waves
breaking in the distance. Warm sea breezes swept through the
open hut, making the silk wick against her skin.

Her body felt deliciously, deliriously alive as she stretched,
turning to face the man sleeping on his stomach beside her. Her
eyes traced the lines of his bare torso, the white sheet hanging
low on his trim hips, just above the rise of his buttocks. The
material left nothing to the imagination as it draped across his
body—outlining his well-muscled thighs and legs. Her eyes
drifted to the curves of his back and the shining silver tattoo
that inked the length of his spine.

"Christian," she said, her fingers tickling his rib cage. "Are
you awake?"

"I am now," he said dazedly, tucking an elbow beneath his
cheek. His silver eyes met hers, traces of sleep still in them. "You
look beautiful in the morning."

She felt a flush consume her body from her hairline to her
toes at the look in those eyes of his. "So do you."

He reached for her, scooting her body beneath him and turning his at the same time so that he lifted up on one elbow to look down at her. The sheet slid lower, baring her upper half to his greedy gaze. Fire pooled deep, spreading its hot fingers wide until her entire body felt as if it were burning.

"Christian, wait," she murmured. "I feel so hot."

"Yes," he said, a fingertip stroking down the valley between her breasts and stopping at her navel. Her stomach muscles clenched at the featherlight touch, sweeping back and forth beneath it in a teasing motion. "I know. I want you to burn for me."

His fingers slid lower, brushing against the heart of her, and something ignited. She grasped his shoulders, her back arching as the flames took hold. "No," she gasped. "Wait. Something's wrong."

He reached up to hold her face between his palms, his eyes mesmerizing. "Nothing's wrong," he whispered. "We're in paradise. Can't you see that?"

"Yes," she agreed, but something didn't feel right. Her gaze shifted to him. He looked like Christian, but he didn't *smell* right. Something felt off. The breeze was too perfect, the scent of the ocean too briny. Her blood burned hot in her veins, scorching the inside of her skin as if forcing her to feel the pain and leave the fantasy. Instead, she shied away from it.

"It's too hot," she muttered. Christian smiled, his teeth perfect and white. Her eyes narrowed at the conspicuous lack of fangs. His fingers were cool against her cheek.

"I only want to please you." His lips descended to hers, taking them in a sweet, demanding kiss that left her breathless. Her blood surged in response, licking against the inside of her like an inferno. She was burning up from the inside out. She tore at the sheets, ripping them off of her, scraping at her skin so that red claw marks appeared.

"What's the matter?" he asked. "Is it something I've done? I want to please you."

Something in his repeated words dug at her. Her blood blistered her skin, forcing the fog in her mind to clear briefly. Focusing on it, Victoria embraced the pain of her blood, letting it fill her until she felt nothing but clarity. She sank her nails into her palm, the release of the blood almost her undoing.

"I love you," Christian said, pulling her close.

"No!" she shouted, shoving him off of her.

"What's the matter?" he asked, reaching for her.

She drew the sheet up to cover herself and shook her head. Blackly red blood streaked the silk sheets as the blood magic surged to the fore. "You're not real. None of this is."

Within moments, the tranquil ocean scene disappeared and there was nothing but darkness. Victoria could feel her body, but she couldn't see anything. There was no idyllic ocean hut, no beach, and no half-nude Christian professing his undying love. Reality was swift to return. As much as she had been seduced by the fantasy, she and Christian had broken up. She hadn't seen him. Once she recognized that truth, the world that her mind had created started to collapse. She'd been charmed somehow.

Her head felt as if it'd been hit with a sledgehammer.

Pan.

What the holy hell had he done to her?

She pressed her hands upward and encountered nothing but dirt and a prison made of tree roots. She was buried. Underground. She called upon her magic, but couldn't focus. Her head felt fuzzy as if something was inhibiting her ability to think. She blinked and bit her lip. Hard. Blood flowed into her mouth along with swift lucidity and filtered memories. Pan had blown something into her face, making her a prisoner and compromising her magic with some kind of herbal hallucinogen—one that had created the fantasy she'd just imagined.

It'd been so real. She could still feel the slant of Christian's lips and the hard, male press of his body moving atop hers. She flushed in the darkness. Whatever Pan had given her had made her fevered imaginings seem genuine, when it was obvious they'd been nothing but dreams. Her entire body tingled with the visceral memory of it.

She shook herself roughly. She didn't have much time or oxygen, and as far as she knew, powerful witch or not, she needed to breathe to survive. She pressed upward again, feeling the dirt crumble between her fingers. Pan had been clever—she'd fallen for his naïve act hook, line, and sinker, even though he had known who she was the whole time. He had always known. His words chilled her to the bone.

I know exactly who you are, little bird.

And then he'd blown the yellow dust into her face, and she'd felt the teleportation spell take effect. She'd fallen prey to the pollen immediately, unable to defend herself, and now she was here, trapped in a dark prison of roots and dirt.

Victoria kicked against the walls of the space, blinking as a shower of soil rained into her eyes. She pushed outward—she had absolutely no sense of where she was, whether she was upside down, buried a hundred feet in the earth, or anything. Panic started to set in, sweeping along her limbs in icy-cold bursts.

Focus, she told herself. *You've been buried in an avalanche before. This is nothing.*

But the remnants of the pollen hallucinogen made it difficult to concentrate or pull her thoughts cohesively together. It'd been a brilliant plan by Pan—poison her nervous system so that she was unable to command her magic. She took a deep breath and tried to tap into the blood's magic. It gathered at her core and then dissipated in the same instant. She couldn't concentrate worth a damn.

She had underestimated Pan, thinking him guileless and innocent. But he'd been biding his time until he could make his move. Victoria wondered what that was. He couldn't expect to use the Cruentus Curse himself, and unless he was attempting to use her as a bargaining chip to the witches or the warlocks, or even the vampires, she couldn't imagine what was driving him.

Her breaths were becoming shallower with the increasing lack of oxygen, and she tried again to summon her blood magic, deciding to give in to its powers and assume the risk. She dug her nails into her palms, tearing at the skin there, but nothing happened. Her blood soaked into the earth beneath her. Whatever Pan had poisoned her with had been potent and effective. *Plants.* She should have known.

Victoria pushed her awareness outward. *Leto? Are you there?*

She wasn't surprised at the lack of response. Leto had been more absent than present the last few weeks, caught up in his own doings. Lately, he was preoccupied and surly, so much so that Victoria had taken to keeping him at a distance. Now, caught in this trap, she wished she had done otherwise, especially after banishing him at Holly's house. Leto did not respond. She tried Angie next, but that failed, too. Angie was no doubt somewhere in Paris, wondering why her friend had decided to desert her.

Half-defeated, she sank back against the crumbling walls of her prison. She'd be better off being lost in her fantasy with Christian. The thought of him made something flutter in the pit of her stomach, and she wondered whether he'd still be able to hear her. She reached out into the void.

Christian? Can you hear me? She tried again, but there was nothing.

Victoria closed her eyes and the image of the ocean reformed in her brain. The urge to return to the safety of it was a powerful one and she almost gave in. She reached out for

Christian one more time, hoping beyond hope that he'd hear her.

Tori? The sound of his voice coming back to her made tears spring to her eyes.

Can you hear me? she choked.

You're so far away.

I'm trapped somewhere. Pan buried me underground and fed me some plant pathogen. I can't use my magic to free myself.

Okay. Don't let go, he said. *Hold on to me. I'm coming to you. Tori, hold on and don't let go.*

I will.

Victoria tried to take short shallow breaths to conserve the remaining oxygen in the space, but she could feel her strength failing. She had to stay conscious so that Christian could find her. A part of her wondered whether she had spoken to the real Christian at all or whether it, too, had been in her head. She blinked, confusion numbing her. She couldn't tell the difference between fantasy and reality anymore. Was any of this real? Was *she* real?

Suddenly, the earth around her started to collapse as the roots pushed in to cradle her body, grabbing her like a giant hand and scooping her body upward. A burst of fresh sweet air crashed into her face as she broke free from the soil. She could see that she was still entrapped in a cocoon of roots. Images rushed toward her—a thick grove of trees, a dirt path strewn with rocks. They were in some kind of wood. She recognized a sequoia tree. A forest? In Paris? It could be the Bois de Boulogne. But for all she knew, they could be back in Maine. Witches could teleport anywhere.

Her eyes adjusted to the daylight and Pan's face swam into view.

"Hello, lovely," he said, his voice unnaturally loud. He snapped two fingers in front of her. "Wake up, princess. Looks like I got you in the nick of time."

"You nearly killed me," she gasped, letting the sweet air fill her lungs. She was alive and this was real. Pan had put her here.

"Come now, don't be melodramatic. You're alive, aren't you?"

"What did you do to me?"

He peered at her. "You didn't enjoy it? It's my own special recipe, meant to take your wildest dreams and make them come true." He eyed her. "Knowing everything I know about you, I expect your wildest imaginings to be about your gorgeous forbidden vampire lover."

"You said you liked him," she accused, trying desperately to focus, but her mind refused to cooperate.

"I did like him," Pan said in a conversational voice. "I didn't like that he had you wrapped around his little finger. Or that you were too stupid to see that you were."

"Stupid?" she repeated dully.

Pan rolled his eyes, taking something from a pouch at his waist. "All this power and you sit around, waiting for some vampire to come rescue you. Girls are so blind. They all want the romance when it's the biggest joke. You think he cares about you? How can he? You're a witch, he's a vampire. You're from two different worlds. He's using you, Tori."

"And you aren't?"

"It's not the same thing. He's a *vampire.*"

"I'd trust him at my side more than I would you." She shook her head, fighting to think clearly. "I would have thought that you of all people would understand about differences. Who cares if he's a vampire? He loves me." *Loved me*, she added silently.

"It is forbidden according to all our laws, laws that you flaunt so carelessly. You are nothing but an undeserving foolish girl." Pan stared at her, his eyes narrowing. "And if your vampire prince loves you so much, then where's your white knight now?" he taunted. "Isn't he going to come save you? Rescue you?"

"I can rescue myself," Victoria said.

"If you say so."

Victoria felt her blood boiling beneath her skin as sanity came back in miniscule doses. She focused as hard as she could on the boy hovering over her cage of roots. The magic pooled within her, struggling past the remnants of the hallucinogen he'd given her. Whatever it was, it was powerful. She couldn't remember ever feeling so scattered, as if she could barely hold a coherent thought. She guessed that was the point of Pan's toxin —magic needed focus and concentration, even blood magic. She needed to distract him, get him talking so that she could let more of it wear off.

"When did you know?" she asked. "About me?"

"After that episode in the glade," he said with a smile. "That counter spell was genius. Even the trees were impressed. They told me who you were then."

"So you decided to poison me?"

"On the contrary," Pan said, one white eyebrow arching high. "I wanted to inhibit those magnificent powers of yours." His eyes narrowed. "I'm still working on a synthesis that gets the components just right—psychotomimetics and psychotaraxics and things like that—without killing you, I mean." He grinned as if pleased with himself. "It's a delicate balance, plant study."

Victoria blinked. Her knowledge of botany was sparse, but she did know that many of the worst poisons and hallucinogens had their origins in plants. She should have guessed. "Why? Didn't your precious trees tell you that you can't control the Cruentus Curse? Others have tried and died for their efforts."

"Of course they did," he smirked. "But that doesn't mean I can't control *you*."

"I'll never do what you want."

"Not of your own free will, sure. But there are ways to

induce that." He nodded to the pouch at his waist. "Case in point. With this little mixture, you are completely powerless, unable to conjure the simplest of spells. With the one I'm developing, you will do exactly as I tell you to."

She stared at him, a tendril of fear coiling in the pit of her stomach. "I don't get it. Why would you do this?"

Pan's eyes took on a fevered glaze as something rolled across his features. "You don't know what it's like, do you? To be constantly overlooked? When nothing you do is good enough? When people choose not to see you? I've always felt invisible, and with you, I won't be."

Despite Pan's betrayal, Victoria felt a stirring of pity. She knew exactly what it was like to feel like nothing. "I was like that my whole life. I get it, Pan."

"You're not now."

"Because I chose to change. You can, too."

"I am changing," he said. "I have the Cruentus Curse in my grasp and soon people will really *see* me."

Victoria shook her head, grasping the gnarly bars of her cage. "The curse will defend itself, Pan. There comes a point where I can't control it and nothing is safe. It will destroy you. It will destroy everything in its path without consequence."

"Not if I keep you in a state of mental paralysis," he said. "Your blood magic depends on the state of your consciousness. It has to flow through you, and if you, its instrument, is incapacitated, then it will be too. Don't you see? It's perfect."

Pan was pacing back and forth, his face contorted with all his scheming. She couldn't believe she hadn't seen it before, but in hindsight, she recalled all the circumspect sidelong glances. He'd hidden his true colors beneath a front of friendship that she'd eaten up. Even her blood had been fooled by his guilelessness.

It surged within her and Victoria felt the power at her core growing stronger, although her awareness felt disjointed. She had a choice—she could keep Pan talking until she had enough strength for one good spell, or she could give in to the blood's magic and hope for the best. The latter was a risk, as there was a good chance it would kill Pan without conscience, and despite his betrayal, she didn't want his death on her hands.

"What do you hope to get out of this? Validation? Recognition? Those things don't matter. This is a curse, Pan," she added desperately. "A warlock tried to take it last year and he's dead now."

"I am not some foolish warlock," he screamed, his voice turning deep and guttural. Victoria frowned at the sudden change, recognition crowding her brain. He'd changed before when they'd fought at Belles Fontaines and she had thought she imagined it. Once more, his features shifted, growing sharper and more defined ... more *elfin*. "You will be completely under my control, just as you are now. I want everyone to know my name—witches, warlocks, vampires, humans. I want them to bend, to cower, to grovel before me."

"You're insane," she whispered, a prickling of fear spreading along her spine. Pan's slow chuckle made the fear turn to ice. He didn't seem like the same person.

"It's not insanity."

Her eyes narrowed as a thought occurred to her—he *wasn't* the same person. "Who are you?" she asked.

He fluttered his eyelashes at her, a hand flying to his breast in mock astonishment. "Whatever do you mean?"

"You're not Pan. You're someone else." She studied him. The change in his face had been deliberate—he'd meant to show her. He wasn't possessed by something—she would have sensed a second being. It was as if he were two people in the same body, a two-faced split personality. "You're a Janusite."

"Such a clever girl," he crowed, clapping his hands. "I knew you would figure it out eventually. I didn't think it would be this soon, but I guess this is a lesson for me not to underestimate you."

Victoria's eyes widened. She'd never met one of them before, only heard the urban legends. It was mostly a human condition, but had been known to affect witches from time to time, and Pan had told her that he had human blood in him. Janusites were torn between good and evil. The little she knew of them told her that they could not be reasoned with or appealed to, and when one side took over, the other retreated. Right now, she knew she was dealing with the beast instead of the boy.

"How did you hide yourself from Madame Starke and the rest of the teachers at Belles Fontaines?" They never would have admitted him had they known.

"What makes you think I hid anything? And even if I did, people believe what they choose to believe. I told you, when you are invisible, you can accomplish many things."

"You're not invisible, Pan."

He laughed, his mirth making him double over. "Oh, come now. Tell me you didn't see me coming? You saw what you wanted to believe just like everyone else does. Don't pretend for a second otherwise."

"You were my friend."

He eyed her coldly. "Is that why you trusted me? Told me the truth about who you are? Confided in me? Oh, wait, you didn't. Because we were never friends."

Victoria felt him getting agitated and she knew that she didn't have much time. It was now or never—the magic felt strong enough. "Excindo!" she shouted, pushing every bit of force she had into the spell.

Pan went flying backward and crashed into a nearby tree as the cell of roots exploded outward. Victoria fell to her knees, gasping for breath. The spell left her weak and disoriented as the magic fought the stringy constraints of Pan's toxin. Black spots flared in her eyes and she was momentarily blinded. In her hazy vision, she saw Pan struggling to his knees. The spell should have left him battered, but it hadn't been at full potency. She dug her fingers into the dirt and forced herself to stand as he crawled toward her, fumbling at the pouch at his waist.

Focus, she hissed at herself. If he threw any of that powder her way, she would be at his mercy. She would lose any advantage she had.

Her blood blistered her skin, desperate for release. Victoria bit her lip, freeing the raw power coursing through her. It felt sluggish, but she managed to stand on shaky legs. "Walk away, Pan," she warned. "I don't want to hurt you."

"You can try."

He teleported and Victoria did the same. The magic was draining her more than she expected. With a strangled breath, she tried to tap into the resources of the amulet that usually rested at her breast. Pan's mocking laugh echoed through the trees.

"Looking for this?" He appeared at the end of the small glade, her locket in hand. "Oh, trust me, I know about witches and their trinkets. I figured it was valuable."

"You will regret this."

"I don't think so."

A vine darted out from a nearby branch to loop around her wrist. A root snaked out from beneath her feet, making her lose her balance and her breath. The spell that had been on the tip of her tongue disappeared as her head hit the unforgiving ground and the breath whooshed out of her. Stars spun in her vision.

"Confuto," she gasped, trying to stop Pan mid-motion. But either she wasn't thinking clearly or the fall had knocked her semi-unconscious because Pan kept coming toward her.

"Nice try, but that reminds me," Pan said in gleeful triumph, looking down at her as he straddled her fallen body. "Time for another dose." He hauled a breath into his lungs and blew into his cupped hands toward her. A sprinkling of gold powder shimmered into her face. She tried not to breathe, but it was no use. The dust melted into her skin and seeped into her nasal passages. Within seconds, she felt as if her entire body was floating on a stream of sunshine.

"You're my best friend, Pan," she told him giddily.

"I know. Time to go back to sleep. We have work to do."

She fell back onto the soft pillows of the bed, her eyes rolling in her head. She felt so calm, so at peace. Something tugged at her consciousness—a hot, insistent sensation along the edges that wouldn't calm, reminding her that her feeling of bliss wasn't real. But the truth was, she didn't want to know. She was safe. She was happy.

She *was* home.

DEMON ROGUE

Lucian held his brother by the scruff of his neck and dropped him to the floor in front of his audience. "Delivered as promised," he said to Freyja. The warlock stared at the vampire's twitching body in surprise.

"How did you capture him?"

Lucian laughed. "You see, my brother likes to believe in my repentance and redemptive qualities. I have yet to convince him that I am a lost cause."

"You would give up your own flesh and blood?" Roan asked, his golden eyes flaring.

"My only loyalty is to myself."

Roan opened his mouth to continue, but Freyja silenced him with a glare. "Enough. You have fulfilled your part of the bargain. Why have you brought the one waiting outside?"

Lucian knew she was referring to Lena. "She's with me."

"Would you sacrifice her, too?" Roan drawled, ignoring his leader's warning.

"If I had to, yes."

"Does she know that?"

Lucian met the warlock's stare. "Of course."

"Secure the prisoner," Freyja said, addressing her followers in the underground hall. "Make sure his body is bound by silver at all times. It is the only thing that will keep him restrained. It is time to bring this witch to us." She eyed Lucian. "Lord Devereux and his companion are our allies. An attack on either of them will be considered an attack against me. Now, make the preparations to put the strategy in place and take up your positions. Do what you swore upon your oath as a warlock to do."

Lucian frowned as almost half of the company melted from the massive hall. He'd never heard of any oath, but then again, he wasn't too familiar with the inner workings of warlock culture. He knew that Freyja and the warlocks were organized, but they seemed focused, as if this was a coup they'd been planning for decades. He expected it was—they'd always existed in the shadows of the witches and the vampires. He, himself, never understood why the witches mistrusted them so much. They, too, were magic users, although they veered toward the full spectrum of magic, including the practice of dark magic. Unlike witches, they used their power to summon demons and other shadow creatures that were bound to the dead. But other than that, Lucian did not know much about them.

Freyja dismissed the rest of the warlocks, a silent communication passing between her and Roan before he hauled Christian out of sight to another room. Lucian approached her. "I am curious about something. Why haven't you aligned with the witches? It seems natural that you would, given you have a common enemy."

Her smile was thin. "We align with no one."

"You aligned with me."

"A necessary evil."

Lucian frowned at her cryptic choice of words. "With your combined powers, you could have taken the vampires out centuries ago. Why now? What do you hope to accomplish with

Le Sang Noir? It cannot be controlled by anyone but its wielder and, trust me, I've tried to coerce the witch before."

She eyed him as if considering how much to reveal of what she had planned. Freyja cleared her throat, a host of emotions playing across her face. "We are not attempting to coerce her. The curse must be destroyed."

"You're planning to *destroy* all the witch's power?"

She nodded. "Power that great is corrosive. It is an abnormality that will twist even the purest of hearts, and it cannot be suffered to exist with the threat it poses to all existence."

Lucian's brows snapped together in disbelief. "You would throw it all away?"

"We are not throwing it away, Lord Devereux," she said in a cold voice. "We are sending it back to where it belongs, where it cannot be of harm."

"And where exactly is that?"

"The demon dimension," she said. "It is where most dark magic is born."

"And you'd know about that, wouldn't you?" he said sourly. Lucian felt all his carefully orchestrated plans start to crumble. The warlocks had never intended to use the witch. They wanted to make sure that no one could abuse her power. His eyes narrowed at the woman standing in front of him—something didn't add up. It didn't make sense that they would go through all this trouble. It went against everything he'd ever known about warlocks. "You mentioned an oath before. What were you talking about?"

"Lord Devereux, I think it is time for you to leave."

But as he turned to depart, an explosion rocked the walls of the chamber, sending a shower of rocks and stones descending upon them. Roan rushed in with two other guards at his side as another shockwave hit the building. Freyja took off at a run, climbing the stairs to the upper part of the abandoned church. Lucian followed on swift feet, his eyes finding Lena, who was crouched behind a marble pillar. He made his way over to her, dodging falling debris.

"We're under attack!" someone shouted before a blast of angry red light tore through him.

"From who?" Roan shouted back. "Vampires?"

"That was magic, you idiot," Lucian snarled as he leapt to the destroyed façade of the church. The pale light of the moon filtered down to the lone figure waiting in the courtyard. "Vampires don't command bursts of light at our fingertips."

Freyja joined him. Lucian could feel her entire body tense as she stared at their assailant. "It's a demon."

Roan paled. "That is impossible. Who summoned it? Is it linked to any of us?"

"Not that I can tell."

"A rogue?"

She shook her head, closing her eyes to take measure of the demon. "It's too powerful to be a rogue. That is something else. I don't see a portal to the demon dimension, which makes no sense."

"What does that mean?" Lucian asked.

"It means that this demon lives here."

"Impossible. Demons can't exist on this plane without being summoned by someone like you."

Freyja stared at him and he was surprised to see a hint of fear on her face. "Stronger ones can. The question is why."

"So what drew it here?" Roan asked as another burst of fiery orange light consumed two warlocks in its path. His furious, accusing gaze fell on Lucian.

"Don't look at me," he snarled. "I'm not in the business of consorting with demons."

"It must have followed you here," Roan tossed back.

Lucian glowered at him. "I seem to recall you conjuring a demon not a week ago, so if it followed anyone, I'd say it would be you."

"Enough," Freyja growled.

The beast shifted into view then. It was roughly the size of a lion with glowing red eyes. An acid green and sickly yellow haze surrounded it on all sides. It seemed to be tied to some kind of host—a smaller creature that wasn't human, but Lucian couldn't quite determine what it was. The reek of sulfur filled the air as it drew its bulk closer to the bodies strewn across the courtyard.

"What's it doing?" Lena said, her eyes centered on the demon.

The beast heaved its weight on top of a fallen warlock and Lucian shuddered. "It's feeding on them."

Sure enough, when the creature moved on to another body, the only thing that remained in its wake was a lifeless hollow husk. At Freyja's signal, the warlocks consolidated their attack, but their spells barely deterred the demon. It seemed impervious to their assault, only focused on consuming as many souls as it could. Lucian couldn't help noticing that each life that the demon absorbed seemed to make it bigger and stronger.

"Nothing's working," Roan shouted as he flung a fire spell toward it. "It's not even attacking. It's feeding. What does it want?"

"One way to find out." Freyja's eyes glowed white as she muttered a spell, pushing a trail of glowing iridescence toward the creature. The tendril curled around the monster. The demon froze and locked eyes with Freyja as their conscious energies joined. Bolts of energy exploded around them as the warlocks pressed their attack, but it was as if a bubble encased the two of them. Time stood still as they faced each other. Freyja was strong, but it was obvious to Lucian that she was no match for the demon. Her hands shook as she tried to retain control of herself. But the demon wouldn't let her go. A whimper escaped her lips as she dropped to her knees, her cheeks sunken and gaunt.

"Freyja!" Roan shouted, falling to her side. But there was nothing he could do while the demon had hold of her. "It's killing her."

Lena shouted and shot forward, distracting it for a moment before it slammed her back into the far wall of the church. She vaulted to her feet and attacked it again, dodging its counter attacks with immortal speed. Lucian hefted a fallen piece of concrete and threw it at the demon. It didn't do much damage, but it was enough to release whatever demonic grip it had on Freyja. She collapsed into Roan's arms, breathing heavily.

Without warning, the demon faded and disappeared.

"Is she alive?" Lucian asked as Lena reappeared at his side, bloody but no worse for wear. Roan nodded his silent thanks.

"What the hell was that?" Lena asked.

Freyja sighed and rocked back onto her heels. Her face seemed haggard and drawn as if she'd been sapped of life. Lucian guessed that the interaction with the demon had drained her more than she expected. Her voice was weak. "That, Lord Devereux, was a very old demon. Ancient, if my assumption is right."

"What's it doing here then? Did you find out anything when you linked to it? Did someone summon it and send it after you?"

She frowned. "No. It seemed confused or lost, as if it didn't know what it was. It was powerful and getting stronger by the minute."

"So you are saying that it is from here?"

"Seems that way."

He stared at the bodies littering the courtyard and frowned. They looked eerily familiar. Something occurred to him. "Have any of your people been attacked in the last few months?" he asked. "Found drained of blood?"

"Yes." Freyja stared at him, understanding dawning in her eyes as they flicked to the nearest shell. "But we blamed the vampires. My people have always been at odds with yours."

Lena cleared her throat and nodded. "The Witch Clans found the same. They thought it was us, too."

"The Council also found vampire bodies turned to ash," Lucian mused. "But that is what will happen when we are drained of life, unlike your people. The vampires blamed the Clans."

Foamy blood flecked Freyja's lips. "You need to warn your people," she coughed. "That demon will only grow in power the more immortal souls it consumes."

Lucian and Lena exchanged a glance. "What about my brother and the witch?"

"That will have to wait. If this thing gets any stronger, we will have a lot more on our hands to worry about."

†††

CHRISTIAN FELT the sluggish movement of the liquid silver creeping through his veins like thick molasses. His eyes focused on the room he was held in. It was a small, stone cellar and his wrists were shackled to the wall. Clear tubing ran from a tank on one side and fed into a tube attached to his forearm. He could see the silvery fluid draining into him and dissolving all of his strength with it. It hurt to think, but when he did, he only had one thought.

Victoria.

She was in danger. He wasn't sure he had understood all her words—they had been incoherent—he only knew that she had cried out for help. *His* help. And he couldn't move. He took a deep breath, feeling the heavy casing of the silver. It made his limbs feel heavy and numb. The good thing was that he was awake—this much silver would knock another vampire completely unconscious.

He vaguely recalled two guards being in the room with him, but there'd been some commotion and they had run out. He'd felt the explosion and no one else had come back in. Christian pulled at the shackles, hearing them clang dully against the wall. There was no give in the rings, but he pulled harder, gritting his teeth until the metal tore into his flesh. It wouldn't budge. He sawed his hands back and forth, grimacing as bits of the silver burned into his wrists, but the pain only made his goal clearer.

After a few minutes, his skin had been pulled raw and then healed several times over, but the chains held fast. They'd obviously been designed to contain something far stronger than him. Frustrated, he growled out loud and yanked with brute force a few times for good measure. Christian focused himself and centered on the feeling of silver in his body. He concentrated on clearing his body of the metal, pushing it back toward the duct that fed into his arm. To his surprise, he saw the silver pooling like wet toothpaste around the outside of the tube. It was working. And he was getting stronger.

Once his head was clear, Christian drew a deep breath into his lungs and pulled at his restraints until it felt like his arms would rip out of their sockets. But he felt the stonework holding the chains in place give way. The slumbering influence of his Reii maker rippled through him, giving him the strength of a hundred vampires. With a roar, he tore loose of his bonds and fell to the ground, grunting. Rocking onto his heels, he glanced at the shattered iron shackles and the now healed wound in his forearm. Remnants of dried silver coated his skin and he felt nothing. Christian flexed, feeling new power coursing through him. He was stronger than he'd ever been, that he was sure of.

There was one guard at the door. Ripping the metal graft out of his arm, he felt his fangs elongate as hunger overtook him.

The warlock didn't stand a chance as Christian bit into his neck, savoring the taste of the magic-infused blood. It wasn't near enough. By the time he reached the outer hall where Lucian had brought him, he'd left a trail of unconscious bodies in his wake. It took him a few minutes to make sense of the destruction at street level. But he was only looking for one person—the bastard who had brought him here.

His brother.

He didn't have to see him to feel him, and he was a blur as he tackled his twin to the ground. He swatted Lena away as she leapt toward him, his new strength formidable, not caring that she folded up into a motionless heap. She was a vampire—she would heal. Eventually.

He slammed Lucian up against the wall, his forearm braced across his brother's neck, two hundred pounds of pure rage barreling into Lucian and holding him prisoner. He could see his brother's shock at his escape and the silver flecks resting on his arm.

"Aren't you full of surprises," Lucian drawled in a casual tone as if they were engaged in civil conversation. "When did you become immune to silver?"

Christian's rage flared. "Tell me why I shouldn't kill you right now."

"Go ahead," Lucian taunted. "I can see it in your eyes how badly you want the pleasure of ripping me apart, but you won't do it. You can't do it. You can never do it."

"Trust me," Christian snarled, pressing his arm in harder. He swore he heard something pop as Lucian's face turned ashen. "Nothing would satisfy me more than breaking your traitorous neck. Why would you bring me here?"

"They want Victoria."

Christian pulled back a smidge, his eyes narrowing. "Do they have her?"

"No."

"Where is she?" he hissed, pressing harder. "If a hair on her head is harmed, I will dismember you myself."

"I don't know where she is," Lucian choked. "I swear."

"You swear?" Christian laughed. "As if I would believe a word that comes out of your deceiving mouth. Have you no sense of loyalty? *Brotherhood?* No," he growled. "You are so consumed by jealousy that you would betray your own blood to save your skin. Everything I have ever done has been for you and you spit in my face. I will ask you one last time. Where. Is. She?" He spat the last three words as if they were bullets.

"I don't know." Lucian's eyes dilated with alarm. "We were attacked before Freyja could do anything."

"You are lying."

"He's telling the truth, Your Grace." Those words came from the gaunt warlock lying in the rubble, propped up against the side of the building. Christian's eyes flicked to her and widened in delayed recognition. He'd seen Freyja in the school courtyard and this pale woman who had spoken looked like a ghostly imitation of her. Shadows haunted her emaciated face.

He inclined his head in silent greeting and lifted one eyebrow as her condition and the state of the building swam into view. The place was ripped apart. That would explain the explosion he'd felt in the cell. His eyes narrowed as he assessed the damage, noting the remnants of magical spells on the walls and on the floor. Bodies—ones he hadn't drained—littered the empty hall and the open courtyard. "What happened here?"

"Demon."

"One you summoned?"

She stood weakly, another warlock—Roan, he recognized—rushing to her side. "No."

Christian frowned, his mind running through the options. If the demon hadn't been summoned by one of her coven, it could mean several things. One, there was a rogue warlock on the loose, which wasn't that improbable. Warlocks were a capricious breed, some preferring a life of solitude to life in a coven. Gabriel, Victoria's school friend from last year had not been affiliated with anyone, and he had coveted the power that Le Sang Noir promised. Two, the demon was lost and had somehow slipped through the fabric of the dimensions to the mortal world. Or three, it *wanted* to be here. And that was the worst option of all—because those demons fed until there was nothing left. Drawn to immortal power, they were parasites, a plague on humans and non-humans alike.

"What kind of demon was it?"

She swallowed, her next words confirming his worst theory. "One I've never seen before. Untethered and strong. Old. Powerful. I think it was … a demon lord."

Christian frowned. It was far worse than he'd anticipated. Demon lords rarely strayed from their dimensions and, as far as he knew, never came to the mortal plane. They could not be summoned or coerced and were known to be ruthless. What was one doing here? And why now?

"Where is it?"

"It attacked and disappeared," she explained. "I tried to connect to it to see if someone had summoned it and sent it here, but it overpowered me." Her gaze shifted to the vampire still caught in his grasp. "Lucian thought that the recent killings of vampires and witches looked to be the same as the victims of the demon."

Christian had forgotten his brother hanging limply against the wall. Now their eyes met. Loathing ripped through him. He'd always been able to forgive Lucian for all of his transgressions and his many betrayals, but this time … he could barely stand to look at him. He released his hold and stepped back. "It is over for good this time."

"Just the way I like it," Lucian snarled, his eyes full of hate.

Christian turned his attention to Freyja, the demon's presence overlooked for the moment. "Why do you want her? Victoria?"

"Your witch?"

A muscle leapt in his cheek. She wasn't his. Not anymore. "Yes."

"Her powers are too dangerous, too volatile. She must be ... contained."

"You were going to use me to get to her," he surmised, correctly interpreting her expression.

"Yes."

She didn't have to explain why. Christian knew exactly what that look in her eyes meant—the warlock was planning to kill her. It surprised him. Most people coveted Victoria's power, but it seemed as if Freyja wanted to restrict it by any means she thought necessary, including Victoria's death. Christian thought back to what he knew of the warlocks—everyone believed them to be evil, particularly because of their summoning strengths. In the old days, they used to be called oath-breakers.

"Why?" he asked anyway.

"It is my sworn duty. Her blood is tainted."

Did she think that she was defending the world from Victoria's power?

Christian frowned, blinking as new information passed down from his maker's memories and rose to the forefront of his mind, particularly an ancient Norse myth of the Vardlokkur. These original warlocks were known as the guardians of wisdom and magic, binding and warding evil spirits and demons to keep the magic of this world safe.

Christian met Freyja's eyes and nodded with a short bow. "I understand what you are." He shook his head. "But she wouldn't have come. Her loyalty does not lie with me." Christian did not miss the disbelieving look his brother sent his way before he scurried off to check on Lena, nor did he miss the agonized one she tossed in his direction. She was dead to him too. He eyed

Freyja. "You should know that I will defend her with my life, no matter your oaths, Vardlokkur."

"Our fight is not with you, Your Grace."

He sighed, raking a hand through his hair. Despite Victoria's recent actions, he could never leave her to defend herself alone. She would forever be in his blood. "If it is with her, then it is also with me."

Christian turned on his heel and walked out into the night. The rogue demon would have to wait. Locating Victoria was his only priority and there was only one person he trusted to help find her.

THOSE WHO COVET

Christian and Angie waited in the half-opened foyer as one of the witches went to fetch Aliya, after a long, terrified glance at him and a circumspect one at her. Four male witches entered the room on silent feet, but did not approach them, instead settling at each one of the corners. Christian acknowledged them, but remained relaxed. After all, a vampire and a magicless witch had invaded their sanctuary. He eyed Angie, grateful that she had accompanied him without question. He knew that she had come to Paris to offer support to her friend and he was humbled that she still considered him one.

"Tori loves you," she'd said.

"I wish I could believe that."

"You have to. She needs you more than anything, but she's confused and being pulled a thousand different ways. She'll come around, don't worry."

"I hope you're right."

She'd shot him a plucky smile. "I am."

They had searched everywhere, called Holly even, but there was no sign of Victoria. It was as if she'd vanished off the face of the earth. He knew that wasn't the case—she had to be some-where. If anything, it meant that her powers had somehow been inhibited. An icy sensation had crawled along his spine. That insidious feeling that something had happened to her had made him go to the one place where he wasn't welcome—the high priestess temple that lay hidden in the center of the Bois de Boulogne.

While they waited, Christian's eyes wandered the room. A trickling waterfall graced one end of the space and vines wound across the top, tying into the nearby trees. The temple was designed in relaxing hues of yellows and greens, with the excep-tion of one wall on the far end, which seemed to shift with the room's occupants. Right now, it exhibited a complex landscape of angry reds with swatches of intertwined grays and blacks. It was an accurate representation of his current emotional state. When Angie had entered, it'd been lavender and orange. He knew the minute Aliya walked in because the far wall shifted into hues of soft whites and blues.

Aliya stared at them, shock etched in her features. Her gaze darted to Angie and her frown deepened. "Your Grace, to what do we owe this visit?"

"My apologies," Christian said with a short bow. Angie nodded imperceptibly to him, and he knew that she had just scanned Aliya's aura. He hadn't expected Aliya to be their enemy, but he had to be sure. "I went to your home and was told that you were here."

"I understand," she said, but Christian knew she didn't. Vampires didn't make it a practice of intruding on the temples of the Witch Clans. One, they were warded from discovery, and two, it simply was not allowed. Christian didn't have time for propriety, however, or explaining to Aliya how he'd managed to find their most sacred of spaces. Time was of the essence. "Why are you here?" she asked.

"May we speak in private?" he asked in a lowered voice. "I am here to discuss a matter of sensitive nature."

"Of course." She dismissed the four witches with a nod and they slipped from the hall. Christian noticed that the far wall had darkened considerably with more midnight blue hues taking precedence. She followed the direction of his eyes and frowned. Instantly, the wall shifted into a pale neutral shade. "It's a moodscape," she explained. "It shows the mental state of anyone here. We are alone, Your Grace. You may speak freely. But first, who is your friend?"

He nodded to the girl at his side. "This is one of Victoria's friends. Angie. She is an Aurus."

"Ah," Aliya nodded as if answering an unspoken question. "That is how you were able to find the temple."

Christian nodded shortly and wasted no more time. "Victoria. Is she here?"

"You haven't found her?"

"No. I am sorry I did not contact you as I said I would. I had ... a minor disagreement with my brother, the details of which I won't bore you with. But prior to that, I received a garbled message from Victoria a few hours ago, asking for my help. It was disjointed and didn't seem like her." He stared at Aliya, wondering how much the witch knew and how much a part she had played in Victoria's decisions. "Given that we are no longer together, I didn't expect to hear from her of all people, and by the time I tried to respond, I couldn't reach her." He cleared his throat. "You have been a longtime liaison to the Council, and I know that relations between us have been strained lately, but I need your help."

"Does this have anything to do with the attack at Belles Fontaines?"

Christian's mind was racing. It was something he hadn't considered. His brother and the warlocks had attacked the school together. Had they meant to take Victoria then? And somehow failed? He had believed Freyja when she'd said she didn't have her.

"I don't know," he answered. "Can you and the other priestesses try a location spell?"

Aliya shook her head. "We can try, but it won't work. We have tried it many times when we heard that the prophecy had come to pass. Her blood has a unique cloaking mechanism that renders it invisible to any other magic."

Christian tried not to let his disappointment show. She couldn't have just vanished. If the warlocks didn't have her and the Clans didn't, then that only left the vampires. Was there some power-seeking vampire other than his brother that he hadn't considered?

"Is there anyone at the school who would want to harm her?" Angie asked, interrupting his train of thought. "I would know if they meant her ill."

Aliya shook her head. "No. That is absurd."

"I'm afraid we have to consider all options," Christian said. "It is a valid question. Too many people know of the existence of the curse and one taste of such power can corrupt the most virtuous of hearts. One of her teachers? One of her friends, perhaps? What about Madame Starke or that boy who was with her at your house?"

"Starke is one of our strongest leaders," Aliya said grimly. "She was opposed to Victoria's matriculation to Belles Fontaines because she was worried about the safety of the other students. But despite her personal feelings on the matter, she'd never hurt another witch. She was my protégée. She should have been a high priestess, but was chosen to run the school instead after her training."

Christian recalled Starke's position when the warlocks had shown up and nodded. She'd appeared to defend the school to the last. "And the boy?"

"Panthèse?"

"Would he wish to coerce her?"

"*Coerce* her? He is her friend and her mentor," Aliya said. "And Pan is one of the most gentle people I know. He'd never hurt her."

Angie exchanged a glance with him, pain shadowing her eyes for a second as the memories of the past year resurfaced. "Sometimes the ones we trust the most are the ones we should fear the most. My brother was the warlock who hurt Tori last year. I trust no one. And until I can see their true nature for myself, you shouldn't either. If this Pan is her friend, he'll know where she is or at least be able to help us."

Aliya closed her eyes for a second, concentrating hard for a moment. "He lives in the tenth arrondissement. Rue de Pareil."

"Thank you."

Christian turned to leave just as his senses tingled. Angie tensed, too. When they emerged from the foyer, a semi-circle of three dozen witches met them, their faces grim. Madame Starke stood at the center of their ranks, unveiled hatred on her face.

"Detain this filth," she shouted. "He and his vampires have killed hundreds of our people. And now he has taken the Cruentus Curse."

"Odette," Aliya gasped. "You overstep your bounds. That has not been proven."

Odette Starke stared her down, her obsidian eyes unblinking. "Oh, don't think I haven't noticed your unnatural affection for these blood-drinkers. If it were up to you, the future of our race and this thing"—her scornful eyes scanned Christian from head to toe —"would still be living together."

Aliya approached the witch with caution, as two other priestesses from inside the temple joined the three of them. "This is a place of peace with innocent children inside its walls," she said, frowning. "And Lord Devereux is here under our protection."

"Then you and those with you are as guilty as he."

"Victoria is missing—"

Odette hissed. "Of course she is missing. He took her."

Christian nodded imperceptibly to Angie, whose gaze was unfocused as she assessed the line of witches opposing them. She stared back, her fingers closing around the hilts of the crossbow tucked into her waistband, confirming his suspicion. This was a coup and Starke and her followers wanted payment in vampire blood. Aliya hadn't quite caught on, but Christian knew a rebellion when he saw one. The Clans were scared and Starke was capitalizing on their fear. He wondered what her endgame was and then remembered Aliya's words—she'd been in training to be high priestess. Was this what it was about? Sour grapes? He met Odette's cold eyes and exhaled. That and power. Everything fell into place.

"It was you, wasn't it?" he asked, his voice mild.

"How dare you address me, vampire?" she snarled. A wave of angry murmurs pressed through the crowd at her back.

"You do know where Victoria is, do you not?"

"How dare you?" Odette repeated. "When you are the very one who took her? Admit it—you were against her schooling from the first. You wanted her powers for yourself."

Christian smiled. "I have already sampled the power of Le Sang Noir, and trust me, I wish to have no part in it."

Odette's lip curled as she spat to the side. "Scum like you has no business wielding the magic of our bloodline. That privilege belongs to us. *She* belongs to us."

Aliya stared from him to the headmistress and back again. "What is this?" she whispered as if finally starting to put the pieces together.

"Your time is over," Odette said. "You had your chance to do what was right and you let this piece of filth defile our temple. You let our people die. You wanted peace with these creatures and for what? For a massacre? Well, the time for goodwill is done. And we're going to start by sending this one back to his people piece by piece." She eyed her longtime mentor. "You can join us or join them, your choice."

"This is madness," Aliya said. "The vampires have had casualties as well. We have no proof that they are the perpetrators."

"If we wait for your proof, how many more must die?" someone shouted from the rear of the line. "The vampires have waged war on us for centuries, and now that we have the Cruentus Curse in our grasp, they are picking us off one by one."

Aliya tried one last time. "Listen to yourselves. You are going to war on a whim based on the word of one witch."

"Step aside, Aliya," Odette said, blue fire crackling from her fingertips. "Or die with your new friends."

To Christian's surprise, Aliya stood her ground. "I pledged a sacred oath to defend this temple and the truth with my life."

"So be it."

He dodged the first blast Odette threw his way as the line collapsed toward them. "Run," he shouted to Angie. Without magic, she wouldn't be able to defend herself. Once more, he found himself taken aback as Angie dove behind a stone pillar and pulled what looked like a mini collapsible automated crossbow from her backpack. He could barely keep up with the toothpick-sized darts flying from it. One by one, the aggressors in front of her fell.

At his look, she grinned. "Had to come up with something to defend myself in this world of supernatural crazies. Nothing like a teeny little sleep dart ... works like a charm every time."

He had no time to ponder Angie's inventiveness as a group of witches converged upon him, muttering a variety of curses and hexes. Christian was a blur as he weaved his way through them, his vampire senses taking over. He could see the spells streaking toward him in slow motion and he dodged them with graceful ease. His newfound powers flexed within him, and after a few minutes, he came to a pause, looking at the pile of bodies. They weren't dead—he'd made sure of that. Inasmuch as they'd attacked him, he did not want to start a war. Not now, when they had a new common enemy.

Odette snarled her frustration as Aliya and the other two priestesses finished conjuring a shield spell over the temple. The air crackled with electricity as the rest of their offensive spells bounced harmlessly off its surface. Christian watched Odette carefully as she reconsidered her options. She stood with a handful of her remaining followers and they, too, looked uneasy as if they weren't quite certain of their leader's motives. She was acting on her own without the sanction of the high priestesses.

"You cannot possibly believe a word that she has told you about the vampires. She's only using you," Aliya shouted, coming to the same conclusion. "She is going against all our laws and the truce we have with the vampires. Are you willing to put all of us at risk? I am the moon priestess of this coven. Lay down your arms and go, and I will take that into account when the time for reckoning comes."

"Don't listen to her," Odette snarled. "Stand your ground."

Angie's eyes narrowed as she invoked her gift. "They're not all bad," she said. "You are right that they've been sold a good story by that one. She is consumed by her lust for power—it's hovering all over her like a poisonous green stain." She pointed to the headmistress, whose face had taken on an ugly scarlet hue at Angie's words. "She wants the Cruentus Curse for herself."

"Are you certain?" Aliya asked.

"Yes."

"Aliya, hand over the vampire." Odette's eyes flicked to Angie. "And the Aurus, too. And I promise no harm will come to you or the residents of this temple."

"I will not." Aliya waved a hand. "And you can no longer penetrate this barrier, so we are at a stalemate. Until the others arrive, that is." Aliya would have summoned reinforcements—those still loyal to her. Sure enough, Christian sensed their arrival as shadows appeared on the horizon beyond Odette in an ominous line. She glanced over her shoulder and gritted her teeth, her hands fisting at her sides. Within seconds, six of the remaining seven witches teleported for parts unknown, as if realizing the predicament of their situation, and Odette stood alone.

"Surrender now, Odette, and face the consequences of your actions."

"This is *your* last chance, Aliya," she countered with an icy smile. "Join me and live. Oppose me and die."

"You are outnumbered."

"Not for long." She hiked her chin, her eyes glittering with cold madness. "Do you think it matters whether I am on my own? They are a means to an end—one that is almost in my grasp." Her eyes slid to Christian, now that the pretense was over. "I wanted them to punish you, of course, for tainting one of ours with the stench of your touch. How dare you presume to come between a witch queen and this coven? You are beneath her—a bloodstain on the earth. What lies between the two of you is an abomination, and when I am finished, any memory of you will be nothing but an ember in the ashes. Victoria will see you for the scourge that you are, and soon she will be ready to take her rightful place with me at her side."

"She does mean to use the Cruentus Curse," one of the other high priestesses gasped. "But how?"

"You are mad," Aliya said.

"Not mad, just motivated. I was always meant to succeed you as the high priestess … as the moon leader of this coven. Now I will do so with more power at my fingertips than you could ever imagine."

"It doesn't work that way," Christian said. Every instinct inside him screamed that she knew where Victoria was. "The magic will not bend to you. It only serves one master."

Odette grinned. "But what if its master serves another? What then, oh all-knowing vampire?"

Christian felt his rage consume him at the thought of Victoria being in danger and under this witch's thumb. "Where is she?"

"Safe. For now."

He watched the woman carefully. If she vanished, he would lose any chance he had of finding Victoria. He stepped swiftly past the boundary of the shield into the direct path of the witch.

"Your Grace," Aliya said. "I cannot protect you beyond the walls of this temple."

"I understand."

Angie frowned, stepping forward to catch his sleeve and standing halfway out of the protective barrier. "Christian, what are you doing? She's more powerful than you think. I can see it."

"I know," he said, pushing her firmly back inside the protected sphere. "But so am I."

Malevolent energy arced from Odette's fingers, jetting toward him in blue streaks. He dodged the attack easily. Several more spells spun his way with blistering precision, forcing him to duck and weave to escape their paths. But with each evasive maneuver, Christian edged closer.

"You think your puny actions can save her?" Odette taunted. "By the time I'm finished, she won't even remember your name. She will ascend to the place she belongs as queen of all super-natural creatures."

"She doesn't want that."

"What do *you* know of what she wants, vampire? This is what she was born for. She was born to rule." Her eyes glittered with knowledge, and Christian's heart sank as her next words confirmed his suspicions. "Her blood has whispered its desires to me and I am but its lowly servant."

"What have you done to her?" he snarled, lurching forward, but Odette was too quick and teleported out of his reach. She appeared a few feet away. They circled each other like two predators.

"Don't worry, I'm not hurting her," she said. "I'm only allowing her to remove her limits, allowing her to experience the true power of the Cruentus Curse."

Christian's fists clenched at his sides. He knew too well the corrosive will of the blood magic. Victoria had grown stronger, that was for certain, but that didn't mean that her blood didn't have a live will of its own. If this witch had done something to Victoria, causing her to lessen her control over her blood, that would only invite disaster—Victoria and every living thing would be at its mercy. And it was ruthless, Christian knew.

"You think it will spare you? Is that what you think? The blood magic only cares for itself—it's a curse, surely you can see that."

"On the contrary, I see it as a gift."

Aliya shook her head, her mouth falling open. "Then you are a fool and you invite destruction upon all of us. Don't you remember what happened to the Duchess of Lancaster? The blood controlled her and annihilated tens of thousands."

"Out of the ashes, as they say," Odette returned. "The phoenix will rise."

Aliya exhaled slowly. "Then you are even more of a fool if you think that's you."

"No more treaties, no more truces, no more rules. Anything that remains after the purge will bend to our will. It will be a whole new world."

"You are insane," Aliya whispered.

"Again, not insane," she replied. "We have different visions for the future of our race, that is all. You've never been able to appreciate the bigger picture, Aliya. Why do you think witches were blessed with magic from the Goddess? Because we are a superior race—superior to the mortals and immortals alike." She waved a hand. "We shouldn't exist in secret, slinking around in the shadows like the rest of these monsters. We are the masters and they are the slaves." She gestured to the sleeping bodies scattered around her. "You think these are my only supporters? I have an army at my disposal—hundreds of students who will follow me to their deaths, who know the value of sacrifice for the greater good."

"The greater good?" Aliya scoffed. "You speak only for *your* own greed. And you are wrong. The humans have their gifts as we do, as do the vampires and any other supernatural being. We share this world as we have always done. We do not want a war that will end all wars."

"You are blind, Aliya, because the end is already upon us."

Taking advantage of Odette's distracted attention, Christian seized the opportunity to fly toward her, moving as David had done with incredible speed so that she did not have time to teleport away. But Odette was not to be underestimated and a dozen attack spells hurtled his way. He could not avoid them all and took the brunt of a poison hex in the shoulder, but still he kept coming. Odette's eyes widened as he stopped in front of her, his fingers closing around her throat. It would take considerable effort for her to teleport without taking him with her. Christian gritted his teeth and held his ground as a second poison spell blasted into him at point blank range.

He could feel the venom eating through his blood and followed the witch's triumphant stare as she watched the acid green trails creep up his neck and into his jaw. It infected his face, his chest, and his arm with relentless purpose. Angie was right—she was powerful and her spells even more so. It took every ounce of his newfound healing powers to battle the infection, but bit-by-bit, the spread retreated.

His eyes met hers as the triumph faded into a look of confusion and then fear. "How is that possible?" she whispered. "Since when are vampires immune to magic?"

"Since me. I will ask you one more time before I take it from you by force. Where is she?"

Odette smirked without a care in the world, as if she wasn't at the threshold of her own death. "You'll have to kill me, vampire, and then where will that leave you? Unable to reach her in time, I expect. Toxins are useful things, are they not? They can force the mind to believe whatever you want it to. Suffice it to say that if you kill me, you kill her."

"What kind of toxin?" Christian's mind raced. The only toxin that would be able to inhibit Victoria's power would be something neural. She'd be immune to magical attacks, which meant that it had to be something tangible.

"Tick tock, vampire."

Christian snapped her neck to the side and sank his fangs deep. The taste of her blood was heady, drenched in magic. Flashes crashed into him as he drank—Victoria's face, the boy Pan, a forest. He drew back with a gasp. Such visions had never happened to him before. He'd felt emotions in the past, but he had never seen anything like obvious flashback memories. Oblivious to the stares from the witches, he set his lips to the wound and pulled deeply, focusing on the images. As the witch's body grew limp, Christian released her.

He turned to Aliya, ignoring the terrified, shocked looks from the other two. What he had done was unforgiveable and broke one of the terms of the tenuous treaty between them. Then again, Odette Starke had attacked him, so he'd been well within his rights to defend himself. His eyes met Aliya's. "I know where Victoria is. This one is yours—I've left her alive to face her fate with your people. You need to mobilize the Clans. There's no time to explain, but there's a corporeal rogue demon lord here, one responsible for all the deaths."

"A demon lord?" she whispered.

"Yes, a powerful one. It killed a dozen warlocks in minutes."

He glanced over his shoulder. "Angie, take my car. Meet me back at the château. If I do not return, find Lucian."

Angie's eyes widened into giant orbs as Christian thrust a heavy signet ring toward her. "Lucian? As in your evil twin brother who tried to kill us all last year?"

"Yes."

"Why?"

"Because we are going to need all the help we can get. And my brother is aligned with the warlocks. Give him the ring and ask him to take you to the warlock Freyja. Tell her everything." He eyed the crossbow dangling at her side. "Take that with you and don't hesitate to use it if you have to."

"W—will I have to?"

He shook his head, worried about the position he was putting a mortal in, but he had no choice. "I honestly don't know. Use your power. It will warn you before of whether they intend you harm." He eyed her. "And, Angie, be careful."

KEEP YOUR ENEMIES CLOSER

Victoria had never felt so at peace in her life. She pulled the strap of her backpack over her shoulder and crossed the quad toward her classes. She waved at a few of her friends sitting on the library steps and enjoying the warm Maine spring sunshine—Angie, Charla, and Gabriel. They smiled and waved back as she walked toward them.

"You guys aren't going to class?" she asked.

"Free period," Charla said. "You have one, too. Gabe convinced the teacher that we needed the afternoon off."

"He did?" Her gaze shifted from Charla to Gabriel, Angie's brother. Angie looked sullen and sour, her stringy dark hair falling into her face. The girl stared at her with unconcealed loathing, and a flicker of something unfamiliar pushed at her awareness. Victoria eyed Gabriel. "How did you manage to do that?"

"Magic." Gabriel nodded at the spot beside him. "Cop a squat. Call it mind suggestion—I suggested, he listened."

Charla grinned. "He's being modest. Gabe totally screwed with his mind. And so we have the entire day off. Want to head up to the lake?"

A person crossing the lawn distracted her, catching her attention. She recognized his lithe body easily. *Christian*. She flushed as his eyes met hers, feeling Gabriel tense beside her, as he, too, followed the direction of her gaze. The enmity between them was tangible even across the distance.

"Filthy bloodsucker."

Her eyes snapped to Gabriel's. *"What?"*

"Devereux is a vampire, didn't you know?" he snarled, the rage on his face like a dark angry thundercloud. "Stay away from him."

"A vampire?" Victoria whispered in disbelief. "What do you mean?"

"He's not like us, Tori. He'll kill you."

A sensation of foreboding crept up her spine. Vampires didn't exist. They were the stuff of stories, of horror movies and books. They weren't real. Christian's silver eyes met hers across the distance and something deep within her belly shifted. She knew *exactly* what he was and it meant nothing. Nothing mattered but him and the way he was looking at her. Her breath caught as a wave of longing overtook her body.

Tori.

Gabriel's warning faded into the distance as she held on to the look in Christian's eyes and the sound of his voice. The quad fell away. The steps disappeared. Her friends dissipated into fragments. Gaping nothingness surrounded her and the truth came back in thick surges. She was no longer in Maine. Or at Windsor Academy.

And Gabriel was *dead*.

She had killed him in the underground tunnels in New York City, which meant that none of this was real.

Reality clawed through the fantasy and Victoria found herself in her earthy prison once more. She wondered how long she'd been asleep this time. Minutes? Hours? Days? She felt disoriented and confused. Pan's second dose had been far more powerful than the first. She felt their effects swimming through her, twisting her mind into tiny knots—to the point that she couldn't discern truth from lies.

Tori.

She frowned as the mental voice projected into her mind. Was she still dreaming? *Christian?*

I'm here.

She was surely dreaming. There was no way Christian would have found wherever Pan had hidden her. But the ground around her started to tremble and then a fist broke through the top layer of dirt. It grasped onto her arm and dragged her out into the open. Victoria blinked against the sharp sunlight as Christian gathered her into his arms, shaking the dirt from her hair and her clothes. His hands felt real, but then again, they'd felt real in the dream, too. Perhaps this was Pan's way of torturing her—by making her believe that Christian had come to save her, even after everything she'd done to him.

She closed her eyes, shame and regret filling her. She had chosen the witches over him, but they, too, had only coveted her power. At least she knew where she stood with Christian... where she *had* stood. No, she had thrown that all away when she had broken up with him. And now he couldn't be real, finding her beneath layers of dirt and rock. It had to be a trick.

"Tori, wake up," an urgent voice said. "You need to fight this."

She blinked again, focusing her wits, even as Pan's poison slithered through her veins and her consciousness. The voice's face was fuzzy, but she wanted it to be him so badly that it started to take shape.

"Christian," she breathed.

Her fingers reached upward, brushing the familiar square outline of his jaw and the soft curve of his lips. His eyes shone down on her with so much love that she could live in this fantasy forever.

Gentle hands pulled her close, and she could smell his scent surrounding her like a fresh summer rain. She snuggled into him. "I'm so glad you're here. When I saw you in the quad, I knew that you wouldn't leave me."

"The quad?" he asked. Careful fingers inspected her eyes, forcing her eyelids open. Christian's face swam into view again, but now he looked worried. "Victoria, you need to wake up. Where is Pan?"

Her mind clawed through the fog threatening to drown it and truth eclipsed fantasy for a moment. She felt the sun on her face and Christian's solid body at her back. Her mouth struggled to shape the words, breaking past her parched, cracked lips. "Is it really you?"

"Yes."

She swallowed, a wave of fatigue sweeping through her as if the effort of staying alert was too much to bear. The moments of lucidity were brief, and Victoria knew she had to hold on or she'd be sucked right back into Pan's toxin. "How did you find me?"

"Odette Starke."

Victoria frowned, making a sharp pain riddle her brain. The headmistress of Belles Fontaines? Perhaps she'd known about Pan and had told Christian. But why would she ask the vampires for help? The questions made her head ache and long for the quiet solitude of her daydreams. She closed her eyes, desperate to succumb to the peace they promised.

"No, no," the voice said. "Stay with me. Tori, stay with me. *Merde*, what has he done to you?"

"P—poison," she mouthed. "Pollen."

"Pan did this?" His eyes flared above her. "Where is he?"

"Right here."

Christian turned in slow motion, as did Victoria. Her fear came back in full force. Christian was here and there was nothing she could do to protect him from Pan's machinations.

He stood alone in the middle of the glade, but she could see the lethal pollen fisted in his hands. One puff and Christian would be as useless as her. Or worse.

Placing Victoria gently down, Christian stood. She fought to stay awake, fighting the terror rising in her gut. She wanted to scream that he was dangerous, but her lips wouldn't cooperate. Her mouth was glued shut.

Pan shook his head, his eyes trained on Christian. "Now, now, no sudden moves."

"Or what?" Christian asked coolly.

Pan smiled, his blue eyes glittering. "You've seen what I can do. You think you will be immune? You'll be worse off than she is right now. The only reason she isn't dead is because of the magic beating in her veins. The curse, as they say."

"You think you can control the Cruentus Curse?"

Pan met her eyes. "I can control her."

"Odette Starke is using you, Pan. Surely you see that."

The boy's smile widened. "Or perhaps she is only a means to an end. I needed to get close, you see. Befriend the new witch. Madame Starke came to understand my point of view with a little pollen persuasion."

"*You* drugged her?"

"Not exactly, but she wanted the power for herself, and well, I couldn't have that. Not after all the work I'd put in to get this toxin just right." He eyed Christian. "How did you find us, by the way? I'm assuming the poor headmistress is dead or was in enough pain to give up the information."

"Something like that," Christian said. He still hadn't moved, although Victoria could see his fists clenching at his sides.

Pan pursed his lips. "It is a pity that I'm going to have to kill you, though. You really are quite hot, but you know what they say in the covenant—relationships between witches and vampires are frowned upon, so there's really no future for us anyway."

Blinking in and out of the hazy effects of the poison, Victoria didn't know whether to laugh or cry. Pan was delusional. How had she not seen it before? Had she been so desperate to be accepted and to have a friend that she'd missed all the cues?

"I guess not," Christian said, his voice inflectionless.

"Can't have you spoiling my grand plans either." He smiled. "So how do you want it? The hard way or the easy way? You look like you like it kind of rough."

Without warning, the ground shook as snaky roots appeared to wrap around Christian's ankles before he could move, slamming him to the ground. He snarled, tearing at them with his fingers and springing into a crouch. He rushed Pan, but a shield protection around the witch sent him sprawling backward.

Victoria focused what little energy she could summon. Christian would have no chance if she didn't crack Pan's protection spell. And, well, if Pan got close enough to Christian, who knew what he'd be capable of with his pouch of pixie dust or what effect it'd have on a vampire. Fear clotted her veins as they circled each other.

Another rotation of roots swept the earth, but this time Christian dodged out of their way. His attacks remained defensive as he couldn't get close enough to do any real damage to Pan. And from the smile on the witch's face, he was enjoying toying with his prey. Vines dropped like rain from the foliage above, wrapping around Christian's arms and binding them to his sides. As quickly as he broke out of the restraints, more appeared to take their place.

Think! Victoria urged herself, but finding clarity was a struggle. Pan's toxin was running rampant within her and she knew she couldn't trust herself, not while she was under its influence. But Christian had no advantage without her. She *had* to try.

She needed a kick-start—magic to restart her own sluggish power, and the only person who had magic was Pan. And it was shielded. She could take life from the trees and the animals around her, but Victoria didn't know how much her power would absorb once she got started, and she didn't want to risk taking innocent lives as weak as she was. That was what the blood magic wanted—it craved darkness and that was the last thing that she would ever give it willingly.

Digging her fists into the earth, she pushed her awareness out, the pounding in her head increasing to excruciating levels as she fought Pan's contaminant with every shred of willpower she had left. She stole energy from ants and worms burrowing the soil, mourning the loss of their lives, but she needed them. She needed them to survive. With each life, her lucidity and her strength grew.

Pan's gaze shot to hers as the nearest surrounding trees shriveled and blackened as she stole their life. "Tori," he said in a warning voice. "What are you doing? You know that's not nice."

Victoria gasped. It wasn't enough. She'd need to consume the entire forest and everything in it to even get back half her strength. If she gave in to the blood magic, it would consume life until it was sated, and everyone would be at risk, including Christian. And her hold on it was tenuous as it was.

"You don't have to do this, Pan," she said, watching as Christian fended off a combined dual attack of roots from below and vines from above. His super speed was blinding as he tried to dart out of their reach, but there were too many of them. As fast as he evaded them, a dozen more snaked toward him.

"Oh, of course I don't. But I *want* to."

Suddenly, Victoria felt a deep reserve of something and stalled. No, it couldn't be. She pushed outward again, but she'd been right the first time. It was Christian. *He* had magic. It was impossible, but just as blood called to blood, so did magic. She'd felt it before, too, in the courtyard.

Victoria knew a way she could help him. She turned back to Pan. She had seconds before he reached her, and once he gave her another dose, she would be powerless. She focused the little energy she'd gathered and pushed her awareness toward Christian.

What are you doing? he asked.

You have magic. She couldn't quite keep the desperation from her mental voice. Or was it hunger? Her body shook with the force of what her blood wanted.

It's a new development.

Can I use it?

Tori, I don't know what it can do, only that it is dark, ancient magic. He paused. *I wouldn't risk it.*

I'll only take a little, I swear. Enough for me to help you. The words couldn't form in her head fast enough. The promise of magic was like the lure of a drug, calling to her every sense. She only needed a touch of whatever he had—enough to free him and to defeat Pan.

Christian stared at her and shook his head, renewing his attack against the serpentine vines curling around his limbs. *No, Tori.*

You're going to die if I don't do something.

With an immense burst of strength, he ripped apart the vines clinging to him and vaulted toward where Victoria was crouching, his body braced like a shield to block Pan's approach. The lacerations on his skin from the barbed plants healed before her eyes, and once more she marveled at the changes in him.

Christian met her eyes. *It's not worth the risk to you, should the blood magic take over. And this magic is not like witch's magic. It's dark. I don't know what it will do to you.*

Her eyes rose to Pan hovering close behind them. "We can't beat him without it," she whispered.

"You can."

Victoria nodded and released the meager energy she'd amassed, slamming it into Pan's shield and feeling it dissipate for an instant. "*Now,* Christian."

At the last second, Christian spun around, his vampire speed untraceable as he cut a blazing path toward Pan. His fist darted out, catching the boy square in the chin, and Pan went down, stunned by the punch he hadn't even seen coming. His shield charm winked out completely as he lost control of his magic and struggled to get his bearings. Christian didn't hesitate as he rushed in for the final blow.

"No, don't hurt him," Victoria cried. "He has ... a disorder."

"He tried to hurt you."

"Please."

Christian stared at her, but just nodded. Clearly, he didn't agree with her leaving a homicidal witch alive. She didn't want to leave him either, not when he was a danger to himself and a danger to others. "We can take him to the high priestesses. They'll know what to do." She sighed, pulling herself up with a groggy movement. "I can't teleport, so we'll have to find a taxi or a metro stop."

"Hang tight," he told her as he stooped to bring her close.

"What?" Victoria was unprepared for Christian to swing her into his arms, but she was even more unprepared for what came next as he grabbed hold of an unconscious Pan by one leg.

She blinked as the ground—and Pan's dangling body—lay below them, and then there was only the breeze against her face and the feel of Christian's strong embrace holding her tightly. "Are we *flying*?" she said.

He leaned close to her ear. "Yes."

"How is this possible?" she said, her brain struggling to catch up to her thoughts. "Vampires can't fly."

His answer was almost lost in the wind. "The Reii can."

Her mind was fuzzy, but even in its incapacitated state, she remembered the Reii. She'd read of them in one of Christian's books when she'd spent half the summer stuck in his château and bored out of her mind. She'd wanted to understand their genesis and whether Christian could ever become human—or whether she could become like him. She'd found nothing that suggested either of those options were possible, but she had discovered the ancestors of the vampire race. Victoria's eyes widened as she and Christian alighted at the witches' temple.

"How did you find out?"

He drew a shattered breath. "Enhard ... left a letter after he died telling me the truth."

Victoria stared at the visible anguish flashing across his face and flung her arms around him. "I am so sorry. I know you always thought he was your maker."

"He was a father to me and that is what is important. It doesn't matter who my true maker was, or is."

"But it does matter, Christian." Victoria's eyes narrowed as she took in his fully healed wounds. She realized that it was the only reason he had survived their last encounter without worse scars. He'd been able to face her one-on-one.

Oh god.

He'd been able to do other things, too. Her body grew hot with the memory of what they had shared and she turned away, composing herself hastily as Aliya ran out of the temple toward them.

"Victoria, are you okay?"

"Getting there," she answered with a wan smile. "It was Pan."

Aliya gasped as her eyes landed on Pan's inert body. "*Pan*? Is he dead?"

"Just knocked out," Christian said.

"He wanted the power of the Cruentus Curse," Victoria explained as Aliya ushered them into the depths of the temple. Two of her people restrained the unconscious Pan behind them. Victoria nodded for Christian to follow, and after a long moment, Aliya flicked her wrist, signaling that he should. It made Victoria feel better that he was close, even though she knew that the attention from the witches inside would make him uncomfortable. Aliya escorted them to her private quarters and dismissed the two witches in attendance.

"What happened? Tell me everything."

Something went fuzzy in her brain and she blinked, staring half into space and half at Aliya who was watching her with expectant silence.

"He used some kind of toxin," Christian interjected after a look at Victoria's face. "One that inhibited her ability to control her magic. It's not wearing off. She had to drain energy from around her to even be this coherent. Odette had suggested that the toxin would kill her if not removed. We brought him with us, but I don't think we have much time," he added with a glance at Victoria. She felt weaker by the second, but smiled at him reassuringly. He didn't buy it, she knew.

A knock on the door interrupted them and one of Aliya's personal guards stepped in. "He's awake and restrained. We found nothing on him, except the pouch of dust you described. He won't tell us anything."

Victoria's heart sank. Of course he wouldn't have had the antidote on him. He was far too clever for that. The room started to spin then and she clutched Christian for support. "I can get it out of him," he growled. "The same way with Odette."

But Aliya shook her head. "He would have prepared for that, Your Grace, knowing who you were to Victoria. My guess is that his blood has been poisoned with a similar toxin."

"I'll take the risk." He stood, but her glare stalled him in his tracks.

"And have the vampires start a war because we killed their prince? No. We will figure this out. It's a witch problem."

Christian raked a frustrated hand through his hair, rage written all over his face. "Don't you get it? It's no longer a witch problem. We need her alive. *I* need her alive. She would have been safe if she had remained with me, but I agreed to let her go with you because we both thought it would be best for her. And look at what nearly happened—a psychotic power-hungry witch and her boy-prodigy would have unleashed the Cruentus Curse upon the world." He jabbed a finger at Victoria, who was feeling more drained by the minute, the buzzing in her head starting to become cacophonous. "Even now, you cannot help her. She is *dying*."

Her gaze snapped to his. "How do you know?"

"Because I can feel it." His voice was measured. "We are connected. We have been since last year, but I could never sense her the way I can now. I can feel her waning heartbeat, trace the venom tracking its way through her system, the tail end of it meant to consume."

Blanching at his words, Aliya stood and spoke to the men at her door. Within seconds, the chamber was crowded with witches. Victoria grasped Christian's hands in hers as they stared at her with varying looks of pity and compassion. She tried to speak and could not. It felt good to close her eyes.

"No, no, Tori, you have to stay awake. Don't go to sleep." That same urgent voice was tugging against her senses. She protested weakly, but pushed open her eyes at his insistent commands. Somehow she'd moved from the chair to the table in the middle of the room. Christian stood beside her. The witches gave him a wide berth too, she noticed faintly. It was because he should not be here … in the sanctified temple. He was an outcast, an outsider. Then again, so was she.

"I'm so tired."

"I know, love, but you cannot go to sleep."

She saw the witches bending over her body, chanting over her. Their fingers brushed her temples, her arms, the soles of her feet as the soft sounds of their voices echoed in the room. A burst of light filled her, pushing against the hot rush of Pan's poisoned dust, but it held fast like a parasite.

"It's not responding to the spells," one of the witches said.

"Magic and science," Victoria murmured, and Christian bent

to catch what she'd said before her head lolled to the side and her eyes rolled back in her head.

"We don't have much time left." She heard Christian shout. A flurry of movement filled her vision as his desperate growl scattered the remaining witches. "Either bring me the boy and I'll tear this place apart to find him."

But as the blood roiled beneath her veins, Victoria knew that it was already too late. Too late for all of them.

THE COURAGE OF ONE

L ounging in an armchair, Lucian stared at the defiant dark haired girl before him, holding his brother's ducal ring in one hand and a small crossbow in the other. He didn't know whether to kill her himself or let Lena kill her. His gaze slid to where Lena sat, watching the ludicrous situation unfold without a glimmer of expression on that icy face. He knew that what had happened in the warlock's quarter would have affected her, but at least now he knew where her loyalties lay. When it had counted most, she had chosen him over Christian. He frowned—he didn't understand why she had allowed the girl entrance, however.

Lucian's attention turned back to the girl and his eyes narrowed. Recognition was swift as he studied her face. "You're the sister of that warlock. Gabriel."

She nodded, her fingers tightening on the weapon at her side. "Angie."

It wouldn't help her cause if he chose to put an end to whatever game his brother was playing, but he let her keep it. The illusion of security went a long way in getting to the bottom of why she would risk entering a house full of vampires and claim to be here on Christian's behalf. In truth, Lucian was surprised that she even made it past the foyer. It was Lena who had seen her and prevented her untimely execution by one of his overzealous followers.

Lucian inhaled her scent. It was rich, but not remarkable in any way. "You are not a witch."

"No."

He smiled. "Considering that, you are either very brave or very stupid. How did you know I would not kill you on sight?"

She stared at him, lifting a cool eyebrow. "I didn't."

"So why did you come here? What do you owe my brother that you would risk blood, breath, and bone to deliver his message?"

"I owe him nothing. I came because I wanted to. I trust him."

Lucian made a derisive sound. "Really? You trust him? A *vampire*?"

To his surprise, Angie smiled at him. "I would trust your brother with my life, Lord Devereux. Just as you do."

He laughed, but the way she was looking at him unnerved him more than her stupid comment. What this poor little human didn't know was that he would kill his brother if he had to. "You seem to know a lot about me, even if you are misinformed."

"If you say so."

His lips curled back from his teeth. "I do. My brother and I are estranged, you see. So I, unlike you, owe him nothing whatsoever."

"I only see what I see," she replied as if that explained everything.

Her lack of fear was beginning to grate on him along with her cryptic responses. Lucian's eyes slipped to the ring in her grasp and he held out his hand, beckoning her forward. She did so without hesitation, although her grip on the crossbow did not relax, and dropped the piece of jewelry into his palm.

The heirloom was indeed Christian's. He glanced at the near identical one on the ring finger of his left hand. Although Christian's gem was a sapphire and his was a ruby, the family ducal crest stamping the setting on both was the same. Their parents had given the rings to them on their thirteenth birthday and Lucian would have recognized it anywhere. A part of him didn't believe that his brother had sent this girl with it, especially given what had happened between them. But the ring was genuine, of that he was sure. He palmed it and closed his eyes.

Lucian's heart clenched as he remembered the promise they had made to each other when they were thirteen, after the rings had been bequeathed in a special Devereux coming of age ceremony.

"If you are ever in trouble," the young Christian had said to him. "Find a way to send me your ring. And I will do the same. I will come to you no matter what."

"Agreed," Lucian had responded. "Blood promise?"

He remembered the sting of the knife cutting into his palm like it was yesterday and the feeling of slippery hot blood between Christian's palm and his. They had never used the rings.

Until now.

As much as he wanted to kill the girl and be done with it, something—a residual sense of honor perhaps—tugged within him. He sighed. Pocketing the ring, he pulled himself to his feet then and closed the distance between them. She raised the crossbow and pointed it at his chest. "You think your arrows can hurt me?" he scoffed.

She shook her head. "I don't want to hurt you. I came here with a message, but I assure you these arrows aren't meant to hurt, they're meant to kill. I designed them specially after what happened in New York." Her eyes slid to the shiny pointed head of the dart sitting in the crossbow's sights. "Pure silver with a core of UV light. It's a hollow point so it explodes on contact.

Auto reload. And I'm a crack shot. At this range, I won't miss no matter how fast you think you are."

He grinned at her boast. Despite himself, he was unwillingly impressed. Narrowing his eyes, he shifted, using all of his vampire speed to move toward the fireplace. To his surprise, the crossbow followed him with unerring precision. He frowned—it had to have been a lucky guess.

"Lucian," Lena warned, her voice low. She, too, now stood, her body tensed for attack.

He shot her a quelling look. "I want to test our new friend's theory." He turned his attention back to Angie. "I'm intrigued. What are the odds you could shoot me before I reach you? I give you my word I won't kill you." He paused, baring his teeth. "Yet."

"Your word?" Laughter threaded her voice. His glance moved to Lena, who was watching them will ill-concealed agitation. "One on one? I think my odds are better than good."

"Just me," he agreed, nodding for Lena to resume her seated position. She wasn't happy about it, but she obeyed.

He watched as she pressed a button on the side of the crossbow and a whirring noise filled its chamber. She met his eyes. "Non-lethal wooden darts. I don't want to kill you, after all. Are you sure you want to do this?"

"I want to see how good you are."

Angie shrugged. "I'll tell you what. If I get a strike, you agree to get Freyja and go to Christian."

"That's two things."

She rolled her eyes. "Then there'll be two strikes. Now are we doing this? I don't have all day to play your silly games."

His amusement waned at her arrogant words, and he crouched into position. "Very well."

Angie cocked the weapon. "Your move."

He charged, blindingly fast, heading directly toward her, but she sidestepped to the right at the last moment before he reached her. He heard the click of the crossbow and the soft swish of its reload, his body bending backward as the dart lodged into the wall behind him. It had passed inches from his shoulder. He scowled and lunged again. She wasn't fast, but she seemed to anticipate his every movement, only moving when he was a hair's breadth from knocking her over. Growling savagely, he dove forward, his arm darting out to catch her in the stomach. She flew back and crashed into the bookcase.

Lucian grinned in satisfaction, watching as she stood, crossbow still in hand, and wiped a smear of blood from her mouth. His senses fired at the sight—and scent—of the bright crimson trail. Snarling with savage rage, his fangs lengthened to their full length, and the beast in him begged for its reward. But before he could grant it, to his surprise, Angie smiled at him, her eyes falling meaningfully to his chest. He looked down. There, lodged directly above his heart was a small wooden dart. He'd barely felt it.

"Got you," she said, panting slightly. "And might I remind you that if I'd used my other darts, you'd be dead. Now honor our agreement, summon Freyja."

He plucked the projectile out and flung it to the floor, nodding to Lena. With a disgusted look, she walked to the door and passed on the instruction. "You still have one shot to get me to go see my dear brother," Lucian said as Lena resumed her position. Her face remained expressionless, although her eyes conveyed her opinion of his continued interaction with the girl.

Angie shook her head, looking mildly embarrassed. "Actually I got you the first time you came at me. I just didn't want to make you feel too badly." She pointed at his thigh, and to his infinite disgust, he could see the tip of a brown arrow protruding from his pants. Lucian glared at her. There was no possible way any human could do what she'd just done. Not without super senses or super speed. He scented her again, his nostrils flaring. She wasn't a witch or a warlock—their blood was like nectar to vampires. No, she was pure, untainted human.

"I suppose that that was fairly won," he capitulated without an ounce of grace. "Despite not knowing what tricks you had up your sleeve."

"Coming from a vampire, that's rich," she shot back. He noticed that the cut on her lip where she'd smashed into the bookcase was starting to bruise. He could still smell her blood, rushing beneath the surface. He smiled inwardly. As he'd agreed, he'd hear her out once Freyja arrived, and then he'd drain her to the bone. She may be able to take one vampire on, but she would not be so lucky with a handful. The thought gave him great satisfaction. He did not like being humiliated, and certainly not at the hands of a teenage girl. But for the moment, he'd be civil.

"Drink?" he asked her, pointing to the bottle of cognac.

"I'm underage," she said. "So no thanks."

"You're in Paris. The drinking age, I believe, is eighteen."

She shook her head. "It dulls my wits."

"I should have offered you some earlier." It was the closest he'd go to giving her a compliment, but she took his meaning. A true smile graced that resolute face of hers.

"You remind me of him a little," she said.

Lucian vaulted his brow. "My brother?"

"Why do you hate him?"

His glance slid to Lena. For a moment, he considered ignoring the probing question, but then resumed his place in his armchair. He raised a palm toward the empty sofa across from Lena, but Angie declined, as he knew she would. Although she seemed calm, he could see her tension in the rigid slope of her shoulders and the thinned line of her mouth.

"He came first."

She laughed and the sound was hollow. "That's not a reason to hate your twin. So what, he came first. Big deal. One of you has to be the older one—and it just turned out that fate decided it would be him and not you. Let's talk about hate when you have a brother who murdered your parents, who punished you daily because you weren't like him. We can have a drink and commiserate when your brother decides he's going to kill you because he can't stand the sight of you." She laughed to herself, a spasm of pain flashing across her features. She met Lucian's eyes. "Get over it. He's a duke and you're the second in line brother. Stop wallowing in your misguided sense of injustice. Grow the fuck up."

"How dare you?" Lucian hissed, her words as effective as those little wooden darts. He almost changed his mind then and there—he'd kill her and then offer his apologies to Freyja for a fruitless trip. "Who do you think you are?"

She eyed him, resting the flat of the crossbow in the other hand. "Truth hurts, right?"

"You know nothing, *child*."

"That may be, but I see enough," she said and his eyes narrowed once more at her choice of words. "You tried so hard to make your brother hate you so that you can feel justified in your actions against him. When your mother died, he was the only one who stopped you from taking your own life."

"How—?" Lucian started, his jaw dropping into a snarl and eyes narrowing, but Angie ignored him, unfazed by his anger.

"All you do in return is push him away. And the sad thing is in his hour of dire need, *you're* the one he turns to. It's baffling." She stared blindly through the floor to ceiling windows, the city of Paris laid out like a carpet of lights below them. "Since we seem to be having a moment, you asked me before if I trusted Christian. I do. He and Tori saved my life. Just as he has saved yours countless times." Her gaze flicked to Lena. "And yours, Baroness von Kurzberg."

Lena half stood, her glacial blue eyes snapping to Angie. "How do you know that name—?"

"I know a lot about you," Angie said, meeting her incensed gaze. "I know about the girl whose sense of justice trumped all, even though she often came out on the wrong end of her brothers' temper. I know about the girl who hid her compassion because she feared it would make her weak. I see a lot, Baroness, including what you have become."

Angie didn't elaborate, and for that, Lucian was grateful. He didn't want to know any more of this girl's truths, least of all Lena's. Her words had troubled him, digging past all his walls and slipping beneath his layers. How could she have known about his mother? About the guilt that had sent him to the middle of an icy lake? He was the reason his mother had died, after all. The girl had stripped away everything, even his own defenses. It made him feel vulnerable and exposed. He didn't like it one bit.

Was she some kind of psychic? Able to see the future as well as the past? He asked the question, despite himself. Her mouth twitched. "No. I don't know what's going to happen, and I only know about the past from reading history books and going online like everyone else. I only see the now *because* of the past."

"What do you mean you *see* it?" he snapped.

But Angie didn't have time to answer Lucian's question as a knock on the door interrupted them. Freyja had arrived and was waiting in the entrance salon. Her presence—and her blood —would cause a stir among the vampires, Lucian knew. While he wanted to hear more of what the girl had to say, it wouldn't be long before someone did something stupid.

He drained the contents of his glass and nodded to Angie. "Come, you have your audience. Let us hear what you have to say."

Angie followed them at a discreet distance until they crossed the wide hall to the receiving room at the far end of his apartment where Freyja was waiting in the foyer. Lucian took a deep breath. She did not look pleased to have been summoned on some fool's errand. Her second in command, Roan, was ever present at her side, and he looked like he was on the verge of declaring war. Lucian dismissed the hovering vampires with a nod, with the exception of Lena and two of his strongest vampires—Marc and Leon. If things went south, he wanted them close.

"What is this about, Lord Devereux? Your messenger said it was urgent."

He cleared his throat, flinching from the acid in her tone. "My brother is in trouble, and he bid this girl bring you here." He swept a hand toward the open door and Angie walked in. He noticed that the crossbow was back in its holster on her hip. Obviously, she did not view them as a threat as much as she had him.

Lucian was not prepared for the reaction that swept the faces of the warlock contingent as the girl strode into the room. The very air turned electric, so much so that Lena took a hurried step to his side.

"Angelique?" Freyja's whisper was ragged.

"Aunt Free," Angie said in disbelief, her eyes widening as she came to a dead stop just inside the doorway. "What are you doing here? How is this even possible? Gabriel told me you had died. You're the warlock leader?"

Aunt Free? Lucian's brows slammed together. The warlock was this girl's aunt? But she couldn't be related by blood—he'd sensed no magic within her. Perhaps she'd been adopted or taken in. He remained quiet, waiting to see what would happen.

Freyja marched forward to take her niece's face into her hands, her fingers running up and down the girl's face. "Where is Gabriel? Is he with you?"

The color drained from Angie's face. "He's dead. He tried to take the Cruentus Curse. I'm sorry. I didn't know he lied about that, too. He told me you died."

The silence was deafening. "*What?*"

"What do you know of the curse?" Roan snarled.

"Hello, cousin," Angie said with a startled smile, peering around Freyja's body. "You're as angry as ever." Lucian couldn't have agreed with her more. She shook her head and sighed. "I know a lot as it turns out. The witch is my best friend." Angie threw a look to where Lucian stood. "And she's dating his brother. Well, they're broken up now, but they were together. Anyway, there's trouble. Christian said I had to get the two of you. You need to come with me to the witches' temple."

"Victoria Warrick is your best friend," Roan said as if he hadn't heard anything else. "Did you not learn anything when you were a child?"

"No, I was busy being adopted by people who weren't magical."

"Adopted?" Freyja looked confused. "I received letters from your mother for years. They stopped a few years ago when she said she wanted nothing to do with any of us anymore. I tried to find you, but you had all disappeared. I respected her wishes, of course, even though it broke my heart."

"Gabriel cloaked us," Angie said. "And he wrote the letters. They died a decade ago."

Freyja's eyes clouded, a soft huff escaping her lips. "I am so sorry I wasn't there, Angelique. You must have felt so abandoned all these years."

The girl shrugged, as if she was all too used to dealing with pain. "It's just Angie now, and you couldn't have known. No one did."

Lucian cleared his throat, watching as Freyja pulled her niece into her arms, with more emotion written all over her face than he'd ever thought her capable of. Turned out she did have a heart, only it was buried deep. Not that it mattered. He wanted nothing to do with either of them, especially now that he knew that Freyja only wanted to destroy Le Sang Noir. He would have enjoyed killing the non-witch and it rankled that she, too, would be taken away under the protection of the warlocks. He gnashed his teeth in silent irritation.

"Not to interrupt this lovely family reunion," he drawled. "But I'm busy and I don't have all day to waste watching you two make nice."

Angie's eyes swiveled to his. She took a step back so that she could face each of them. "Christian sent me. He needs your help to gather your combined forces." Her eyes slid to her aunt and to Lucian. "Both of you."

"Our help?" Roan snarled. "We do not align with vampires."

"You wanted to align with me," Lucian interjected in a silky voice.

"That was a means to an end."

"Ah, yes, all those empty promises you made. I remember." Lucian felt the beast within him start to stretch. Maybe he would teach this warlock a lesson, release some of the tension of unfulfilled desire building up in his veins. Magic or not, they were on his turf. He shot a sidelong glance to Lena, who hadn't moved from her position at his side. His teeth pushed forward through his gums, elongating to lethal proportions as adrenaline and bloodlust lanced through him. He didn't even have to signal to the vampire near the door before Leon lunged toward Angie.

Lucian wondered if she would sense the imminent attack as she had with him earlier. Watching it from an outside perspective gave him pause. Leon was so fast that Lucian could see Freyja and her two guards moving into defensive positions as if in slow motion. His eyes narrowed as the girl ducked into a crouch seconds before Leon reached her, crossbow armed and notched. There was no way she'd have been able to sidestep him, but that was exactly what she had done. She didn't hesitate. She fired the dart right into Leon's heart. It was not a wooden dart as she'd used with him, he realized, as Leon's body crumbled in a blazing inferno of blue and white light before scattering to ashes on the polished mahogany floors. For a second, Lucian felt an odd twinge of relief that she hadn't used those darts in their sparring.

"Wait," Angie said to Freyja, who had already started chanting a counter spell. She turned to Lucian and held up a hand to stop any retaliation from the scowling warlocks pressing at her back. "I'm sorry about that, but I told you what would happen. We have no time to lose with any more of your games."

"What are you?" Lena snarled at his side. "You have no magic. What you did is not possible for a human."

"I am an Aurus," she answered, hiking her chin a notch. "No magical power, but I can see what people are, along with their motivations. Not that it matters, but for every minute we stand here arguing, one more of our people dies."

Lucian's eyes settled upon her with fascinated interest. He'd heard of such individuals. Their gift to see the true nature of beings was a valuable one. He thought back to that brother of hers he'd faced in New York—no wonder he'd kept her close. She'd been the secret to his success. Something hot lanced through him as he recalled her earlier comment of him trusting Christian with his life. He didn't like the idea of anyone being able to see through the core of him—or knowing things that he himself couldn't know.

"My brother can go straight to hell," he said. "Along with anyone else stupid enough to get in that demon's way."

"Your sentiments do not match what's in your heart, Lord Devereux," Angie murmured, her words like slender daggers piercing through the chinks in his armor. "And the threat has grown far bigger than a rogue demon. The more souls it consumes, the more powerful it gets. The only way we can defeat it is to come together."

"What about your precious Victoria?" Lena said. "Le Sang Noir. The savior of us all?" Her tone dripped sarcasm, but it was a valid question. Surely such a powerful witch could dispatch a demon without so much as blinking.

Unfiltered pain rocked across Angie's face as she related what had happened with the headmistress in a few short sentences. "Tori has been wounded. A poison."

"What kind of poison?" Freyja touched her niece's shoulder.

Even Lucian could read the bleakness in those dark eyes. "The kind with no antidote." She drew a deep breath. "There's a war coming, but it's not between us. It's against all of us, and even if we put up a united front, we don't have a fighting chance without her. So you have one choice—choose to stand and fight, or hide and die."

THE CURSE AWAKENS

limmers of light swung in and out of Victoria's vision while hot and cold bands of fire and ice riddled her body. Her blood boiled beneath her skin as her consciousness floated in and out. It wanted to escape so badly, but it, too, was trapped, just as she was. Right now, things seemed normal, but she knew that her hold on reality was tenuous. Pan's toxin was slowly erasing any ability to control her own mind. And soon, she would slip away entirely.

Perhaps this was the best way for her—and the curse—to die. So many coveted her power—even those she had trusted, those who had taken oaths to defend the Witch Clans like Madame Starke. She would always have enemies.

"Tori," a soft voice said as gentle fingers stroked her jaw.

She pulled what little strength she had left to focus on that sonorous sound. Her lips formed his name. "Christian."

His face swam into view as did the upper, white-gauzed airy rooms of the temple. She was lying in a bed and he was sitting beside her and locking the clasp of her amulet back into place. They were alone. "My necklace," she managed. "Thank you."

"You are welcome. I know you wouldn't want to be without it."

Victoria nodded and turned her face, pressing her lips to his warm palm. "I'm sorry ... about what happened."

"I know."

She hauled a labored breath into her lungs. "I'm glad it was with you."

"Stop saying your goodbyes," he said, his finger sliding to her chin and forcing her to look at him.

"This is goodbye," she whispered. "And maybe it's for the best. Maybe Pan did me a favor. All this power can't be good. It's a curse, Christian. And I'm tired. I'm so tired of being in control all the time."

"You don't have to be."

"But you see, I do. If I don't, the blood ... will do what it wants without conscience, and I cannot allow that to happen."

"You're strong, Tori."

"But maybe I don't want to be anymore." A hot tear traced a path down her cheek as a wave of fatigued rolled its way through her. "I need to say goodbye now while I'm me ... while I know *you*."

Pain rocked her to her core as she stared at his silent, handsome face, memorizing every last detail of it from the slope of his cheekbones to the rise of his upper lip and the straight arch of his brow. His eyes were storm gray, the black ring around them almost invisible. She lifted a hand and drew a finger across that unsmiling mouth. The poison would make her forget she knew, but for right now, she devoured everything about him.

"Will you tell Holly that I love her? And Leto ... I don't know where he is." Something zinged in her conscious at the thought of the familiar. He'd been missing for weeks. She'd know if he were dead. *Wouldn't she?* "Do you think that demon killed him?"

"No."

"How do you know?"

"Because he's here."

She frowned, hot white lights appearing behind her eyelids. "Why can't I sense him?"

"You're weak, Tori," Christian said. "But you need to hold on. Pan is cooperating and we will have a remedy in no time."

She eyed him with a wan smile. "You never could lie to me."

Christian grasped her shoulders, enfolding her into his arms. "Damn it, Tori, I need you to fight. Not give up. Heal yourself, do something. *Anything.*"

She inhaled his scent, sealing her lips to the cool skin of his neck. "Did you know that I loved you from the first moment I saw you? Love at first sight when you crashed into me at registration an eternity ago. No one else has ever made my heart scatter the way you do." She parted her lips and tasted the sweetness of him, hearing his indrawn breath and feeling powerful. "I didn't care that you were a vampire because I was already so far in love with you that it wouldn't have mattered *what* you were. And when we were together, it felt so *right*. More right than anything. I'm so sorry for what I did and the things I said. If I could go back in time, I would. Forgive me?"

"Of course I forgive you."

He turned his face then and she kissed him, settling her lips to his with single-minded purpose. Her mouth slanted sideways, drawing his tongue into her mouth and sucking on his lower lip. She wanted to remember the way he tasted, the velvety feel of his tongue rubbing against hers, the way his kiss made deep tremors shoot to her breasts and between her hips. Christian made her feel alive. He made her feel anchored to his strength. After an eternity, they broke apart. Victoria felt dizzy, but in a good way. Truth was, kissing him felt more normal than anything else had. Perhaps it was an after effect of Pan's toxin, but the second her lips left his, the panic started to set in.

A sharp rap on the door interrupted them. Leto sauntered

in, his gray coat looking patchy and worn. Victoria hardly recognized him. His green eyes lacked their usual luster and an odd darkness hung over him.

"I'll give you two a minute and then you should get some rest," Christian told her, pressing a kiss to her forehead before exiting the room. She wanted to tell him to stay, but she needed to talk to Leto alone.

Where have you been all these weeks?

He licked a paw and proceeded to wash his face as if she weren't sitting in a bed dying. *Around.*

Around? she repeated. *That's all you have to say.*

What do you want me to say?

Victoria narrowed her eyes at the feline. It looked like Leto, and sounded like him, but something didn't strike right. "Who are you?" she whispered aloud.

Leto. Your familiar. He loped to the side of the bed and peered up at her. *You really do not look good.* He cocked his head to the side, his green eyes penetrating. *You know, there is something you can do.*

"What's that?" she asked, a foreboding filling the pit of her stomach. She knew even before he said the words what he was suggesting.

Invoke the blood magic.

"I cannot." Her insides twisted in horror at his cavalier proposal.

You can.

Leto hopped up on the bed and Victoria fought an instinctive urge to recoil. Something about the cat seemed dangerous. It was *him*, but it wasn't him. Her head ached with confusion. The toxin made it difficult to think clearly—perhaps it was that addling her brain and making her believe that Leto was the enemy.

Do you know the entire story of the Cruentus Curse, Victoria?

She recalled fragments from her conversation with the high

priestess—that her blood was demon blood. The thought made her shiver. "Yes, Aliya told me."

Your blood is very powerful.

"It's evil."

Evil is a state of consciousness. It is power, nothing more. And your blood belongs to me. Why do you think I went to such ends to see you this way? It was easy to convince the Janusite to concoct his poison.

"What?" The floor disappeared from beneath her, and Victoria felt the terrible sensation of tumbling backward without anything to break her fall. She fought to catch her breath as Leto's calm words made shivers erupt all over her. Leto—her protector—had been behind what had happened with Pan? "You made him do it? Why?"

He wasn't too hard to convince. He nodded. *And I knew that you would be the only one who could stop me.*

Victoria gaped at him. She frowned, blinking as he drew closer, his weight making the mattress dip. He seemed bigger than she remembered. His fur was matted and almost gone in patches as if something had attacked and torn his hide. She met his eyes and shrank back at what shimmered there. Something rippled in the periphery of her eyesight, and for an instant, she had a vision of something large and hulking. Whatever this cat was, it wasn't Leto. It was something else.

"Leto?"

One of my many names, yes.

"Who are you?" she whispered, but god help her, she already knew. The pieces fell together like building blocks of something monstrous—a possibility that drained the blood from her body and the breath from her lungs. It all stemmed from the one question he'd asked about whether she knew of the true story of the Cruentus Curse. "You're the demon who took Thaia, the mother of the first Cruentus Curse witch."

Something that looked like misery flashed in those dull

green eyes staring steadily back at her. *Her* eyes ... the ones she'd inherited from him. She felt sick to her stomach.

Cursed to walk this plane for eternity to watch over my progeny. He bowed his head slightly. *And might I say, you are the most promising of them all.*

"Where's Leto? What have you done to him?"

I am Leto, but I am also me.

"How?" she breathed.

You see, I wondered the same thing at first. Bits of my own consciousness started returning after the torture spells your friend Gabriel performed, cracking through the curse that has bound me for millennia. Not what he intended, I assume, but fortunate for me none-theless. Circe's bonds grew weaker the more powerful I became.

"By taking innocent lives."

Not all innocent and a necessary sacrifice. He made a grimace, one that only looked odd on his cat face. *I only wish to return home. With you, my daughter, at my side where you belong.*

"I'm not going anywhere with you."

And how pray tell are you going to do that? You have no power and the curse will bend to me, its only true master. The boy's poison was a brilliant touch; I'll give him that. He has ambition. Leto blinked. *Perhaps I shall spare him if the vampires don't tear him to pieces.* He licked his lips at the prospect, making Victoria's blood curdle. His stare returned to her. *Now do what you were born to do. Invoke the blood magic.*

"No."

He advanced toward her and Victoria drew her knees up as if to ward him off. She could barely move her own body, much less keep her thoughts straight. But she knew she had to stop him. If he made her summon the blood magic, there was no telling what it would do. It would take power wherever it could find it—which meant all the innocent witches in the temple or any life within a five-mile radius. Her blood would be ravenous. Uncontrollable.

The blood rushed in her veins as if sensing that freedom was imminent and Victoria gritted her teeth. Her strength came and went in waves. Leto lurched toward her and she cried out, kicking with all her might. She caught him in the belly, but he came at her again with a growl. This time, she caught him squarely in the face, and her vision started to blur as the demon took corporeal shape. Its red eyes focused on her, its scaly hide visible in the haze. Bile pooled in her throat.

"Don't do this."

I need to do this. Your blood must bend to me and it can only do so free of your control.

"It will kill people without conscience."

Yes.

"Please," she begged. "I don't want to be responsible for genocide. I'd rather die."

This is what you were born for, Victoria. You are a witch queen. Your destiny is to rule. These creatures mean nothing to you. All they covet is your power. You should have no loyalty to them—they will all betray you.

She thought of Christian. "Not all of them."

Your vampire? he scoffed, reading her thoughts. *He only keeps you close so that he will have you at his side and no one else's.* The cat shot her a sly look. *He's more powerful now because of you. Because of your blood. The blood magic is what made his powers appear.*

"I gave him my blood to save him!"

Or perhaps that was what he wanted all along.

"No. He would never do that."

Demon Leto hissed, making the hairs on the back of her neck stand at stiff attention. *I grow weary of this conversation. Invoke the blood or I shall do it for you.*

Victoria set her lips and shook her head. She still had one weapon at her disposal. She opened her mouth, but the spell was lodged in her throat as if the blood, too, was against her. The shifting demon version of Leto eyed her, watching and grinning as she choked on her own breath. He extended his paw forward and raked a stinging path down her calf. Victoria's entire body sagged backward as the blood welled along the four channels, its color blackly red and luminescent.

"No," she whispered, feeling something dark and hot consume her insides. But it was too late. Blood magic suffused her veins, racing along her limbs like an inferno. She fought valiantly to control it, but it resisted and she was weak … so weak. The blood magic filled her to bursting, consuming her every conscious thought until all she could think about was her hunger. She'd told Christian once that she was the vampire, but she was wrong. She was something far worse.

Demon Leto prowled toward her and she didn't have one iota of willpower left. He would teleport her away, where she'd be the cause of untold destruction, just as her ancestor Brigid had been. She'd taken her own life in an effort to subdue the blood magic, and Victoria vowed to find a way to do the same if push came to shove. Her fingers clawed the bed sheets, her body arching with brutal force as her blood fought Pan's toxin. Once it was free, it would consume magic from every possible source. One thing she'd learned over the last year was that her blood would do anything—short of killing her—to survive.

Suddenly, with a strangled breath, she grasped the amulet Christian had placed at her throat. She didn't stop to think of the cost, only that she had seconds before her own will was overpowered. The amulet's magic slammed into her like a tangible force as she invoked its stored power.

"EXPELLO!"

Shock hung over Leto's features even as his shape started to crumble and wane as the banishment charm took hold. Victoria had no idea where she was sending him, only that she wanted him far away from her. She could barely hold on as it was. At the last minute, she focused on the château in Fontainebleau. It was the only safe place she could think of.

Victoria, what are you doing?

"What I should have done from the start."

The amulet will not protect you from me. The rest of his words faded as he disappeared from view. The last thing she saw were those green eyes delving deep into the marrow of her soul.

Victoria fell back onto the bed, drained. She took a deep breath and dragged herself to the side. She wasn't finished. She forced her legs to bear the weight of her body, grinding her teeth together with such force that her entire skull ached. Pain was good. Pain meant that she was still in control. Pushing each foot one step in front of the other with the help of the amulet, she reached the door. Hundreds of dragging steps later, she reached the main receiving room. Two young witches rushed forward.

"No," she rasped. "Don't touch me." They recoiled at the growl in her voice, but Victoria didn't care. She wasn't sure how much power was left in the amulet, but she didn't trust herself not to drain the two of them to nothing. The scent of them was too appealing. She wanted to absorb every ounce of their magic. She licked her lips and focused. "Where? Aliya?"

One of the girls pointed toward two large doors and Victoria made her way across the room. Several other witches appeared, but they, too, gave her a wide berth. Victoria was aware of how she must look, dressed in bloodstained white nightclothes, black streaks coloring the length of one leg. She hoped it frightened them—they needed to run.

She drew a shuddering breath at the door before pushing it open. The sight that greeted her was a shock—all the leaders of the major otherworldly factions were convened in the massive hall. Vampires, witches, warlocks, werewolves . Christian stood at the front along with Aliya, Freyja, Angie, and others Victoria did not recognize. Lucian was there too, she noted with distaste, with the ever icy Lena at his side.

Their eyes converged on her as her will struggled to control the rampant desires of her blood. Coming here had been a mistake—there was so much power in this room that the feel of it drugged her senses, made her delirious. She slid along the cool, smooth wood, her mind collapsing onto itself with want. Digging her nails into her palms, she focused on the blossoming pain.

"Tori?" Christian was at her side in an instant. "What's wrong? Why are you covered in—?" He pulled away, his nostrils flaring at the scent and sight of her blood. The other vampires in the room shifted, the tension skyrocketing.

Angie raced toward her without fear for her own safety, her eyes wide as she saw what only she could see. Her friend grasped her shoulders and Victoria slumped forward into the embrace. "Pan's here," Angie said. "Christian compelled him to fix a counter potion."

"It's too late," Victoria whispered. "He only wanted me weak enough to invoke the blood magic."

"Pan?" Christian and Angie said in unison.

"Leto."

Christian exhaled. "*Leto?*"

She raised heavy eyes to them. "He's the demon. He's the creator of the Cruentus Curse, trapped in a cat's body for millennia."

"You're not making sense, Tori," Angie said. "Leto is your familiar."

"Leto is a demon."

Aliya joined them, nodding with slow understanding. "According to the Cruentus Curse legends, part of the Goddess Mother's curse was for the demon to serve his descendants until the end of time. We assumed that was in spirit or it was a part of the story that had become myth instead of truth." She shook herself. "I should have guessed. My familiar, Dante, sensed that Leto was an Ancient, only he isn't the familiar successor of a witch queen. He is so much more than that."

"No one could have known," Victoria said weakly. "I used the amulet's power to banish him to the château, but not before he invoked the blood magic. No one's safe."

Angie sucked in a breath, her eyes unfocusing as she used her special sight. "Tori, your aura is going all black and blotchy again."

"What does that mean?" Freyja asked from behind them.

"It's beyond bad," Angie whispered, wide-eyed. "The curse has been invoked and it's taking over everything that is *her*."

"The curse?" Freyja gasped.

Angie nodded. "I saw it possess Christian once, and now it's trying to do the same to her. With the effects of the neural toxin on Tori's control, it has a chance."

"What do you mean by *possess*?"

Christian answered Freyja's question. "Victoria's blood has a mind of its own, and it is consumed by a lust for power and its own immortality. Put simply, the blood magic is a beast that she must keep caged, and now that her mastery over it has been compromised, the beast is free."

Angie's eyes turned upward as the stone walls of the temple started to rattle. It felt like an earthquake was erupting beneath them, but Victoria knew that it was far more than that. It was by sheer force of will that she didn't kill the people standing around her, but a half dozen witches, three vampires, and a warlock near the entrance collapsed, their figures drained to empty husks. The stolen magic surged into Victoria's body like the purest drug. The high was exhilarating. *Consuming.* And heaven help her, she wanted more.

"Get. Everyone. Out. Of. Here." Victoria's words came in a violent staccato as if she could barely control her lips. Her eyes lifted to Christian's, tears pouring from them. "Take … me home."

Christian nodded to Aliya and the rest of the people behind him. "Do as she says," he said before scooping Victoria into his arms. "Get the younglings to safety and rally anyone you can. The demon is at Fontainebleau. I'll take her."

Lucian's voice cut through the fog of the panicked chatter. "Christian, what you are doing is suicide. She will kill you."

"If that is my fate, then so be it. My life has always been bound to hers."

THE RULES OF SURVIVAL

Christian held Victoria close as they flew through the night sky. She felt so fragile in his arms, but he knew that the power within her slim frame was capable of destroying the entire world around them. Her skin was cold, her fingers clasped in a death grip around her amulet. The scent of her blood was maddening. He knew he could resist her, but this was different. This was the same blood that had called to him, that had seduced him months before without a qualm. It was like an old lover offering herself and he could barely resist its siren song. Christian's teeth grazed against his lower lip, and for the first time in weeks, hunger speared his insides with violent irascible touches.

"What are you going to do?" he asked close-lipped as they alighted on the lush manicured gardens of Fontainebleau.

Victoria's fierce eyes were like pieces of onyx in the shifting moonlight at odds with the shaky tenor of her voice. "I'm going to kill it."

"You can't do that alone."

She blinked, her hands gripping his as she fought for balance. "The demon only wants me."

Christian shook his head, frowning. "I don't understand."

"He wants me to do what I was born to do. Take the power around me and feed it to him so that he can become strong. He was afraid of me ... that's why he made Pan do what he did so that he could control the blood magic."

"Why?"

"Because I'm the only one who can stop him." She drew a shaky breath. "Who could have stopped him. Now my blood no longer answers to me—it bends to his command."

Christian grabbed her by the shoulders, his fingers skimming down the softness of her bare arms. She was so cold, too cold. "You're too weak. I can see what the blood magic is doing to you—it's eating you alive."

"I can do this, Christian," she said. "I have to do this."

"How?"

She didn't answer him. Instead she knelt at his feet and placed her hands flat on the grass. Her eyes met his and he realized what she was going to do. "PROTECTUM," she whispered in his direction. The dark magic at his core responded to the power of the shield spell even as the grass at her fingertips faded to a rusty brown. The circle of death widened, sparing him because of her protection spell, as Victoria leached the life from around them. Trees wilted and withered before his very eyes. He could feel the life around him dying as she absorbed their living energies.

After several long minutes, Victoria stood. Her skin pulsed with stolen energy and her eyes were the color of gleaming jade. It almost scared him how easily she could take power from other living things to satisfy the insatiable thirst of the blood magic. She stepped toward him, the air about her crackling with electricity.

Christian felt something surge in his body. Even surrounded by the field of destruction she had created, she had never looked more beautiful. Or desirable. Her face was flushed, her blood rushing beneath the surface, its scent subtle and tantalizing. His teeth elongated in automatic visceral response as other parts of him lengthened, too. Embarrassed by the heated response of his body, Christian inhaled sharply, fighting to rein himself under control. It was a losing battle, especially when she closed the distance between them and plied the length of her body against his. Paralyzed, he held his breath, unwilling to tempt fate.

But Victoria had no such compunction. Her gaze captured his as if she felt the inexorable pull between them, too. Her free hand slid down the bunched muscle of his back to the rise of his buttocks. She kneaded gently, drawing him even closer to the heat of her own body. It made him think of thoughts he'd banished—thoughts of her lying half clothed in his bed. He closed his eyes, his shameless thoughts agonizing. Her hand slid around his hips to the front of his trousers.

"What are you doing?" he gritted, his jaw clenched.

The melting look in her eyes was his undoing even before she spoke, her voice husky with want. "Kiss me, Christian."

His brows snapped together with confused restraint. "Kiss you now?"

"Yes." The word was a growl as she grabbed the lapels of his coat and dragged his head down to hers. He sheathed his teeth, keeping his lips closed, but Victoria would have none of it. Her tongue pushed past them and forced his mouth open. And Christian was lost in the taste of her, the silky feel of her. His tongue slid against hers, their lips grinding together. The tips of his teeth grazed the inside of her mouth and he held his breath. It wouldn't take much to break the fragile skin and one drop of blood was all it would take to reduce him to a slave. She sighed against his mouth as if she knew exactly what he was thinking.

He pulled away, knowing he was losing her by the second. He could see flashes of the girl he knew in her eyes. "Tori—"

"I can control it, Christian. I'm already stronger from the magic—" Her voice faltered as if the thought of where she'd obtained the strength was too distressing to bear. "And Pan's toxin won't last much longer."

"Take whatever dark magic I have. Use it." Christian knew it was a gamble offering it to her, but he'd meant what he said—every last breath within him belonged to her and her alone.

"I'd hurt you." She shook her head. "No, I can't risk it."

"You won't."

"How do you know?" she whispered.

"Because I trust you," he said. "And I told you once that my life was yours. It still is and now you need it more than I do. I love you, Victoria. Now do what you need to do. Or else I will be forced to do something rash like attempt to drain your blood to keep it from harming you."

She didn't answer, but her eyes went wide with alarm. She, too, knew what her blood was capable of when it had possessed him before. After a long, charged moment, she leaned up to press a whisper soft kiss on his lips. Her eyes never left his. But he could feel the moment she started to absorb his energy. Pinpricks of burning light prickled his skin. He felt weightless and suspended, as if caught in a magnetic field, and he could feel his strength diminishing with each passing second. Her green eyes widened as his dark magic filled her. Christian's body felt sapped as she drew her lips from his with an indrawn gasp. Wild and unhinged, his hunger returned in full force. His earlier lust was eclipsed by a need for blood and only blood.

"Is that better?" he gasped, falling to one knee, and stared at the ground. The hunger clawed at him, making him see red. The smell of her was torture, and Christian realized that if he so much as looked at her, he would rip her throat out. "Do you still feel weak?"

The woman in front of him laughed, the humorless sound brittle in the silence, and it made his stomach clench. "This host may be weak, but I am not, Your Grace."

"Tori?" He frowned, but by the time he looked up, Victoria

had already gone. He was alone. And ravenous. Christian loped into the surrounding forest with a single deadly intent—to feed.

Ten mindless minutes later, he wasn't sure how much he'd consumed or how far he'd run, only that the dull insistent throb in his throat had finally disappeared. Sated, his senses sharpened with acute awareness. Christian knelt, placing his hands onto the damp earth of the Fontainebleau forest, letting the rich soil crumble through his fingers. He'd raced far beyond Victoria's sphere of devastation, deep into the wood. He could hear the chatter of night animals, feel the pulse of life beneath and around him. The magic of the night called to him, and for a moment, he let himself be cradled in its embrace.

"Christian?" The voice was shocked.

He looked up to find his brother and Lena standing there watching him. Christian stood, feeling the life force of fresh blood coursing through his veins. For the first time, he noticed the grounded fear in both their gazes and frowned. "What is it?"

But they didn't have to answer as his eyes took in what lay before him. Dead carcasses of every possible animal littered the forest floor, the landscape a bloody tableau—one far worse than Victoria's brown canvas. How many had he killed? Despair struck him with the raw edge of its blade. The death toll sickened him, and he was the only one to blame. He had allowed this to happen.

David had cautioned that his hunger would be uncontrollable if he let it get too deep, and when Victoria had taken his energy, she had sapped him to the very bare bones of his humanity. His single grateful thought was that he'd been alone in the forest instead of in the middle of Paris. The body count would have been same, only it would have had a far different outcome. Raw power coursed through him and he flexed his arms, feeling its tensile strength as replenished dark magic shivered along the inside of his skin. Every inch of him felt *alive*.

"Are you okay?" Lucian asked.

"Fine." Christian shook away the remnants of self-disgust and met his brother's eyes. There was something in there he'd never seen before—a measure of respect. It surprised him. Lucian's expression where he was concerned was primarily loathing. Lucian stepped forward and handed him his signet ring, which he placed on his finger with a nod. A third figure stood in the shrouded darkness, whom he hadn't noticed, likely because she hadn't posed a threat. Angie. "Where are the others?"

"They have come en masse."

"Have you seen Victoria?" he asked, even though he knew she was close. He could feel the pull of her like the barest brush against his senses. His brother shook his head. Christian's gaze slid to Angie, who stood beside Lena. He didn't bother to disguise his surprise.

Lucian quirked an eyebrow at his unspoken question. "She impressed me."

"She tends to do that," Christian agreed, remembering that it had been Angie who had come to him with Victoria's where-abouts last year. Her courage had saved them all. She met his stare with an even one of her own. "Are you okay?" he asked her.

"Are *you*?"

"I think so. What do you see?"

She cocked her head as her irises unfocused. "I see power." Her eyes widened. "And magic. So many tendrils of it, tethering you to the earth and to the shadow."

"Am I strong enough?"

She stared at him. "To face Tori?" He nodded, and Angie frowned. "I don't know. You're strong, but there's still a part of her in you. I can still see it—webs of stringy black slith-ering just below the surface." Her gaze slammed into him as if she belatedly realized why he was asking the question. "Why?"

Christian cleared his throat. "If she becomes lost to the curse, I will be the only one who can retrieve her."

"She'll kill you."

"I've heard that before," he said with a crooked smile. "Shall we?"

Angie hefted her crossbow. "We follow you, Your Grace."

†††

VICTORIA ENTERED the dungeons of the château, following the tingling in the pit of her stomach. Cool, stale air rushed against her face along with the smell of long decayed death. Leto had passed through here. She could see the malevolent taint of him like little breadcrumbs left behind for her to find. He knew she would follow, after all.

Her body felt tight and coiled, bursting with the power she had stolen … and been given. Christian's magic had shocked her —he had grown more powerful than she had guessed. But he was the descendant of a Reii. She'd had an inkling of what that meant, but until she had drawn his energy into herself, she hadn't truly known. Christian was stronger than strong. As a vampire, he had superhuman gifts—ones that made him a fearsome predator and a force to be reckoned with. As a Reii, his powers superseded those and more. She shook her head. She'd always been a little bit afraid that she could hurt him, but now she thought that maybe they would have a chance.

If she didn't die.

He'd told her that he still loved her, but impending doom had a way of making you say things that you wouldn't say in ordinary circumstances. She had told him the truth. She'd give anything to take back the choice she'd made … and choose to stay with him instead of being afraid. In the end, the very people she'd put ahead of him had betrayed her. Lost in her own insecurities, she'd fallen prey to Madame Starke's lies.

Victoria stopped at a point where two tunnels broke off from the main passageway and closed her eyes. The air was thick and musty. She focused her energy on Leto's essence and chose the right-most corridor. It was the narrower of the two and seemed to suck the darkness toward it. As a precaution, she removed the amulet from her neck and placed it upon a nearby stone ledge. She knew it was a risk facing Leto without it, but it was also her only way out if things went bad. Heaving a deep breath, she ducked and took tentative steps into the space.

"Illustro," she murmured and a ball of light flickered to life in the center of her palm. Smears of what looked like caked blood covered the cobwebbed walls. Despite herself, she shivered. Monsters, she could handle. Vampires, no problem. But spiders were part of a whole other universe of nasty.

The skin on the back of her neck tingled as a webbed skein caught against her collar and she fought to keep from gagging. The spiders down here wouldn't be small either. They'd be monstrous. As if on cue, something skittered at her feet and she throttled the scream in her throat.

"Focus," she hissed to herself. Spiders should be the last of her worries. She should be worrying about the rogue demon lord that was the father of the Cruentus Curse—the one who had possessed her familiar's body and been trapped within it for millennia. He was still bound by his corporeal feline form, which meant that his power was not at its peak. But that would not last long. He'd slaughtered hundreds of supernatural creatures over the past few months, absorbing their energy and growing stronger with each kill.

Gabriel had unwittingly fragmented the curse when he'd tortured Leto last year, and since then, the demon within had been fighting to break loose. And to do that, he needed power—

lots and lots of otherworldly power. Sure, he could have taken it from humans—they had magic, too, in minuscule amounts—but when a dozen humans equated to one supernatural creature, he'd chosen to go for quality rather than quantity. It'd been a relief to Victoria that he hadn't opted to kill people. The death toll would have been staggering and would have drawn more attention from the humans than they could handle. And fear drove people—even supernatural ones—to do reckless things.

The blood surged beneath her skin. It resisted her control, testing her will for weaknesses like a beast trapped within a cage. It was responding to the presence of its true father—the blood was part of his, after all.

And part moon priestess, a voice reminded her. The mother of the blood curse had been a powerful witch in her own right and one of the Goddess Mother's own handmaidens. The demon had stolen Thaia from this world and condemned her progeny to a life of horror and pain, one shadowed by the darkness of his blood. Victoria remembered what Aliya had told her, that the Goddess Mother had deemed their child an abomination and had condemned her to death. Circe couldn't bear the thought of killing her own granddaughter and had hidden her away from the Goddess Mother, trying—futilely—to bind the girl's powers.

Leto had said he wanted to return to his demon dimension and take her with him. Victoria would die before she let that happen. But best of all, she vowed that she would use the very powers he had given her to destroy him.

"I know you're down here," she called out. "Show yourself."

The faint echo of mocking laughter reached her as the passageway finally widened into a cavernous room. She stretched to full height, feeling the weight of fresh air on her face, and frowned. It wasn't so musty anymore and she could feel dampness seeping from the crumbling walls around her. She'd lost her bearings with all the twists and turns of the underground tunnels, but at some point the ground had started to shift upward. Her gaze narrowed at a change in the light at the far end of the space. Was there an exit point leading outside? Into the forest, maybe?

But before she could reorient herself, something slid out of the murky shadows—the same half-cat, half-hulking creature that she'd seen.

"You bring me gifts," demon Leto said in a conversational tone.

The shock of his guttural voice was like a physical blow. Leto had never spoken. His words had always been mental. She shook it off and focused her power to her core. She'd need every ounce of strength she had if she was going to best him. She eyed him, watching his form shifting into solid mass and then retreating into shadow. It made it hard to look at him—a monstrous amalgamation of the cat she knew and loved and a formidable demon that only cared for its own survival. "Why are you doing this?"

"I told you," he said. "I want to return to my home."

"I won't go with you."

"You do not have a choice," demon Leto growled. "If you stay here, the Vardlokkur will do what they have been tasked to do."

Victoria frowned—she did not recognize the word. "The what?"

"What your people call warlocks."

"The warlocks have been tasked to kill me?" She laughed, the sound echoing off the walls. "The warlocks are not out for the good of mankind, trust me. Gabriel was a warlock and he wanted the curse for his own gain."

"There are always stray sheep to every flock."

"The warlocks are evil."

Demon Leto pinned her with an intelligent green gaze that made her think of her many debates with Leto the cat. "As are humans, vampires, witches. No one race is pure. They all bear the stain of the very first one to fall from the grace of the heavens."

"They consort with demons," she seethed, power racing along her limbs and crackling across her fingers. She sensed that he was toying with her.

"I'd hardly call summoning consorting. But yes, they will use their power over my race to bind your very real demon blood. And then they will kill you. We do not belong here. You do not belong here. That is their call to arms as the guardians to the portals between the dimensions, Tori."

"Don't call me that!" she snapped.

"As you wish, *Victoria*," he mocked. Demon Leto shifted forward and she automatically tensed. "Regardless, your time here on this plane is over. You belong with me. So now that we are done with pleasantries, why don't you give me what I want? Release the curse and free me from this prison of fur and bones. Do your duty, daughter."

Her lips pulled back in a disgusted sneer. "I am no daughter of yours."

"Shall we put that to the test?" He smiled and murmured two words. "Cruentus effero."

She frowned at the summoning charm that had fallen from his lips and braced herself for a secondary attack, but none came. Instead, demon Leto stared steadily at her, and the minute her eyes locked with his, something started happening. Her blood pushed against the surface of her skin, shoving her toward him with mystical force. She fought it with everything she had, but the pull was inexorable. *Inescapable.*

She only came to a stop when she was directly in front of him. She would have preferred to be where she'd been standing before. Now, this close, she could see the green mottled color of the demon's skin beneath Leto's ragged fur and smell the cloying scent seeping from his pores. She was surprised. She'd expected something far more foul. Victoria peered at the demon

—and was shocked to see that it looked vaguely human in features. The sight of the handsome, if stringent, male face made her blood crawl.

The demon lifted a scaly talon and dragged it down her cheek. Victoria didn't have to look in a mirror to know that the touch had welled blood in its wake. "Even buried within the familiar's consciousness, I watched all the others, you know," he told her. "But none were like you. None had your courage. Your daring. Your fearlessness. Deep down, I knew you would be the one to liberate me."

"But Gabriel—" she blurted out.

"It was easy to suggest the kind of spells needed to crack the Goddess Mother's bindings to him." At the look on her face, he shrugged. "Don't feel sorry for him. Trust me, he enjoyed every second of inflicting such pain. Those spells were not for the faint of heart, and your friend was cut from a fetid cloth." His grip slid to her shoulder. "Now, come, give me what you have. We have a long night ahead of us. It will be enough to break the last of the bonds, but I will be weak in my true form."

"How many will have to die?" she asked in a weak voice.

"As many as it takes."

Her stomach clenched. "Do you truly relish taking all those lives?"

"Relish? No. Require it? Yes. I *require* their souls to sustain my existence and my endurance."

"Why don't you just give up and die and be done with it?" she scoffed, trying to come up with a plan that didn't lead to the loss of tens of thousands of innocent lives.

His breath feathered into her face, his claws digging into the soft flesh of her arm, the slight stinging tell her that he had drawn blood there, too. "Survival instinct? And to right the fact that I was wronged."

"Wronged?"

"Thaia chose to stay with me."

Her sneer was shaky this time. "You coerced her."

"A powerful moon priestess?" he returned evenly. "She could have left in an instant. No, my child, she chose to stay."

"With *you*?"

He stared at her, that gaze of his compelling and intense. "Some of us choose to love those that others deem to be monsters. You, after all, should know all about that."

"Christian is nothing like you," she whispered.

"Isn't he?" he said as a scaled talon raked across the tender skin of her shoulder. "He takes life from others to live. People fear him. He, too, is trapped by his own immortality. I think we are more alike than you'd care to admit."

The demon's words made her blood boil. Or maybe he intended to incite her anger. She stared him down, refusing to even dignify what he'd said with a response. Christian didn't murder innocents—he took blood judiciously if and when he needed it. Victoria frowned as something occurred to her. The demon had said that once he broke free of his corporeal bindings he would be weak. That would be her chance ... her opportunity. She'd give him what he wanted for now, and when he was least expecting it, she would do what she was meant to do.

She would give him the liberty he craved.

BLOOD WITCH

"Okay," she agreed. "Take what power I have."

Demon Leto smiled then, one that crept beneath her bravado and slunk into her heart. She could see a reptilian sheen cast over his deceptively human face. Even in demon form, he bore an odd resemblance to her, and it made her stomach turn. The look in his eyes made her worried that she hadn't thought of something. She knew that she'd be weak, too, once the transfer was complete, but she was hoping that Christian and the others would be waiting to take advantage of the windfall.

She pushed her energy out, reaching for him. *Christian?*

"He can't hear you."

"And you can?" she shot back, her gaze slanting to his.

"My blood tells me everything." His words made her blood run cold as the demon looked up toward where the shadows started to merge into dimly lit speckled moonlight. "But your lover is close. Spoils for the taking once I am released. Now come, daughter. Let us begin."

Demon Leto's fingers closed around her throat, and Victoria felt her breath catch, a feeling of foreboding filling her. There

284

was something she hadn't thought of, only it kept eluding her. She blinked, forcing herself to remain calm. Christian had rallied everyone. They were ready. They *had* to be ready or all would be lost. Once demon Leto assumed his true form, he would consume the life of every creature within a certain radius. It wouldn't matter—human or supernatural—it would be a purge that no one would see coming.

The demon drew her close. For once, her blood wasn't surging within her like a wild wave, desperate to defend itself from harm. It no longer needed to protect her, not when it was being commanded by someone else. No, instead, it trilled with delight as if it, too, was finally going home. Victoria hauled a strangled breath into her lungs and swallowed her revulsion as the creature pulled her to him until they were nearly nose-to-nose.

Intense green eyes bored into hers, heat blooming across every inch of her skin as the magic coursed into a frenzy. Her breath slowed to shallow gasps as she felt the blood magic inside of her start to coalesce. It pushed to her center and then up her throat. It felt as if her very soul was being sucked through her body into her skull. And then the expulsion started.

Her mouth opened in a soundless scream. Victoria's entire body convulsed, rocked by spasms that shook her from head to toe as every last ounce of her power was drained from her body into the demon standing before her. Disoriented, she slumped onto her heels, feeling as if her bones had been liquefied. Her entire body felt like it was made of nothing but air, and her mind became filled with imaginary bees. A dull, buzzing sound filled her head. It hurt to think ... to even open her eyes, but she forced herself to focus on Leto.

Flashes of light burst from his body as he, too, staggered backward. Black bands of iridescent magic swirled around him, faster and faster, until it was blinding. The frenetic movements made her feel nauseated and bile pooled in her throat as she pushed herself to her knees, her body swaying unsteadily. No wonder he hadn't been threatened when she'd given in so easily —she could barely think past the mush in her brain.

Suddenly, the cavern grew bright as if the sun itself had appeared between them. Only there was no sun—it was the sight of a curse being broken. Victoria shielded her eyes, feeling the burst of power hit her like a hot blast. The light winked into darkness, and when she blinked the stars from her vision, all she could see was a form huddled on the ground.

A man's form … one bound to nothing.

Leto was gone.

She fought the urge to shudder, knowing that what lay there was the furthest thing from human, and wished that she had the strength to slip the dagger tucked into her boot into his black heart. But making wishes when you didn't have any magic at your disposal was a useless prospect. Gritting her teeth and grasping the dagger in hand, she willed herself to crawl forward on her hands and knees. Dirt caked beneath her fingernails, but with each grunt, she inched closer. She could do it.

A foot away from his nude, shivering form, the man turned, and Victoria blanched. He had her face. She'd seen the resemblance before, but it was nothing compared to *this*. His dark hair was long and framed a heart-shaped face. Those green eyes, the mirror image of hers, held her captive.

Why didn't he look like a demon?

Instead, he looked as if he could be her father. Her *real* father.

"No," she hissed. She swallowed past the lump in her throat. Her fingers tightened on the dagger. It was now or never—he was weak and she'd never have another chance like this. His eyes flicked to the weapon in her hand and he smiled.

"CRUENTUS FAMULOR," his lips murmured, and Victoria felt her body jerk in response as every remaining drop of blood within her obeyed his command. Her hand holding the dagger trembled as it curved upward, moving toward her own torso. Victoria's eyes widened at the path of the blade, but nothing she did could stall the movement. She was sure he was going to kill her, but a hair's breadth from her chest it stopped.

"We are one now," the man said. "And you are my instrument to control."

Victoria hauled a breath into her aching chest, her gaze never sliding from the dagger's tip at her breast. She pushed forward, a drop of blackly red blood smearing the front of her white bodice as she impaled herself on the unforgiving point of the blade. Pain flowered along her nerve endings, but with it came clarity. "There's one thing you need to learn about me," she said, "I am no one's instrument."

Something like anger flashed in the man's eyes as he stood. She could see the shaking of his limbs even as he drew himself to his full height. He crooked his wrist and a black cloak appeared out of nowhere. He shrugged into it, a spasm of pain shimmering over his features. Victoria frowned. She needed help—she needed Brigid.

"Effero amulet," she whispered, her tongue thick in her mouth. Nothing happened for an extended moment. Suffocating her fear, she repeated the command, her nails digging into her flesh, and after a second, something whizzed through the air. She caught the amulet in her fist and summoned the strength of her ancestor. "Evoco Brigid," she screamed with everything she could muster. "I summon you."

Brigid hadn't failed her yet. Victoria knew that she wouldn't now.

The crystal flared red in her palm as her fist closed around it. Energy stormed toward her as Brigid's full power leapt from the jewel to her body. The crystal crumbled to dust in her hand as her starved body absorbed every last bit of magic Brigid had to offer. *Thank you*, she told her ancestor silently as she stared at the colorless fragments of the pendant.

The amulet was gone and this was her last stand.

Without hesitating, she flung a blast toward the man. It caught him square in the chest, pinning him against the wall. She strode up to him, dragging the dagger from her chest inch by painful inch. Her blood still obeyed him, but her mind was strong. Holding him in place with the force of her will, Victoria fought the blade, twisting it with brute force and pushing her palm against it until it bled. Finally, her hands slick with blood, it was pointed toward him.

"You will never control me," she hissed and slammed the heel of her palm against the dagger's hilt. It smashed into the rippling skin of his rib cage and met steel-like resistance before falling to the floor. He wasn't human, she reminded herself. He may appear to be human, but even now she could see the greenish reptilian cast of his flesh and the imperceptible scales that only *looked* like skin.

Leto was a demon ... and a powerful one.

His face registered no surprise at her failed attack, and to her surprise, Leto laughed. The sound was devoid of any humor. "I expected as much from you. I did not see the amulet coming, but believe me, I shall take great pleasure in consuming Brigid's magic once you learn your place. I can taste it now, along with the pungent tang of your fear." He closed his eyes and licked his lips.

"I am not afraid of you."

"You should be."

Her lips curled back from her teeth. "Why? You are a demon, but I am the product of so much more than you alone. We both know why you felt you had to poison me—it was *you* who was afraid of me. Just as you are now. The scent of your fear reeks to high heaven."

"You confuse fear with respect."

Victoria frowned at the tinge of pride in his voice and leaned close. "Neither of those sentiments will save you."

"Show me."

Maybe it was the condescending tilt of his words, or the apathetic look on his face, but Victoria had a sudden desire to inflict pain. She'd meant to kill him to rid the world of his scourge, but now she wanted to punish him. She wanted him to feel the panic she felt. She wanted him to *fear* her.

"INCENDO MALEFICUS," she said, watching as a yellow-rimmed ball of fire formed between her fingers. It was a spell she'd learned from Gabriel, born of dark magic and evil intentions. She felt it was fitting for the occasion. "Demons deserve to die in hell," she told him as she released the fire. Victoria didn't wait to see the fire engulf him in flames—she shoved both hands forward and focused on magnifying the spell so that the fire fountained from top to bottom in the cave.

She was so intent on burning him to ashes that she didn't realize that her own skin started to blister and peel in sheets from her exposed limbs. She screamed as the cut of a thousand blades whittled across her skin, but when she looked down, she saw nothing. There was no fire touching her. It was at the far end of the cavern, obscuring Leto from view. She frowned and released the spell.

Leto stood there—singed but alive. And watching her, a calculating smirk on his lips.

Victoria stared down at her arms, watching the bubbled and roasted skin there. *Impossible.*

"CURO," she said. Her skin healed and flattened, the redness disappearing. She didn't want to look up to confirm what she already knew, but she had to. Her eyes slid to the man and her breath caught in her throat. He, too, had healed.

"No," she whispered, eyes going wide.

"Yes," he said. "I told you that we are one. You cannot hurt me with magic, no matter how much you want to."

Victoria swallowed, her mind racing. She'd lost the only advantage she had if she couldn't defeat him with magic. He had to have a weakness! What *was* it? If she couldn't overcome him, she needed someone who could. She needed someone who could banish him to his own dimension. She needed the Vardlokkur.

She turned and ran.

†††

"Is that *Tori?*"

The incredulous voice belonged to Angie, but Christian didn't care. His tortured gaze fell on the slim figure running at top speed across the landscaped lawns. His relief was cut short by the second figure not far behind her. It looked like a person, but he was too far away to be certain. He squinted, but his senses tingled like a livewire. That was no man.

"Demon," Freyja said at his side, her thoughts echoing his.

Lucian cleared his throat and frowned. "It doesn't look like the demon that attacked us. Is that its true form?"

"It's the form of choice in this dimension," Freyja said.

"Why doesn't she use her magic and kill it?" Angie grabbed the crossbow at her side and raised it to look through the sights. "He's gaining on her."

Christian frowned. The same thought had occurred to him. Unless … somehow the demon had found a way to inhibit her magic, or even worse, had taken it. A cold sensation unfurled at the base of his spine at the realization—*that* was how the demon had broken free of the curse tying him to the cat familiar. Victoria was running because she had nothing left to fight him with. But if it did have her full power, why would it hesitate to kill them all? Unless it needed her.

His nostrils flared, adrenaline coursing through his body as he turned to give the signal. Supernatural creatures of every persuasion gathered behind him, with Freyja and her army at the fore. Every single Vampire Council member was there, along with Aliya and an enormous contingent of witches. All in all, they totaled nearly a hundred strong. Surely they could take down one rogue demon, or at least distract it enough to give Victoria a chance to escape its clutches.

Christian's gaze fell on his brother. He didn't know what had caused his crisis of conscience or why Lucian was suddenly so solicitous of his wellbeing. His brother's face was blank and so was that of the female at his side. Lena. He had released her as her maker and now her loyalties were tied to Lucian. She'd proven that earlier. Once he'd been able to count on her, but betrayal had a way of undermining centuries of trust. No, his brother had a secondary agenda—Lucian did nothing that did not serve his own interests in some way. He did not trust either of them where Victoria was concerned.

He nodded to David and the other elders—their strength would be needed—and gave the sign. Half of the group melted into the surrounding forest. They would have a better chance of success if they attacked from the rear.

Christian stared at Freyja. "The demon is the target. Get Victoria to safety if you can. Angie, I want you to stay here."

"No!" she argued. "She's my friend and I'm not going to stand here like some useless human."

"You could get kill—"

"You're not the boss of me, Christian Devereux," she said and Christian fought back a grin. "Why don't you worry about what you have to do and let me worry about me? Stop staring at me like I'm nothing but a blood bag—go save my best friend from that lunatic."

Christian shook his head. Angie's courage never failed to impress him. "As you wish, but stay with Lucian." His brother's gaze slammed into his before nodding tightly. Christian hoped that he wasn't putting Angie in danger, but given that she'd arrived at Fontainebleau with Lucian and Lena, keeping them together meant that Angie would be safer and she could keep an eye on Lucian. Angie nodded after a long moment, and Christian sped down the steps as the first wave of the attack began.

The witches' spells bombarded the demon, but he deflected them easily. Some kind of barrier spell around them prevented any of the vampires or werewolves from getting too close. They touched the invisible line and howled in agony, which left the witches and the warlocks as their only line of offense—at least until they could take the demon out and bring down the barricade.

Victoria's arms were waving madly and she was shouting something that he couldn't decipher. Aliya and the other high priestesses redoubled their efforts, their spells exploding like fireworks in the twilight sky, and Leto stumbled. Christian frowned as he noticed Victoria stumble and fall, too. He could feel her agony as if it were his own.

His eyes darted between the two fallen bodies, both struggling to stand, and the understanding was swift and cold. From his vantage point on the garden steps, he could see that they were attacking the demon, but somehow, Victoria seemed to be bearing the brunt of it. No, his eyes had to be deceiving him.

Get up, he willed her. He knew she couldn't hear him—he had tried to communicate mentally with her before and had been unsuccessful.

As if she'd heard him, Victoria dragged herself up, crouching on her hands and knees. She must have gotten hit with a rogue spell and the timing was coincidental. Christian vowed to find the witch or warlock who had hit her and grind his fist into their face. He willed her to move, begging her to get out of the strike zone, but for some reason she wasn't moving.

"Christian!" Angie's scream made his ears ring as she nearly tumbled down the steps in her haste to get to his side. "You have to do something."

He braced his palms against her shoulders, his heart tripping at her terrified expression. "What do you see, Angie?"

"She's dying," she gasped as she tried to describe what she was seeing. "Tori's *dying*. They're connected. You have to stop them. Every attack on that thing is an attack on her. And the blood magic ... it's taking over. Soon there'll be nothing left of her and then ..." She trailed off, horror written all over her. She didn't have to finish what she was saying. He knew only too well what would happen if the blood magic took over. Victoria would cease to exist and history would repeat itself.

All the strength drained from his body as Angie's words sank in—he'd guessed that Victoria and Leto were somehow joined, but he'd refused to consider the possibility. And Angie was never wrong, not with what she saw. Victoria crouched and faced them then, and what Christian saw in her face nearly rocked him to his knees. Rivers of black ran down her cheeks as she wept tears of blood. Her fingers clenched into fists at her sides as her body was wracked with assault after brutal assault.

Without hesitating, he took to the air, flying toward them and shouting at the top of his lungs. "Stop!"

But it was impossible to halt the attack now that the demon was down. The warlocks had started chanting and a portal was solidifying before his eyes. If he didn't get to them first, Freyja would banish the demon and Victoria would be tethered to it. The closer he got, the more powerful the energy field around him became. There was no way he could reach her *and* stop the Vardlokkur's portal. He opted for the portal, tackling Freyja to the ground mid-chant.

She snarled and hurled a blast toward him as the other warlocks surrounded him, fear and mistrust on their faces. He dodged her attack, and out of the corner of his eye, he saw the portal start to fade. "What are you doing, vampire?" Freyja growled.

"She is tethered to the demon."

"Good," Roan said. "Two for the price of one."

Christian gnashed his teeth together. "That was not what we agreed."

Freyja eyed him evenly. "We are not bound to you, vampire. We are bound to our oaths to protect the dimensions. If they are joined as you say, then your witch is as dangerous as he. We cannot take the chance that what happened centuries ago won't happen again. I'm sure I don't have to remind you that that Cruentus witch decimated our kind without even brushing the full resources of her power. She took her own life, but it could have been a hundred times worse. We have a chance to banish the curse once and for all, and I will not let your paltry *feelings* on the matter put millions of innocents at risk."

As if on cue, the ground quaked beneath their feet and all eyes converged on the creature that stood in the midst of a swirling storm of black energy. Victoria was standing, her hands wide and palms to the sky. Blackly red blood streaked her clothing and rimmed her eyes, and for a moment, Christian felt real uncertainty settle in his stomach. The tips of her toes dragged on the grass as the magic held her in thrall.

Suddenly, everything went deadly silent and she eyed those surrounding and crooked a finger. "Come if you dare."

The voice wasn't hers. It was guttural and harsh. Christian recognized it deep within his core, feeling the call of the blood magic. His eyes met Angie's, standing with Lucian so far away, and the tears streaming down her face were her answer. She could see what he so clearly felt.

The blood magic had won.

"Don't!" he yelled, turning to those at his back, but his warning was lost in the shouts as the vampires rushed forward once they realized that the barrier preventing their approach was down. She let the first wave get within inches before a gratified smile stretched across her lips. Flashes of electricity burst around her like exploding light bulbs and Christian felt the energy being sucked out of the air, creating a strange kind of vortex. Whatever it was, it wasn't good.

"Get down!" he shouted, just as a giant blast spread outward from her body, making the ground split apart and the leaves piston off nearby trees. To his horror, those closest to her disintegrated to ash as the magical flare incinerated their bodies. The witches and the warlocks screamed protection spells, but even so, the potency of Victoria's magic forced them to their knees. Christian, too, was thrown to the ground, waves of acid fire raking across his face. He healed in seconds, but others were not so lucky. They screamed in agony as their skin peeled in sheets from their bones.

Black flames surrounded Victoria's body as the electrical storm intensified. The demon at her side stood, feeding off the stolen energy. He smiled, his eyes glittering as his progeny became the thing of legends.

"Do you see?" Freyja hissed. "We have no choice."

Christian shook his head, refusing to believe that Victoria was lost. She was still in there somewhere. "No. Let me try."

"You won't survive," Aliya said, her hand on his arm.

"Maybe," he said. "But I have to try. I promised her that much. I can't give up on her now."

"That's not Victoria, Your Grace. That is a monster."

His smile was bittersweet. "We are all monsters."

Freyja stared at him, compassion flickering in her eyes for a brief second. "You have as long as it takes for us to generate the portal."

Christian nodded, his gaze flicking to his brother standing atop the balustrade with Lena and Angie at his side. He had his arm around Angie as if holding her back from running down onto the field, and for that, Christian was grateful.

Take care of yourself, brother, he said.

Anger threaded Lucian's words. *What are you doing, Christian?*

What I have to do.

Is her life truly worth yours?

Her life is mine. Christian paused. *Je'taime, Luce. Until we meet again.* He hadn't used the childhood nickname in over a century, and something within him cracked as he said his goodbyes to his little brother.

Christian—

But Christian had already started walking forward, cutting off the mental conversation. He needed to be strong and sorrow was something he couldn't afford to let in. He took a deep breath and faced his fate.

THE MIND OF THE MONSTER

As he faced the Cruentus Curse witch in all her dreadful and terrible glory, Christian had no doubt that these could be his last moments on this earth. His faith faltered that Victoria was even in there. There was no recognition on her face, no love in her eyes, nothing of the girl he knew.

The demon at her side eyed his approach, but made no move to stop him. And for a half-beat, Christian hesitated. If Leto believed that Victoria would spare Christian out of whatever residual feelings she had for him, he would have surely intervened. His lack of action meant that he wasn't concerned, which didn't bode well for Christian.

Heat buffeted his face as he approached. It felt like he was walking into a fiery sandstorm, the edges of each sand grain whipping into his exposed skin. Black trails of blood coiled like snakes on her body, and her eyes glittered like chips of onyx.

"What do you want, vampire?" she asked.

"Tori, I know you're in there."

"The girl you seek is gone."

He inched closer as the black flames scorched him. "You

have to stop this. I know you can stop this. You are not like him. There's love and grace and beauty inside of you. You are not this killer."

The witch threw back her head and laughed. "Your sentiments amuse me." Her eyes narrowed on him. "You are familiar to me, which is the only reason I allowed you to approach. I have tasted the inside of your mind and swept through the limbs of your body. But something is different now." She leaned forward, as if scenting him. "You are far more powerful than you were last time we … met."

"Tori—"

"I told you—she is *gone.*" A hot rush of anger made her flames shoot outward, searing his face with its force. Christian fought through the pain and drew from his well of inner strength. His burned skin healed instantly.

He ignored her warning. "I know you're in there, Tori. Please."

"I tire of his whining," Leto interjected, and something clicked within Christian based on his earlier theory of Leto's disinterest.

He stepped forward, bracing for more pain as he settled his hands on her arms. It was like holding burning cinders. "Tori, I love you. I always will. And if need be, I will die at your hands, but you have to stop this. Angie's out there, and Aliya, and many others who continue to stand by you."

"Cease!" the witch screamed, clutching her head as if she were being attacked by an unseen force from within.

"I believe in you, Tori. You control the blood magic, not the other way around. *You* control it."

"Shut up!" she screamed, ripping his hands from her arms and propelling him to the ground. "Excrucio."

The pain spell connected squarely in his chest, robbing him of breath and thought before agony erupted like wildfire along his limbs. He fought against it, subduing it, and lurched toward her only to find Leto blocking his way. Out of the corner of his eye, he could see the portal beginning to take shape. It wouldn't be long, he knew, before it solidified, which meant he had minutes. Or less.

A blast of magic whirred his way and he rolled to the side with inhuman speed. Leto was playing a clever game. He knew that Christian would not attack and risk hurting Victoria, which left him at a distinct disadvantage. Christian dodged a few more attacks, his heart starting to race as the purple of the portal glowed more brightly. He was running out of time and he knew that Freyja would not grace him with any more.

Suddenly, the energy in the air shifted.

"CONFUTO," a voice shouted. The spell was joined by another and another until Leto could not move. Christian spared a glance over his shoulder and saw Aliya deep in concentration. She held hands with each of her high priestesses as they united behind the spell. One by one, all the other remaining witches joined in, focused on the effort of binding the demon. Even the warlocks lent them their strength.

Grateful for their effort, Christian rushed in, uncaring of anything but getting to Victoria. Because of the spell on Leto, she was immobile too. She eyed him, fury flashing in those black eyes as the blood magic fought the restraints. "You think they can hold me?" she snarled. "They are no match for the Cruentus Curse."

"Maybe not, but Victoria is."

"She is *dead.*"

"I don't believe that," Christian said raggedly. *Please, Tori, come back to me.* He chanted the mantra in his head as he pressed his lips to the witch's burning ones. Holding on to her was torture. The pain ripped through his mouth, tearing apart his throat with bladed fire, but still he kept his mouth on hers.

It was a losing battle.

She turned the tables on him, the blood magic sucking his

strength like a ravenous beast. He felt himself failing, growing weaker by the breath in her arms. She was too strong and he had miscalculated the power of the bond between them. He had gambled his life and he knew in no uncertain terms that he would lose.

Tori, please, come back to me.

The chant grew feebler and feebler, but he couldn't stop himself. Victoria had stopped when she had taken his power before, but this witch would not be so inclined. She would drain him to the last drop, until he was nothing but a husk.

Come back to me.

Please.

The plea was shuddering. Soul destroying.

But no response came—Victoria was lost to the blood magic that consumed her.

Christian felt the life force within him ebb. This was it. This was the end. He focused on every memory he had of Victoria and let them fill his head. He wanted to die thinking of her. His eyes shifted to Freyja, who stood on the edge of the circle. He blinked once and she bowed her head in response, deep melancholy in her gaze. She'd wanted to believe in him, but she couldn't take the chance that love wouldn't win out in the end. And it hadn't. The portal flared brightly. Connected to Victoria, he felt its compulsion through her body.

Leto screamed his frustration, struggling against the magical bonds constraining him, and Victoria wrenched her head away. Bright red light surrounded her in a haze as she fought the collective spell. She would break it, he knew. Christian closed his eyes, watching as all three of them were drawn closer to the portal.

"No!" someone shouted. Dully, Christian recognized the scream as Lucian charged in, ripping him from the witch with wild strength. Dazed, Christian staggered backward, his legs like jelly. He flopped like a ragdoll onto the earth as Lucian thrust himself between them.

The witch turned burning eyes on him. "Lord Devereux, is it? How much you look like your brother," she exclaimed, her smile gaping. "But your soul is so much darker, isn't it?" She frowned at him, a knowing grin on her lips. "Why the sudden sacrifice? Surely you don't seek redemption after all this time?"

Lucian smirked. "I am long past redeeming, as you well know. But I welcome death with open arms if it is indeed my time to go."

"Lucian," Christian protested weakly. "What are you doing?"

"Returning the favor," he said with a sardonic twist of his lips. "You saved my life more than once. It's time I do the same."

"Don't be foolish."

"Better a fool than a coward."

The witch laughed. "So touching, but it matters not for you will both die." She reached for Lucian, but he spun out of the way, his claw darting out to rake her side.

"What are you doing?" Christian gasped. "Don't hurt her! It's still Tori."

Lucian set his jaw, compassion visible for a brief moment on his face. "I may not know much, but I do know that pain is the one thing that will loosen the blood magic's hold, brother. Trust me. She's a witch, she'll heal."

He struck again, this time his nails scouring across her middle. Her back arched, her shriek of rage piercing as she twisted to get him in her sights. But Lucian was fast, dodging the spells that flew his way. He crouched and appeared behind her, his eyes meeting Christian's.

"I am sorry for everything—"

Christian stumbled forward, hands outstretched, as he realized what his foolish brother was about to do. "Don't do it, Lucian. It will kill you."

"And you'll have a chance. Don't waste it." And with that,

Christian watched in horror as his brother sunk his fangs into Victoria's neck. She fought to dislodge him, but he hung fast. His eyes flared as her blood coursed into him. It was poison, Christian knew. And it would kill him. Or control him as it had Christian. Whichever best served its interests.

Lucian ... you fool! What have you done?

Au revoir, mon frère.

Regardless of Lucian's ill-conceived attempt at heroism, Christian couldn't stand and watch his brother die. He lurched forward, but was distracted as movement above him caught his attention. A figure descended from the sky. And then another and another. They surrounded Victoria and Lucian, barring them from Christian's view. Something in his chest awoke, like a deep-rooted awareness, stretching out to connect him to one of the new arrivals—a woman. He recognized her face instantly in his memories—the long silky hair and that striking olive-skinned face—the one that had given him immortality.

Sezja.

His maker.

Sezja and the ethereal glow that surrounded her mesmerized him. She was otherworldly, like an apparition.

The Reii had come.

Christian didn't have time to process what was happening, only that the three immortals surrounded Victoria. Like Lucian, they fastened their fangs upon her. They would be far stronger than Lucian was, Christian guessed, with a greater chance of survival against her blood.

Lucian tore away and reeled backward, his eyes black like the blood that stained his lips. Christian hobbled to his brother's side, his body still drained and weak. The smell of Victoria's blood consumed him, and god help him, he wanted to take the blood Lucian had just consumed. He stalled himself with effort and pulled his brother into his arms. Lucian's entire body convulsed against him.

"Why?" Christian asked, his voice tortured.

"You. Know. Why." Each word was a pained gasp.

"You owe me nothing."

Flecks of bloody foam spotted his lips. "Owe ... too ... much."

His brother's body went ramrod straight in his arms, his skin mottling as the blood magic did its worst. Black tendrils wound their way down his limbs and across his cheeks. His dark silver eyes met Christian's and suddenly they were twelve years old again, lying beside each other in the field beside the château and staring up at the glistening stars.

"What do you want to be when you become a man?" the young Christian had asked.

Lucian had smiled. "I want to be remembered."

Tears filled Christian's eyes at the memory as he gripped Lucian's poison-ridden body. "You won't be forgotten," he whispered as the last light of life left his brother's eyes. His body shuddered and then went still. "I promise you."

Christian howled his grief to the sky and stood. He didn't want his brother's sacrifice to be for nothing. Sezja beckoned to him, her lips black with Victoria's blood.

Come, she told him. *Find her.*

He understood what Sezja was saying to him. He had to go into her mind and connect to what was left of her consciousness. Figure out a way to bring her back. Victoria was in there somewhere and his window of time was swiftly closing if the color of the glowing portal was any indication. Leto's eyes met his, full of primitive, impotent rage, and Christian knew what he had to do. There was no way he could let her go without a fight.

Sezja put her hand on his shoulder. He stared at his maker and felt a strange peace descend upon him. Her touch filled him with strength and purpose.

You were going to die for her. Choose to live instead.

Christian nodded and stood in front of the love of his life. Victoria's eyes were black and her mouth a slash in her face. He could feel her vitriolic rage center upon him. He closed his eyes and pushed his essence out. He focused on the core that was Victoria and entered her mind. They had done this before, torturing each other with sexy mental games, but now it wasn't about lust. It was about life and death.

And before, she'd been receptive.

Now, her mind was closed and angry and vengeful.

A person's mind was like a living backdrop, capriciously changing with quick turns of emotion and evolving states of being. When Victoria was in a playful state, exploring her mind was a joyful, wondrous experience. When they flirted and made out, it was a wildly sensuous one. The one time she'd been angry, he'd found it full of rough seas and dangerous predators, but *she* had still been present. Normally, she'd come to greet him and welcome him into her private sanctuary.

Now, not only was it was a dark barren landscape and nothing of the Tori he knew, there was no sign of her. Black bands of shadow scattered between the hollows on either side of an ash-colored maze. Spindly burnt trees surrounded him like a demon labyrinth. It was bleak and desolate. Christian trod carefully, knowing instinctively that whatever remained of Victoria would be trapped somewhere. Deep down, he also knew that this was nothing like what she had endured with Pan, where her fantasies were of her own making. This was the blood magic—and he knew that the blood would not want her to be found.

In the mental world, he was also powerless. He did not have any super speed or vampire strength. He only had his wits and the power of his own mind. Shadows moved around him as if they were alive and something slithered across his feet. He forced himself to keep moving forward. The worst thing he could do was to get caught up in any of the blood magic's tricks.

He'd only taken a few steps when something snaked around his ankle and snagged tight. He fell like a sack of bricks, slamming into the ground so hard that the breath was knocked clear out of him. Agony lanced through him.

Christian had to remind himself that the pain was not real. He kicked at the python winding around his legs and grabbed for a nearby rock. He managed to dislodge the creature and stood, only to realize that the blood was testing him. If he had panicked, it would have no doubt sent more snakes. He took a deep breath—staying calm was critical.

Christian made his way through the speckled pathways until he reached the other end of the maze. It led him to a lush meadow that had a glistening river running through it. As he got closer, he realized that the river wasn't clear as he'd thought. It was red. *Blood* red. He felt an answering pressure in his jaw and ran his tongue along perfectly flat-edged teeth. He wasn't a vampire here, but hell, the sight of the river of blood did shaky things to him. Christian shook himself roughly, forcing himself to focus.

"Tori!" he called out. He waited, sure that he'd heard a whimper of a response. He shouted again, and this time heard another whisper of a cry. It was coming from a cave cut into the hillside. Christian made his way carefully upward, through the razor-sharp blades of grass that nicked at his skin. There were larger plants, too, ones that looked far too carnivorous for his liking. He tried to steer clear of them, but tripped on a rock that appeared out of nowhere and plunged headlong into a field of the beasts.

They snapped at his face, taking huge gouges out of his flesh. He was being eaten alive. Christian pummeled his fists and tried to rip them out of the ground, but the more he fought, the more aggressive they became. Poison from their venom slid into his veins and he felt himself slowly turning to stone. He struggled as they slowly ate him alive, feeding on his calcifying flesh. He looked down—he was covered in vines. He was going to die in a coffin of creepers. Even in his state, the irony was not lost on him.

It's not real, Christian.

He had no idea where the voice came from, but it made his panic dissolve. He blinked and suddenly he was lying in a boat that rocked on the ocean. He had to get back to that cave! That's where Victoria was. The bottom of the boat held nothing, not even an oar or a piece of wood he could use. His eyes scanned the horizon—there was nothing for miles, no land that he could see. The only thing disturbing the glassy surface of the water were the pointed fins circling the tiny vessel.

Christian gritted his jaw. He could handle sharks. Using his hands, he knelt and started paddling. The sharks followed, but kept their distance from the boat. It was as if they wanted to see how far he would get on a journey to nowhere. Christian knew that he would paddle until his arms fell off. After what seemed like hours, he could see land looming in the distance. Suddenly, the sharks started circling more fiercely. Christian frowned—the fins surrounding the boat were too perfect. Too evenly spaced. The realization surfaced moments before the creature beneath him did. They weren't fins, he saw. They were *teeth*!

He did the only thing he could. He dove into the swirling water and started swimming for shore. Gasping, he pulled himself onto the sand just in time to watch the boat disappear into the maw of the sea monster. He knew it wasn't real, but nothing would make him relish the sensation of being swallowed alive, not even if it was all in his head. Or Victoria's head, as it were.

"Tori!" he shouted, cupping his hands to his mouth. He heard the faint cry again, and this time, Christian sensed that she was close. He ran up the beach and saw a gilded cage sitting on the edge of a green wood. It was too perfect—too *obvious*. But there she was, shackled to the bottom of the enclosure. She wasn't moving.

Christian advanced with caution, but nothing untoward attacked him or jumped from the bushes. He half-expected the sand to turn to quicksand beneath his feet at any moment, but it held firm. He reached the pen and frowned at the gate. It was unlocked. Something wasn't right. It was too easy.

"Tori?"

She blinked and turned weakly to stare at him. Every cell within him leapt with recognition. It was Victoria, not some trick. Her hair was matted and her face haggard. Oozing wounds covered her entire body and both her legs looked broken. In addition to her apparent battered appearance, the look in her eyes was utterly defeated. "Christian?" she whispered as if in disbelief. "How did you get here?"

"I came to find you."

"You have to leave. It will kill you."

He shook his head. "Not without you. Can you move?"

"My legs and some of my ribs are broken."

Wincing with sympathy, he unlocked the gate and stepped in, lifting her into his arms. "I'll carry you. Which way?"

She pointed down the beach and Christian took off at a run. He raced down the beach and into the woods, past the carnivorous fields where he'd seen the cave, and back to the shadowscape where he had entered. He met no resistance, but Christian was prepared all the same. Her blood would not let them go that easily. Sure enough, they came to a looming black wall. It's sides looked like polished onyx granite. It stretched for miles on either side. He looked upward—they'd have to find a way over it. He set Victoria down and she clung to him.

"Don't leave me."

"I won't," he said. "I need to figure out a way over this."

"Can you hold me for a second?"

"Of course." He sat beside her and drew her shaking body

into his arms. He pressed a kiss to her temple at the same moment that she turned her face up to his. Christian's second kiss brushed her lips. In response, she plastered her body to his and kissed him as she'd never done before. He couldn't help his body's instantaneous and fiery reaction. He wanted to be gentle, but she would have nothing of it. Memories of the last time they had kissed like this tortured him.

"I love you," she said against his mouth.

"I love you, too."

"But not more than her."

His eyes narrowed. "More than who?" he repeated carefully.

Victoria smiled at him, brushing a lock of hair out of his face. Her features shifted and Christian flew to his feet, dumping her unceremoniously off his lap. White blond hair framed a face of startling perfection. Ice blue eyes drilled into his. "Lena," he huffed. "What is this?"

"You killed Lucian," she snarled. "You *murdered* your brother."

"No," he said, the pain still raw.

"You wanted him to die." She advanced on him. "Because you wanted this." She pulled her shirt apart, exposing breasts as perfect as he remembered. Before he could utter his denial, she closed her mouth on his, her tongue sweeping in like a sweet, seductive devil.

Something shifted again and the body in his arms was once more Victoria. "I told you that you loved her more than me. You made her."

"No, it's only you," he vowed.

Her face morphed into Lena's again. "Tell her the truth. You wanted him to die. *Murderer.*"

And once more, Victoria's, making his head swim. "You never loved me. You're a liar."

He shoved her away, clutching his head as the voices around him intensified into a cacophonous noise, and fell to his knees.

"Stop," he begged. His fingers dug into the sharp gravel at his feet. "You are not her," he screamed. "Where is she?"

Victoria/Lena's face transformed into a demon and he lurched forward, catching her about the throat. He squeezed, guilt driving him to madness.

Christian. It's not real.

His heart stopped, his grip loosening. The landscape disappeared until it was nothing but a blank gray slate. A body flopped against him, unconscious. He stared at his fingers still wrapped around her throat in horror "Tori? Oh, god, Tori. Please. I'm sorry. I didn't know. Please. Be alive. I'm begging. *Please.*"

A huff escaped her lips, her eyes fluttering open, and they were the brightest, most vivid green he could have ever imagined. He knew that green.

This time, he knew it was real. *She* was real.

"Hi."

Christian brushed her cheek and she leaned into the caress. "I almost killed you."

"I know, but you didn't."

"Are you okay?" he asked, his thumb stroking her jaw. "To face the blood?"

Victoria blinked and took his hands in hers. "I'm sorry about Lucian. I saw what he did." Christian swallowed hard and nodded. She slid her fingers between his. "Let's finish this."

THE FINAL STAND

As Christian pulled away from her mind, Victoria gathered what was left of her magic. She was the wielder of the blood magic, not the other way around, and no matter what its endgame was, she would be the one in ultimate control. It had to bend to her will—not her father's or whoever he was.

She reined herself in, taking sharp hold of her mind. The blood magic swirled hotly in her veins in protest, but eventually, she felt it capitulate. Pan's toxin had weakened her willpower and dominion over the blood magic, which Leto had taken full advantage of and had so very nearly succeeded in spiriting them both away. But now she was back. Her mind was strong. *She* was strong.

And she had a demon to vanquish.

Her palm solidified in Christian's very real one as everything around her came into sharp focus. Including the demon who had once been Leto. He growled at her, leashed violence shimmering in acid green bands along his limbs as if he could read her mind. She blinked, realizing that he probably could because of their connection. She frowned and blocked him from her.

Her eyes darted behind her. Almost three quarters of their number had been decimated and those who hadn't fled remained behind them. Aliya was still alive, she noticed, focused on the spell keeping Leto—and her—transfixed. So was Freyja, the head of the warlocks, but her energies were directed toward the dimension portal. Three stunning vampires, a female and two males, stood to Christian's right. They were Reii, she knew. She could sense the power emanating from them—they were old and powerful. They were the ones who had drained her blood without dying. And thank goodness they had, or who knew how many more she would have killed.

The woman turned to stare at her with dark impenetrable eyes, holding her gaze with an assessing, curious look, and Victoria felt an odd recognition in her gut. She inclined her head graciously and Victoria did the same.

That's Sezja, Christian said, noting the interaction.

Your maker?

Yes.

She came to your rescue.

Not just mine. Everyone's.

Victoria squirmed inwardly at the thought that the Reii had been awakened from the self-imposed sleep because of her. She was the extinction level event that had roused them. She sucked in a deep breath. She'd be lying if she said she wasn't grateful for their intervention.

Her eyes narrowed as they shifted from the Reii to the ranks behind the warlocks and settled on Angie, who stood next to Lena. The vampire's face was impassive, but oddly, Victoria didn't feel any of her usual animosity toward her. Perhaps it was because of Lucian, or perhaps it was because of the way she stood next to Angie, almost like she was protecting her.

Angie made her way forward, and Victoria frowned. She would prefer that Angie be out of harm's way, but she knew that

Angie was going to do what Angie wanted to do. They'd always joked that her superpower was pigheadedness.

"Are you okay?" Victoria asked her.

"Yeah," Angie said, hefting her crossbow. "Although I have to say that your dad has some serious issues."

Victoria rolled her eyes at her friend's dry humor. "Making new friends?" she tossed back as Lena edged toward them.

"She's okay." The quiet way Angie answered made Victoria quirk an eyebrow, but she didn't push the matter. She had more crucial things to worry about, like a very pissed-off demon, as Angie had noted, standing not a stone's throw from them.

The witches' enduring immobility spell held him fast, but Victoria could sense their control waning. They were tethered and she, too, was bound by their magic, but it was weakening. She could feel it. Leto had gorged himself on the lives she'd taken and she could feel the power emanating from his form. She frowned. He wasn't even trying to fight—he just stood there watching her with a heavy malevolent stare.

What was he *doing*? The answer to her question came in the next breath. He was waiting for the portal, she realized. It was his out. But Victoria knew that he wouldn't leave without taking as many souls with him as he could. A desire for vengeance shone in those chartreuse eyes. It curled along the link between them, making her blood boil with anticipation.

No. She steeled herself against her blood's willful influence. *I am your master and you will yield.*

Momentarily thwarted, the blood magic simmered beneath her veins. She felt its resistance keenly and now, without the power of the amulet, she was on her own. But Victoria knew that she was its ruler. She was the alpha. Not Leto and certainly not the blood itself. It was a matter of dominance and she had to assert her will or become the one subdued.

Her eyes slid to the shimmering sphere that was nearly fully formed. She had minutes before they were both pulled through it, which meant that Leto would be free and she would be trapped for an eternity.

Use my strength, Christian told her as if sensing her agitation.

Her fingers brushed against his and she shot a sidelong glance at Leto. *Thanks, but I think I'll take his. I've earned it.* Christian frowned at her and then his eyes widened as he took her meaning.

Victoria released him and focused her magic on the bond that stretched between her and Leto. "DEVORO," she whispered. She sensed Leto freeze as the spell whispered along the space spanning between them. Her blood trilled in her veins. She latched on and extracted the power that they had both stolen, and with each passing second, she grew stronger and stronger. He would fight her, she knew, once he felt the drain.

Sure enough, it wasn't long before his eyes snapped to hers. With a snarl, his lips drew away from his teeth, his will pitting itself against hers and slamming into her with such force that it made her dizzy. Her fingers shook and she felt the warm slide of Christian's grip. She didn't take his strength, but she took comfort from his touch. He believed in her. He always had.

With an inhuman grunt, Leto tore free of his magical restraints and howled. The sound was full of wrath and power. With the exception of a few, nearly every single creature within the immediate vicinity—witch, warlock, and vampire—dropped to their knees and clapped their hands to their ears. Victoria felt something pop in her eardrums as she, too, was released from the witches' broken spell.

Christian's grip yanked on hers as his legs buckled. Her gaze fell to the vampire at her side, and with horror, she saw a thick trickle of blood seeping from his ears. Only the Reii remained erect, although they seemed visibly disoriented by Leto's battle scream.

"Are you okay?" she asked Christian.

He nodded and swiped at the blood, shaking his head to settle himself. "Already healed." His eyes narrowed, alarm brewing in them. "What is he doing?"

Victoria followed Christian's gaze, watching as midnight blue energy dribbled from the open portal toward Leto. The demon manipulated it into a sphere around his hands, a globe that was growing bigger and bigger.

"That's dark energy," Victoria whispered. "I can feel it."

"From the demon dimension?"

She nodded. "It's not from here."

Christian glanced over his shoulder. Scrambling to her feet, Freyja looked as afraid as they did, but still the warlocks kept the portal open.

"Close it!" he shouted.

"We can't," she yelled back. "Something has to go through it."

"What do you mean?" he asked.

Victoria stared at him. "She means that it's a reverse summoning. It won't close unless something is *summoned* back. We have to get him in there."

"How?"

"I don't know. He is getting stronger. Whatever power he's drawing from that dimension is not going to be easy."

Just as the words escaped her lips, a blast of *something* spread outward, and Victoria felt a writhing sensation in her stomach. All around her, vampires and witches dropped like flies, clutching themselves.

"Oh my god," Angie whispered, her eyes flying wide. She seemed unaffected, but perhaps it was because she was the only human there. Her eyes were unfocused as she used her second sight to see something that only she could. Victoria linked her mind to her friend's and sucked in a sharp breath. Tentacles of dark energy reached outward from Leto's body to encircle those closest to him. He wasn't killing them. No, he was doing something else ... something far worse via his dimension's energy.

One by one, those who had fallen stood. But they weren't the same. They were possessed by whatever dark matter Leto had summoned via the portal and were now his first line of defense. He controlled them like puppets. Spells flew toward her head and she ducked, taking Angie with her.

"Stay down."

"But I can help," she insisted.

"I don't want you getting hurt or anywhere near that portal." Victoria's eyes slid to Lena and they exchanged a look.

"I'm right here," Angie said with an eye roll, "and I don't need a babysitter."

But Victoria was already gone. She chanted under her breath, forcing her rogue magic into submission and spread a protection spell wide to the fighting few that remained uncontrolled by Leto's darkness, including Angie, Lena by default, Christian, the Reii, Aliya, and Freyja. "PROTECTUM!"

His army surrounded him like a sphere as vampire attacked vampire and witch attacked witch. He was using their own powers against them. Leto had blocked her, too, and cut off the lifeline of power between them.

Suddenly, across the field Aliya screamed as four witches swarmed her. Victoria recognized two of them from the temple earlier.

"Aliya!" Their eyes met over the distance and Aliya smiled, sorrow and acceptance written all over her face—as if she knew she was going to die. "No," Victoria shouted, shaking her head in denial. But it was too late.

She blinked in shock as members of her own coven tore Aliya's body in four different directions and the scream throttled to a choked gurgle in her throat. Her limbs popped with wet sounds, and the possessed witches pounced on the severed pieces with unrestrained glee. Bile rose in Victoria's throat and she felt the ground start to sway.

Focus, she growled to herself.

Victoria rolled her neck and set her jaw. She was part demon and the sooner she accepted that the better. Leto would kill everyone without conscience. She had to beat him at his own game.

She took several purposeful steps forward before a hand stalled her. "Tori, where are you going?"

Christian looked worried. His face and body were streaked in blood and her heart clenched before she realized the blood wasn't his. Her eyes fell to the bodies he'd left in his wake. She sensed his misery lying like a shroud upon his shoulders. Because of Leto's possession, it was either kill or be killed. But every time they were forced to kill one of their own, another took its place. Leto was doing what demons did—taking control of malleable hosts.

"He killed Aliya."

"But it's *you* he wants," Christian shot back.

"Then let him have me." Victoria raised her hands and pulled herself into relentless focus. The beast had already been unleashed. It was time to become what she loathed the most.

Christian grasped her shoulders. Tension radiated along his arms—having just been in her head, he knew intimately what was at risk. "Tori—"

"I have to." She lifted a hand to stroke his mouth with her fingers, edging over the razor sharp incisors just visible beneath his upper lip. Leaning into him, she stood on tiptoe and pressed a kiss where her thumb had traced. "If I forget to tell you later, I love you."

There in the middle of that blood soaked common with her lips joined to the man she loved, Victoria understood her purpose. She may have been born to destroy, but she was also meant to protect. She was the daughter of a demon and a witch and her magic was *hers*. Her power was an extension of her, *not* the father of her line. Releasing Christian and striding away to the line of rogue vampires, she faced Leto.

It was time to become the demon.

She waved a hand, and the vampires and witches in her path collapsed, creating a gap. She stared him down, even as the severed tentacles sourced new hosts.

"CRUENTUS DEVORO," she snarled, invoking the blood magic within her. The spell amplified a thousandfold. It sucked greedily and dark power coursed into her, rippling along her veins like an incoming tide.

Leto's eyes snapped wide as he tried to stop the outward flow, but he couldn't do that *and* keep control over the bodies at the end of his phantom arms. Victoria was merciless, focused only on absorbing what she could. The blood magic bucked and rolled within her, but she held it under unbending control. She would release it when the time was right.

Leto growled and bellowed. "You can stop this, daughter." He nodded to the creatures around him. "Their lives for yours."

"There's only one more life to take," she said. "And I already told you—I'm not your fucking daughter."

She flew at him then, magic crackling from her fingertips as she barraged him with spell after spell. He dodged, shoving his minions in front of her to take the brunt of her attack. They didn't die because the spells were not fatal. Victoria didn't mean to wound him. She wanted to distract him.

At the last moment, she twisted and ran straight into the dark energy. She felt it sink into her, making her gasp. God, it was powerful. *Leto* was powerful. More than she had imagined. Victoria swallowed hard. Which meant that she was strong, too. She pushed into the remaining tentacles until the dark magic sizzled between them.

"You think to defeat me, child?" He wrenched against the

connection, drawing her toward him in a burst of midnight blue light. "With my own power?"

She eyed him and held her own. "Yes."

"You would save *them* over your own blood? Their souls have been corrupted and dishonored by the actions of their revered ancestor. Yet you would call them family?"

Victoria nodded, hearing an odd note in his voice. "What do you mean, them?"

"Witches." He spat the word. "This plane must be cleansed of the taint of the Goddess. She and her descendants must be punished for what they brought upon me."

"You stole their daughter."

A spasm of pain rippled across his face. "Thaia came willingly."

"You *killed* her."

Something undulated between them. "She knew they were coming for the babe. She tried to defend against those the Goddess sent. *They* killed her, not me."

"You lie, demon," someone—one of Aliya's priestesses, maybe—screamed from behind them. "She died in childbirth."

Leto's eyes slid to hers. "She died at the hands of your own. You were fed a concocted story. This is the *truth*."

Victoria's body trembled with the force of his pain ricocheting along the link between them. She would know if he was lying. And he wasn't. Understanding filled her—he'd been punished for an eternity after his child had been stolen from him. No wonder he hated the witches.

"The actions of one doesn't define an entire race, Leto," she said. "You taught me that."

"They must be cleansed."

"Then I must also be cleansed, as I, too, am part witch."

"You are part of my Thaia, not these diseased creatures," he snarled.

Victoria drew a long breath. His bitterness and anguish

consumed him and deep down she knew she would not be able to talk any reason into him. But she could not allow him to eradicate an entire species just because he was wronged by one of them a thousand years ago. Still, a part of her couldn't give up on him.

"Let go of the past, Leto. Forgive and leave it behind. It is done and nothing can change that."

"The past—and the pain—are all I have."

"You have me." She felt him waver then, but the moment was brief. He was too riddled by his own acrimony. No, Leto only wanted vengeance, and he wanted her to be his right arm. "I am sorry for what you have lost, but they do not deserve the cost of your anger. They are innocent, too."

His gaze hardened as he released his hold on the blue-black energy. "If you are with them, then you are against me."

"So be it," she whispered and braced herself.

Leto whispered an ominous chant. Dark magic swirled from the portal, surrounding him and starting to take shape. Victoria felt the breath steal from her body as she realized what he was doing. He was summoning demons.

"Close the portal, damn it," she heard someone shout dully. But she knew that the portal would only close if something—or someone—went through it. She took a deep breath. She was the closest. It would mean leaving the rest of them here to face Leto, but at least he would be alone. They would have a fighting chance. She did not know what lay on the other side of that glowing sphere, but she would survive. Her demon blood would protect her, she hoped. She moved toward it.

"Tori, no!" The scream was feminine. She heard the thud of darts as they sank into Leto's corporeal body. They wouldn't hurt him. Unlike vampires or witches, demons weren't susceptible to silver or poison. But Angie wouldn't know that.

"Angie, stay back."

But it was too late. A tendril of darkness snaked toward

Angie, quick as a striking cobra, and gathered her close. Victoria halted in her tracks. Leto's eyes glittered in triumph. "You care about this one. I will spare her if you give me your loyalty."

"Leto," she began. "Release her."

"Your bond."

"Don't do it, Tori," Angie shouted. "I'm nobody."

"You have ten seconds to decide." Leto held her body aloft. Angie, for her part, didn't give one inch. She struggled against his magical hold even as more demons materialized around them.

Victoria glanced over her shoulder. There were only a handful of them left, and if he continued at this pace, they would be outnumbered ten to one in a matter of minutes. She had no choice.

"Tori, no."

She met Christian's eyes and then each of the others in turn. Her silent message was clear. Seal the portal at any cost. She would do what her ancestor Brigid did before allowing Leto to have any control over her or the blood magic.

"Fine, you have my bond," she said, walking forward. "Release the girl."

She waited until she was within inches of them before her right hand balled into a fist at her side—the signal to bring down the portal. Movement filled her vision as bodies rushed the gateway. Leto snarled in rage, his attention drawn to protecting his means of escape. He did not release Angie as Victoria had hoped he would. So she threw herself between them, severing the demonic tether. Angie fell in a heap to the grass and rolled to a stop directly in front one of the spectral shapes.

Leto growled, unleashing the demon wraith toward Angie. This would not be like the dark energy he had cast forward before. The wraith would consume her soul and take over her body. Angie scrambled to her feet, her face contorted. There was no way she could get away and no way for Victoria to reach her before the wraith did.

Impotent rage flowered like an explosion in her chest. "Angie!"

A blur streaked in front of the wraith, catching it squarely head-on an instant before it connected with Angie's body. Lena twisted and convulsed as the specter shuddered through her. She was immortal, but the pain would be agonizing. It wouldn't consume what was left of her soul. Instead, the possession would incinerate them both. Within seconds, a hot red glow spread like a stain over her alabaster skin and she fell to the ground, writhing as her vampire nature fought the demon writhing inside.

Victoria reached her contorting body at the same time that Christian did. Out of the corner of her eye, she saw Freyja fall to her knees at Angie's side, her face wracked with concern. She tried to draw her away, but Angie shook her head as she crawled to Lena's side.

"Lena."

But Lena's unseeing ice blue eyes shone with pain. They turned to Christian. Blood flecked her lips. "You were right about them. The humans." Each word was a gasp of agony, but she had more to say. Her gaze slipped to Angie. "Out of all my years as a vampire, I never wanted progeny. No human was worthy." Her smile was pained. "Never, until now."

Angie inched forward. "Then fight, Lena."

"My fight is over." Her body arched as the heat scorched brilliant crimson that streaked into amber. Her mouth opened in a soundless scream, her skin graying to the color of burnt ash. Her eyes met Christian's as something passed between them. "You know what to do."

The sounds of the battle raging on behind them drew their collective attention. David, a vampire Elder, stood battling four of the wraith demons, while Roan and the other warlocks took on a half dozen others. Sezja and the other two Reii had sequestered Leto's attention, and from what Victoria could see, they'd gotten in a few good strikes. Nothing lethal, but every little bit helped.

Christian stood with the dying vampire in his arms, and without a sound, he tossed her body toward the portal. Leto's shriek pierced through the silence as Lena hurtled through the space between them. He struck out an arm of dark energy, but it was too late. She sailed through the glowing disc and the portal winked shut. The demon spawn he'd conjured faded as the power tethering them to the earth disappeared.

"Confuto," Victoria said.

The Reii converged then as Victoria held Leto still. "You gave me your bond," he said, his eyes glittering with malice as he shrugged off her spell and sent the vampire ancients sprawling with a burst of power that came directly from her body. "Your blood magic is mine to command."

"Maybe she did," a voice said from behind them. Eyes swiveled toward where Angie stood wielding her crossbow. She had Leto in her sights at point blank range. "But if there's one thing I know about, it's being forced into involuntary bondage to tyrants, and it never ends well. People don't like being controlled and, well, some bonds are meant to be broken."

"Your puny little darts won't work, little one."

She arched a cool eyebrow. "This one's special."

Leto grinned. "I'll tell you what. Take your best shot. I'll give it to you. I'll come back from anything you've got."

Angie didn't hesitate. Her shot was true, piercing him right above his black heart. Victoria summoned her magic to her, expecting that Angie's strike would do nothing—Leto was impervious to human weapons. What she did not expect was the look of incredulous shock on Leto's face as he fell backward, clawing at the dart's point of entry in his body. His body shriveled as a black dust coated his skin and then liquefied into a greenish black ichor. His death was instantaneous.

"Come back from that, bitch," Angie muttered.

Christian exhaled, and once more, a dozen pairs of incredulous, disbelieving eyes fell upon Angie. "What the holy hell was in that dart?"

"Dead blood magic."

THE BEGINNING OF EVERYTHING

As it turned out, Angie had saved the bit of blood that had tried to possess Christian back in New York.

"I didn't want to leave it there," she'd explained later inside Christian's château. "You know, in case someone found it. It was alive, after all."

"What do you mean?" Victoria had asked, amazed by her foresight.

She shrugged. "I could see it shimmering with my other sight. It wasn't quite dead, so I scooped it up and meant to bury it or throw it into the river or something. When I started making the darts, I made it into one. I never thought I'd actually use it. I just kept it as a ... memento of what could happen if I didn't protect myself."

When Victoria asked her how she knew that it would work, Angie had explained that she didn't. She'd hoped, but she didn't know. Turned out that blood magic had transformed into the worst kind of venom when it'd been exorcized—the demon side of it anyway. And thanks to Angie, Leto had met his end from the very blood he sought to control. Victoria felt hollow at the loss of her best friend and mentor, but he'd been too consumed by his hate to let it go. It had festered for too many years.

In truth, she missed the stupid cat.

A hot tear trekked a pathway down her cheek as she sat in the foyer waiting for Angie to finish packing, and she swiped it away. She missed his stupid cat giggles and his infuriated expressions when she did something idiotic. He wasn't the only loved one she'd lost. Victoria mourned the deaths of Aliya and a handful of witches she'd met. Aliya had been replaced by one of the priestesses she'd been training, a woman named Arielle. She'd be a worthy successor. One of her first acts as high priestess of the coven had been a proposal to strike the law forbidding relations between the witches and the vampires. As far as Victoria knew, both parties were seriously considering it.

Not that it made one hoot of difference for her and Christian. They would do whatever suited them. But the more she thought about it, the more she realized that it was the judgment of others that pushed people to unforgiveable extremes. Whether an elephant loved an ant should be of no concern to anyone but to the two of them. Leto had been cursed through several lifetimes because the Goddess Mother had deemed his love for one of her priestesses an abomination. But Thaia had loved Leto, too, and she had died defending the product of their love.

The truth was: love was *pure*, no matter its form and no matter its participants.

Victoria even mourned Lucian's passing, though that was more for Christian than for herself. Despite all of his brother's treachery, he'd been desolate at the loss of his twin. The vampires had suffered more than their share of fatalities. Victoria hadn't seen it, but Christian had told her that David, one of the Elders, had been killed by two of his own progeny. David had been part Reii, but neither his age nor strength had been enough to save him when they tore his heart out. Christian hadn't taken the news well—it was far too close to the death of his own mentor, Enhard.

"Hey," Angie said, interrupting her thoughts. "I'm ready."

Victoria looked up to where Angie was standing with her backpack. She'd spent the last few days of her break with Freyja, who, as it turned out, was her aunt. The leader of the warlocks was Angie's birth mother's sister. Angie had explained that Gabriel had kept them away because he didn't want them to affect his hold over her gift. She had also explained that warlocks weren't evil—they'd just gotten a bad reputation over the years because of a few rogue warlocks who had abused their powers.

Supposedly, they were descendants from the great Norse Vardlokkur. Christian had explained that they took oaths to safeguard the magic of this world against evil spirits and demons from other realms. Despite knowing that Freyja had fully intended to banish her, Victoria liked the warlock, and she especially loved how protective she'd been about Angie.

"I don't know about you," Freyja had told her. "Your magic is too capricious, too volatile, but we vow to watch and protect you. There will always be those who covet your power, and if it falls into the wrong hands, we invite destruction upon ourselves. We will not allow that to happen."

"Nor will I."

She'd meant it. The Cruentus Curse was a part of her for better or for worse and it was time she started accepting that. It was akin to the old adage of a glass being half full or half empty. It was time to start seeing her curse as a gift, one that she could use to safeguard others ... not just witches, but *anyone* who needed protection.

"I wish you didn't have to go," she said to Angie.

"Me too, but classes start tomorrow. I'll see you soon, though. Aunt Free wants me to visit next month."

Victoria hugged her friend. "I'm glad you came. Pretty sure

the world would have gone to hell in a hand basket if it weren't for you. And I would have been the one to deliver it there."

"I think the deliverer was your friend, Pan."

"He wasn't all bad. Leto coerced him."

"What's going to happen to him?"

Victoria shrugged. "They're going to try to help him with his Janusite disorder and maybe erase his memories. He remembers everything he's done and he's in bad shape about it. He refuses to see anyone, even me."

"I'm not surprised. Knowing you were the tipping point to making us all extinct has to be a heavy load. Will he be okay, you think?"

"Maybe. There are some powerful memory spells. I'm going to go over there tomorrow to see how I can help."

"And the headmistress? Starke or whatever her name was."

"Stripped and exiled." Victoria shook her head. "I never even saw that coming. She was supposed to be there to teach young witches, and all she craved was the Cruentus Curse and its power."

"Demons come in all shapes and sizes."

"Tell me about it."

Angie eyed her, the somber look on her face replaced with a mischievous grin. "Speaking of, how are you feeling? Any murderous inclinations? Blood magic behaving today?"

"It's under control," Victoria said, swatting at her.

"That's good to know," Angie said, her grin widening. "And not just because you have a super-hot boyfriend, who, by the way, is now powerful enough to handle you, being Reii royalty and all. Maybe you can, you know, continue where you left off last time now that you have your house to yourselves."

Victoria felt the blush consume her from tip to toe at her suggestive tone. "*Angie!*"

"What? I'm just saying. Nothing wrong with taking advantage of a windfall, right? Carpe diem, as they say."

"He's not ready," Victoria confided as they walked out to the car where Christian was waiting. "I don't know that either of us wants to go there so soon after ... everything."

"Understandable."

Christian's slate gray eyes met hers in the driveway, and Victoria's knees almost buckled at the look in them. Stupid vampire hearing. He'd likely heard every word of that last part of the conversation. She fought a second flush and hopped into the passenger seat. Christian loaded Angie's bag into the car and they got in.

"Thanks for driving me to the airport," Angie said. "I could have taken the metro." Victoria rolled her eyes. She could have easily teleported Angie, and Christian could have *flown* her back to the States in a vampire minute, but Angie had insisted on normal human travel. Victoria guessed it had something to do with decompressing after the events of the last few days. She didn't blame her one bit.

The ride to *Charles de Gaulle* airport was quick. Too quick. And soon, they were exchanging tearful goodbyes at the curb. "I'll pop in to visit," Victoria promised. "We'll be back stateside soon."

"You better."

She watched as Christian hugged Angie and handed her a blue box. "What's this?" Angie asked, opening it. Nestled on a bed of velvet was a gorgeous ring. It was old, inlaid with sapphires and a delicately carved crest.

"It was Lena's," he told her. "She asked me to get it before she died. She wanted you to have it. It was her mother's."

"*Me?* Why?"

Christian smiled. "I think she saw something of herself in you—the Lena she used to be. I agree," he added. "You have the same force of will and the same strength of spirit."

Angie blushed and stared at the ring. "This looks priceless."

"It is. The Kurzberg Dynasty fell during the war. This is one of the few remnants of their House." He placed a hand on her shoulder. "In the old days, the gift of a family heirloom was a great honor. She told me that you made her remember who she really was—the girl before the vampire."

"She saved my life."

"I think in the end you saved hers."

Angie's voice shook as she answered. "Thank you." She tucked the box into her backpack and hugged Victoria hard before walking toward the sliding doors, her face rigid as if she was determined not to cry. "See you around. Love you guys."

Victoria stood staring at the spot where Angie had disappeared for a long while until Christian placed his hand on her shoulder. She turned to stare at him, surprised to see him standing there with the morning sunlight glimmering off his hair. The immunity to sunlight was yet another of his Reii gifts, he'd explained. Normally, he'd be sticking to the shade or sitting in the comfortably dark interior of the car, and Victoria still hadn't gotten used to seeing him moving around in the daylight. She slid closer to him and told him so.

"Me too. I feel like I should be running for cover. But the sun feels nice. Warm."

They climbed back into the car. "Did you talk with Sezja?"

"Yes. She was sorry she did not get to speak with you more, but she wanted me to tell you that she approves."

Victoria laughed. "Good to know. I wouldn't want to piss off the only prospective mother-in-law I have."

Christian quirked an eyebrow, shooting her a sidelong glance. "Mother-in-law? Do I take that to mean getting married is an option?"

"Do vampires even get married?"

"On the odd occasion, yes."

"Well then, I suppose it's something to look forward to. I'm only eighteen, after all." She glanced at him and giggled. "Even though you're an old man. We're such a creepy couple."

"Speak for yourself," he tossed back, his teeth glinting in a wolfish grin. "I am a spritely young man and not creepy in the least."

"You're a perv who's dating a teenager."

"And in my day, you would have been well on your way to being ensconced on the shelf. A spinster by all accounts."

Victoria swallowed an indignant gasp and chucked him in the shoulder. "Are you calling me an old maid?"

"What of it? You're going to fight me, young slice?" He squinted at her, those silver eyes teasing. Victoria nearly snorted at Christian's ridiculous slang.

"Name your time and name your place, old timer."

"Now. In bed."

The jovial atmosphere in the car turned electric at his low response. Victoria felt her bones turn to water and every cell in her body fired at his words. She swallowed hard as he reached across the center console to grab her hand. The breath left her body in a wild rush as his thumb stroked across the sensitive skin of her wrist. She could have whisked them home in a second, but she couldn't move, much less think.

By the time they pulled into the driveway at Fontainebleau, her entire body was humming from the light touch of his fingers. She glanced at the house and stiffened, drawing her hand away as if burned. She'd thrown herself at him the last time for all the wrong reasons. A rush of shame filled her at the memories. She had lied to Angie—*she* wasn't ready, not Christian. And not because she was afraid … she was ashamed. She had bartered her body in return for the cost of breaking up. He'd accused her of twisting his love and she'd deserved every bit of it. The truth was she didn't deserve him.

Christian switched off the engine and turned to her as if he could read her mind. "I love you, Victoria. And regardless of what happens between us moving forward, that is never going to change."

"But what I did ... and said—"

"Is forgotten." He stroked her face. "We have had so many beginnings, you and I. What's so different about this one? Bumps in the road have never stopped us. I told you before, when we make love, it will be my pledge to you. That hasn't changed. But I will wait until you are ready to take that step, for however long it takes."

Victoria stared at his face, her misery threatening to choke her. "I made it ugly."

"Nothing you do is ever ugly." Christian smiled, making her heart leap. "Even your breakups have an innate grace."

"I hurt you."

"As I have hurt you in the past, and as I expect we will continue to do so over the next hundred years. We're two different people, Tori. While I would never *want* to cause you pain, we are going to say things we don't mean and make foolish mistakes. But that's part of life and love. We take the good with the bad. My parents argued like cats and dogs, but they loved as hard as they fought. I'd rather have a life of passion than one without it. Wouldn't you?"

She sniffed through her tears and nodded. "Why are you so amazing?"

"With advanced age comes great wisdom."

She wanted to laugh at his solemn tone, but something deliciously warm was spreading inside of her ... something that had its own agenda and its own goal. She leaned forward so that her lips could brush his. "Take me upstairs, Christian."

She didn't have to ask twice, and within the space of half a breath, they stood in the bedroom they shared. She stared at the bed and looked away, the memories—and the humiliation—coming back in full force.

"Forget about what happened before," he told her and she nodded, even though it did nothing to calm her sudden feelings of inadequacy. "Wait one moment," he said.

"What are you doing?"

"Running you a bath."

"Oh."

By the time he returned to the bedroom, she had worked herself into a frantic state of nervousness, but Christian scooped her into his arms and took her into the adjoining bathroom. He'd lit candles, she noticed, and the oversized soaking bath was full of steaming scented bubbles. Two glasses of wine sat on the edge of the bath. She didn't know where he had gotten the wine so quickly and then she smirked—vampire super speed, of course.

She moved to take off her clothes, but Christian beat her to the punch. She held her breath as he lifted her hands high and drew off her t-shirt. But other than the slight flare in his eyes, Christian kept his hands clinical as he removed the rest of her clothing with deft detachment. She fought her shyness as he stripped away the last of it before helping her into the tub.

"Is that better?" he asked, his voice husky. "Temperature okay?"

"Yes," she squeaked.

"You looked like you needed to relax."

He pressed a swift kiss to her forehead and handed her one of the glasses. Victoria stared at the love of her life sitting on the edge of the tub. She'd fought a demon, for heaven's sake, and now she was letting her own insecurity get in the way of her happiness. She swallowed hard. "Don't you need to relax, too?"

"No, I'm—" he began and then his eyes slammed into hers as he realized what she was getting at. "Are you sure?"

"Yes."

She tried to look away as he peeled his shirt off, but she couldn't help herself. His sculpted shoulders and the sleek ridges of his stomach mesmerized her. Christian had a beautiful body with not an ounce of excess fat on his broad frame. His legs, like the rest of him, were lean and well-muscled. Her breath caught as he tugged at the waistband of his boxers and she dragged her eyes away. They only returned to him when she felt the slosh of the water as he entered the bath.

Victoria handed him the second wineglass and practically gulped the rest of hers. Her entire body felt like it was on fire at his nearness. He took the glass from her shaking fingers and drew her to him. When his lips took hers, she forgot everything but the exciting taste and the feel of him. The velvet touch of the water enveloping her body maximized every sensation and Victoria clung to him. But other than the decidedly passionate kiss, Christian didn't make any other moves.

Instead, he grabbed the soap and started lathering her skin.

"What are you doing?" she breathed.

"Relax."

His hands skimmed her shoulders, kneading the tension out of her muscles. She didn't make a sound as he turned her around and pulled her back against his chest, his hands continuing their gentle ministrations. His fingers massaged her arms, her lower back, her sides, and wherever he touched, he left a trail of fire. She held her breath when his palms slipped around to her stomach and slid lower still to rest at the juncture between her thighs. All rational thought deserted her. He stroked briefly before kissing her again and then stood, taking her with him.

He stepped out of the bath and looked around for a towel, but Victoria whispered a word and within seconds, they were both dry.

"Handy," he told her with a smile.

"I have my moments." She stared at him, wondering at his ironclad control. He was still a vampire after all, and despite his new gifts, she didn't want to hurt him. "Are you sure you're okay?"

"Yes." Christian claimed her lips in a passionate kiss as laid her gently down on the chaise lounge sitting in front of the fireplace. He stretched out beside her. "You are beautiful," he murmured, drawing his fingers through her hair and skimming the side of her body. "Like a Persian goddess."

His mouth settled on hers once more and Victoria felt heat start to pool in her abdomen as his hands explored her back and her stomach. They fluttered lower. His fingers resumed their probing caresses, and soon, the only thing that filled her mind was desire. When his body hovered over hers, she braced herself, but Christian was inordinately gentle as their bodies met. He slid forward and her eyes widened as he began to move.

"I love you," he said.

Those three words made her heart—and her body—melt. Her hands traced the ridges of his powerful shoulders as his body pledged itself to hers in an age-old ritual. A forever dance. Christian brought her skillfully to the edge and then nudged her over, his lips sealing to hers as she arched against him, pleasure streaking through her like a thousand falling stars. Christian joined her swiftly thereafter, cradling her in those unbreakable arms of his.

"Oh," she breathed as he shifted to lie next to her. Victoria blushed and brushed a lock of hair out of his face. "If it'd been like that the last time, I'd have seriously reconsidered breaking up."

He kissed her. "If it'd been like that the last time, I would have kept you under lock and key as my vampire concubine."

"That's romantic," she laughed and then sobered. "Are you okay? Hungry?"

He reached for her playfully. "Always."

"Not that kind," she said, feeling as if her face were on fire. "Blood kind."

"No."

She eyed him. "No inclination, nothing? Not even when …" she trailed off, embarrassed, but he only shook his head. "Well, I guess that's good that neither of us tried to kill the other."

"It's a start." Christian grinned and kissed her nose. "You should get some sleep."

"I'm not sleepy in the least."

She eyed him, blushing, and he laughed low in his throat before pulling her to him. "I suppose I could think of something to keep us awake."

EPILOGUE

Christian watched Victoria sleeping, her dark hair strewn across the pillow and the sheet resting across her slim back. He inhaled deeply as the scent of her blood reached his nostrils. It was alluring, seductive ... and deadly.

He hadn't been fully honest with her before. He *had* been affected earlier. In truth, his craving for her blood had not diminished, and he was beginning to realize that it never would. Yes, he was Reii, and he was strong. But her blood would always be his arch nemesis—torturing him, enticing him, and tormenting him at every turn. Christian closed his eyes, fighting his ravenous thirst.

He'd meant what he said—he would rather take the bad with the good than have nothing at all. The monsters within were always going to be there. Hers, his, it didn't matter. What mattered was whether they gave in or chose to fight. He stared at the sleeping woman in his bed and felt something deeply protective flower in his chest. Deep down he knew he would always choose to fight.

She was life and death, darkness and light. She was the keeper of his immortal beating heart. She was *his*.

THANK you so much for reading Bloodcraft! I hope you enjoyed this story as much as I loved writing it! I know there are so many books to choose from and I'm so grateful you chose to read mine. If you have a minute, please consider leaving a review. Word of mouth and reviews go a long way for authors and even one or two sentences can help! I appreciate them so much!

GOOD NEWS! The next book in the series BLOODBOUND is available now. Want to know more about the dark and sinister twin, Lucian Devereux? Or learn about the mysterious, deadly Lena? Read Lucian and Lena's story, and see why broken hearts never truly heal! One click this novella now! FREE in Kindle Unlimited!

ETERNAL LIFE COMES AT A COST

Love or freedom…the choice is hers.

VIENNA, AUSTRIA, 1892. Lady Leandra Von Kurzberg is a hellion. Raised with seven older brothers, there is only one thing Lena fears: marriage. She has no desire to give up her freedom to be any lord's broodmare.

When Lena meets the dangerously attractive Devereux twins, , she is smitten. Inexplicably drawn to both men, the brothers are polar opposites—as much as Christian is every inch the debonair Duke of D'Avigny, his brother Lucian is a roguish scoundrel bent on hedonism.

But the captivating twins aren't what they seem…

As frightening truths are unveiled and a one-of-a-kind offer is made, Lena will have to decide whether love is worth the loss of her freedom, or if freedom is worth the ultimate cost...her life.

WANT to stay up-to-date with the latest news on Amalie Howard's new releases, giveaways, contests, and ARC opportunities? Join my mailing list and get a FREE copy of my exclusive science-fiction short story from the world of THE ALMOST GIRL, *THE SOLDIER.*

WATERFELL BY AMALIE HOWARD

Need something new to read? Try WATERFELL: An alien sea princess pretending to be human must take back her crown and fight to save her undersea kingdom from the forces conspiring against her.

The Little Mermaid meets Pacific Rim.

"A coming-of-age story complicated by regicide, superhuman powers, the duty to protect a kingdom and one hot surfer. A fantastical surf-and-turf romance." ~ Kirkus Reviews

THE DEEP CAN BE DEADLY...BUT LOVE CAN BE DEADLIER

Nerissa Marin is far from home. Though she lives an anonymous life on land during her cycle of human study, she is Aquarathi royalty by birth—and the future monarch of a hidden, undersea kingdom. But when her father is murdered, the human world becomes her only refuge.

Adrift and indifferent, Riss indulges her every whim, including her feelings for the new surf king of Dover Prep, Lokeane Seavon. But as the day she comes of age looms closer, old enemies appear and challenges are issued: If she forsakes her throne, her people will suffer for it.

To win her crown, she must become the queen she was born to be.

Praise for Waterfell:

"A coming-of-age story complicated by regicide, superhuman powers, the duty to protect a kingdom and one hot surfer. A fantastical surf-and-turf romance." Kirkus Reviews

"A page-turning blend of magical realism and fantasy." Booklist

ACKNOWLEDGMENTS

First and foremost, this book is for my fans. So much gratitude goes out to those of you who fell in love with this series and waited so patiently (years) for this book. Thank you for not letting me give up on finishing Christian and Victoria's story. To the reader who wrote me last year asking whether she should give up hope on waiting for book two, this one's for you.

To Angie Frazier, who inspires me and keeps me off the ledge, thank you for being such an amazing colleague and friend. I adore you. To Damaris Cardinali, whose passion for books always astounds me and who always goes over and beyond— thanks for everything, babe! Huge thanks to Kate Kaynak who helped me come up with the brilliant idea of a plant toxin—you rock, woman! I'm sending some pixie dust your way. Don't go crazy now. To Brianna Lebrecht, who did a fantastic job of keeping all my commas in check, thank you so much! Massive thanks to Alan Pranke, whose cover design skills are epic. To my warrior princess agent, Liza Fleissig, who is always in my corner, you are the real deal. Seriously, thank you. And to all the bloggers, readers, librarians, booksellers, and event coordinators who spread the word about my books and humble me with their enthusiastic support, thank you for everything that you do!

Lastly, to my wonderful family, thanks for making this ride worth every single second.

ABOUT THE AUTHOR

AMALIE HOWARD is the bestselling, award-winning author of several young adult novels critically acclaimed by Kirkus, Publishers Weekly, VOYA, School Library Journal, and Booklist, including *Waterfell*, *The Almost Girl*, and *Alpha Goddess*, a Kid's INDIE NEXT selection highlighting East Indian mythology. She is a national IPPY silver medalist and Children's Moonbeam Award winner. She is also the co-author of the #1 bestsellers in regency romance and historical fiction, *My Rogue, My Ruin* and *My Hellion, My Heart*, in the *Lords of Essex* historical romance series. Of Indian and Middle Eastern descent, she grew up in the Caribbean but currently resides in Colorado with her husband and three children. Visit her at www. amaliehoward.com.

ALSO BY AMALIE HOWARD

YOUNG ADULT BOOKS

THE CRUENTUS CURSE SERIES

Bloodspell

Bloodcraft

Bloodbound

THE AQUARATHI SERIES

Waterfell

Oceanborn

SeaMonster: A Novella

THE RIVEN CHRONICLES SERIES

The Almost Girl

The Fallen Prince

THE ALPHA GODDESS SERIES

Alpha Goddess

Dark Goddess

Made in the USA
Monee, IL
22 October 2025

32665489R00208